IRON LOVE

● ▮● ▬▬▬ ● ▮●

MARGUERITE POLAND, who lives in KwaZulu-Natal, wrote the acclaimed *Train to Doringbult* in 1987 which was shortlisted for the CNA Literary Award. This was followed by her second novel, *Shades*, published in 1993 and shortlisted for the M-Net Fiction Award. It is a prescribed work for high school students.

IRON LOVE

●∙●∙▬∙●∙●

Marguerite Poland

PENGUIN BOOKS

PENGUIN BOOKS

Published by the Penguin Group
27 Wrights Lane, London W8 5TZ, England
Penguin Putnam Inc, 375 Hudson Street, New York, New York 10014,
USA
Penguin Books Australia Ltd, Ringwood, Victoria, Australia
Penguin Books Canada Ltd, 10 Alcorn Avenue, Toronto, Ontario,
Canada M4V 3B2
Penguin Books (NZ) Ltd, Cnr Rosedale and Airborne Roads, Albany,
Auckland, New Zealand
Penguin Books India (P) Ltd, 11 Community Centre, Panchsheel Park,
New Delhi – 110 017, India
Penguin Books (South Africa) (Pty) Ltd, 5 Watkins Street,
Denver Ext 4, Johannesburg 2094, South Africa

Penguin Books (South Africa) (Pty) Ltd, Registered Offices:
Second Floor, 90 Rivonia Road, Sandton 2196, South Africa

First published by Viking 1999
Published in Penguin Books 2000

ISBN 0 140 29705 7

Typeset by CJH Design in 10/12.5 point Plantin
Cover design: Bureau Connexion
Printed and bound by The Rustica Press, Old Mill Road, Ndabeni

For Andreans remembered,
For Andreans loved,
For Martin, Susan and Verlie,
And for Dimmie, who believed.

Dedicated to the memory of
CHARLES WINTON FRASER

Morning marches into the valley, overwhelming
The strong-points of the mist; unseen
Creatures of half-light, foresaking the haunts of man,
Withdraw to the pathless hills.
But you, invisible inhabitant
Of thought, hold out against the thrusting sunlight.
For death is more than a rifleman's misjudgement,
More than whatever material accident,
Choice of wrong cover or failure of vigilance
Brought upon you.
Death itself is your claim to compassion,
Illusions vanish with dew but no evaporation
Of private fiction, sentimental detail,
Breaks down the substance of your right to memory.
And I see you as guardian, sentinel over
Life's secret frontier, because you lie
Here . . .

From: *Trooper Temple Pulvermacher* by William Branford

ACKNOWLEDGEMENTS

So many generous people helped me during the course of researching and writing this book that it would take pages to name them all and to write of each individual contribution. I can only say that, without them, I would not have been able to proceed and each contribution is reflected somewhere in this story. There were those who phoned, wrote, sent school magazines or related anecdotes. There were those who lent me family albums and photographs and gave generously of time and memory. In meeting them, my belief in the greatness, warmth and generosity of the Andrean Community was confirmed. Every contribution, great or small – newboy to nonagenarian – is enormously appreciated and old friends and the new that I have made along the way, are much valued and loved.

With this in mind, my particular thanks go to my publishers, Viking-Penguin, my editors Alison Lowry and Pam Thornley, production manager Claire Heckrath, and marketing and publicity manager Nicky Stubbs; the Headmaster, Antony Clark, the staff and students of St Andrew's College, Grahamstown; the staffs of the Cory Library, Rhodes University and The Campbell Collections, University of Natal; the keepers of the St Andrew's College archives especially fellow researchers John Axe, Percy Callaghan, Lynette Paterson and Lettie Rivett. I would like to thank Dr Robert Morell of Natal University for access to invaluable research material, Duncan Thomas (OA) of the Commonwealth War Graves Commission for doing so much to seek out the graves of Andreans who fell in the

First World War, and Dee Nash for scouring the State Archives for me. I gratefully acknowledge all who loaned photograph albums, family letters, memoirs or who spoke to me at length about their own experiences at school. My warmest thanks to Professor William Branford (OA) for graciously allowing me to use an extract from his moving poem, *Trooper Temple Pulvermacher*.

Besides the Andrean Community and many others with an interest in my subject, my loving thanks go to my proof-readers, Susan Clarence, Antony and Brigitte Clark, Elizabeth Compton, Lynette Paterson, Gill Pringle and Brenda Richardson and to all my friends for their support and laughter and for putting up with the eccentricities of the writer.

My love and thanks to my family: my husband, Martin Oosthuizen, who provided so many of the insights, all of the laughter and most of the inspiration; Susan and Verlie for being the caretakers of 'the boys' and, in the end, the keepers of their hearts; my brother-in-law, John Oosthuizen, who went so far to photograph the battlefield at Latema Hill. And in the heartland – my mother, Nemmie, for shining days; beloved Dimmie Randell and her garden; Bee Rennie who remembered Charlie; Jean Branford for gathering us together; Liz Currie for her pilgrimage to Taveta; Lynette Paterson and her wonderful poems; Gilly Pringle and times at Fair Holt; Mervynne Danckwerts and a day to remember; Dave Woods and the journey east; Bren and many other journeys; College – my loyalty and love. And always – those young men, especially Charlie Fraser, who gazed back at me from the team pictures and the schoolboy albums – the companionship, the inspiration and love during the writing of this book, have been memorable and moving.

A full list of contributors is printed at the back of the book.

PREFACE

Iron Love is a work of fiction and must be judged as such. Consequently, in the text itself, I have not identified the school and the names of the young men who inspired this story have been changed. One of the protagonists – Charlie Fraser – is based closely on the truth, others are a combination of fact and fiction, others, entirely imaginary. The story has been constructed from fragments of boy-history, family legend, a passing anecdote from an old boy, the experience of a present pupil. These have been absorbed and used in different ways in an attempt to breathe life and authenticity into the characters. Most of the events in the tale arise from my conception of how it might have been, set within a carefully researched time-frame and in a much-loved place in which the real history of the school and the recall of the community provide texture and background. I acknowledge that some will recognise flashes of their own relatives' lives and I hope that the mixture of conjecture and fact will neither be judged as intruding too far nor disappoint for fictionalising dearly held histories that some might have wished to be told more accurately or fully.

The fifteen boys who gazed at me from the 1913 First XV photograph in the school archives have been the source from which much of the story sprang. Those fine, valorous young men embody the spirit of the time. Within five years, seven of the fifteen had lost their lives in battle. In writing of them, I hope I have restored them to memory – and if I have taken liberties with them, I hope I will be forgiven on the grounds of my loyalty and commitment to the school they represent and my admiration for the brief honour of their lives. In my experience of sharing in their story during the time of writing *Iron Love*, I feel that the tribute paid to one by a Commanding Officer, so long ago, could stand for all:

> *'If I ever have a son, I shall be proud to know he was like your boy –*
> *lovable, courteous, brave and altogether delightful.'*

Marguerite Poland
Durban, 1999

ONE

Charlie Fraser.

For some, just a name, just a boy. For some, not even a remarkable boy. Not like Rudd had been – god himself; not like James Seymour or Georgie Holmes, trailing all that glory about behind them still. Charlie Fraser: just one of the good fellows in the House with a particular facility with a rugby ball.

–Remember Fraser?

–Fraser?

–Charlie Fraser.

–Ah . . . yes. Quiet fellow. Full-back, of course.

It was written in the school magazine of that year:

'Fraser is a splendid full-back, solid as the proverbial stone wall, a courageous tackler and an accurate kicker with both feet. Can always be relied upon to be steady and cool.'

Herbert had that magazine still. If unconsulted now, he could recall the contents without fault. He kept it with the photo album 'Sunny Memories' with its grey-blue cover and a rising sun engraved in the upper left hand corner.

It was Charlie Fraser's album, full of Charlie Fraser's photos, taken with the camera he'd been given by an uncle. It was the only new thing he'd ever owned. On the back of each print he'd written his initials – CWF – in his firm, round hand or 'my effort' when the subject inclined to horseplay round the swimming pool or mock fights on the lawn behind the House. 'Not for public scrutiny; dressed in Nature's garb': a picture of the fellows at the public pool, bunched together, naked and cross-legged, just their grins immodest.

For years Herbert had meant to put the album together again, return the pictures to their original ports, with the kind of care Charlie would have taken. Charlie had always pretended they were inconsequential. If anyone came in and glanced over his shoulder at them, he would stretch, his left eyebrow drawn down but lifting at the edge, a kind of self-mocking frown, and push them aside as if they didn't matter.

But they did matter.

Herbert had seen him often, late at night, half reclined across his desk, sorting, choosing, discarding, arranging: an absorption. And he remembered the day that Robbie, their Housemaster, stamping about in search of some culprit who'd evaded him, had glanced into Charlie's study in passing and said, 'Fraser, for pity's sake, are you always at that wretched album of yours? I'd suggest a little more application to mathematics and a little less to pictures. Put it away at once and don't let me catch you at it except on Sundays. What possible use could it have beyond wasting your time and pleasing your mother in her old age?'

Charlie Fraser had closed the album and left it where it was – not put aside, but there, under his lamp, defended.

–What possible use could it have beyond wasting your time and pleasing your mother in her old age?
She had given it to Herbert herself, smoothing the binding of the spine which had come away from the cheap cardboard underneath.
–Take it, she had said. –I would like you to have it.
He had turned the stiff pages, not looking at her.
She had glanced over his shoulder. –That's my favourite, she had said, pointing to a picture of Charlie and Dan Grant, laughing, holding Highland Terrier pups. –Aren't they dear little dogs?
Dear little dogs: all that redirected tenderness.

She had turned away then and made the tea. Neither had spoken.

Among the photographs, at odds with the content of the rest, was a faded snap of Davey Bennett's hut on some bleak mountainside at home. Herbert had always hoped to see it, though Davey was pretty secretive about it. In a corner on the front, as if he had autographed a picture of himself, Davey had written: 'D.B. Bennett, My Hut!' On the back, in indelible pencil, Charlie's older hand, denying ownership, 'Jones' hideaway' and a date.

That date was indelible too: 10th April 1913.

There was also a cutting from *The Journal* among the pages of the album, yellowed and without a picture, an advertisement for Lea and Perrins Sauce on the side. Again, Charlie's writing in a margin, almost rubbed away: 'Big Match. June '13'. Herbert knew the contents of that too:

'In the dying moments the visitors worked their way towards the home side's territory. The day was saved by Fraser. This sterling young Rugbean gathered near the halfway line, and absolutely wormed his way through the whole of the opposing team, until he was practically under the goal posts. Had he wished he could possibly have notched a try, as he had a beautiful opening, but instead he coolly dropped a goal.'

That day, GB, Charlie's fag, had almost had hysterics in the stand, he'd been so proud. He had sat with the mascot and the camera, his face shining. When the team came off the field, it was Charlie the juniors had mobbed, flapping their blazers and pushing in for a chance to be noticed. They were so excited, Herbert had to duck a salvo of small unchallenged farts and elbow them to get some air. GB was punching Parkes to reach Charlie first. Herbert had to give them a shove to clear the way for the rest of the team. They'd been quite out of hand. But Charlie Fraser never minded them hanging on his shirt tails. He just shook them off good-naturedly and went on walking.

'Splendid drop, Fraser,' said the coach.

3

'Thank you, sir.' No swagger. He took the water mug from Herbert and had a drink, his back to the crowd. He didn't seem to hear the cheering from the boys, just for him. He wiped his forehead with his sleeve, rolled it up, looked off across the field towards the Zeederbergs' hedge where a little group stood watching under the fig tree. The glance was brief – then closed away.

Percy Gilbert took a photo of the team after that match. He used Charlie's camera and the fellows sat and stood about, arms linked, disreputable socks, jerseys pulled awry. In that picture, Charlie was standing behind, not pushed to the fore though he'd won the match for them. He had a towel slung around his neck. Herbert stood beside him, half his height, leaning into his shadow.

Call it devotion. It was as good a word as any.

It had started on Herbert's first night at school. Temporarily billeted with the more senior boys of the Upper Four to make place for the assistant chaplain's sons, he'd been caught unarmed. Changing for bed, he'd glanced out of the window and seen the sky – a pale, high-riding light after sunset – and the eastern hills just lifting in the dusk. Out there was space and distance. Out there was wind. Home: the only light far-off in the valley and his dog, running down before him in the veld, dodging tussocks. No matter how he'd sent her off, she was there, just behind his eyes. Nothing helped. He'd felt the burning in his throat before he could retreat. As if he'd stumbled on an ambush, he had panicked: against every instinct of self-preservation, the solemn vow of abstinence to his brother, Herbert had cried.

Then Boag, the prefect, had come, filling up the dormitory with derision. He'd stood, as if scenting something in the air, his chin lifted. He'd barked suddenly, 'Who's snivelling? I won't have snivelling.'

–If I hear you've blubbed I'll kill you! That's what Herbert's elder brother had said. –I'll kill you stone dead, d'you hear?

Boag patrolling, 'Where's the mother's brat?'

'It's me,' Herbert's neighbour had cut in quietly. 'I've got a blood nose.'

Boag, perilously close, stopped just short of Herbert's bed. 'You're disgusting, Fraser,' he'd said, looking him over. 'I suppose you've been fighting again?'

'Yes.'

'Yes, who?'

'Yes, Boag.'

Boag's prolonged scrutiny had been returned quite calmly, without insolence. Disconcerted, Boag had gone back up the row, cuffing someone out of his way. Herbert had turned to Fraser. 'Thanks,' he'd whispered. Charlie Fraser did not seem to hear. He had stretched on his bed with his arms folded across his chest, staring at the ceiling.

But after that – for ever after that – it was a matter of honour, Herbert's due to Charlie Fraser: if he *had* to cry, then it would be silent. Let sorrow just leak out without a sound, without a breath. Lie still, quite still. And in the end, it would leak inward, undetected.

When the lights were out and Boag had roared for silence three times, Herbert had turned towards Charlie Fraser's bed. He had not hunched himself away, back to the little space of floor and dividing chair. He'd watched Charlie Fraser in the gloom: he was very still in sleep, stretched out across the whole of the bed, one arm dangling over the side, blankets kicked off, unprotective of himself. Herbert had felt defended by his calm.

And in the days that followed – in the hall, the dining-room, the library, the passageways, even with a senior standing against him, palm screwing his head to the wall, knee in his groin, he'd imitated Charlie Fraser consciously. That stillness was an unexpected armour.

It was from him that Herbert learned the First Commandment in the school: Silence and Denial.

And from him, in time, the Second: Not to Fail at Footer.

Charlie Fraser did not fail at footer. Nor did Herbert.

And Silence and Denial?

Again, they were triumphant.

Such resolution: such wanton innocence.

Silence and Denial: he had the album as a consequence.

There were two pictures of the dormitory. In one, the fellows were unpacking: wooden trunks, tuck-boxes, Arthur Graham fooling about, dragging at his braces with his thumbs. In the other, the room was empty, just the beds lined up, row on row with their iron heads, old school towels draped on each foot, the shower room in the corner at the end. Herbert could tell by the neatness and the glow of the windows that it was taken in the morning when all the boys were in class. There were ten beds on this side and ten on that and the light floated up against the angled ceiling, making pools above. He had always felt as if he was in some watery grotto up there, with the sun just out of reach, or in a chapel, for the tops of the lancet windows at the end framed the sky and all of the town beyond.

Even now, reciting like a litany, he could recall who slept in each of the beds in that first term at school. Here, in embryo, the core of the next XV, side by side:

Vincent MacCallum.

Danny Grant.

Sparrow Bell.

Douglas Morgan.

The fifth bed was Arthur Graham's. In the picture, the bedspread was unruffled, the towel neatly hooked across the foot-rail. But when Arthur Graham had occupied it, day or night, the end had always bulged with cast-off pyjama tops or stray socks, the surface burrowed and excavated – for the cover never lay smooth when Arthur had made it. He was the despair of Miss Maltby, the matron. And even he, with all his clowning and the way he crinkled his eyes, could not beguile her.

On the first night, Arthur Graham had looked Herbert and Davey Bennett over as they'd stood forlornly and misplaced at the door in their long pants, temporary intruders in an Upper Four dorm. Arthur, all elbows and wrists, decreed – with a grin – that Herbert's name was 'Apie' because he was skinny and dark and his ears stuck out. In time he'd grown into them, but then, after slaughter in the barber's chair, they met the breeze full on, without protection. And 'Apie' he'd remained, throughout his school years and beyond.

The sixth bed was Charlie Fraser's.

In the picture, the light from the window just above fell across the head and then dipped, slanting to the floor. It was the last picture in the album, stuck in the bottom right-hand port. The end of school.

For Herbert, that empty room, that sunlit bed, the reflection of the summer morning drifting on the ceiling, were more telling somehow than the picture of the new Memorial chapel, the grey stone edifice of the House, the Clock Tower, even the great iron-bolted door where the sports teams posed for photos. And the sixth bed, lit by the window, was the vantage from which Charlie Fraser used to prop himself against the sill and look out, quite detached. Once Herbert said, 'What are you looking at, Fraser?' but he'd made no reply. Herbert had climbed on Charlie's bed and gazed out himself one day, to see what it was that interested him so much. There was nothing. Only the playing fields and the roofs of the classrooms and the Drill Hall and the little *sloot* at the bottom of the footer field. It was only later that he guessed that Charlie must have been tracing the road leading north-east, up past the stone pines which crowned the last hill.

From that crest the valleys fall away on either side, the vegetation changes, it is wild and inhospitable: aloes, euphorbias, kiepersols, prickly pear. The dense green enamelled leaves catch the sun, glinting sharply and way, way off the Amatolas rise up out of that green-blue distance. For Charlie Fraser that was home. Herbert hadn't thought about it then, having his own homesickness to contend with. In afteryears he knew – Charles Fraser had been homesick like the rest of them. But he'd never said.

In all their albums, it was the photograph of the rugby team that was placed reverently on the centre page. Herbert had pictures spanning four years. In three of them – stern mouth, victorious eye – he sat cross-legged on the jackal-skin kaross at the feet of the full-back.

But in Charlie's album there was only one picture of the team. It was a clear, small print, glued in a corner of a page full of other pictures. It was not at the centre, surrounded by scrolls and annotated with names and captions. It was simply there for the record. Charlie sat, centre row, extreme right, quite at ease with himself, seemingly unconscious of the glory. He had always been unburdened by his reputation: he acknowledged applause but did not bask in it; he kept his honours cap in a drawer, not hanging on the wall above his bed; he just got on with the job of putting the ball over the line or through the uprights. He practised unceasingly. He would take a ball down to the field and he would kick it at the posts, over and over, from every angle, into the sun, away from the sun. Kick and see it fly. Fetch it, head bent and going at a slow trot. He had an accuracy few could match. He would stand with the ball poised before him, legs braced, looking at the posts. Strong legs, strong knees, honed by training every day. Feet together, step back three, then swift: that precise, practised boot. He stood astride to watch the ball fly, arms folded. Trot, head down, gather, start again. No one went near him then. He was not just kicking the rugby ball.

And when a match was played and won, he had no need to carry fame around with him beyond the final whistle, to nudge it about wherever he went or fill up the road with it like Vincent MacCallum or Douggie Morgan when they sauntered into town. He did not take the long way past the girls' school on an errand and stop to put his foot on their fence to tie his lace or jog along the edge of their sports field in his XV footer jersey. And yet, he acquired a kind of enigmatic fame beyond the rest of them. He was the object of extreme interest – not just to breathless first-year 'nubs' who swapped stories about tries and goals or, like Davey Bennett, cut out little extracts from the sports page of *The Journal* – but to the girls at the sister school as well.

If he knew, he gave no indication.

Yet, in their final year, no one who had ever passed the pews of girls in the cathedral on a Sunday morning to take Communion with him, could doubt their own rating. James Seymour, the Headboy, might be reviewed by some, but only if Charlie wasn't there did Vincent MacCallum or Doug Morgan or Arthur Graham get the nod. Herbert used to laugh, he and the younger boys, watching the others strutting. Charlie never strutted. He didn't have to.

'Fraser!' Nudged by Arthur Graham in the pew so that he started.

'What?' Rather loudly.

'Clarice White is staring at you.'

'Who's Clarice White?'

'Don't be an idiot! You know who Clarice White is! You know ... *that* one!'

'Which one?' Unmoved but for a slight tilt of his brow.

'Don't *do* that!'

Arthur knew him too well: it would be easier to try and prise barnacles off a rock with his bare fingers than to get Charlie to react like any other fellow.

What was it, this devotion? Why Charlie? Why not Danny Grant or Vincent MacCallum or dear old Sparrow?

Herbert only knew it to be so, for Charlie Fraser, despite the odd detachment and silence of the fellow, had that quality that only those unique as Rudd had shared.

Presence.

And whatever presence was, it ensured, in his final year, the absolute devotion of the junior boys, gained not by favour or familiarity and quite at odds with the tendency of senior boys to patronise, belittle or ignore. If Fraser passed, a junior such as Parkes, standing back respectfully to say 'Evening, Fraser' as he would to any senior boy, would be acknowledged with an easily offered 'Parkes'. There was no need to shrink into the doorway or dissolve behind a locker or stand with eyes bent on the floor in the hope that the great boy would go away. For Fraser, nubs like Parkes existed.

Not that he paid them undue attention.

He did not speak to them, was never chummy. And yet it was he who knew their names, no matter how small or insubstantial or unworthy they might be. And somehow, if he was near, in a gathering of the great boys, it was clear they felt protected.

When, as a prefect, he had chosen a fag, his choice had been surprising. Even Herbert had been disappointed. It seemed eccentric for Charlie Fraser to have acted as he had. Herbert had discussed it at length with his friend, Davey Bennett. Neither could understand it. Fags were picked with care. A boy who would grow to be a reflection of oneself, could be roughed into shape, was clearly a fledgling member of the XI or the XV, was the first to go. The timid, inept or unattractive – like Unwin, for example – were the preserve of boys with little rank. Charlie Fraser could have had the best. He chose Giles Braithwaite – 'GB': with a face like a moon, a neck like a heron's and hair so thin and flat it lay limp on his head like fish scales from which protruded, at right angles, a pair of delicately formed but epic ears. He came from a trading station in Pondoland. He was so thin Miss Maltby gave him a dose of worm medicine that must have revolutionised his constitution and increased his misery a hundredfold in the first week of term. His only recommendation was a rather old-world courtesy, that was confident without the slightest hint of familiarity and a bird-like alertness that seemed to amuse Fraser in a private but undeprecating way. The little fellow blossomed. He became, in time, an estimable scamperer. He began to grow into his ears. He was, by the term's end, quite famous with them all.

But the advantage seemed to be GB's alone for Charlie's choice of fag could not serve his need for good connections. GB was as unknown, as unconnected in the greater world, as he. Perversely, this seemed to please Charlie Fraser. They sometimes spoke in Xhosa together, when no one else was around. Their provenance, each from an outpost quite unknown to most, isolated, inhospitable, seemed to be a bond.

But Charlie suffered for it too. He had no immediate family history tied to the College, no predecessor who would make a senior master say, 'Fraser? My dear fellow, I taught your father in '83. The finest three-quarter I can remember.' He did not even *have* a father any more. And his father's estate, despite his having been a District Surgeon, amounted to a few personal items and a very large debt. His mother eked out a living on a small allowance from the State and he was kept at the College through a scholarship from the Bishop awarded to the sons of needy clergy: a missionary grandfather was qualification enough. He was clothed from the mission-box and there was no great man on the College Council who might have known him. At the Founders' Dinner, no dignitaries to whom he was related sat at the top table or occupied the front pew in the chapel, no plaques commemorating fallen uncles, no heroes staring from the ranks of photos ranged about the dining-hall, were his. And, in his choice of fag, no prospect of a pleased and prosperous father who might put a word in where it mattered: a little fillip offered, on leaving school, reward for fairness to his boy.

'He'll be a clerk, perhaps,' the oracle, Percy Gilbert, Second-Head-of-House, had once said when all Charlie's peers were preparing applications for English universities and taking breakfast with the Head to discuss preparatory reading for the voyage. 'He's quite as bright as all of them' – expansively – 'but you simply have to have connections. An ancestor is crucial in this business. Never mind,' and he had sent Herbert a sly glance, 'the fellow's so heroic-looking, some heiress might take up with him. Pity about the Blue.'

Percy Gilbert knew he had a captive audience in Herbert. And Herbert, being so young, was far too circumspect to contradict him. 'He'll get on in some large office or department – Civil Service, Public Works, Native Affairs' – Percy warming to it – 'Perhaps some Old Boy will take him on because Robbie will recommend him as "sound".'

'Sound?' Herbert had said, with a snort.

'Sound! What else does anyone know? He won't be playing footer in an office.'

Percy had missed the point. Everyone had missed the point entirely.

Herbert knew it. So did Arthur Graham.

For them, connections did not count, where a fellow came from did not matter. Charlie Fraser was Herbert's hero. He was Arthur Graham's friend.

Arthur was the laughter in the House – a great, glad, uncomplicated clown. He had made the first weeks at school bearable for Herbert and for Davey. Without losing sight of their very junior status or sinking to familiarity, they were included through a kind of chummy teasing. Arthur made them laugh. And laughter was a way to counter strangeness and overlook the slights of other senior boys. Arthur's antics were something to recount in letters home and to regale each other with when that familiar hollow ache lodged under the ribs on Sunday nights after chapel. Arthur was always a welcome topic.

Arthur was tall and gangling: big knuckles, big feet, long arms, bits of Arthur everywhere. He had a narrow face and eyes which crinkled when he laughed.

He was always laughing.

And he was always being beaten by Robbie. For untidiness. For noise. For high spirits. As a junior he was sent up for horseplay in the dormitory almost daily. Through his five years, he was also sent up for poor marks in class. There was a difference between being beaten for high spirits and beaten for something he could not help. And a difference in how he took it. Arthur was a past master at walking straight from Robbie's study, smiling, making a perfectly nonchalant progress from the door to the stairs. Then, out of view, he would hop and jump, clowning down the steps – all legs and knees and exaggerated expressions on his face – and run twice round the field to dispel the sting. His arse, in the showers, was a matter of wonder to most boys. His stripes were inspected with some fascination, Robbie's accuracy measured and admired. No one could give a six like Robbie. They were proud of him. He had a perfect swing.

'Cupid hits with a clothes-brush!' was the derisive rejoinder to boys from another of the houses, displaying any signs of self-congratulation. 'None of you have ever had a decent thrashing in your lives!' An arse, well thrashed by Robbie, taken like a man: that was honour. And Arthur was the best example of such manly cheerfulness when Robbie administered for pranks. But a hiding for bad marks pained him immeasurably and the boys would keep away when he was sent up for that, out of deference. Arthur's ears burned then and he would walk the passage without the devil-may-care in his eye and turn down the stairs, taking them evenly and walk out and keep walking. It was then that Charlie Fraser would appear from somewhere, as if by chance, and go with him, not saying anything, but setting a pace, and by his presence, keeping others away.

Arthur had no brothers but three married sisters who seemed to dote on him and from whom he received, at intervals, unexpected parcels of tuck. He was generous with it, often giving Herbert a suck from his condensed milk tin. He kept the best bits of biltong for Charlie.

Charlie never had tuck-boxes.

If Arthur's tuck was abundant, the letters he received were also more numerous than most. His mother was devoted and wrote twice a week, never flagging. Like everyone else, Arthur dashed off the obligatory letter every Sunday afternoon. His mother kept every one of his letters in perfect sequence throughout his time at school, never minding that – from nub to senior – his spelling was appalling:

'My dear pearence,
I hope you are well. I hope that Bokkie has had her puppys. Please keep a little male for me. I got beaten four today for getting out of bed and making a aughful row. Robbie is an old fool. He wouldn't let any of us watch the match between our inferier houses. It's 30 days 'til the holidays. Please send a pound for the train ticket. A fellow called Pauter told me to clean his boots so I said he must go where it does not snow. Fraser is in my dorm. He is very good at footer. He is a deesent chap. I am quiet well.
Your loving son,
Arthur Graham.'

When, as a senior, he had graduated to a study of his own, with a prime view of the street and a window that looked directly onto the path on which the girls from the sister school would walk to church, he wrote:

'Dear old Moth,
My study is terribly bair. Please send pictures (of girls) (no relations). MacCallum has a picture of a Red Cross Nurse all the fellows are in love of. North played South today and we won. I scored a try. Fraser converted. Seymour made a splendid dash from half way to score again. The ref. was running backwards and tripped over and we all laughed. Last night there was an organ recital in the chapel. A Miss Van Ryneveld sang. She is a tall lady with kind of giant teeth.
Please send tuck. I'm starved.
Your loving son,
Arthur Graham.'

Arthur Graham was a special favourite of old Jarge, the porter, whose turn of phrase Arthur could imitate to perfection. Like Herbert, he was also one of Jarge's 'Rabbits' – a novice golfer whom Jarge loved to coach, taking his recruits down to the rugby field and teaching them to swing and chip. He would watch a bad shot, sent wildly, squinting into the sky to retrace its trajectory and say consolingly, 'That were all right. It gives you the proper hangle for the second shot.' He convinced Arthur that he would be a great golfer. But unlike Charlie, who could kick the rugby ball with dogged determination by himself for hours, Arthur was too sociable to putt or swing alone. He had to have a group or Jarge to keep him company and such sessions were attended with high glee and much laughter and the loss of rather too many balls, especially when Sparrow or Danny was with him. Herbert, an eager observer at the edges, was always discovering strays in the bushes round the Lower field and retrieving them for him.

But for all the high spirits outdoors, once confined to the school-room or his study, Arthur struggled with his lessons. He was subject to distraction but when time was running out on him, Sparrow Bell could be relied on to sit down and coach him in the mysteries of Latin. Very straight in his chair and very earnest in his approach, Sparrow would poke his fingers at the words in the primer and Arthur would attempt to read or translate. But, in the end, Arthur – grasshopper-like – would find something to joke about and Sparrow, struggling to remain stern, always ended up convulsed himself. It was enough to bring the other boys to the study door to find out what the joke was all about.

But no one could put in what nature had left out. And Arthur, despite any effort on the part of others or himself, was unable to master mathematics at all. Rugby honours cap or no, cricket colours, athletics cups, his fortnightly visits to Robbie's study after 'mark orders' became a painful ritual, his appearance before the Head each term, an ordeal. And one time the sunshine went out of him, as if it had been extinguished. He closed his door and set his cupboard across it. Alarmed, Parkes, his fag, called Vincent MacCallum, the new Head-of-House. Mac went to the door and knocked. There was no reply. He stuck a note underneath it. Its edge could still be seen and it lay untouched for several hours. Arthur did not appear at supper. He did not appear at prep. MacCallum made excuses to the master, saying that he thought that Arthur Graham was ill. At last, risking it, after lights out, Charlie Fraser climbed up the wall outside. It was a perilous journey with only the dressed stone and the old Virginia creeper as toeholds. The watchers below could barely look, so painful and slow was his progress. Herbert turned his back, certain of a coming thud and seeing Charlie smashed on the paving stones. But Charlie made the window at last. He was silhouetted against the small glow of a single candle, clambering over the sill.

GB, Charlie's fag, crept to his bed once in the night to see if he had returned, but it was empty. When he went to look in the morning, Charlie was there but he was still asleep in a tangle of blankets. He hadn't heard the bell. GB approached tentatively and put out a hand and shook his shoulder. Charlie did not stir.

'Fraser?' such a small voice, urgent now, for any moment Robbie would be down. 'You'll be late for breakfast.' GB peered into his face. '*Vuka*, Fraser, wake.' He had never stood so close before. He inspected, open-mouthed, the square chin: Charlie Fraser must have been shaving for years. He put out a finger again and prodded gently at the shoulder but Charlie only twitched. Indecisive, GB stood between the peril of leaving him and being responsible for him being rowed by Robbie or waking him and finding himself staring into the eyes of a colossus at close quarters. He could not decide and already the boys were clattering down the stairs to breakfast. He went after them and called Herbert, who was pulling at his tie, trying to knot it on the run.

'Cummings.' GB was breathless, a little bead of sweat on his lip and his pale eyes blinking. 'Fraser won't wake up.'

'Why? Is he dead?'

'I don't think so, Cummings,' said GB earnestly. 'I think he is breathing.'

'Well wake him, then.'

'Please, Cummings,' GB tugged at his sleeve but Herbert pulled it impatiently away. 'Cummings, please!'

Herbert made a face, retraced his steps and dashed up the stairs again.

Glancing at GB and daring what he never would have dared alone, he approached the bed and yanked off the bedclothes. 'Up, Fraser, up. Robbie's coming.'

Charlie Fraser sprang up and handed them off as though they were opponents. It was strange to see so great a boy so startled, pulling his open pyjamas around himself defensively with his head tousled and his straight, fair hair in his eyes. 'Right,' he said in a way that ensured their instant retreat without another word.

GB put his piece of buttered breakfast bread inside his jacket pocket. The stain of the little lick of dripping left its mark for weeks to come. Whenever his fingers touched the greasy patch in it he recalled that he'd gone hungry that morning and taken the bread to Charlie Fraser and offered it tentatively.

'What did you eat?' said Charlie sternly.

'Parkes was feeling sick and didn't want his so I brought you this.' He looked at the floor because he couldn't lie straight-faced. 'I am sorry it isn't much, Fraser. I can go to the tuck-shop for you after school.'

Charlie Fraser put out a friendly hand and cuffed him on the head. 'Thanks GB. You're a good nub. Now scat.'

Charlie had appeared in class on time and so had Arthur. No one said anything. One look from Charlie was enough.

They played a match against the public school that afternoon. They won 24-3. Arthur wrote to his father:

'We gave the local lads a wopping. I scored two tries. Daniel Grant scored as well. Fraser converted all of them and did a beautiful drop as well. He's a good touch-kicker too. Dan got hurt. He has consuction of the brain. Miss Maltby was furius because she'd just had the doctor up and he had to come back again. He took Dan home. It's lucky he lives close. If I got consuction I'd only have Miss Maltby to look after me. I'd rather be dead.'
Your loving son,
Arthur Graham.'

16

Nothing was written of the hiding, or the humiliating interview that he had had with the mathematics master.

'Graham, your work is a disgrace.'

'Yes, sir.'

'Did you apply your mind?'

'Yes, sir.'

'If that's the case, the deficiency in that organ is astounding.'

'Yes, sir.'

'I put it to you, Graham. You are nothing but a lazy, dissolute fellow.'

'Yes, sir.'

'Quite unworthy of your place . . .'

'Yes, sir.'

'Boys like you, Graham, are not a credit to this school.'

Unjust. Untrue. Arthur did not answer then.

'What have you to say?'

Nothing.

'What have you to say, Graham?'

Nothing.

'Get out.'

'Thank you, sir.'

Once the Head had written to his father with his usual bluntness: 'Your son, sir, though a sound, straight fellow, is an ass.'

He knew he was an ass. That was fair. That was right. But he knew he was a sound, straight fellow too. Robbie had made him feel that way. So had the Head. So had the others in the House. An ass, but not unworthy of his place. An ass, but still a credit to the school. In the agricultural class. At cadets. At rugby. At cricket. As a prefect. In his heart.

Now, he was a dissolute fellow. Unworthy. Improvident. Untrustworthy?

His honour had been impeached, his self-esteem stripped. Everything he did carried the stigma. There was no escape. The master did not care about his prowess in the agricultural class – and what good was it anyway? He had no farm to go to, his father was a magistrate. He did not care that he'd led manoeuvres at cadets in a

17

way that had earned Robbie's special praise. He did not care that his batting average almost equalled Daniel Grant's, that his keen interpretation of the play in a rugby match had often helped to win the day. No, to this dry and churlish little man, he was an ignorant oaf: 'There is no getting by without mathematics, boy. And if I have to beat it into you, I will. I'll have you singing out your theorems by the end of the term.'

He had gone away to his study and stood by his desk and stared at the wall. He'd kept his eyes wide as if he would choke them open. He wanted to lash out. Butting it with his shoulder, he had pushed his locker across the door. One word from anyone and he would have fought them blindly. Yet shame transcended anger. He did not want to see their faces, finding pity there. Perhaps, like the master, secretly, they also thought he was a fool.

Charlie came, heaving himself through the window and seating himself on the chair, leaning his forearms on his knees. He didn't say much. He sat there quietly, knowing what was wrong, unable to change it. He talked about other things. About techniques in footer, finding touch, proposed a strategy for the back-line move which made Arthur half laugh because it was so outrageous. His breath stopped catching unexpectedly, the blood surging in his ears slowed down. He fished a secret tuck-box from under the bookcase and, with a penknife, carved slivers from a last heel of fruitcake, scraping off the bits that had taken on a pale crust of mould. His hands were not quite steady, a lumpish shame in them for their lack of dexterity and promise. His arse ached and this time blood had been drawn. Charlie did not expect that he should sit. He flicked a mouldy raisin at Arthur. Arthur flicked one back. He grinned. Charlie glanced at him then: that look with one eyebrow tipped at the corner, half quizzical. For now, it would be all right. For now, they'd see it through.

Arthur was no ass and Herbert knew it too. But then, his assessment had nothing to do with algebra or trigonometry. And if Herbert had lost, over time, the pitch of the voice that yelled 'Croc coming' down the dorm when the sound of girl-feet from the pavement outside, marshalled into pairs, alerted him, the calm reassurance, 'It's all right, Apie. It's all right, old chap,' the pressure of a cool hand, were still clear. Clear as that greater and more distant sound, captive in his head: the heat and tumult of the guns.

And that calm reassurance was presaged in the photo of cadets – D Company – which filled a space on the album's final page, next to the empty dormitory. If he had examined any, it was over this that Herbert, in his time, had lingered most of all. Here were embryonic soldiers, boys metamorphosing into men. The officers stood ranked behind: Captains James Seymour and George Holmes, Lieutenants Sparrow Bell, Vincent MacCallum and Daniel Grant. Here were Douglas Morgan and Arthur Graham, tall and upright, arms stiffly to their sides. And then the small boys – Parkes, GB – and a host of others, cross-legged at their feet. Lying in front – chosen because he looked the most heroic in his sergeant's uniform, in the slouch hat with the College colours on the band – was Charlie Fraser. The midday sun slanted the shadow of his brim across his face, dividing it diagonally like the stripes on the hat band, mouth set, brow stern and his eyes distant and narrowed against the light.

Herbert liked that photo best of all: drill on the field; Harry Zeederberg wailing on his bugle; the precision of presenting arms, the feel of the carbine and the smell of its barrel; the billycans over fires and the fellows smoking their pipes. Best of all was the camp at the Kowie where, for a few glorious weeks the corps went on serious manoeuvres, in and out of the dunes and along the river.

'The corps is living in a state of the most appalling hugger-muggerdom at the Kowie,' wrote the Head to the Bishop.

Arthur Graham to his sister: 'Some of the fellows haven't barthed for three weeks.'

When it was time off they dug mud prawns in the tidal banks and went fishing. Sparrow Bell caught a nine pound elf one evening, Danny Grant gaffed it for him and they returned to camp triumphant. A fire was built and the gutted fish reverently laid on a grid on the coals. Each had a mouthful of the white flesh, delicately veined in black. It was a communion, eating it under the stars with the drift of wood smoke in their coats and the white bones charring quietly in embers and the milkwoods dark against the sky.

At night, in the tented camp, the smaller boys laid the fires and lit them and tended them. GB, overcome with the glory, standing close to Fraser by the cooking fire – fag turned batman – said, 'If you cook my chop for me, you can have it.'

Herbert laughed and GB looked at him bewildered, but Charlie Fraser took the proffered chop without comment and cooked it, turning it with a wooden stick and then, taking up his own enamel plate, gave it back to GB. GB looked at it and up at Fraser.

'Go on, then,' said Charlie. 'Cummings will eat it if you're not careful,' and he nudged him away from where Herbert stood prodding his meat with a wire prong.

So GB carried it reverently to the edges of the bush, sat alone in the sand and ate the chop, slowly, as if it were sacred, and sucking the little T-shaped bone until it was clean and smooth. He fell asleep where he sat, the plate tipped in his lap. Between them, Herbert and Charlie picked him up and put him in the tent with the younger boys and Charlie pulled his blanket up around him, squashing it in to keep out the draught and covering the cold little fins of his ears.

Herbert took an early watch, walking the boundaries with the wind blowing off the sea and the pale pewter gleam of the river far below. The officers and seniors were sitting near the fire: Arthur Graham, mess-hand, traced idle patterns in the air with a slim burning twig as he waited for the kettle to boil for their coffee; Seymour, Guard Commander, wrote notes by the light of the flames. Vincent MacCallum was blowing smoke rings at the moon. Percy Gilbert sat at a little distance, in a trance. Somewhere among the tents was Unwin, ousted from companionship. Edwards and Mostert were squabbling noisily in one of the outer tents. Beyond the voices and the firelight, the stars hung in a clear sky: such dark and the sound of the sea, the sucking of the waves and the echo of them in the dunes as if the water was deeply subterranean, currents deep beneath the sand. Much later, Herbert could hear its sighing under his ear, pressed to the ground, as he lay wrapped in his blanket in his tent. He rested his cheek in his hand. He could smell river elf on his fingers, taste the salt. He drifted with the sound of the waves. Some time towards morning, he woke and opened his eyes. Through a wedge, where the flap of the tent breathed in a small wind, he could see the embers of the fire pulsing gently and, beyond the fire, the watch standing with his carbine. He heard him walk along the perimeter of the camp and turn and stroll back, stand for a moment, looking out over the bush towards the shore.

Herbert followed him with heavy eyes. He did not stand hunched against the dark – but at ease, great-limbed, the wind lifting his hair. His tread was soft but firm, his movements steady. Herbert could hear their weight, feel them in the sand under his hand. He slept.

Sentinel: Charlie Fraser, watching for them all.

TWO

●▪●▬▪●▪●

'House Juniors: 1911.'

Nubs: small boys, bunched together, hanging on each others' jackets, shoving. Those knees, even in the old sepia picture, were scaly and dry. Herbert knew the smell of them. Iron and dust: dust from floorboards, dust left from the mud at the edge of the Cradock Dam where they made tracks and bridges. Flaky little knees and small boy heads, still downy in unexpected places at the nape or forehead. Here, a plume on the crown, like Sparrow Bell's ubiquitous crest which wavered on unquenchable, no matter how much gob was applied. There, the cow-lick slicked against the ministrations of the mothers who seemed to love them so. Herbert recalled his own mother tracing a proprietary finger over his. And that look! Wet it, brush it flat, grease it down *hard*! No fellow with sense would let such an aberrant little give-away spoil the glory of the XV photo! Turning to it in the album, scanning it, every one of them – manly chins, manly noses, manly ears – would have scorned to let a cow-lick show. Poor Arthur: the kink was evident despite the stiffness of his back, the way he held his head as if it was a jug in danger of spilling and let his eyes slide sideways to the front: in breathing, that cow-lick might spring out, betray him as his Mother's Boy.

But nubs were a different matter. Nubs were ignorant of such things still. They did not know to keep their chins held up, challenge the sun when a photo was taken. They had no idea how to present themselves. They'd incline their heads and squint one eye at the light. They were happy to open their mouths and let their tongues edge out, counter to screwing up their faces. They would stand, knock-kneed, with nowhere to put their hands and keep their caps on their heads as if they were a glory! And pushing – you could see that they were pushing to be noticed, grinning for the mamas.

There was no picture in the album of Charlie as a nub. If there had been, he'd have stood at ease, hands linked behind his back, no squirming for the camera. But Herbert and Davey were both in the 'House Juniors: 1911', looking their worst: caps, tongues, idiot smiles. Davey Bennett stood with his stomach thrust forward and his shoulders slouched and his feet pointing outwards. You could see, even then, Davey Bennett was not going to be a rugby player. At his side, Herbert – at least – was upright: he had observed Charlie Fraser well already. He stood, jaw lifted just enough to show that small dent of manliness and resolution in his chin. It was fine, except for the ears!

Herbert was thirteen when he came to school. And what he remembered most – it had bewildered and distressed him in those first few weeks – was the unexpected disappearance of distance and of light. The hills at Molteno, the width of sky, the great unending vault, horizon to horizon, miles and miles apart, were what he knew. Here, he was sunk in a bowl of hills with the two church spires and the neat gardens, the white-fronted houses and the shops in the High Street where everything was out of bounds. And at school, all around him, the stone buildings leaned in and made deep shadows which touched each other without the sun to warm them in between.

He came to school on the train, alone with his trunk. Woken long before dawn, the candle flame had wavered down the passage and his mother had sat on the end of his bed and looked at him in that half-wakeful moment when he had wanted to creep down under the blankets, feeling her there, and pretend to sleep still, so she wouldn't move. But he had got up briskly and dressed and wished her away for she had no business with him in these unfamiliar clothes, handed down by his brother. And when he had washed, he walked out of his room without looking at his *slagyster* in the corner, or his mouse traps or his wagon made of wire or the buck heads on the wall: his first reedbuck; his first grey rhebok, dassie skins, and a *rooikat* pelt, copper-gold with sooty ear tufts, draped across the back of the *rusbank*. He had not touched his rifle. He had paid no attention to his dog whining at the door. He sat in the dim light of the kitchen at the table near the stove with the shadow of flame leaping suddenly across the room when his father lifted the cover-plate and gave the coals inside a stir with the poker. He had drunk his tea but eaten only half a rusk and pushed the porridge away. His mother had stood by the iron rail of the stove, with her fingers curled around it. She spoke very quietly every now and then – not much, only small words, as if to herself more than to him. She touched his hair but he had wetted it flat and it did not yield to the quick brush of her fingers. Her tweaking his lapels or straightening his tie must be discouraged: he stood at the other side of the table, not looking at her.

A last visit to the privy in the garden, a word behind the house with his dog where no one could see him, then he went to the trap. He did not grumble. This – he was trying to convince himself – was an adventure: too soon to regret, too immediate for retreat. As they drove past the little schoolroom where his mother had taught him and his sister and all the neighbouring children – stone-walled, iron-roofed, the bell askew – it suddenly seemed no more significant than the wash-house or the goat kraal or the water tank. He would leave them all behind. He had kissed his mother rather stiffly, not wanting to crease his shirt and had made small embarrassed snorts to counter all her snuffling. He had not kissed his sister at all and he could see that she had wanted to cry. To stop her he'd said goodbye rather severely and waved, looking in another direction. They drove out of the yard and he did not turn. He had gates to open and it was a chore to keep his boots from getting dusty. First gate, easy on the swing; second, lift and turn and push and lower into the drift of sand; third, a tricky twisted hook and the *gwarri* post smoothed to silk by fingers softened from shearing wool. A little knot high up on the gatepost had always looked like an eye. It gazed from some interior, deep inside the wood, something of the spirit of the tree was there, peering out. He did not glance at the wooden eye then. It had no power that day to hold him in its gaze as it could in the evenings when he had ventured out to fetch a horse. And the hills he had climbed, rising to the grasslands high above, had not folded into krantz and shoulder in the light yet. They still stood, dark and featureless, against the cool green of early dawn. Herbert did not salute them. He jostled against his father to the rhythm of the horses' hooves, sniffing the fresh scent of an early pipe. His brother had ridden with them to the station, gone off to speak to the stationmaster about a consignment for the store. Three months out of school and he was an old man. 'Look sharp, Boet,' was what he said. It might have been the best advice Herbert had ever had.

Only on the dusty platform did any detail impinge on his thoughts: things his brother had told him when they walked in the veld or sat on the bean bags in the storeroom while his brother smoked. There were words that he had invested with a certain visual meaning of his own. They loomed suddenly, despite the familiar sweep of hills still around him and the sound of milk pails being loaded and the long pant of the waiting train on the tracks. Robbie. Lower. Jarge. And Benji, the cane. And the names of the fellows in the footer team, written underneath the newest photograph that hung in his brother's room, the captain, splendid in his colours cap. Some of the younger ones would still be there, fellows just a year behind his brother, seniors now, whose names he'd have to know within a week or bear the consequences of derision and a well-thrashed arse: Tanner, Bryant, Gilfillan, Hugo. He couldn't remember them all. Pauling? Cowen? Meintjes? And for the rest: –Do as you're told; Hold your tongue. Watch out for senior cops, whoever they might be. Never give buck. Look sharp. If I hear you've blubbed, I'll kill you.

He had been practising kicking his ball against the fowlhouse, to make his boot accurate. –No matter what, you'd better be good at footer. That's what his brother had said. Herbert knew he would be good at footer. He could hit the same spot on the fowlhouse wall over twenty paces, time and time again. His record was twelve in a row.

He shook hands with his father, his brother, carried his luggage aboard and sat by the window. The train jerked, was silent, gathered itself, paused, gathered itself again and trudged away. His father and brother, standing in the dust by the siding gate receded and were gone – the mountains gone, the veld he knew, the last dam he might recall. He had never been this far from home before.

He guessed the time by the sun. At midday he thought he should be hungry and so he reached up and lifted down the box his mother had packed for the journey. He opened it. She always folded a napkin like that. And the bread wrapped in it was spread a certain way. Her again. There was an apple from the old tree near the reservoir. It still had a little leaf and a stalk that held a wisp of lichen. She must have picked it in the dark. He took out a sandwich, poking his fingers in where they shouldn't be but she had packed them tightly, enough for a day and a night. What it is to eat bread which tastes and feels so familiar and yet which seems so suddenly displaced. It came from the big oven in the backyard, where he used to wait to see it brought out, four loaves in the black metal pan, loaf on loaf, side by side. He would make his choice by the knobs and bumps on the crust and beg some slices. The loaf would be cut, steam bursting out, fragrant with wheat and brown with baking. He would take a piled plateful to the orchard with his *kwedinis* and a little tin of lard. They would dip the crusts and eat, the lard dissolving in the warmth. Herbert looked out of the train window at *besembos* streaming in the wind. He put his sandwich away unfinished. There was a taste of salt which he had to swallow and the bread was cold and heavy in his mouth.

At Conway, he was joined by another boy. Herbert saw him standing with a woman by an old conveyance drawn up near the track. A man and a servant brought his trunk and thrust it through the door into the passage outside. Herbert poked his head out of the window and looked down. The boy, his own age, was as slight, as small, with red-brown hair cut in a straight even fringe to his eyebrows. He said, 'Can you take these through the window?' lifting a tennis racquet of great age and a large roped box with a carrying loop of worn leather. Herbert leaned out and pulled them up, dumping them on the floor. He looked at them, deciphering a name on the box: Basil Bennett.

The door opened. The boy stood there. 'Are you Basil Bennett?' said Herbert.

26

The boy laughed. 'I hope not!'

'Who's Basil Bennett then?'

'Gramps,' he said. 'It was his tuck-box when he was at school. He gave it to me, in case I felt homesick.'

'Is it your first time?'

The boy nodded. 'And yours?'

'Same.'

They shook hands.

'David Bennett,' said the boy.

'Herbert Cummings.' He was burying any nickname for ever.

The train was beginning to draw away and David Bennett's mother was tapping urgently at the window. David Bennett leaned out. His mother was hurrying alongside the carriage, calling his name. 'Davey. Davey.' She put up her hand to him, holding onto her hat with the other. He was obliged to take it. It seemed so urgent to her.

Herbert was glad no one had seen his mother. She had not come to the station – it was too early and too dark.

This mother was crying. It was a great embarrassment.

What could one say when the mother cried? It put a fellow on the spot.

Herbert took out his food parcel again and offered David Bennett a sandwich. It seemed to distract him. Herbert's didn't taste so bad then – it was David Bennett who was having difficulty now with swallowing. So they talked about goats and pasture and drought: two old men discussing the weather. They outdid each other on the hunt. Herbert suddenly acquired two extra reedbuck in his bag. He crossed his fingers. Never lie. Well, he had helped his brother stalk them, hadn't he? David Bennett knew a lot about rifles. Herbert was impressed. No one came to disturb them and they hardly noticed how the veld changed, drier and more distant, going south-west.

At Cookhouse station they'd bought ginger beer on the platform. Herbert was an authority on Cookhouse ginger beer – more information appropriated from his brother. He had never tasted it before but he hoped it would be there, like his brother had said.

It was. They bought two bottles, comparing them. One was a whisky bottle, the other must have had Rose's cordial in it. The contents had raisins bobbing on the surface.

'Looks like gorged ticks,' said Herbert.

David Bennett made a face and laughed. They fished the raisins out, splashing themselves and making the seats sticky. Herbert's finger got stuck in a bottle neck and turned blue until Bennett managed to wrench it off. Ginger beer flew all over the compartment.

After that they squashed their hats to make them look less new and sat on their blazers and pulled their ties sideways and tried to feel at ease. They laughed at everything and nothing, keeping the anxiety away by clowning. They talked all the way to Alicedale, far into the night, where the train groaned and settled, groaned and settled, going forward, hesitating, going back. Herbert taught Davey Bennett – secondhand – the lore of the House: do as you're told; hold your tongue. Watch out for senior cops, whoever they might be. Watch out for bucks. Look sharp. Whatever you do, look sharp.

They were grubby and a little subdued by the time they reached their destination in the still grey morning. Herbert's bravado and his salvo of names and instructions evaporated at the sight of the master standing on the platform, surrounded by other boys and a heap of trunks and boxes. A porter was loading luggage on a scotch cart. They had emerged dishevelled and the master had consulted a list and barked, 'Cummings, H.O.; Bennett, D.B.' and ticked them off. They were marched down the hill in a line with the others, two abreast, across the bridge and up the slope. Herbert had hardly dared to look at the others, sticking close to David Bennett. The big boys swung along, but the small seemed to shrink as they progressed, the murmurs subsiding into silence as the great grey stone buildings of the school loomed in sight. Herbert and David had moved closer, jostling, two young animals bunching at the brink. They grinned as if they were unconcerned: they had each other to pretend to. When they'd reached the House, they had plunged inside together.

A great boy sauntered into the dormitory, hands in his pockets. The seniors standing at the door had parted for him, drawing back. He paused. Framed there, he seemed prodigious in every way. Herbert could tell, just by the hush, that god was among them. He walked in and looked the small boys over. They, so swamped by large shoes and jackets bought two sizes big and trousers with a turn-up half way to the calf, could never move as he did: in command, his shoulders strained at their seams and his collar seemed too tight. Just his presence stirred a knot; just his walk, something close to awe. Lined up before him, they did not dare gaze closely. Herbert stood mesmerised. He scrutinised the toes of his shoes, breathed slowly.

This was Hugo, Head-of-House.

–You'll know him by his nose. That's what his brother had said.

Herbert did not dare raise his eyes high enough to look.

Then the great boy said, 'Where is Cummings Two?'

Herbert stepped forward.

–If you get a senior cop or Head-of-House, you're made. His brother had said. –You're lucky you've got me to put in a word.

Implicit in this was the obligation to perform a number of menial favours in return. Throughout the holidays Herbert had gone out every time it had rained to close the gates or supervise the milking or take their father his bottle of tea in the shop. His innate discretion outweighed the instinct to rebel. He complied with whatever was asked. He knew what 'looking sharp' was all about.

And so, Herbert had become fag to 'Grotius' Hugo, Head-of-House. His future was assured. David Bennett, without connections, had gone to Maximilian 'Bog' Boag. It was not an auspicious start.

When the prefects had chosen – two each – the juniors who were left unclaimed were allotted to seniors without rank. The last, overlooked and standing damply with his eyes on the ground, was fobbed off – an afterthought – as third fag attached to Boag. His name was Unwin. Herbert watched him shambling to his place, a bewildered sort of boy, oblivious of his sentence. 'Perhaps he should run away at once,' he had murmured to David Bennett.

But, in time, it was not Hugo or Boag they feared. It was 'Goens' Archer – with size, not rank. To a man, they feared him, Unwin most of all. In the second week at school, Archer had found Herbert and Davey and trapped them in the dorm when they'd come up to fetch their cricket things, late for practice, going quietly, listening for

Robbie's tread, hustling each other to be quick.

'Come on, Apie, hurry up,' said Davey, pulling on his shirt, eye half on the door. 'Robbie will be after us.'

'I've lost my ducks. Someone took them. Maybe Miss Maltby didn't bring them back from the laundry.'

'We'll both be thrashed if we're caught up here.'

'Go on then, leave me.'

'Don't be an idiot!' Davey, bouncing quietly on his toes. 'If you roll up my spares, they'll do.'

'I don't need to roll them!' Indignantly.

'Hurry!' Davey tossed them at him. Herbert took off his trousers and dragged on the proffered ducks. He used his school tie to knot them up. They'd pleated high about his waist, hung over his bare feet. Davey started to laugh.

'Sshhh!' Herbert was suddenly alert. 'Quick! Under the bed.'

Concealed in an instant, the cover pulled down, Herbert could fit with ease. For Davey it was more awkward. His legs were longer, his arms all angles. But one fitted somehow, anyhow. One always fitted.

They could sense the shadow at the door. They could sense the listening. Archer. He was standing there for sure, to catch a sound; waiting with his footer boots, even though the season hadn't started. Slow steps came down between the rows of beds. Cringe lower and smaller. The predator stopped, his boots laced in white, his great legs astride. From that angle Herbert could see six inches up his shorts. The skin on the inside of his thighs was surprisingly white for so great and dark a boy. To stare in fear so closely, it seemed a shocking sight. He could almost smell him. But it was Archer who could scent a victim: he reached down, quite nonchalantly, and scooped Herbert out by the collar.

'Why are you hiding, snot-face?'

There was nothing to say. No one went under the bed for fun.

Down on the floor, face pressed against the nail-heads, cheek nipped blue by the thin, spiteful groove between the floorboards, Herbert was pinned by Archer. He dared not struggle.

Herbert and Davey had both been raked that afternoon. Face to face, they had submitted to the cruel, blunt stub of a rugby boot catching the tender skin at the side of the eye. They made no sound.

Robbie came. They knew his tread. Archer looked up. Open-palmed, he twisted Davey's face into the floor once more and then he was gone, out of the lower door and down the side stairs. They had lain still, breath held.

Robbie looked in, but they were on the floor, obscured by the row of lockers. He stood a moment, hesitating, and then he walked on down the passage. They could hear the brush of his old grey flannels and the squeak of his shoes. The door to his quarters closed behind him.

'Archer is a great bloody sod,' said Davey under his breath. 'We should report him to Boag.'

'Are you mad?' Herbert got up on his knees.

'Why not?'

'It's not good form.'

'Why?'

'He's older.'

'So?' said Davey.

'So, he's older. He's allowed.'

'Why's he allowed?' Mulish.

''Cos he's older.' Really!

'So?'

'So!' For God's sake!

Davey was still an ignorant nub. He would learn.

He did.

He and the other nubs learned very fast. And the fastest thing they learned was never to question rank – no matter whose. If Robbie had told them the world was flat they'd have agreed. If a buck, one form up, had told them to wait while he lumbered through a door, they would wait – even if he was twenty yards behind – or be pulled back by the scruff of the neck, like a dog, and have their faces pushed in. There was no room for dissent or impertinence. Standing order was unquestioned amongst nubs.

Their sojourn in the Upper Four was brief. The assistant chaplain's sons, who had displaced them in the junior dorm at the start of the term while their parents were away in Port Elizabeth, were restored at the fortnight's end to the cottage beyond the footer field: eight little Zeederbergs patched, scrubbed and quite unruly. They left berths in the junior dorm for Herbert and Davey. Herbert did not want to go. He liked being called 'Apie' by Arthur Graham and to be included by Sparrow Bell when he gave out tuck. He liked bowling balls to Daniel Grant in the nets before chapel in the evenings. And if he waked at night and thought of home, he would turn on his stomach, like Charlie Fraser always did, a yard or two away, and crook his knee and let his arm dangle over the side of the bed, as if, by his weight, he might smother it. And even if he and Davey knew they were on the periphery, unnoticed by most of the other occupants of the dorm, Sparrow and Dan, Arthur and Charlie had never made them feel that they'd intruded.

Arthur christened Davey 'Davey Jones' and by this small group of boys, one form up, he was always known as 'Jones'. Herbert called him 'Jones' as well, unless, in teasing or exasperation, he was 'Basil'.

And in the time of their stay a companionship grew up between them all and Herbert knew, because of it, he would not have to fight to keep his place. In standing order, he and Davey would be first among their peers. And when he went to bed at night, back in the junior dorm, he felt he could lie quite comfortably with his hands behind his head and stare into space and think of footer before he went to sleep. That's what Fraser did himself, frowning at the ceiling, chin up, square. Herbert wondered if he thought of footer too – but he could never bring himself to ask.

If Herbert chafed inwardly at removal from the more senior dorm, Davey Bennett did not seem to mind demotion. He was the most accepting sort of chap: an easy companion, an affable, unhurried boy, the sort who shared his marbles, ignored fights and was genial to have around. He always laughed at other people's jokes and listened to their stories. His hair was so straight, it never stood up in a cow-lick like Herbert's – it always flopped, just so, neat and even to his eyebrows. His eyes were dark and mild. He had a good tuck-box, kept clothes tidy in his locker, didn't interfere with other people's property. He played cricket for the junior house team as eighth bat. Herbert soon discovered he was clever, in an unostentatious way. His place on the prize list was assured. He was the sort of boy – to the consternation of both – that Robbie would be unlikely to beat.

'We'll have to do something about it, Jones,' Herbert had said. His own backside had been well warmed within a week. By the end of the term, Robbie knew him rather better than he'd hoped.

'It's not for lack of trying,' Davey had said.

'You just don't *look* bad. You're like Sparrow. He'd have to be ten times worse than anyone else for Hugo to send him up.'

When they were restored to their proper place, Miss Maltby put their beds at the far side of the dormitory, facing down the row, at the opposite end from the prefect who slept near the door. They made friends with those around them, secure in their status, and in the afternoons, if they had no sport, they went with the other juniors up to the commonage around the Cradock Dam. They rounded up the woodcutters' donkeys that grazed there and raced them on a track they'd made. Secretly, David Bennett found it a relief from games. But he never would have said it to Herbert for Herbert was impassioned. He practised his kicking all the time, preparing for the season. Nor did he ever miss watching a first team cricket practice and he whitened Hugo's boots so well they were a beacon on the field.

For Davey, the good times were not in the House or on the playing field. They were in the fort that he and Herbert built. It was here that they were equals – no Hugo versus Boag, no cricket scores, no footer talk. And it was here that Davey Bennett could forget, for an afternoon, that, as the season loomed, he wouldn't be allowed to play rugby. He did not bring the subject up: he simply couldn't do it. And then, one day, breaking in on other thoughts, Herbert said, 'Are you trying out, Jones?'

'Don't know,' Davey said, planing planks; two shillings worth of wood requisitioned from the carpentry master.

'Don't know?'

'Never thought about it.' Drive a nail in, hard and true.

'What?' Incredulous.

He was not allowed to try. His heart was weak from rheumatic fever. What could he say to Herbert, a man possessed? He wouldn't want to be his friend. 'Pass the nails.'

Herbert passed the nails. 'Did I hear you right?'

But Davey sent the hammer down. Perfect aim, perfect balance. 'Who d'you think will be the captain?' He did not look at Herbert, put a pair of nails in his mouth.

'Hugo.'

'Uh, uh . . .'

'Of course he will.'

'Bet not.'

'Who then?'

'Tanner.'

'Rot.'

Davey was right. Tanner it was.

But that was after, when the autumn came.

In those limpid summer afternoons, the sound of cricket practice drifting up the hill towards the Cradock Dam and there, against the small busy rustlings of bulbuls in the trees or a boubou in the undergrowth, Davey and Herbert had hollowed out a place in a clump of bush and built their shelter. They came there at the weekends when they were not at prep or chapel, when their cricket side wasn't playing and their own practices were over. Inventive as each other, they constructed a pulley to raise a basket of supplies from the ground to the platform and a sort of rustic ladder which acted as a drawbridge.

Others followed suit and a rash of forts grew up. Mock battles were held between rivals. They bombarded each other with *kleilatte*. But Cummings' and Bennett's fort was the best and being there together, the ladder stored and the view out through the leaves uninterrupted by buildings or spires, it did not seem to matter quite so much that the space, the distance and the veld were far away, beyond their reach. They knew, unchanged beyond the northern ridge, the *garingbome* still marched home across the Dikkopvlakte and far off the Winterberg were indigo against the sky. For now, they

34

brought their tuck up to the shelter in the basket on the pulley and shared it out between their friends and forgot to be homesick. Dried fruit, biltong, *tammeletjie*, bull's-eyes bought from Dicks'.

No seniors came here. Rank was decided among themselves: good forts, strong forts, inventive forts. That was what counted. Herbert and Davey knew theirs was envied. Tom Edwards' fort was good too. Pringle had made it with him. Like Herbert and Davey, they could build. Farmers' sons, they had known all their lives how to lash or nail, plane and lathe. Good forts: Ross and Mostert and White. They found an old pipe and hoisted it at one end, burying the other in a pit they'd dug under the tree. 'We have a bog in our fort,' they announced triumphantly. The chosen were allowed to test it. Herbert and Davey were the first to be brought up to see it. Anyone with faulty aim wouldn't be invited back. No one messed, even in laughter.

Someone, trying to outdo 'the pisspipe', stole a bucket from the House bogs and tied it on a rope beside his fort. Robbie discovered the loss and the culprit was thrashed. He earned the nickname 'Tangy' after that: 'Tangy-boys', the word used for the men who came to remove and renew the buckets in the lavatories. They came and went with their mule cart, well after midnight. Mostert, preoccupied with bogs at that moment – foolishly, for the incident of the bucket had only just occurred – had suggested, one Friday, that they lie in wait for the 'Tangy-boys' and pelt them with soap as they passed below the windows of the House. The mess and stench the next morning had put the Headmaster in an uproar. To be summoned before him – the whole of the junior dormitory – and to watch him walk up and down, he in his dark coat, his watch chain eye-level, jerking between the buttons of his waistcoat and his fob pocket, his pale blue eyes ablaze, so tall, so awesome, even Robbie standing off – here was instant death: it was a heroic moment.

Robbie had been well warmed in beating them all after that. He'd felt the after-effects in his shoulder. Miss Maltby kept wintergreen for just such exertions but he did not allow her to minister it. He did it himself.

When the boys had been beaten they had had to clean the mess, Edwards had thrown up twice but was not excused from duty. It was

.pandemonium. When they were done, Hugo detailed Boag to ensure they showered properly and went off to smoke in his study in peace. It was a snub to Boag. He knew it and he took his cricket bat to the ablution cubicle and used it vigorously to prod the unwilling. He lined them up, naked as new-born mice. Scamperers, blue with cold, one by one they hopped up and down in the shower, not daring to meet Boag's eye. Then Davey Bennett said – clearly, he had forgotten himself – 'Imagine being a Tangy-boy . . .' There was a silence and only the sharp spatter of the water on the floor. Herbert winced. Idiot. Davey looked bewildered a moment.

Boag kept Davey Bennett in the shower with his bat poised just under his chin, pushing it up. The water streamed into his face. He was almost choking. Two minutes, three, four. It was for ever. When it seemed that he had drowned – standing on his feet – Boag let him out. The square-tipped mark of the bat on his backside, next to the first stripe Robbie had ever inflicted, was clear. Was the nub touched? Why should anyone, for God's sake, care what it was like to be a Tangy-boy?

But the forts were beyond the reach of Hugo and Boag and Robbie and any of the seniors, even one form up. It was the small boys' domain. And if the bucket had gone, Ross and White and Mostert's pisspipe remained and who could use it and who couldn't was concomitant with standing orders. Pissing down the pipe was a privilege. Without compunction, they chose whom to exclude. The little throng gathered eagerly below the tree were summoned one by one.

But there were those whose names were never called.

The last boy allowed almost stumbled up the ladder with relief. He'd never feel quite the same about his mate, left behind. Or about their fort. He'd have to join another. After all, he really had no choice. The boys denied the privilege milled below the tree, like ants dispersed by a predator. They retreated, cast out.

'House Juniors: 1911.' There they were in the faded old picture in Charlie Fraser's album – Edwards and Pringle and Ross, White and Mostert of the pisspipe. And at the edge, Unwin. Lamentable Unwin, pale as unbaked bread. Herbert could have heard their voices from the page.

He might have smelled them too. Small boy smells – grubby, not offensive; a halo of little lost farts, of stiff, sandy socks, of shirts which had been bundled into lockers instead of wash bags, and forgotten. The bark-green stains from the trunk of the guava tree in African Street might go a little mouldy, the juice of *dinnebessies* take on the smell of moss. There was nothing to recoil from. Their laundry could be inspected openly, piled in a cauldron and half boiled over a wood fire, stirred with a paddle and a good bar of blue soap by the housemaids. No cricket ducks from the men's department at Birch's. Nothing animal and strong. Such objects were for the attention of fags.

A footer jersey, ripening in the heat of eighty minutes, was not spread out and inspected by Miss Maltby before washing. It was gathered up gingerly, dumped in an enamel bucket and taken to the pump at the bogs to be washed. The potency came through the suds. It was not a matter for discussion. One squatted, arms immersed to the elbows, letting the sweat ooze out into the water, turning it grey. Herbert's view of Hugo's socks was undisclosed, Unwin's contemplation of Boag's under-drawers sacrosanct to Unwin. To recoil was to break the First Commandment. To recoil was to undermine the second. No one did.

Herbert had not minded Hugo's laundry: he was Head-of-House. It must be unimpeachable. He was brisk about it though, just as Davey was with Boag's. Herbert did not squat on his haunches with his arms resting in the suds or pop the bubbles idly. When Rudd was still at school, his nub – Danny Grant, to his everlasting glory – probably drank the washing water or kept some in a bottle to anoint himself. No wonder he could bowl so well and send a six far beyond the boundary fence; no wonder he could run.

Had Charlie Fraser dawdled over someone's suds? The great Nothard's? The epic Barber's? Somehow not. Did GB dawdle over his? Undoubtedly.

When he was a nub, Herbert had tried to admire Hugo enough to linger. But he couldn't. Perhaps it was his Adam's apple, peaked a little too decidedly at the opening of his cricket shirt, the odd, dark mole on the inside of his arm where it was very white, the unfamiliar smell of his discarded boots from which he must stand back in silence. He'd made Hugo's bed without looking too closely at it or smoothing his hand across the bottom sheet to straighten it. He'd pulled it from the side and tucked it in. He'd rearranged the pillow by tugging at equal corners. If a hair should have fallen on it, he'd blown it away with a brisk exhalation. And Davey had been the same. They had not patted and plumped their fag-masters' pillows or played with them, throwing them about or putting them on their heads as Herbert had seen GB do with Charlie Fraser's – a mouse under a toadstool – happy to squat there and pick his nose and gaze off into space. GB, so small in his long pants, could have curled up in a corner on Fraser's pillow and slept, imbibing the master's smell, content.

When they were nubs, Davey and he had washed the footer things together and pegged them neatly but did not pry or comment on the holes that pushed through the seams of Hugo's socks or draw attention to the tatty age of third-hand under-drawers. They folded the jerseys, carried them up together, not holding them against their chests, but presented and detached.

For Herbert and for Davey, their heroes were somewhere else.

Closer than Herbert imagined, for Davey Bennett held Herbert half heroic himself. 'My friend, Apie. He's in the footer team. Athletics and aquatics. Second XI now – but wait 'til next year comes.'

'Who won the high jump?' Some pushy nub needing to know before his mates. One-upmanship was never subtle.

'Cummings.'

'I think it was Edwards.'

'It was Cummings.'

'How do you know?' Impertinent.

'Of course, man. He's my friend.'

'Cummings is your friend?' Disbelieving.

'Is Cummings really Bennett's friend?'

Why shouldn't Cummings be his friend? Look there, in the picture, sitting in costumes on the benches by the indoor pool, Davey leaning back between Herbert's knees, Herbert's forearms folded along his shoulders. Evidence enough. A hundred photos.

It would have been different, Herbert knew, if he hadn't been selected for the First XV so young, if he hadn't felt the need to play the hero and left his friend behind.

Oh, Jones, how he had betrayed him.

He could recall Bennett's face looking back at him, fleetingly, on the night that he'd been chosen, as he'd been borne away by the stalwarts for a ducking. He recalled the grin and the small uncertainty in it: Davey knew, as Herbert knew, that somehow, This Was It. There would be no more afternoons with hours to build their fort in the bush; no more fruit raids; no more laying of their pennies on the railway line and hiding in a culvert and waiting for a passing train to flatten them. No more riding on the donkeys by the Cradock Dam. Herbert simply wouldn't have the time.

'It really doesn't matter, Apie,' Davey said unexpectedly one day. 'You're a lucky sweep, that's all.' Still, that smile and the small regretfulness.

There was nothing grudging in Davey's support of Herbert when he played. He watched practices, he watched matches. He sometimes took care of the mascot and sometimes the coach allowed him to be linesman with a small white flag. He did it very well. But, by the way he trailed back up to the House after a game, among the motley and the undistinguished and unknown, it was hard for Herbert to accompany him when he could be walking with the victors on their way to the showers.

Davey Bennett knew he'd have to find another friend.

He joined the photographic society instead. He did not have a camera, so he ran errands, cut pictures to accurate size, carried tripods for the master and, by his third year, was often given the task of delivering films to the photographer's shop in the Church Square for developing. A week later he would return with a new batch and wait for the prints of the previous week. The master who oversaw the activities, deemed him reliable enough. Charlie Fraser's pictures were the special charge he gave himself. And Charlie always let him into his study saying, 'Checked for duds, Jones?'

'No, Fraser, I was waiting for you to see them first.'

'Well, have a look, will you. I'm busy at the moment.'

Included then, Davey Bennett would open the envelope and spread the pictures out while Charlie Fraser fiddled about in his locker – Davey never knew if it was a pretext or not – until they were on the desk top and he had had a chance to admire them himself. Then Fraser would come and lean over and glance at them, half frown or a half smile. Charlie Fraser – by a gesture – offered validation.

THREE

In those pictures there is a cipher, easily read – a hand on a shoulder, the inclination of a head: Sundays, Howieson's Poort, Michaelmas holidays in Port Elizabeth. House teams in victory, sure enough of momentary brotherhood to elbow-hook, fingers loose inside a collar, skin to skin, heads touching. Here the spaces are diminished. Here, fellows are propped together so that Davey Bennett, bearer on these occasions of Charlie Fraser's camera, could record the winning moment on some late, triumphant afternoon. They stand, eyes narrowed against a lowering sun, legs entwined, hair unbrushed, coats piled over a fence behind. Everything in disarray.

Here was evidence of friendships, linking page to page. Charlie had put them there, firmly annotated by initials, connecting them in each grey-blue frame. Arthur clowning. With Charlie; without him. Arthur on Charlie's shoulders – Davey Bennett's effort – perched, hands in his hair. Charlie, gruff under teasing fingers, shaking him off. Arthur was the only one allowed such liberties. He sat aloft, beaming like a jester.

How easy to follow it – oh, with hindsight, Herbert knew. And with age, the augur's eye, unfaltering.

Here, the classrooms, Jarge at the Bell, the Second Master with his hat and cane, the Head on Sports Day. Sparrow Bell and Danny Grant: always together, cricket pitch, cadet camp, fishing. Dan and Charlie: fooling in the backyard of the Grants' tall stone house, a picture with puppies in their arms some Sunday afternoon, and tea by the fig tree.

    –It's my favourite picture, Charlie's mother had said. –Aren't they dear little dogs?

    Sparrow Bell and Arthur in a study when Arthur was in trouble, looking grave: Sparrow sitting like a tutor, hair neatly parted, collar starched; Arthur, just behind his chair.

    'Sparrow!' Arthur yelling down the dorm. 'Help!' Latin test tomorrow and not a declension under his control. 'Spaaaarow!'

    'Shut up, Arthur,' John Barham being prim. His Latin books were thoroughly digested.

    'Spaaarow!' Pulling his hair in mock despair.

    Sparrow, wherever he was, paid no attention.

    'Sparrow' – Arthur leaning out of the dorm window – 'Clarice White's just walking past the chapel. Come quick!'

    It was an infallible formula. Sparrow would appear, leaping down the dorm to stand at the side of the window. If she wasn't there and Arthur was bluffing, he would low-tackle him, pull him down, sit on him, pummel him, breathless, with his dark freckles standing out across his face and his down-turned eyes fierce and beady and the little plume at his crown, bobbing. But if she was, he would chew the edge of his lip and watch, rapt, unconcerned with ragging.

    Clarice White knew that they were there, but she was too pretty and assured to mind – or to have the need to choose another route.

    'You're a beetroot, Sparrow!'

    'So what! She can't see.'

    Arthur would nudge him hard, pushing just enough to provoke.

    'Get off, Arthur!'

    'Let's carry him down to her . . .'

    But Sparrow didn't care: if people teased, it was always so affectionate, he let them play the fool. He was the only boy who could admit – quite freely and without the slightest hint of shame – that he adored his mother. But then, anyone who'd ever been to Sparrow's house admitted secretly she was the only sort of mother one could publicly own. She was quite the sort to fall in love with.

    No one teased him about his mother – and everyone hoped for

an invitation in the holidays. No one teased him about being a chorister in the Cathedral Choir either: under the cassock, the little white ruff about his neck that made the mothers twinkle at him from the pews, he could give a blistering kick to the shins. He was not past wearing his rugger shorts under his robes to be ready for practice in a moment. Besides, he was the House boxing champion and was not to be trifled with in competition. At a match, no matter how popular his opponent, the shout was, 'Go Sparrow! Go Sparrow!' He was unstoppable. If he won, he grinned. If he lost, he still grinned. And shook hands and never showed any rancour.

The chaplain once expressed the opinion that he had a vocation. Sparrow was alarmed. His face – the sort grandmothers took between two hands spontaneously – invited such a notion but his humour was decidedly unclerical. It was the way his shirt tails nudged out of his pants unnoticed that gave him, perpetually, the air of a small, dear boy. It deceived them all.

The girls at the sister school doted on him: he was a favourite at dancing classes. It was because, when he looked down at his feet – to ensure he was positioning them properly and always deeply apologetic should he tread on a toe – his eyelashes were so surprisingly dark and long and thick, there was the urge to touch them softly with a finger.

'It's not fair that Jack Bell has got such long eyelashes!' – a flutter: the younger girls a little more possessive than the rest.

'Have you seen them?'

'Next time, look.'

'He's such a pet!'

A Pet! Sparrow would have aimed a few kicks for that. There was nothing he could do to change the fierce maternal competition he inspired in the big girls or the homely vivacity in the younger: he was invited more than any other boy to have tea in private houses where the mothers petted him outrageously.

'Ah Jack, get invited to the Carters and wheedle some cake out of Lovell to bring back to school for us,' begged Herbert.

'Sparrow,' Arthur messing his hair and making baby faces at him, 'how about asking if you can take along a pal next time you go to your

Aunt Dimmie's? I've been starving for a week.'

But no matter who Sparrow's friends were, no matter how heroic an association, no matter what berth he had in the XV or how ferociously he boxed or how strongly he could catapult the cricket ball to the boundary, no matter how he grew, or made valiant attempts with the cut-throat razor – 'I hate you, Apie,' when Herbert had made his first successful shave before him – he would always be 'Sparrow' or 'Little Jack'.

'Poor Sparrow will always be a boy,' observed Percy Gilbert once.

'Why do you say that?' said Herbert.

Percy had shrugged. 'It doesn't seem he has a choice. No one wants him to grow up.'

Sparrow's friend was Danny Grant. As Sparrow was small and vivid in his movements and his speech, Danny Grant was big and lumbering. Big shoulders, broad neck, dark skin, straight brown hair. Always sheepish. Gentle Dan.

And if Sparrow could stand at the window and stare at Clarice walking by, while Arthur fell about heaving mock sighs behind his back until Sparrow either laughed or thumped him, Danny Grant went to the most extraordinary lengths to hide his own unrequited longings.

Danny's secret.

But everybody knew.

You only had to look at Dan to know. That subterranean flush, despite the olive skin, if Mary Clifford should appear.

No one teased. It made Dan stutter. No one liked to make Dan stutter: they ranked behind him in support. In class, under scrutiny, his mates leaned forward in their seats when he was questioned, as if to urge out words for him. And when he made a sentence whole, without a pause, they breathed collectively, Sparrow most of all.

Sparrow knew what Mary Clifford meant to Dan. They all did. Douggie Morgan knew what Danny meant to Mary Clifford too. His sources were impeccable: his sister told him everything. Dan was on a winning streak.

'Sparrow, sit Dan down and tell him, man to man,' Douggie said, exasperated. 'Mary Clifford's mad about him too. You can see it written all over her face!' Doug hauled Sparrow into the common-room and closed the door to keep out intruders. 'I can't bear the suspense any more. Fetch him here and kick his arse.'

'Now, Dan, just *talk* to her,' said Sparrow earnestly, handing his friend a cup of tea, brought up from the tuck-shop by Percy Gilbert to emphasise their good intentions.

'*Talk*?' Incredulous.

'Well, roll up your sleeves then and show off your manly forearms!' Percy Gilbert was being flippant. 'The sight will dumbfound her and you can both be silent together.'

Dan folded his arms away from Percy's gaze and frowned.

'Come on, Dan,' Sparrow turned back to him. 'You never stutter with us.'

'Why should I stutter with you?'

'Why should you stutter with her?'

'There *is* a difference.'

'Pretend I'm Mary Clifford . . .' Arthur posing. 'Just say, "Would you like to come to the Cathedral Café for tea, Miss Clifford?"'

'Would you like to take yourself off, you big idiot,' said Dan.

'We'll get you right,' said Sparrow, absently taking Danny's cup and sucking up the contents in a noisy gulp.

'Thanks for the tea, pal,' said Dan.

'Get him some more,' said Sparrow.

'Send Arthur,' said Percy.

'Why me?'

'Mrs Woodman's daughter's serving in the tuck-shop.' Percy inspected his nails.

'Tuppence for tea!' Arthur was scratching in his pocket and was out of the door and down the stairs.

'Is she?' said Charlie, eyebrow raised.

'No,' said Percy. 'But he falls for it every time.'

Charlie laughed.

'Now, Dan,' Sparrow with his hands on his hips. 'We will have to make a plan. . .'

So much anguish for nothing. Such a waste. So little time. Danny Grant, with all his rank and prowess – the best cricketer the school had had in years, batsman supreme, Captain of the XI, stalwart of the XV – remained speechless. And red.

But in the end, taking up the challenge, he joined the debating society with Sparrow and after the initial terror and frozen jaw, he had mastered his fright and debated with the best of them, only succumbing when he became excited. His school-mates willed him through House debate after House debate, Sparrow mouthing words unconsciously, trying to unstick them in Dan's throat. He'd race then – with himself – to reach the final phrase and Sparrow would wipe his top lip and shake his shoulders a little, in relief.

In the end, Danny had led his team to victory more often than not in inter-house debates.

And then the invitation came from the girls' school. A senior team. The best debaters. The English master would not hear of Danny stepping down, after all the glory. Dan demurred. The master insisted. Dan made excuses. None was good enough.

'What, lad? Am I thinking, perhaps, that a few girls' – just a touch of condescension from the old fellow – 'are going to frighten you away? And after the century you made last week?' Eyebrows disappearing into his hair. Would they ever come back?

'No, sir.'

A frown, then, quite ferocious, brows pulled down again. 'I should think not, indeed!'

Dan had prepared for days, knowing the challenge, Sparrow coaching, Mac for seconds.

'Say it again, Dan. Take a breath. Begin again. You're doing fine. Splendid, Dan!'

The subject was a good one for a sparring match with girls: 'Only qualified women should receive a parliamentary vote'. The opponents would be looking for a fight: *all* women should receive a parliamentary vote! Couldn't you hear them whining?

Danny had practised his opening remarks over and over, walking up and down his study, his words unfaltering, Sparrow bobbing with each emphatic point.

'You can do it, Dan. Perhaps she won't be there. She's such a quiet girl, they'll never have her in the team. It's those harridans that always end up in debates. Suffragette types with big shoes and big noses and big opinions.'

'And big arses,' said Mac absently.

But Mary Clifford *was* in the opposing team. First speaker.

She sat on the stage in her starched white blouse, her thick dark hair in a brand new ribbon tied at the nape of her neck and her little boots burnished, neatly crossed under her chair.

It was as if Dan had been hit by a brick in the solar plexus when he saw her, sitting serenely with her papers in her hand, opening for her side. Dan had nowhere to put his eyes. Sparrow, beside him, decided to look fierce. He composed his mouth, frowned when he remembered, leaned in and spoke to Danny every now and then, like a trainer in the boxer's corner.

Mary Clifford directed her argument entirely to Dan. He sat mesmerised, staring, not hearing a word she said. The sweat started to creep inexorably down his cheek. Percy, on his other side, had to prod him to his feet to reply. Sparrow put his head in his hands as if he were reading his notes. Herbert, sitting in the audience, knew that he was praying.

Herbert sat clenching his knuckles fiercely in his lap: –Go on Dan, go on.

Danny Grant began, looking out at the audience, catching Herbert's eye. Herbert winked.

Danny managed well, four minutes, five. Then, gaining confidence a little, turned towards the girls' team, quite emphatic. Mary Clifford gazed up at him.

Daniel Grant paused to breathe.

And then he stood.

And stood.

Crimson, the words stuck, choking him. He was unable to proceed or retreat. No one could look at him. Sparrow slumped, pushed his hand through his hair. It stood up damply and he took out his handkerchief and blew his nose. He glared at Mary Clifford – but she was unaware of what she'd done. It was her proximity: all that

47

sweetness and those dark brown eyes exploring Danny's face and her curly mouth. Wretched female!

Percy had taken over quietly, picked up Dan's notes and, without a trace of fluster, delivered the rest of the argument.

Reading in even tones, the text unseen – 'Women are incomprehensible . . .' Percy paused. 'Mankind belongs to two classes: men on one hand and lunatics and women on the other.' He raised an eyebrow delicately and glanced at Dan. Really!

There was uproar among the girls, cheers from the boys. Herbert turned round to stare at the ranks. Josie Zeederberg, the assistant chaplain's daughter, was there behind him. She was laughing with a little patronising tilt to her nostril. She saw him and stared him out a fraction longer than was fair. 'It's true about them,' he muttered to Davey next to him, 'Lunatics!' and pulled at the lobe of his ear.

Argument was heard from every side, the adjudicator calling the boys to order several times.

'May I ask the Speaker, ma'am' – some supercilious great girl – 'to withdraw his last remark.'

'The remark was not mine, madam.' Percy, haughtier than she. 'I am only reading what is in my colleague's notes. However, if we consider the commotion in this room at the present moment and reflect that ninety per cent of the occupants are young women, we will recall that Bedlam . . .'

Howls and hoots drowned him out.

'Madam Chair,' Doug Morgan, as third speaker, shouted them down. He was standing in a most embarrassing way with his legs apart as if he were leaning back against a headwind. 'Give a woman a finger and she will take a hand,' he said and made a gesture as if he were encompassing all the girls in the seats below the stage. His palm gleamed a little: Douggie was not quite as confident as he seemed. Knuckles to hip now and striking another pose – such a heroic fellow – 'Women' – he paused – 'are not guided by reason but are a slave to every passing whim. In medieval times, ma'am, a talkative woman was publicly ducked. It is something that should be reinstated. Especially in this town!'

'Shut up, Doug,' Herbert heard Percy say. '*I* am supposed to be speaking for Dan.'

Doug sat, looming in his chair with his ankles muddled with the legs of the table and the girls staring up at him. He did not stare back but he touched the end of his nose as if checking it, to be sure it appeared at its best advantage.

The girls carried the day and Percy conceded defeat on behalf of his team. He did it with the utmost grace. But the jubilation of the girls was an affront and Percy had tapped Danny's notes together and left the platform like the Bishop in retreat. He'd consulted his pocket-watch with an air of resignation: a pipe in the common-room would have suited him far better than refreshments in the draughty dining-hall with all those girls.

At tea, only Danny had stood, great and forlorn, among his fellow debaters and friends. The rest were in high spirits. But Douggie Morgan and Arthur, Charlie, Sparrow and Mac had ringed him round against the stares of the gauche. Then Mary Clifford had come over and offered a plate of buns and looked up at him with such a smile that Herbert had feared that Dan might ignite spontaneously if she didn't go away.

There was complete silence.

Even Arthur was lost for words.

Even Sparrow stood quite still, the little plume on his head frozen upright.

–Say something, Dan.

No one breathed.

–Dan! Speak, for God's sake!

But Dan had only closed his mouth and shaken his head severely at the buns and, rebuffed, Mary Clifford had dropped her eyes and handed the plate around to the others. Each had taken a bun, silent too, not looking, as if in speaking they'd betray their friend. No 'thank yous', no 'much obligeds'. She'd offered it to Dan again but he'd looked out over her head at the far wall as if she wasn't there. Sparrow had taken one for him, edging it off the plate, like a dog sneaking a titbit from another's bowl. Her colour high, Mary Clifford had turned and walked away.

Sparrow put the extra bun in his pocket and gave it to Danny later. He suspected Dan had kept it for days in his drawer – or, at least, a part of it – because of its origin.

But on the cricket pitch or rugby field, it was different. There Danny didn't have to speak at all. And everybody knew, as he knew, that Mary Clifford was present when the public games were played. She used to sit in the stand with the other senior girls and brothers and cousins and any who could approach without remark, and watch him. No one could see where she looked from under the brim of her school hat, so still, so neat, so rapt was she. But everyone guessed. And Daniel Grant, from a distance, delivered heroic performances.

But despite the cajoling of his friends, Sparrow's arguments, Percy's careful rationale, Arthur's frustration at his sheepishness – and the offer to be emissary, to carry letters, messages, gifts – Dan could not be persuaded to approach Mary Clifford again and though she watched him, drifted along the street in full view of the House and though she glanced up at his window often when the croc passed beneath the old grey stone walls, he remained resolutely out of sight. If he could not speak, he had no way of showing his devotion. And he dared not speak, in case his voice got stuck and he stood before her, seemingly an idiot. Nor did Mary Clifford have any way of showing him how little she minded and how many team pictures she had procured from the photographer and hidden in her dictionary and how – behind his head in each – there was a little cross, carefully placed, and 'DG' written with a small, self-conscious flourish.

He never knew.

It was all so innocent then. Like lamplight, like tuck-boxes, like Dicks' buns on Saturdays and the ringing challenge of the bowler making an appeal and the high, apricot-coloured clouds of evening riding far above them. Crocs, chapel, the smell of Robbie's pipe coming round a corner first to give them warning; the first production of *Princess JuJu or the Golden Amulet* where one could stare at Clarice White as the La La Maiden, swathed in silky bits with rather frayed edges, without being mocked. It had to do with Herbert glaring and kicking up dust and cursing under his breath when Miss Josie Zeederberg went by with her hat dangling and her snout to the fore, not looking in his direction and he wearing his brand new heraldic footer jersey, emblazoned with the wide blue glorious stripe: just trotting past in her boots with the hem of her serge skirt trailing where her heel had caught it and her black stockings with a run and a look that said 'Why should I care what jersey you are wearing? Idiotic boy!' Innocent, like tennis on Saturdays and who was invited; weekends at the Seymours' farm when Jamie's sisters were around; playing with the puppies at the Grants and asking Danny's sister, for the hundredth time, what their names were: –I've told you, Herbert! Cantie and Baldie! Why can't you remember?

It was really love that had preoccupied them all.

Percy had said it.

Herbert had dismissed it.

But Percy had been right. A thousand different kinds of love – but love, nonetheless. Among it – iron love: undisclosed, undisclosing.

It drifted there, trawling quietly under everything. It went onto the rugby field with them. It went to chapel. It went to bed with them at night. Some, like Unwin, did not know where or how to find it. Some, like Archer, wanting it so much, had killed it. Some, like Mac, had made a little shrine to it. Some, like Arthur Graham, just rejoiced in it, unashamed. Some, like Charlie, had it in abundance and he wasn't sure what it was he had, or why.

Some, like Percy, grieved at it.

It was needed. And denied. Explored voraciously. And silenced. It had many forms.

'Everyone, croc coming!' Sunday morning and Douggie Morgan, always vigilant of the corner of the street, sent the words echoing about the rafters of the dorm.

There were no curtains in the windows but, standing to the side, the walls were thick and the sills deep. The girls, walking two abreast, could not see if there were watchers. Except, of course, they guessed. So the knowing ones pranced up a little as they passed. Among themselves, it was clear that they were taking airy bets as to who was watching. Except it was not *who* was there but who they *hoped* was there: past the first house, it would be Seymour or Oosthuizen they'd be wishing for, and Holmes or Wentzel at the next – how could you choose between them? Past the big House, maybe Douggie Morgan or Vincent MacCallum.

And Charlie Fraser. Always Charlie Fraser.

But Charlie Fraser never looked. Everyone knew that.

Of course, it was the boys the girls never talked about who watched them most, the younger boys, shouldering each other at the sides of the windows and trying not to laugh. Some of the littler girls, bringing up the rear, might crane and titter, even with a mistress near. And then there was Josie Zeederberg, with her one thick plait and her quaint nose and her down-turned eyes, who knew exactly who was there and didn't give a fig for anyone.

The great girls at the head of the column were grave, except they lifted their chins and tilted their heads, just a fraction. Herbert knew who for – just in case, in passing, he might glance from a window – just in passing, and be forced to see: but Charlie Fraser never bothered when the shout went up. And if he noticed them at all, he'd never show it.

'Here comes the croc,' the hiss would go down the dorm and everyone jostled for a place. Round the corner they marched, across the road and under the windows. All that was visible from above were hats, capes and narrow shoes and sometimes the fleeting glimpse of a face turned up.

'Clarice White's the prettiest!' announced Morgan.

'Rot!' Snorted Arthur.

'Shut up, Arthur, Sparrow will hear.'

'Mary Clifford,' said Arthur.

'She's too dark,' said Doug.

'Rot yourself!'

'She is too!'

'Dan will beat you up if you speak against her,' said Arthur, giving him a shove. Doug fell against a chair and tipped it over. It clattered to the floor. Twenty pairs of eyes looked up from below, scanning for watchers. So did the mistress. She stopped and surveyed the windows of the House frostily.

'Idiot,' hissed Doug and Arthur flopped down on a bed and started to laugh.

'You boys' – a bird-voice floating up – 'Mr Robinson will know about this.'

'You boys . . .' mimicked Arthur.

Once there was a step on the stair and everyone scattered. Charlie Fraser came in.

'We thought you were Robbie,' said Arthur, swinging his legs over the side of his bed, stretching out and putting his hands behind his head.

'What's up?'

'Just watching the croc. They'll be back from church in two hours. Do you think Clarice White is the prettiest? Or Mary Clifford?'

'Neither,' said Charlie.

'Why neither?'

But Charlie paid no attention.

He was infuriating. Everyone knew exactly who it was the other fellows watched. But they didn't know who Charlie watched. He never gave a sign.

It was Josie Zeederberg who was the cause of Herbert's getting a beating. Her father was the assistant chaplain to Mr Dowsley and she was the third of eight children, polished up and patched in her sisters' hand-me-downs. She had no regard for boys – she had three brothers of her own – and she was the captain of the junior cricket team at the girls' school. She could hit a six with the best of them. Josie Zeederberg came to chapel with her family when her father took evening prayers, uncaring of the fellows ranged in ranks behind her pew. She sometimes turned and looked at them quite candidly and other times she didn't look at all, just as the inclination took her. Josie Zeederberg was fifteen and had learned to play the trumpet. It was her brother Harry's – he was bugler for the cadets – and he made it whine and grate with every note to set the teeth on edge while she could blow it like a regular, cheeks puffed out, her nose quite white from the effort. Not that she came to school to demonstrate, but she tooted away in the garden of her house which backed onto the playing fields. Once Herbert lobbed a cricket ball over the hedge by mistake and she fetched it. She had a gruff voice. She appraised Herbert with her down-turned green eyes and said, 'Are you in Charles Fraser's house?'

'Yes.'

'Good.'

'Why good?'

'Good.' That's all she said, without explaining and she tossed the cricket ball back, over-arm like a boy, so that it whizzed past his ear and sent up a puff of sand and Davey Bennett and the other fellows, waiting on the field, who were close enough to see, all laughed. Herbert knew he'd hear of nothing else all week. He was not pleased and he left her with a glare.

That was why she stuck her tongue out on the way past the House the next time the croc went to church, so, seeing her, Herbert leaned out and stuck his back and almost fell over the sill. Robbie, the old fool, came in at that moment and picked him up by the seat of his pants where he was dangling and booted him into his study and gave him four for his troubles and a long lecture that the whole House could hear about gentlemanly behaviour. After that there was a score to settle.

She had wanted to know if Herbert was in the same house as Charlie Fraser. So, in chapel, he observed her closely after that, to have something on her, but she paid no one the least attention. Not Charles Fraser, not Arthur Graham, not Danny Grant, nor Vincent MacCallum nor Georgie Holmes nor Doug Morgan nor James Seymour nor any who the great girls watched so avidly.

And sometimes when the school went to the cathedral for a special service, Herbert might just find himself standing behind her when the Communion queue was long. He didn't mean to look at her but there was nowhere else to look – that's what he said to Davey Bennett when Davey nudged him and told him to close his mouth and breathe through his nose. She was very small, but she stood as straight as a cadet. She had surprising little tendrils under her plait. And her neck was most surprising of all. Herbert wasn't quite sure why, so he looked at it a lot to find out.

54

She must have heard Herbert had had a beating on account of her because she sometimes used to glance at him, out of the corner of her eyes and her nose would move, just a fraction, as though she were sniffing him out. It was a funny little gesture, almost friendly. It used to make him want to laugh, there in the queue with old Robbie hovering over them. But then, he remembered that even her brother said she was an infuriating girl and certainly not to be noticed. He once asked Arthur Graham what he thought of her and Arthur said, 'Who's she?' – puzzled – and then, looking Herbert over with a grin, 'I say, Apie, is she someone I ought to know? Be a sport and introduce me.' He cuffed him on the head in jest and winked at him in chapel the next time Josie Zeederberg walked in but Herbert ignored her for at least a month to show him that he'd got it wrong.

But why she'd asked if Charlie Fraser was in his house remained a mystery at the time. He soon forgot about it, for the rugger season was starting and he had his mind on lofty things.

For love was rugby too. And in the second term, love was rugby most of all. The great *esprit de corps*. Anticipation of that moment – new jersey, stiff with glory – when the team ran together onto Lower field for the first time.

–You're supposed to be quite a *bok* if you play on Lower.

Everything Herbert had done in the two years at school was in preparation and when the summons came, his heart flopped about uncontrolled and there was no restraining it. He'd had to put his head down between his knees. Younger almost than any boy before him, as small still in stature as a nub two years below, his feet only a size four, it seemed preposterous that he should take the field with Douggie Morgan, towering at six foot two.

But the coach had chosen him.

Scrum-half in the First XV. Cummings, H.: 15 years and ten months.

'Cummings took the field for the first time today at half-back. A small, dark-haired lad, quite the youngest in the pack, his pluck and dash were unrivalled. This spirited young player should be an asset to the College side with many years ahead to prove his worth.'

55

His first notice in the press! He cut the piece surreptitiously from *The Journal* and put it in a book. The passion and the practice had paid off.

But nothing could rival the moment when he'd heard that he had made the side, nothing could touch the exultation.

The lists were put up after prep one evening and Robbie, coming up the stairs, when the lads were washing after games, saw Herbert in the stairwell with his towel and he said, 'Cummings minor, you had better go to Birch's and order a footer jersey and socks.'

'Sir?'

But Robbie went on, calling stentoriously for the juniors who'd been caught on a fruit-raid that afternoon: Herbert heard them lining up, subdued, outside his study door.

And then Arthur burst into the dormitory and strode over to where he was messing about with Davey Bennett and scooped him up and slung him over his shoulder triumphantly. 'Well, Apie, now we'll have to give you a ducking, old pal. Under the showers with you! Help me, lads.' And there were MacCallum and Doug Morgan and Holmes and Seymour and Sparrow Bell and they carried him shoulder-high down the stairs. Charlie was coming up from the prep room and, grinning, joined in the triumphal procession. Off with his clothes and a right royal ducking Herbert had, the water sluicing into his nose. He laughed and choked all at once. There was no feeling like it. No feeling ever. Under the hands of demigods, he was a demigod himself. They dressed him in Doug Morgan's jersey. It reached past his knees. To put the arms into the folds and to work the fingers down that sleeve through the cuff and for hands to appear stretched out, was a whole reclothing of his life. It was burning in his chest to feel the glory. They set him on top of the lockers and gave him a pint of ginger beer to swallow in a gulp. His throat ached with the great intoxication. His head spun with lights. Choirs sang. The trumpet call of far off battles. The chant of boys. The eyes of the others – the younger ones, those in waiting and those who would never make it there – watching him. He felt suddenly detached from them, even from Davey Bennett, his friend who'd built a fort with him, his co-conspirator who'd manufactured stink bombs with him in the lab; his companion of the train: he stood there grinning like a fool, his face receding. It was as if Herbert had passed over into a brotherhood from which there would be no return. Even if he played only one game and died for it. Standing in between them all then, they punched him, roughed his head: Morgan, MacCallum and Danny Grant; Sparrow and Arthur. Seymour and Holmes, MacGregor, Jansen, Wentzel, McIntosh, Lotter and Oosthuizen all came across from the other houses. Charlie Fraser hooked his arm about his neck, pulled his head down to his shoulder briefly. 'Welcome, Apie,' he said.

–I'll kill you if I hear you've blubbed.

Herbert laughed instead. It was a close call.

And then, when the team photograph had been taken and Herbert, the only new cap – the youngest ever – had had to sit on the kaross at Charlie Fraser's feet, not knowing how or where to look, Charlie Fraser had given his shoulder a friendly nudge. It seemed, because of that, the picture came out right.

And love was something sunk in each of them and in the very stones, just as bound to them as the great door of the House was bound to the rugby team in each immortal annual photograph posed against the backdrop of winter creeper and iron-studded wood. Love was belonging: on the field, in the Drill Hall when a bout was fought, shoulder to shoulder in the dining-hall, hiding stringy boiled pumpkin in a pocket when Robbie wasn't watching.

Love was Robbie too: love and awe together:

'Cummings minor?'

'Sir?'

'Why are you loitering about up here?' That sarcastic nasal edge, foretelling trouble.

'I came to find my footer boots, sir.' The only acceptable excuse.

'Then why are you staring out of the window?'

'Sir.'

'Idle boy. Loitering gives rise to every kind of mischief.' Sloth and sin are synonymous.

'Sir.'

Herbert could not think of the House without Robbie, without the sound of his old grey flannels and the squeak of his shoes and the smell of tobacco and lozenges that preceded him and followed him. He could not believe that now he was beyond footer boots and idle boys, up in the cemetery beyond the station. There was a new housemaster in his quarters with a wife and a baby in a pram. Robbie would never have considered a wife! One could not care for sixty boys with a wife.

–Such unnecessary distraction.

–So much expense. Baleful Robbie, casting his eye over the poor deluded lads in their senior year, settling in and complacently smoking their pipes in his study and asking permission for a dance, if you please!

–A dance? Devil take it! Such a commotion for nothing. Grumble, grumble and they, still cajoling.

–Go hunting, boys.

–Take up a Commission.

–Try prospecting. It'll keep you out of trouble.

But Robbie had his secrets too. Oh, a little chink discovered.

'Did you hear the rumour?' Douggie Morgan.

'What?' Herbert.

'Robbie went to a boarding house in PE in the hols and there was a lady who sat at his table. John Barham says he's going to marry her.'

'What unadulterated rot. Robbie wouldn't even talk to one. He'd be too scared.'

'Robbie scared? A big game hunter like him?'

'Bet he'd rather face a buffalo than a woman.'

There were three buffalo heads in his quarters. All well-horned and mounted.

'Barham said that he went everywhere with her.' Doug was insistent.

'How does he know?'

'He saw them at the beach.'

'Robbie at the beach?' Herbert was incredulous.

'So' – gleeful Doug – 'this morning at break, Barham, the fool, goes up and says to him, "Congratulations, sir. I hear you are getting married".'

'Arse!'

'I thought Robbie would decapitate him.'

Perhaps Robbie wandered round the House at night now, checking up on loiterers: that all-knowing, rheumy eye. Perhaps nubs, taking the long, cold trot to the bogs after lights out, smelled lozenges and tobacco as they passed the boxroom door.

–What's that smell? Bunching together.

–Someone's smoking in the boxroom. Peering in, bolstering each other.

–No one's here.

–It's Robbie. Some gormless ignoramus.

–Who's Robbie?

–Don't you know? A know-all with a brother who'd preceded him.

–Run!

Herbert wouldn't have been surprised if boys met Robbie in the hallway or on the stairs. He had nowhere else to go. The House had been his life.

Robbie always kept his bush knife at his hip and patted it every now and then to make sure that it was there. Pat, pat, pat: when he was worried. Pat, pat, pat. But he fingered it when he taught, caressing it when he was explaining or making a point. It was a talisman of earlier times. He'd hung his hunting trophies from his young days on the walls along with the best of the team photos. Prefects took tea with him once a fortnight. He made it in a battered old pot which must have accompanied him on countless hunts, been warmed at countless thorn-wood fires. It had a glamour, belonged in an era before house duties and curricula and small boys' misdemeanours. Sometimes the seniors could inveigle a story out of him. Not often though. He never bragged.

'How did you bag that tsessebe, sir?'

He would regard the head, mounted up above his desk, with an intimate glance and then fob them off. The story was between the tsessebe and himself. He would describe techniques in tracking, discuss the merits of weapons, recommend taxidermists. But the chase itself – his part in it – was undisclosed. Hunts and wars: it was bad form to discuss either. It could lead to exaggeration or boasting; blowing the trumpet or worse. So each, whoever rose in rank to be admitted to the sanctuary, invented his own version of the buffalo, the tsessebe, the waterbuck, while Robbie maintained his gruff detachment.

Bad form. One did not do or say – or even *think* – something that Robbie might judge 'bad form'. That was the worst sin one could commit. Second to that was insubordination. One would be soundly beaten or banned from watching a rugby match for that. Banning was worse than any beating. Much, much worse. Robbie held footer sacred. So did they.

And they were proud of Robbie's reputation to terrify. Proud of Robbie's swing, the resounding six, equidistant, welts perfectly aligned. Proud of Robbie's mangy dog, which only growled at other boys, scenting difference: it could out-fart a class of nubs and have them running for the windows, gasping. Robbie didn't seem to notice. He'd pop another lozenge in his mouth and pull at his moustache. It was bad form to remark on farts.

They were proud of Robbie's scorn of hot water, interior bogs, warm beds.

Robbie made men.

At any price.

Love was all the heroes who still gazed out from pictures on the dining-hall walls. The great House door, the creeper, the kaross, the half-moon of chairs, the little table with the cup, the rugby ball with the date carefully inscribed. Cricket, Athletics, Footer.

Examine them. Know them. Absorb them.

Here is Sampson: The best full-back ever. Here is Taberer: played against England in '04. Here is Broster.

Here is Rudd.

As a newboy, Danny Grant had polished all the trophies on Rudd's study shelves. For him they were the Holy Grail. He'd been chosen to succeed, to follow. And so, now, Love was watching Danny Grant hit a double century and now, some little nub, a tadpole growing legs, was tending Danny's cups, metamorphosing quietly himself.

Love was anyone who wore the dark blue velvet colours cap with silver edging and the little tassel spiralled to the crown. Love was cheering Fraser's drop goal, pitched across the crossbar in the fading minute of a match. Love was watching him trot away, head down – as if it was nothing – while the School went wild. Not a word: bad form.

'Well done, Fraser.'

'Thank you, sir.'

Simple as that.

Love found expression in the rush to the photographer's in Church Square for copies of official shots. From the smallest nub to the heroes themselves, the copies were acquired with the fervour of gamblers hoarding lottery tickets.

'Lend me half a crown, Davey. I'll pay it back next week. I want some snaps.'

'There's a board up in the window with a picture of cadets.'

'Are we in it?'

'Can't see us, really.'

They bought it anyway. No one needed question why. It had to do with the heroes in another guise: bandoliers, officers' swords, pipes in the corners of their mouths, firmly clamped. Heroes, cut out and pasted in albums, thumb-tacked to the picture rail on a wall, framed in a home-made paper border and kept in a locker.

Those pictures became, in time, the most tangible testament of having been there. For some, of having existed at all. The choice of picture, distributed over and over among so many albums, linked them: we were there. We were there when the MCC came. We were there when Rudd set up the record for the half at one minute, fifty-eight and a half seconds. We were there when Grant made two twenty-three. We were at the cricket dinner with the great backdrop of the Victoria Falls thundering within a fretwork of sunset palms, painted by old Lucas, the Head presiding and the team sitting at the top table, all eleven in their wide-striped blazers.

Those pictures were the only proof of bonds, fixed in faded sepia. They could be glanced over and dismissed. Or re-read. Team-mates, arms linked; swimmers braced to dive, a human pyramid teetering on the lawn behind the House. Herbert knew them all. And, in later years – in a newer world, quite changed – he had examined them, searching for their clues. Like an archaeologist with a little brush lifting dust, layer on layer, to uncover the essential artefact beneath, he'd searched his own collection.

The clues were there: like the picture of them all, piled up against each other in the grass, straw boaters at an angle, eyes squinting at the sun. Charlie had taken it at the Seymours where they'd gone on a half-term leave-out, easy legs and knees, arms relaxed along a thigh, ankles crossed. And in that picture, MacCallum, usually so upright, was recumbent against Percy Gilbert's shoulder, face turned up to the warmth, eyes half closed to its brightness. They were all laughing, except Percy. Percy, his hair perfectly parted just off centre, smooth to the touch of the brilliantine he always used, was looking down at MacCallum, his hand poised at the instant that the shutter opened, just above the crown of MacCallum's head, not touching.

There was something in that gesture: a caress, frozen suddenly within the little space between the hand and the curve of the upturned forehead. Mac, face to the sun, arms out to its simple benediction, was unaware.

If the cipher had been uncomprehended by the boy, the man – brush in hand? – had understood. Herbert had mulled it with himself. And one December Saturday, returned with those who had been left – stunned survivors mustering (were the others there, gathered just beyond the known frontier?) – he'd met Percy Gilbert wandering under the trees by the new school chapel, hat in hand, as if the intervening years had been some strange aberrant dream.

'Cummings minor, dear fellow,' Percy had said. 'I might have known. It had to be you.' He had addressed Herbert as if he'd taken up the sentence from the last time they'd spoken – neither continents, nor seas, nor wars, nor a decade in between to interrupt the even flow of words, the continuity of thought. He had smiled. 'I divined you, long before I saw you!'

And together, through that day, sitting in the pavilion, watching present pupils and past play each other at cricket, through the reunion dinner and recital, through the memorial dedication and cadet parade

– through all the resurrected rituals of their boyhood, participants in some old rite to reaffirm belonging – their words had drifted back and forth. And in between, the silences had been reflective and companionable.

'I wonder why we make these pilgrimages, Cummings. What are we looking for?' Percy Gilbert had said.

'A way to put off dying,' Herbert's words had echoed Percy's from long ago.

Percy had smiled then. He had remembered. 'Metaphorically or literally, Cummings?'

'Both.'

'Both, indeed.'

FOUR

Percy Gilbert had grieved at love and no one knew. For Percy was beyond conjecture – an adult, not a boy. It seemed impossible that he had ever been a nub, preposterous that he had polished someone else's boots. No one could recall the time.

But Percy *was* a boy, just like all the rest. He'd also been a nub. He'd learned the First Commandment too. Silence: absolute. Denial? No – but sacred to himself. And when he had rank and was Second-Head-of-House, he never sent the small boys up. Corporal punishment distressed him. He could still feel the knot from his own junior year.

–Gilbert, I shall have to conclude this punishment for now and hold the rest over for another day. The Head stopping after two, gingerly rubbing his elbow. –I shall administer the other four when I feel more disposed. You may go.

No denial. Only terror in the waiting.

And still, five years on, the sound of caning made him close his study door – firmly – to keep the echo out. He could not detach himself or stop the anger. He read aloud Newbolt's 'True Friends'. And if he had to punish, he set the juniors essays for their misdemeanours, looking at his victim from an airy distance, spelling out the topics to the ignorant: 'Nepotism: an assessment of Hannibal's performance in the Alps' or something equally obscure. He did not expect facts – only wit. He rarely got either. Nubs scattered when they saw him. They'd rather have a beating any day.

Percy was treated as an adult, even by the masters. If he had wandered into the staff room and helped himself to a sherry and settled down by the fire and read *The Journal*, no one would have noticed. The Head might have poured a glass himself, said absently, 'Gold Shares falling, Gilbert?'

'Hhhmmm. I wouldn't sell quite yet. Indications show an upswing on the way . . .'

'Really? Well, I never . . .' Looking over the half-moons of his spectacles.

Percy, forever in the university classes, had hovered over all of them, some stork-legged bird, exposing, by a word, a look, the underbelly: all the things kept concealed, unadmitted. And most dear. He had a way of leading into the shallows, preventing retreat and finding out – a quick thrust, incisive always – some evidence to validate his notion of the human heart. They called him 'the oracle', with reason. Even Robbie did.

'Gilbert, a word,' Robbie pulling his moustache.

'Sir?'

'Come up to my study, Gilbert. A conundrum, I'm afraid.'

'I'll do my best.'

In his final year Percy had said to Herbert, a pronouncement, almost ominous, 'You are the next oracle, Cummings.'

'Pardon, Gilbert?' Herbert, arrested as he passed, brought up short by Percy sitting on the garden bench outside the House.

Percy glanced up at him, scanned him as if observing something. He rested his arms along the back of the bench. Herbert waited impatiently, anxious for escape.

Percy smiled. Herbert rubbed the heel of his shoe in the sand, making a pattern.

'*Tibi est successio*,' said Percy Gilbert. 'To you is the succession.'

Herbert kicked his heel in harder. Percy, shifting his gaze to a point just ahead of him, said, 'The augur is a visionary, a wise man, Cummings. A seer.'

Herbert frowned. Percy unfolded his legs and crossed them the other way and said, 'You will be a magistrate, Cummings.'

'I won't. I'll be a farmer.' It was a retort.

Percy ignored the rebuff. 'When you were a little fellow, Hugo's fag – not like that dratted Buckerbridge of mine who is unable to polish a teaspoon let alone a shoe – I could feel it. You attended to him with such discretion, despite his being an oaf. It really was remarkable. I thought then – Cummings will be a magistrate, a justice of the peace. He debates matters with himself. Right-wrong. Wrong-right. You can see the fellow churning up his head, you can see him watching.'

Herbert stopped kicking and screwing his heel into the ground. He put his hands in his pockets, thought better of it, took them out.

'You are something of a philosopher, Cummings. An artist even. Not always a happy lot in life.'

'Sorry, Gilbert?'

Percy did not explain.

Undismissed, Herbert had to wait.

'Do you know,' Percy said, changing tack, 'my tuck-box has been plundered yet again? Do you think it could be Barham?'

'Barham?'

'Yes, Barham.' He made a gesture with his hand, as if conjuring him up. 'I can only suspect him – but he'll have some IOU clause up his sleeve to confuse me and put me off the scent. Barham will be a merchant or a broker like his father. His inclinations are entirely exploitative. Why would he take such extreme pains to secure a portion of everybody else's tuck without committing himself to a reciprocation clause?'

Herbert did not contradict him: his tuck fell prey to Barham as well. He'd thought of bringing a *slagyster* from home and setting it inside the tuck-box to trap the thief. The satisfaction would be worth the risk.

'I've been working out our destinies,' said Percy. 'It's been a diverting change from Greek. Georgie Holmes – let's look at him. Perhaps he'll be the next Rhodes Scholar. So many centuries notched up on the pitch. Splendid really. Seymour? Maybe. Being Headboy will help. Brains – and all that talent on the field to boot.' He smiled at his own little pun. 'And so they should be' – as if the choice was entirely his – 'but only one can go, so which are we to choose?' He looked up at the sky. 'Thank God for Holmes and Seymour to counteract the crop of farmers! I can tell them from the moment they walk through that door, no matter how well they're scrubbed and got up. Just look at Douglas Morgan, poor fellow! He will still be Douglas Morgan, as he is, in fifty years from now. He will produce flocks of goats and children and send them here to garner honours in the rugger team. It's a pity it's so difficult to distinguish between the two.'

'Doug Morgan's a very decent chap!' He was one of Herbert's heroes.

Percy glanced at him and smiled, folding his arms and staring off in front of him again. 'No one disputes that.'

Herbert was easing away. He wanted to kick a ball about before chapel and the light was fading. But Percy was not inclined to let him go. 'Holmes and Seymour, of course, will be great men. Daniel Grant – perhaps . . .'

Herbert breathed out slowly. Blast. Here he goes again.

'Almost as great as Rudd – but not quite. Not quite. After all, *he* was god. You only get one in a generation, you know. Poor fellow.'

'Why poor fellow?' No one said anything deprecating about Rudd.

'Such a burden, if you think about it. All that expectation.'

Herbert looked up at the windows. The lights were on. The chapel bell would ring.

Percy said, 'We'll all put in our pennyworth of how we knew Holmes and Seymour once. We'll rush off to reunions in the hope they might remember us. It's so predictable. It would be so much more interesting if, say' – he seemed to search – 'Archer or Unwin were famous instead and we all turned into sycophants for them!'

Herbert did not know what sycophants were.

Percy sighed. 'You are not diverted, are you, Cummings? But there is no point in discussing things with Buckerbridge, is there? He appears to live in a fog. Most days I'd like to drop him head-first out of a window.'

Irritated and impatient, Herbert said, 'I'm sure MacCallum will listen.' It was a great impertinence but it was out before he could bite

67

it back.

Percy Gilbert did not move. Neither did Herbert. Ten seconds, twenty. Idiot! How could he have said it? It wasn't Herbert's business.

Percy seemed to be regarding the toe of his shoe along the line of his outstretched legs. 'I see no MacCallum in all of this.' He said it gravely, overlooking the impertinence. He did not take his eyes from his shoe. 'No MacCallum. No Arthur Graham. No Sparrow Bell. They are uncertain still. Great men or nothing.' He paused. 'And that object of your scrutiny, dear fellow,' – ah, he hadn't got away with it – 'I see no clear direction there. Charles Fraser is entirely enigmatic.'

Herbert felt the flush on his neck. He'd asked for it. He'd got it in the gut.

Percy glanced at him then: he'd won the round. But he said, with a small, wry smile, 'You're a seer, Cummings, whether you want to be or not.'

Herbert remembered still the heaviness of his own steps going up the stairs that evening. He had put aside the idea of kicking the ball around. Feeling exposed, he'd fetched his soap and stood in the queue for the shower – rush in behind the last fellow, hit the wall at the other side, bounce off and roll on the bedspread to dry off any stray drops – and only just stopped himself from punching Tom Edwards for flicking him with a wet towel in jest.

Percy Gilbert had not spoken to him again for some weeks but somehow, the conversation was resumed – and ended – late one afternoon, when he was minding his own business after lessons and had come back to the House to collect forgotten prep books. Percy Gilbert had wandered into the locker room from his study and said, 'What position are you hoping for next season, Cummings, when the seniors go and you are in almost sole possession of the Firsts?' He had leaned against Herbert's locker.

Irritably, Herbert had scratched in the cupboard. 'Same as I always play, Gilbert.'

'Scrum-half?'

'Yes, Gilbert.'

'An interesting position, but not for the old man of the new team.'

'Why not? It's as important as any other!' Herbert had retorted.

'Of course – and you are slight for your age. But I think it is a position associated with youngsters. Am I right? Then again, there are some positions which have a certain cachet and others which don't. I wouldn't have you as a forward, Cummings, heaving and grunting in the front rank like Morgan and MacCallum. All that gladiatorial gristle!'

'It's a team game,' Herbert had said briskly. 'All positions are necessary.'

'True. But if I were a player, I'd want to be Holmes at centre, perhaps, or to be a splendid wing, like Arthur Graham. All that diving about . . .'

Herbert had rummaged noisily.

'What would you have?' Percy had persisted.

'Scrum-half, as I said.'

'What about full-back?'

Herbert was silent. Only Charlie played full-back.

'Someone will have to take his place,' said Percy.

Herbert threw out his tennis racquet and his cricket boots, searching.

'Who will the exalted be? Edwards?'

Herbert snorted, tossing the boots back in. 'No one can take Fraser's place.'

'Ah-ha' – Percy, as if he'd achieved his goal, dropped the piece neatly in its place. 'Indispensable?'

Herbert glowered at him. He was not getting into this debate. It could only lead to misunderstandings. He extracted the wrong book from the jumble in the locker and shoved it under his arm.

'His father shot himself, you know.' Percy said it quietly.

'Who said?' Herbert stood quite still.

'I heard.'

'Graham told me he died in an accident.'

'He did. Suicides are always accidents. Of another kind perhaps, but accidents, nonetheless.'

'That's rot!' Herbert had felt an unreasonable anger rising. No one mentioned suicides. Except in terms of some disgrace. Or cowardice, or worse. He closed the locker door with a snap. 'That's prying.'

'It's not the sort of thing I'd say to someone who I *thought* would pry' – and there had been nothing satirical in his tone – 'I thought it might be important that you knew, that's all.'

Herbert didn't want to know. Absolutely not. 'Why should it be important to me?' he'd said.

'Well, it is to Fraser.'

'He's fine!' Herbert had retorted, even supercilious: what did Percy know about Charlie Fraser, anyway? They never hung about together out of prefects' studies. 'He's always fine.' His face had burned. 'He's never said anything.'

'Precisely.'

Herbert had gone off, taking the stairs in doubles, not looking back.

He'd caught the quiet note in Percy's voice. He'd understood. He could deny it ever after, but he'd heard.

Percy knew it too. Whatever he had said would be protected. It was safe with Herbert. Percy looked out of the window, leaned against the window sill. The street was empty. Just the shadow of the house was laid along the dusty pavement, the young trunks of stone pines intersecting it. The bell on the roof rang the quarter. It measured their hours so precisely. If he could silence it, there'd be no need to bargain, no thought of its inexorable allotments. In its tongue, there was such finality.

It was inevitable that Percy should have chosen Herbert as his acolyte for chess. No one played voluntarily except Robbie when it was appropriate and he could take the time. He could give Percy a game to remember but no one in the House could compete with him. He required a high level of competence to keep him from getting irritable. It was as if he were playing with himself, pitching the contest far beyond the valiant attempts of Mac or Sparrow, devising permutations on their simple themes. He was like a clever musician entertaining himself by transforming, to full orchestration, a two-finger nursery rhyme.

One afternoon, in the last term of Herbert's third year, Percy had come upon him and said – was it a punishment, in lieu of an essay, for something he had done? – 'You will play chess with me, this afternoon, Cummings.'

Herbert had balked. 'I don't know how to play, Gilbert.'

'I will teach you.'

Herbert did not want to learn to play chess. He wanted to go with Davey to the Cradock Dam and ride donkeys. He did not want to come to Percy's notice.

'You have a good brain, Cummings Two. It needs cultivation. You won't be sorry in the end.'

In the end, he wasn't.

And all his life since then he'd loved playing chess. There had been times when it had been a panacea, the only antidote to boredom and to fear. He'd remembered Percy then, with some affection.

But, for Herbert, it wasn't just the learning of chess or that Percy always beat him but explained afterwards with particular patience where he had gone wrong, it was the little room with its Turkish wall-hanging that was strung up, seraglio-like, that made it different from being in another fellow's place. His study was like no one else's: not at all the Zulu shield and crossed spears and fighting sticks affair in Danny's or the great muddle of books, matches, discarded boaters, ginger beer bottles and disreputable coats in Arthur's, nor even the spartan bareness of Charlie's. In Percy's room one sampled the lemon cordial in small sips and didn't wipe the back of the wrist across the mouth. And if Percy decided to intersperse a game with a reading from his burgundy-bound tomes, Herbert listened and tried to think of something pertinent to say. He never could. Percy didn't seem to mind. He would sit with fingers linked about his knees and regard Herbert with his head on one side. It was as if he was waiting, but Herbert never knew for what. It was both absorbing and disconcerting. Herbert could always feel the sweat behind his knees.

'I think you waste a lot of time, Cummings Two, galloping about in your footer boots. There are other things to pursue,' Percy said.

–Nothing like footer. But Herbert didn't say it. Percy did not play footer, so he wouldn't understand. Nor did he discuss sport. It seemed to bore him, despite his elegant appearances for the First XI and being quite famous as a long-distance runner. When Herbert had asked his times for the mile he seemed to have forgotten and had to consult the engraving on the tarnished back of last year's trophy in which he kept his locker keys.

His preoccupations were somewhere else and once he'd said, absentmindedly but rather suddenly, 'We all need affection, Cummings. Even those you'd least expect.' He paused and Herbert had been at a loss, his pawn poised in his fingers. Percy resumed, 'Look at Unwin. The fellow is dying for want of it. Look at Archer. All that rage for nothing. Someone just needs to tell him he's not such a bad fellow after all. It's what we all want, Cummings.'

Herbert shifted. His shoes felt big. What could he say? His dog was affectionate. 'Yes, Gilbert.'

And he remembered most how Mac came in from footer practice just then and barged through the door without knocking or greeting them and glanced at Herbert sitting at the table with Percy, the chess board between them and swept him in with a small, ironic smile. He took the lemon cordial bottle in his fist, fished a glass from the cupboard, poured a measure and added water from the jug. He ensconced himself on the window sill, elbows resting on his knees and yawned. 'Got a fag, Daisy? I've run short.'

'In the drawer,' Percy did not take his eyes from the board.
Mac opened the drawer, found the Westminsters and the matches, neatly set, side by side. He extracted one, looking over Percy's shoulder at the game, winked at Herbert, making a slight indication with his head, looking pointedly at his queen. He struck a match, bent to it and sent a long trail of smoke to the ceiling.

'Don't encourage Cummings to cheat, Mac,' said Percy without looking round. He put his hand up, reaching for the cigarette. Mac placed it between his fingers. Percy put it to his lips. He showed no reluctance at the damp tip. He did not look at Herbert.

Mac retrieved the cigarette and went back to his seat on the window sill and Percy made a move – one, two, three and the game was over. 'Thank you, Cummings.'

Herbert stood, easing the trousers away from the backs of his legs.

'Good fellow,' said Percy. 'You're coming on grandly.'

Mac had his feet up against the edge of the window-frame, he did not look in Herbert's direction as he left.

Herbert started away but he heard Mac say with a laugh, 'Still looking for undying devotion, Daisy? First Sparrow, now Cummings.'

'You owe me two boxes of cigarettes to date.' Percy's voice was brisk.

'I'm going to town tomorrow.'

'So I've been told before.'

Herbert walked away. He wiped his face with his sleeve. That was it. Despite all his rank and fame and the people that came in and out of his room and drank his cordial and borrowed his cigarettes, Percy Gilbert was alone. And no one knew.

Unaccountably, uninvited – and in retreat – Herbert thought of home. It was not a good idea. He hurried off in search of Davey and Tom Edwards. Damn chess. Damn Percy. Damn the dog. He'd run fast. Faster.

He had heard Tom and Davey long before he saw them. They were shambling about in circles on the donkeys, clowning. Pringle and Ross were making *kleilatte* at the water's edge. They were yelling at each other in Xhosa though they squatted on their haunches five yards apart. Herbert yelled too as he ran down the slope towards them. Pringle aimed a mud ball at him and it hit him in the chest. He staggered about dramatically, tripped over his own laces, rolled in the dust. Pringle came and pummelled him. He laughed then. He laughed until – at last – all of him was laughing.

Percy grieved at love and only Herbert, with the augur's eye, had seen.

And in his last term, Percy had written Herbert a note, leaving it on his desk, ostensibly to wish him well for the Senior Higher, its purpose – in the postscript – dashed off, as if offered as an afterthought:

> 'Your nature and your character made a great impression on me.
> I never realised that all those little games in my study were merely
> to drive away despondency.'

How the paradigm had shifted. Unaccountably, Percy had revealed his need: the patron was, in fact, the supplicant. Herbert did not know what to do with the letter. He wished to stand off from it, change it. But he couldn't. Nor could he tear it up: it would be like jeering at a cripple who had been a soldier once.

Unfair – he knew it. He pushed the thought away: hand it off; pay no attention.

In writing it, Percy had dared to flout the First Commandment. Herbert put the letter into his Greek grammar where he wouldn't find it again.

He did not know then about the other letters Percy wrote in a penny notebook in a small, indistinct hand to conceal his words. They were for copying out onto the good heavy paper that he'd brought from home, tinged faintly blue with watermarks. They were composed to be sent, but never were. They remained untranscribed, tucked inside his leather writing case. He kept it out of reach. Perhaps the wretched Buckerbridge might look in it and know.

Know what?

'Mac, I have longed for you to realise me as I am, to see beyond my half heroics, to know you mean a very great deal to me . . .'

There was more but it was indecipherable. And then he wrote:

'There, I've let myself go entirely.'

And letting go was something Percy didn't do. But in writing it, he'd loosened a need that had remained unassuaged. And like Charlie Fraser's pictures, pasted in a dozen albums, those letters had remained extant. And, like the pictures, in years to come, some vague enquiry – following up some family record – had called them forth.

If these had been destroyed – the letters and the albums – they would all be gone, unremembered. All that life, that vigour, that sheer presence. All of these, expunged from memory.

Without them, the names and faces might have drifted away, been sometimes dredged from the sketchy memories of old men. Without them, love would have been misplaced or forgotten, redemption lost. They were not merely sentimental icons from the past: in the end, they were the only form of validation left – as long as there was someone who believed.

   –I think you are a seer, Cummings, Percy had said.

He had scorned it. He had not wanted to be aligned with Percy. 'Difference' was an aberration in boyhood, no matter what form it took. If Percy saw it in him, it should be repressed. He would avoid any notion of it. He would not see what he did not wish to see: Davey Bennett in his last year; Unwin at any time at all; Charlie Fraser on Lower field, feet together, legs braced, step back three, then quick and let the ball go up, a keen trajectory across the posts. Kick and let it fly.

   He could simply hand it off as he'd handed-off in footer. And in doing so, circumvent it neatly. He could always hand-off other fellows in a race for the try-line. He could jink like a hare to avoid capture. He could stop, turn, change direction with heart-racing speed, exultant. 'Watch Apie, watch Apie!' Once the Head had said, 'Cummings, it gives me great pleasure to see the skill, despite your size, with which you hand-off an opponent in a match.' Hand it off. That's what he should do.

   He had then.

   But the seer's eye would not close, despite his resolve. It remained intent and lidless like the knot in the wood that peered out of the interior on the pole of the gate of the homestead.

FIVE

Herbert, at the start of the first senior rugby season: 'God, if I swear I'll never, ever, ever do it again, will You let me keep the place at scrum-half and give Sparrow something else?' A pause. 'I haven't done it often. Only once . . .' Another pause. 'Only sometimes. I am very sorry.'

Sparrow: 'Dear God,' kneeling by the bedside very late – ready to spring up in case someone woke and saw him – 'Do You think You could get Apie moved? He would be good at centre, just as good as he is at half-back. Better, I think. I'm not the only one who says so. And I promise never to mind singing in the cathedral choir and never to say anything bad about it just to be a buck in front of Morgan. I'll even think of being a priest.' He shifted on his knees. The old flannel pyjamas were very worn. 'Maybe not.' He waited. 'Can I leave that 'til later – just as long as You don't mind moving Apie? Amen.'

'I am not asking for Sparrow to be dropped. Amen.'

'Apie has a year more than me to play scrum-half, so if it's possible, just for this season, I'd be glad. Amen. I will remember what I promised. No lies. Amen.' Then he thought it: saying it was admission, 'and no impure ideas . . . or anything. Amen.'

'Or anything' was having read his mother's book – the one she kept in her drawer wrapped in a little thread-work cloth, 'The Perfect Woman', with the opening lines:

> 'Men must rule the Race, but Women govern its Destiny. We must not lose sight of her most divine and sublime mission in life – womanhood and motherhood.'

That was all right. Sublime. Divine. But then – in contrast – it was full of drawings of the most alarming kind in between the plates depicting 'Maiden' and 'A Happy Home' and 'Mary, the Mother of Jesus' and a chapter on 'How the Faces of Madonnas are Reproduced' (through self-restraint, lofty thoughts and never giving way to 'Animal passion'. Animal passion?). But there, interspersed among the paintings, diagrams of little bunches of livid grapes lodged inside a sectioned breast, and a pop-up anatomy with a thing like a golf ball on a peg – 'the bladder – at capacity'. There were lurid and inadmissible others in a colour-tinted body, draped in a cloth, the face of a goddess, distant but demure, labelled 'Internal Organs of Chest and Pelvis'.

The cure for constipation was not of interest although the Glossary had words to be pondered: 'enceinte' and 'Graafian follicle' and 'genitalia – birthplace of the egg'. 'Sanguineous.' Sanguineous organs, sanguineous cycles: it made him wretched to think of all that blood. 'Nates' – he had a pair himself. Nates: it didn't sound right. Fat Nates? Kick his nates? Sparrow laughed. 'Ovum.' There was a lot to do with eggs. He wasn't quite so keen on poached or boiled for a while after that.

> 'If conception takes place in the early part of the menstrual cycle a girl will be born, in the latter, a boy. Queen bees lay female eggs first and male after. The same is true of domesticated fowls.'

But it was page thirty-four, 'Go Teach Your Boy', that had to be reviewed each hols. The idea would enter his head and he would push it off. But it lodged there, waiting, until his mother went out and then it would nudge him and nudge him until he went up to her room and opened her drawer and unwrapped the volume carefully. And looked again.

Page thirty-four: 'Go Teach Your Boy'. His mother hadn't taught him anything from page thirty-four. It didn't seem as though she would, so, to save her the trouble, he had read it, covertly and fast. Hot in the ears. Hot all over. Skip the first sentences – reading them was complicity.

> '... the whole body is abused when the organ is handled or excited in any manner whatever. Teach your boy to shun all children who indulge in this loathsome habit or who talk about these things.'

Was he a loathsome child? He had talked to Danny once. But Dan had started to stutter a bit, so he had talked to Arthur instead. Arthur had laughed. He said his mother had told him everything – but clearly she hadn't read the book or he would know better than to grin like that.

> 'The sin is terrible! These organs too are closely connected with the spine and brain by means of nerves, and if they are handled or thought of, these nerves get excited and become exhausted and this makes the back ache, the brain heavy and the whole body weak. It makes boys lose their minds. Others, when grown, commit suicide. ...'

But – a page or two on – there was an odd duplicity: the case of little Cyril whose mother found that he was the victim of the vice:

> ' –Do you know, my son, that if you keep up this habit a brown spot will come on your abdomen and grow darker each week until it eats a sore into your system? It will eventually kill you. When Cyril was asleep she applied to his navel a dab of iodine from the cork of the bottle, the size of a pea. –Look, look, the worthy mother exclaimed – it has come! The boy cried out in very fear! The next night the mother put a second application,

still darker and a trifle sore. Cyril watched the spot as he would a reptile that was lurking, about to do its deadly work. . .'

In triumphant conclusion: 'that Mother was never again obliged to use iodine as a deterrent.'

Surely that was falsehood? Would his mother stoop to it and cause such terror and revulsion? He inspected his stomach nevertheless. It was possible – just possible – that the Devil, ever-vigilant, would find him out and do the deed instead?

No spot. Yet.

But he was not complacent.

No deeds, no thoughts. The first was manageable. The other difficult. Did dreams count as thoughts? They must. What else were dreams but thoughts? Except a fellow couldn't help his dreams. If he could, why would he dream so often that Robbie'd beaten him senseless? The only predictable dream was thinking you were in the bog when you weren't – and that was your own fault if you were too much of a ninny to go down after lights out or in the rain. And there was always the window and the creeper that hid the stains, if you were desperate. But if thoughts and dreams were one, he would have to stay awake. If he didn't sleep he wouldn't dream and then the Devil wouldn't catch him unawares and God could not punish him. But Sparrow always slept as soon as he got into bed. He often dreamed.

And God, in His compassion, did not punish Sparrow for dreaming. He didn't punish Herbert either. He accommodated both of them as long as they kept the bargain consciously.

But then Herbert sinned. Consciously.

He was moved to centre for a week or two when Holmes was injured and Sparrow took his place at half-back and performed dazzlingly. Herbert also got a huge carbuncle behind his ear. It was so full it squeaked when he finally managed to pop it: a reminder of what he'd done, defying God and breaking his promise. Disgusting boy. He was too shamed to say he was sorry, but he was. Bitterly sorry and guilty and low. 'I will never do it again, God. Just don't let Sparrow keep my place.'

The carbuncle was not the only evidence of sin. Herbert inspected a rosette of little heads on his chin in the small mirror in his locker. He could also feel them painfully on the back of his neck, even without touching them, subterranean and sore. He knew why they had come, malignant as fungus budding in the dark. He even had a wart starting on his index finger. Wasn't that evidence enough? What would Miss Maltby have to say now? She, who trod down the dormitory on Monday mornings every fortnight to strip the beds herself with the air of a Chinese laundry agent, inscrutable and all-seeing? The evidence on a boy's face was concomitant with all she guessed about him on a Monday: they knew her small, stiff despising, the way she treated certain boys and the way she treated others.

'Douglas Morgan, strip that bed yourself, my lad.' Doug was rash from forehead to chest, from ears to scapula.

'Graham, you're a disgrace!' Eye beaming in on Arthur's nose: a veritable beacon. Arthur let it glow, unashamed.

Archer, for a while, was quite beyond the pale. He was so scrofulous, Miss Maltby could not look his way.

Despite his fears, Sparrow never sprouted spots at all, neither on his face, nor in pea-sized stains on his stomach. Dan Grant's were far too mild for him to be suspected and, besides, Miss Maltby loved them both, despite their sheets. Contradictions did not ruffle her: she knew a good lad when she saw one.

Charlie Fraser got a pimple only once, right in the middle of his manly chin for all to see. Everybody stared, but only Arthur said, 'Hallelujah! Let me see, Charlie! Let me see!' Pinning him to the wall. 'It's a beaut! What've you been up to? Charlie? Hey?'

'Get off, Arthur.' Charlie growling.

But on every other Monday evening, at prayers, Robbie – after clearing his throat in a particular way – brought the subject around to 'vice'. He never said *what* vice, he didn't have to, but, rubbing his knuckles at the small of his back and looking just above their heads, he'd say, 'Boys, boys, don't make pigs of yourselves. D'you hear, boys?'

Back straight, neck stiff, do not look at your neighbour.

Think of footer. Do not let your ears burn.

Pimples were evidence of secret sin, the Devil's joke, exposing them. The almost-senior boys were sinners to a man. Miserable fellows. And the larger nubs with rashy little pustules on their chins – look at them! Only GB and Parkes wriggled at the back and swung their legs and thought about tuck.

Herbert considered, then, whether he was mistaken about the Devil. Perhaps the Devil was a huge, devouring woman. Or even a little one. Whenever girls walked down the road and Robbie caught the fellows hanging from the windows watching, he would always mutter 'the very devil' glaring down above their hatted heads and shooing the fellows off as if he were protecting them from pestilence. Herbert wouldn't have been at all surprised if he'd fetched his shotgun and let it fly at the rear end of the column.

And when a case was reported in *The Journal* of a poor derelict girl who'd been loitering in New Street, Robbie swooped into the common-room and took the paper away – but not before Douggie Morgan saw it and said, 'I say, you fellows, have a look at this.'

'The Seamy Side'
'Young Girl's Degradation'

They all bunched over his shoulder to read:

'Lettie van Aas, a young girl of 17, was arrested for vagrancy. She had left her parents' home after a misunderstanding regarding an apprentice in her father's workshop. Mrs Huggins, of the Salvation Army, has taken her in. In this good lady's care, she will be given an opportunity to reform.'

'Wonder what they did?' said Sparrow.
    'Who?' said Dan.
    'Her and the apprentice.'
    'Rather an appropriate name,' said Percy.
    'Why?' said Sparrow.
    'Well, you know, van Aas . . . van Aas.'
    'I don't get it.'
    'Wake up.'
    'I don't get it. . .'

81

'Hang on fellows, it goes on,' said Doug, turning the page and reading aloud. 'Lettie van Aas was brought before the Magistrate – that's Holmes' father, maybe Georgie can find out details – and sentenced, but Mrs Huggins, our own Good Samaritan, interceded on her behalf. Lettie van Aas admitted herself that her father's apprentice . . .'

'The very devil. . .' Robbie nabbed it before Doug had got to the end. 'Leave this muck, lads. Leave it now. Trash. All of it. Pure pollution. . .' He folded the paper and stuck it under his arm and departed with it to his study.

'Bet he reads the whole thing . . .' said Doug.

'He wants it for the article on Captain McQueen's Lantern Show called "African Exploration", Shaw Hall, 8 pm on Tuesday,' said Percy who had read the paper from end to end long before anyone had noticed it. 'He'll read that first and maybe Miss Lettie van Aas second – just to see what we saw, so he can lecture us on the difference between woman and woman.'

'What on earth are you talking about?' said Mac.

'Woman the goddess. Mother and all that. . .' said Percy. 'And Woman-Thou-Art-My-Downfall. . . you know, that bit in the Bible. How does it go?'

'You mean Adam and Eve and the snake,' said Doug, brightening.

'Whatever,' said Percy drily, but Douggie missed his tone. Poor fellow, the sooner he got on with it, the better.

'It's rot,' said Arthur. 'It's all a lot of rot.'

'What's rot?' Dan said.

'All this nonsense about the Devil and snakes and things.'

They looked at him. Percy smiled, rearranged himself in his chair and settled in.

'You're filling your heads with rot. There's no such thing as the Devil. It's all an invention to make you feel guilty about everything.'

Sparrow frowned. He'd have to copy out that bit for Arthur from page thirty-four. It was printed in a book, after all, written by a doctor . . .

'Maybe this Lettie was in love with whatshisname,' said Arthur.

'That's not love,' said Mac.

82

'Why not?'

'She was a vagrant.'

'She didn't choose to be.'

'Still . . . she was . . . sort of . . . low.'

'So, does that mean she can't love anyone?'

'It said in the paper about degradation,' said Mac. 'It's got nothing to do with love. She must have *done* something.'

'And if she did, what's that to you?'

'Nothing.'

'It is – or you wouldn't be so interested,' said Arthur, trouncing him.

Girls were not the very devil. He should know, he had four sisters. They weren't goddesses or madonnas either. They were simply girls. Nor did he believe there were connections between his sometimes spotty face and anything he did – or didn't – do. And if girls preoccupied him – so what? What was all the fuss? They were his favourite subject after footer. And sometimes, when a match was won, the result safe, they even edged the footer out. Nor did he give a hoot about his spots, unless he played a public match and sisters from the girls' school came to watch. Then he inspected his face the night before, picked at it with unashamed absorption and ate a teaspoonful of nutmeg and sugar every morning in the hope of a cure. His mother, quite sanguine about the spots, sent a supply of the remedy in a little jar every term.

Arthur fell in love with remarkable regularity. Mrs Woodman's daughter, when she served in the tuck-shop, was diverting enough on Tuesdays and Arthur wasn't past borrowing a few pence without permission and bringing back the spoils, delivered without expectation of a taste, or leaving an IOU which was honoured promptly when he fetched his week's shilling from Robbie's care. Then why go? Well . . . it was Mrs Woodman's daughter's day to serve.

There was a mutiny, however, when he took to buying a foul form of sherbet in little cones with a liquorice pipe to suck it up which Miss Woodman had been trying to get rid of for weeks.

'I don't want bloody sherbet!' Doug Morgan said. 'I hate the stuff.'

'Well, I don't want it either.'

'Then why the hell did you buy it?'

'It was Bertha's turn today.'

'Idiot!'

She could have sold Arthur anything.

Miss Woodman on a Tuesday and Katie in the holidays: once, at Michaelmas, he and Charlie had gone to John Barham's family in Port Elizabeth. There were boating parties at Redhouse and picnics on the windy rocks at Schoenmakerskop and walks around St George's Park to visit Sparrow's family in Bird Street. There was Poppy Bell, Sparrow's sister – reincarnated Sparrow with two long plaits and a dimple just the same as his – and Sparrow's darling mother, all buttermilk pudding and slices of thin bread and butter sprinkled with sugar and mugs of cocoa made with creamy milk for tea. Poppy and her friends, Katie and Connie, went with them to the conservatory in the park with its musty palms and orchids and painted wrought-iron pillars weeping little rivulets of rust. Was it Katie or Poppy or Connie he'd watched as he wandered along the narrow gravel paths among the yucca plants? Or was it the little flock of girls who were sitting on the red-painted swings outside, wafting to and fro with the creak of chains in the windy afternoon? It didn't really matter which. He and John and Charlie had had a splendid photo taken by a man in a booth nearby. Poppy and Katie and Connie had tried to make them laugh but the bigger girls swirling on the roundabout were watching and both he and John had come out startled and rather stiff. Only Charlie was relaxed in the picture. He had looked the camera straight in the eye, easy in his old jacket, hands loosely linked, a little flower he'd purloined inside the hothouse perched on his lapel.

It couldn't have been Poppy whom Arthur'd fallen for because she looked too much like Sparrow, so it must have been Katie because Connie was too young and didn't speak and stared at Sparrow all the time. Katie with the brown skin and little chip on her front tooth that made her grin beguiling. Katie with her long, long legs and polished boots. Whoever it was – whatever – he'd had a watery feeling in his stomach all afternoon and had nearly thrown up at the kitchen table at Sparrow's when they went back for tea. Sparrow's mother encircled his head with her arm as she stood behind his chair and felt his forehead with a small, firm hand to see if he was feverish. 'Too much rich food, Arthur dear,' she said, holding his head against her briefly, her fingers pressing at his temple. It was like sinking into sleep. He closed his eyes. She gave him a dose of milk of magnesia. He'd have drunk the entire bottle just to have her coax him with the tablespoon.

When they left at the end of the week, Katie said she'd write. She did. And he replied, becoming quite extravagant, despite his spelling. She didn't seem to mind. So Arthur mooned about with great exaggeration for a term and spent his afternoons loping off to the post office in town. He didn't lose his appetite so it couldn't have been terminal but he sat in prep and languished over his desk in a way that made it clear he wasn't working.

Thinking of Katie had nothing to do with his spots. She only had to do with swings in the park and the dusty scent of palms; with the seashore and the wind blowing her straw hat down the sand and his fetching it and brushing her fingers with his when she took it from him. It was entirely different. It had nothing whatever to do with the Sunday prayer '. . . and from the sin of fornication, we beseech Thee, Good Lord deliver us.' They were unconnected.

'. . .And from the sin of fornication, we beseech Thee, Good Lord deliver us.' They said it often enough and just to drive it home, the Reverend Dowsley gave a sermon once a quarter, for the edification of any newboys and as a warning to all suspected miscreants. It was more interesting than most. They knew the content well.

'Love is a sacred thing,' the Reverend Dowsley said. 'It comes from God and is sanctified by God' – putting Miss Lettie van Aas in her place – 'and in marriage, and marriage only, it finds its true expression.'

'Here we go.' Arthur took up the Book of Common Prayer from the shelf on the back of the pew and picked quietly at the binding, mouthing in unison, with exaggerated sanctimony, to make Charlie look away so he didn't laugh.

'Sanctified by God' – dipping the voice and accelerating like a gramophone being wound – 'and not to be abused in vile ways by man.' He meant boys. Shiftings in the pews, so many glowing necks. Percy crossed his legs, folded his arms, looked at the arches above and flared his nostrils gently.

'Self-abuse!' said the Reverend Dowsley, giving the word its full, awesome weight and dropping it over the heads of the small choirboys into the laps of the row of seniors, 'is worse than lying or stealing . . .' softer now and Arthur raised a finger surreptitiously as if holding a musical note suspended. 'Self-abuse . . .' louder now and Arthur's finger dipped and rose, poised once again for emphasis, 'damages both the body and the soul. It brings with it lethargy, weakness and disease. It is the work of the Devil!'

Herbert, sitting behind Arthur, wanted to look round then to see if the Devil had come in through the back door to pitchfork offenders out: he'd have to look sharp. He did not turn. Someone might guess.

Dowsley's voice swelled, the cadenza coming. Arthur raised the index fingers on both hands, ushering in the trumpets and drums. 'Beware of the sin, my sons!' – Arthur drew a breath, not quite steady, Charlie had started to shake beside him – 'of the sin – the dreadful sin – of Self-Abuse.' Silence. Arthur mouthed in perfect pitch: 'Preserve your Jewels!'

It was too much. At the pew along the way, Mac blew his nose loudly. It parped out, off-key. Arthur exploded. The pew rattled. The Reverend Dowsley's eye beamed in. The Head's. Charlie turned and thumped Arthur on the back.

'Is something wrong?' said the Reverend Dowsley.

'Stuck!' said Charlie, giving Arthur a whack that was hard enough to wind him and to stop any breath at all. 'A lozenge.'

Percy, three seats down, locked and unlocked his jaw and looked at the toe of his shoe. Danny Grant's eyes were bulging: he had his hands clenched on the edge of the seat. Beside him, Sparrow shook but only the little plume on the top of his head registered the tremor.

'A lozenge?' the Reverend Dowsley said, bewildered.

'Stuck,' said Charlie, louder. He whacked Arthur again without looking at him, caught him on the edge of the shoulder and sent him sprawling across Sparrow. They tumbled between the pews together.

There was a general eruption then.

'Will you boys go outside,' said the Head from the Chancellor's seat. 'I will see you after the service.'

Charlie ushered Arthur out before him, 'Cough, you fool!' he hissed under his breath. Arthur coughed. And coughed. And coughed all the way down the aisle. Sparrow rose to follow.

'Sit down, Bell,' said the Head peremptorily.

'Preserve your Jewels!' said Arthur when they were outside. He crinkled up his eyes and kicked at a jacaranda pod and watched it fly. 'Preserve your Jewels!'

'Never mind your bloody jewels,' said Charlie. 'We'd better think about preserving our backsides.'

'The Old Man would never thrash anyone on a Sunday.'

'What's wrong with Monday?'

'He'll be too busy to remember.'

'I wouldn't count on it.'

'I don't want to Preserve my Jewels, Charlie,' said Arthur soberly, hands in his pockets, gazing off intently across the rugby field. 'I want to squander them all over the place.'

Charlie laughed.

'Don't you?'

Charlie folded his arms and looked up at the trees.

'D'you think it's really a sin?' said Arthur.

'Perhaps.'

'D'you care?'

'Bugger off, Arthur,' said Charlie mildly, raising that eyebrow, half a frown, half a laugh: as if he'd say.

'Graham?' said the Head.

'Sir?'

'Eating lozenges in chapel is disruptive.'

'Yes, sir.'

'Lozenges may help the voice when one is singing solo, Graham. But I observe that you are not in the choir.'

'No, sir.'

'Perhaps you are keen to join?'

'No, sir.'

'You are not keen?'

Arthur was silent.

'Should I have a word with Mr Abbott, Graham, and tell him you would like to audition?'

'No, sir.'

'Ah . . . so, in truth, you had no need of lozenges, Graham?'

'No, sir.'

'Then why were you eating them?'

Arthur said, 'I didn't have a lozenge. Sir.'

'You didn't?'

'No, sir.'

'Fraser was mistaken then?'

Arthur cast Charlie a helpless glance. But Charlie was standing there, quite calm. 'Yes, sir.'

'You were rather over-zealous in your treatment of Graham, Fraser,' said the Head, turning to Charlie.

'Sorry, sir.'

'One can stop laughter by simple control,' observed the Head, after a pause. 'One doesn't have to assault a fellow and fell his neighbour.'

'Yes, sir,' said Charlie.

'Did you find what Mr Dowsley said so very amusing, Graham? Perhaps you don't agree with him?'

'No, sir.'

'No, you don't agree with him?'

'Yes, sir,' stammered Arthur.

'Yes, you do agree with him?'

'No, sir.'

'Extraordinary, Graham. Could I have some clarity?'

'I mean, yes, sir, I do agree with him.' Arthur scrutinised his feet. His face burned.

'Fraser? Do you agree with him?'

'I can't answer, sir.' Charlie Fraser looked back at him.

'Why not?'

'I need to think it out.'

'Indeed?' The Head regarded him a moment. Then he said, 'Graham, go down to the pantry and select a cane.'

Arthur went. The Head took a turn about his room. He did not speak to Charlie. Arthur returned and the Head took the cane and tapped the end of it in his palm. He indicated a chair with the tip, prodding it. 'I can't have you setting a bad example in chapel,' he said. 'Graham first. Over there.'

A desultory four each.

'Thank you, sir,' they said and shook his hand. 'Good morning, sir,' and they were gone.

The Head stood at the window and watched them as they walked back to the House, giving each other a friendly shove, laughing at something he could not hear as they went through his gate, the sun shining on their heads. Great, glad, vigorous boys, full of energy and sap. Of course they didn't agree with the Reverend Mr Dowsley. How could they, bursting with life like that?

Great, glad and vigorous. But what of those who weren't? The motley, drifting through the school unnoticed, seldom vigorous and neither great nor glad. Or those who went Proclaimed-to-All – objects of scorn – like Furry Huddlestone and Fatty Harman.

'Are you a gorilla, Huddlestone?'

The hair grew like vines up his stomach, his chest and on his back: a little ape-man always in an overcoat to hide his wiry arms.

Some self-complacent senior: 'We should pack him up and send him to a museum, or to Mr Darwin. He's such a specimen!'

Some sensitive nub: 'He must be crawling with bugs.'

On Fatty Harman: letters home on Sundays.

'You should see the fat boy in my class. His brother is almost as fat, but not quite. They are the fattest boys you've ever seen. It's funny 'cos I never see them eat that much. Miss Maltby says it gl/ans . . . galands. Glands.'

To friends: 'Harman's got disgusting *dobies* from sweat 'cos the air can't get in his pants. Have you seen them?'

Miss Maltby, brandishing a bottle of gentian violet, 'Harman! Come along and bring an old pair of drawers. I don't want complaints from your mother and stains on your trousers.' Harman, scarlet under scrutiny, too large to skulk unseen, follows obediently.

Then there was Unwin – lamentable Unwin. The most Proclaimed-to-All in the House.

Unwin was a tearful, needy boy. He was a disappointment to his father.

When they were juniors, Herbert had always been glad Tom Edwards slept between them for Unwin was a boy who, if the smallest attention was paid to him, grasped at it and then became a leech. He always needed things: to borrow sixpence, to have help with his prep, to ask if another fellow had seen his pyjamas. Tom, impervious to his whining, paid him no attention at all except to direct well-aimed blows at his head with a pillow if he heard him snivelling at night.

Unwin had a subscription to *The Boys' Own Paper* and, in order simply to have a conversation, he would lend it out. No one would borrow it after a while, the dues were too uncomfortable, being seen talking to Unwin too demeaning, so the less scrupulous took to stealing it from his locker and returning it tattered at some later stage. This threw Unwin into a state close to apoplexy. Seeing this, the boys preyed on it. Unwin, from what had been to his advantage, now owned the paper at his peril.

'Where's your paper, Unwin?'

'I don't know. You fellows have taken it.'

'Which fellows?'

'You fellows! You fellows!'

Someone would have it and consult it elaborately, keeping it out of Unwin's demented, snatching reach.

'Give it back. It's not yours. I shall tell Mr Robinson if you fellows go on teasing.'

They knew that at some point Unwin would lose his composure

and lash out. They waited for it. Then they waited for the tears of rage. They would start up at the outer corners of his eyes and he would scream out in a high voice that was like something wounded and ugly. 'I've had it! I've simply had it!' A high, chilling keening. Then they would scatter, keeping from his grasp with ease, leading him within range of Robbie's door. Robbie, who seemed to despise Unwin as much as they, would emerge, grip the unfortunate boy by the shoulder, push him into his den and deliver a swift caning for disrupting the peace of 'quiet time'. This seemed to calm Unwin down. He would twitch involuntarily then, mumble the obligatory, 'Thank you, sir' and leave. He would go to his fort at the edge of the field, way off from where the others had built theirs, and sit like a shadow among the leaves, alone.

It seemed to trouble Davey Bennett. He had mentioned it to Herbert but Herbert, hardening up, had said, 'There's nothing to be done with Unwin, Jones. At least, not here at school.' Unwin might have irritated Davey Bennett as much as any, but he never could be cutting or unkind. Unwin, sensing this, and with some small life-force fighting to survive, dogged him. He would offer tuck to Davey if he looked his way. 'I say, Bennett, I was sent some fruit cake. Would you like a piece? Come up to my fort. I'm going to keep it there.'

'No, thanks, Unwin.'

'It arrived this morning.'

'No, thanks, Unwin.'

What was it about Unwin's cake? Was it that when he cut it, with his pale bony fingers, he was like a frog dabbling in spawn? Not even Davey, if he accepted it, could bring himself to eat it.

Unwin had a certain self-destructiveness as well, as if, in the end, as he moved up the school from form to form, he wanted others to despise him.

'Unwin!' – the prefect, each breakfast time – 'You're slurping your tea! Are you spitting in it?'

Sometimes Tom Edwards would leap out of bed and run down the dormitory, his face screwed up as if he was about to be sick. 'He's eating snot again!'

Unwin was unmoved.

91

Or, on waking: 'Unwin, isn't it time you changed your pyjamas?'

Unwin would remain dumb and lumpish.

Miss Maltby, on laundry inspection, fingers poised at the corners of his bed linen: 'D'you know what the Devil does to boys like you?' Every eye was on him. Unwin simply looked bewildered.

But, in the end, he seemed to court degradation. It was as if he wished Archer to bring his rugby boots and rake him apart. He would have lain there like a snail without a shell and allowed the dismembering, only the twitch of exposed flesh to show that nerves had once been there, alive.

No one would shower near Unwin, even from the first. He was a deathly, mottled colour as if the blood was too close to the surface of his skin and made a blue mosaic on it, like the thread-veins of a fish. As a junior he avoided showering as often as he dared and, by his third year, took to hiding away at wash time. He did his ablutions in secret. They were sketchy, at best.

'Tell me, Unwin . . .' – on instructions from Miss Maltby, MacCallum took a stand – 'Do you have some sort of aversion to water?'

'No, MacCallum.'

'Perhaps you have run out of soap?'

'No, MacCallum.'

'Then when are you going to shower, Unwin?'

'I have a cold, MacCallum. I think I should avoid it 'til I'm well.'

'We'll all be ill ourselves if you don't do it soon, Unwin.'

'Yes, MacCallum.'

'I think you should understand that you stink, Unwin.'

Unwin did not answer. The sweat oozed. In heat or cold. There was nothing he could do to stop it.

MacCallum looked at him, saying nothing, but all the world's derision in his glance.

MacCallum did not stink. Even after footer. Unwin knew the reason: he was not afraid. There was never any need for flight. He never smelled of fear.

'Did you hear me, Unwin?'

'Yes, MacCallum.'

'Well, get on with it then.'

'Yes, MacCallum.'

But he'd waited and crept down after lights out to wash, strictly out of bounds. Goens Archer, returning from the bogs, found him. He heard the running water and took his candle in. Unwin cowered away from the flame. Archer stared at him for a long moment. He came up to the senior dorm and said with a smirk, 'Unwin's in the shower at last. No wonder he never washes with the rest of us. The fellow has endowments past your wildest dreams!'

Boys looked up, a laugh started. 'What? Unwin?'

'Dream on,' said Charlie Fraser with a swift glance at Archer.

He could have killed Charlie Fraser then. Anyone who knew him understood the slight. The laugh was turned against him. Even Percy Gilbert laughed. Only Charlie Fraser continued reading the paper with perfect equanimity, ignoring further conversation, but he might as well have struck Archer in the throat. Archer could have pulled the building down.

It festered. Oh, it festered: –Dream on!

How could Fraser have defended The Maggot, been such a bloody prig and put him down so publicly?

It festered quietly. And then, a few weeks later, at the start of the rugby season, it burst. And Unwin, with a strange self-destructive instinct of his own, courting it, was there as catalyst.

Archer did not make the Firsts.

When the lists went up, Charles Fraser had the berth. Archer had stood stunned. He had read the name over and over. *Fraser, CW; Fraser, CW; Fraser, CW*...

It was catastrophic.

For a year, Archer had played at full-back in the Seconds. He was waiting for his turn. One day Sampson would leave school, depart for Oxford and take his reputation away with him for ever. Archer had played in Sampson's place once or twice when the great man had been indisposed. He'd acquitted himself well. The coach had been pleased enough. But even Archer knew he would never have

Sampson's flair – the dash or the dazzling boot. The intellect.

Sampson had gone, weighted down with a box of trophies from the prize-giving and Archer had been left assured. So assured, he had not thought to prepare for the season. He never took the ball down to the field to punt it over the posts. He did not run. He smoked prodigiously behind the row of lavatories.

Now, Fraser had his place. Fraser wasn't as old as he. He wasn't as big. Fraser hadn't waited as he had. Fraser hadn't played at full-back in the Seconds. He'd been at centre. He might have been full-back in the Junior House team when he was just past being a nub and Robbie might have raved on about how fine he'd turn out to be, silly old fool; he might even be good – but not *that* good! Fraser had belittled him in front of everyone: –Dream on, he'd said.

The berth in Firsts was Archer's. He'd kill the coach. Kill the captain. Kill Fraser gladly.

He came up to the House, taking the stairs in threes. Raging. Anyone else, seeing him – all that anguish under the sullen set of his mouth – would have left him, crept off to mind his own business. But Unwin, meeting him head-on in the doorway of the locker room and panicked into speaking, said, 'Why aren't you at footer, Archer?' The desire to kill could not have been more unequivocally served.

Unwin rose from the floor, flesh and shirt and tie screwed together within Archer's fist. He was thrown down against the wall and Archer was kicking him.

Unwin cried like a maimed rabbit. The more he pleaded, the more it aroused Archer's wrath.

Davey Bennett, hearing him, came running. He stood appalled at the threshold of the locker room, saw Archer raking Unwin's back with his boots. Archer glanced up. 'Get lost, Bennett!' He had Unwin by the ear. 'You're a white slug, Unwin. A maggot.'

'Robbie's coming,' Davey yelled, not knowing what else to do, but Archer did not seem to care. Davey ran back along the passage, opening doors, looking for a senior. The studies and the dorms were empty.

He heard voices below, the sound of boots coming up the stairs. It was Herbert and Sparrow Bell and Arthur Graham, Charlie and

MacCallum, back from practice. 'Quick!' he shouted.

'What's going on?'

'Archer's murdering Unwin,' said Davey Bennett.

They pushed past. Sparrow was the first to reach them. 'Archer,' said Sparrow, his voice going suddenly high. 'Archer! Stop!'

Archer swung round and Sparrow backed hurriedly. Archer dropped Unwin and came bearing down on Sparrow. Sparrow stood his ground. His tongue flicked into the corner of his mouth. There were high red patches under his freckles. Archer put out a hand to grab him, a great fist to lift him. Charlie Fraser interposed, broke the lunge with a well-timed counter movement of his arm that knocked Archer back. Charlie punched him in the solar plexus, hard.

Archer drew a breath.

Here was the object of hate. Unwin was forgotten. 'Fuck off, Fraser.'

The word, in its enormity, hung there. Even Unwin forgot to sob. Such a word! Such a word and all of them standing there to hear it. Thunder might as well have rolled around the room.

Startled. 'What?' said Charlie Fraser.

Archer put his hands on his hips and said again – deliberately, loudly – 'I said, fuck off, Fraser.'

'Would you like to repeat that in my study?' Robbie stood in the doorway, with his hunting knife at his hip and his old tweed jacket hanging about him. No one moved. Sparrow breathed so deeply his nostrils were quite white. Charlie Fraser stood, Arthur stood. MacCallum and Davey and Herbert stood, looking wherever they had been looking when the word was said. The only other sound came from Unwin. A small, sighing sob. Robbie stepped through the doorway and glanced at him and said, 'Off the floor, Unwin, and stop that snivelling.' He turned to MacCallum, 'I'll see you in ten minutes, please.'

'Sir.'

To Archer, 'Come with me.'

They walked away.

Unwin could not get up off the floor. It was Charlie Fraser and Sparrow who bent to him. They hoisted him between them and set him on his feet. He did not look at them. His hair was plastered to his head with sweat, fear oozing out. They could all smell him.

'You stink,' said MacCallum matter of factly in his hollow voice.

He did stink, it was true. It was that sharp, frightened smell that has nothing to do with heat or exertion. Herbert stepped back. He did not want to know it.

Charlie Fraser said, 'Are you hurt?'

Unwin opened his mouth but only a bubble escaped, popped on his lips.

They could hear the sound of the cane from Robbie's study. MacCallum cocked his head. 'Good six,' he said with satisfaction. 'Bloody sod.'

'He'll get another from the Head for what he said,' remarked Sparrow. 'If he's not rusticated, I bet you another six.'

'How much?' said Arthur.

'A ginger beer,' said Sparrow.

'And bun.'

'I'm short of money.'

'Then you shouldn't make bets.'

'Right. A ginger beer and a bun.'

'Bet Robbie won't send him up.'

'Bet he will.'

'How d'you think Robbie will bring himself to repeat what Archer said. "Mr Headmaster, Archer just said . . ." '

'He'll have to.'

'Would you say it?'

'Yes.'

'Bet you wouldn't.'

'Fuck off,' said Arthur under his breath.

'You'll go to hell for that,' said Sparrow severely.

'Rot.'

'Cut it out!' said MacCallum irritably. He wouldn't have levity in his House at a time like this. He took his dignity off with him to Robbie's study for instructions.

Davey Bennett went to fetch a face cloth. He wet it at the basin. Herbert watched him. Davey could do those things and not bother what people thought. He gave it to Unwin. Unwin left a trail of snot on it. Davey Bennett took the cloth as though he didn't mind and returned it to the basin. He left it there unrinsed but he didn't make a face at it.

Charlie Fraser said, 'Do you want some water?'

Unwin nodded.

Sparrow fetched a mug.

Unwin drank. He wiped the back of his wrist across his mouth. 'Thank you,' he said.

'Right?' said Charlie Fraser.

'Right,' said Arthur.

'Right,' said Sparrow.

Unwin did not look at them.

They went then, leaving him. It was all they could do. Davey and Herbert were walking away when they heard MacCallum returning. They heard him say – his voice was quite clear from the passage – 'I wish Robbie would get Unwin sent to another house. He's such a repulsive little creep, he gives us a bad name.'

Unwin heard it too.

Herbert saw him flinch, as if a boot had caught him.

Unwin went to his dorm, like a dog creeping off, skirting a wall. He sat on his bed.

He was still sitting when the supper bell rang.

He was not at his place at the meal. His chair stood empty.

'Where's Unwin?' said Robbie, looking down from the top table after he had said the grace. 'Bennett?' Unwin's closest neighbour on the left.

Everyone stared at Unwin's chair as if it might produce him miraculously, spawn him from its grease-stained seat. Then they looked at Davey.

'I don't know where Unwin is, sir,' said Davey Bennett.

'When last did you see him?'

'Only this afternoon, sir.'

'Well, what's the matter with him?'

'I don't know, sir . . .' Davey Bennett was at a loss. Robbie knew as well as he what the matter was.

97

'You'd better find him after supper and tell him to come and speak to me,' said Robbie. 'Tell him, I don't want to have to search for him myself.'

'Yes, sir,' said Davey Bennett.

'I told you he should run away,' said Herbert under his breath.

Davey Bennett and Herbert searched the boxroom, the bogs, the lockers. They went to the pavilion at the edge of the field and looked in the storeroom. No one was there.

'D'you think he ran away?' said Herbert.

'Where'd he go?' said Davey.

'Home, I suppose.'

'How could he go home?' said Davey. 'He lives in Bulawayo.'

'I wonder why he was sent so far to school?' said Davey.

'Maybe they didn't like him either,' said Herbert. 'What will you say to Robbie?'

'I'll wait 'til after prep. He might turn up.'

Herbert and Davey went back to the House, collected their books and followed the others to the classroom. It must have been there that Davey thought to look in the chapel. He did not tell Herbert but, when they filed out with the bell, he said, 'I'll be up in a minute, just keep Robbie off my back if I'm late.'

He was right. Unwin was in the chapel.

Davey Bennett went in quietly. He did not have to push the door. He made no sound. He almost retreated, seeing the little red light in the sanctuary and the heavy draperies on the altar and the back pews and caught that strange holy smell in the gloom. He stood, hearing his own heart. Being heard.

Someone was talking in there. Davey Bennett turned hastily to retreat. Perhaps he had stumbled in on Zeedy preparing a sermon. But the voice was small and tired and far away. It was Unwin's.

'I hate you, God.'

Silence.

'I hate you, God.'

Davey Bennett could feel the sweat on his lip, hearing the small, hollow frog-tone.

'Archer told Fraser to . . .' he could not catch what was said then, but he knew. Unwin's voice steadied, was louder. 'Well, I say fuck off too.' There was a quaver in the voice, despite the defiance. It slipped into a falsetto, slipped back to its tenor range. 'Because You hate me. So I will hate You too. And I hate Archer.'

There was a pause, as if he were drawing breath. A long, long breath. 'But I hate MacCallum most of all because I have done nothing to him. I liked him, God. He was decent. But he said that. He wasn't even angry when he said it. So he meant it.'

Davey Bennett did not know what to do. He simply stood. Then he turned to walk away and his shoe caught the edge of a pew and the sound echoed round and round the chapel.

'Who's there?' said Unwin in a high, frightened voice.

'It's all right, Unwin,' said Davey Bennett, walking quietly down the aisle towards him. 'It's only me. Robbie sent me to find you.'

'And you'll tell him what you heard.'

'No, I won't.'

'I know you will.'

'I promise I won't tell him.'

'What did you hear?'

'It doesn't matter.'

'What did you hear?'

'Just what you said to God.'

'You'll get me expelled.' There was almost relief in his voice.

'No, Unwin. I won't. Come back to the dorm or Robbie will be after you.'

'I don't care about Robbie.'

Sacrilege.

'Well, if you care about yourself' – echoing Herbert – 'you'd better look sharp.'

'I don't care about anything.'

Davey believed him.

'I'll tell Robbie you're sick. At worst, you'll get castor oil from Miss Maltby. Wash your face and come to bed.'

'I can't.'

'You'll have to, Unwin.'

He did come up and the others stared at him, a murmur starting, but Herbert glanced round at them with such a face they'd shut up fast. He would have knocked any of them down for a careless word: there were consequences enough already. He'd seen Archer, lying on his stomach, face to the wall. Everyone knew there'd be six angry welts in perfect sequence across his arse.

Everyone knew that all his privileges had been withdrawn.

Everyone knew what he'd done to Unwin.

By lights out, everyone knew what he'd said to Charlie Fraser.

Everyone knew why.

Unwin was irrelevant. Unwin had always been irrelevant.

It was the berth in the Firsts.

And, Charlie's words: –Dream on, Archer.

SIX

All Archer had wanted was validation. It's all any of them wanted. Without it, self-esteem was tenuous. Without it they were lonely.

And Archer was lonely.

Unwin was lonely.

Huddlestone and Harman and all the motley struggled on sporadically. They had their moments too but they also had the kindly undertow of approbation, offered by those masters who did not preoccupy themselves with tries and wickets and the exploits of the epic: the chaplain, gentle and avuncular; the choirmaster; the Second Master who remembered everyone; Jarge, the porter, who had never failed to recall a name or incident, to give a boy, however briefly, his moment of regard.

They had each other.

Even they, in time, might come back and think of boys like Archer with a laugh.

–Great bully of a fellow, do you remember? Whatever happened to him?

–Interesting story.

–Really? Not much upstairs!

–Despite that, he was a great success.

Archer himself might return and wander round the House, breathing in the smell of the wisteria on the back porch, glance at windows out of which he'd sometimes hung a hapless nub, and feel refreshed. Dear old Robbie, dear old House, Good Lord – Miss

Maltby's still in harness, our Founders, Governors and Benefactors.

If Unwin's loneliness was circumstantial, Archer's had been earned. It took aberrant forms.

It spawned a kind of treachery.

Like Unwin, Archer did not have the power to earn the loyalty of friends but, unlike him, he had the strength and presence to impress or to coerce. Archer was big. Archer was strong. Archer, fleshy though he might become with age, was vigorous. When unconscious of himself he was even an engaging boy, but most times he cultivated the air of a buck, surly when he wasn't showing off.

But Archer was also manly: it was the great reprieve.

Unwin was not: that was his tragedy.

The bucks were audience enough for Archer. They hung about with him when they felt it safe for him to entertain them. Sporadic rebellion, led by Archer, was one way to counter their insignificance – but a sort of cowardice made them always hedge their bets. Sensing danger, they retreated fast, melting into anonymity again. As long as Archer was ahead and no one was around to see, they'd shadow Archer's back. They smoked with him, they ate his tuck, smirked over pictures he'd procured of half-clad women, were indifferent when he humiliated nubs or challenged other boys to fight. But they slunk off when Archer came to the attention of the great and glorious. No one could defend Archer in the face of Seymour, Holmes or MacCallum.

No one could defend him in the face of Fraser.

They gloated secretly to see him stand exposed: a sly betrayal. Who was Archer then?

But having done that – who were they? Itinerant sycophants. Their cruelty was their indifference. Archer, at least, paid a price for his.

To have been dropped for someone younger. Every hope destroyed since he'd sat at the edge of Lower field and watched the full-back of that year, Sampson, kicking penalties. Archer had burned to kick like him. He could imagine it – he could have done it. But he only thought about the result: he did not observe Sampson's diligence at practice times or how he came to achieve such accuracy. He only knew of the little ditty – all the rage – written in so many autograph books at the girls' school, 'Keep it up 'til . . .' to be filled in with something witty or apt by a classmate. The most common that winter term had been, 'Keep it up 'til Sampson proposes'. So many hopefuls for Sampson, Full-back, First XV!

Sampson's deep blue velvet colours cap had hung above his bed. Archer knew it well. It was silky on the inside and had a pile on the outside that could be smoothed with a finger to shadow or to sheen. A wiry tassel made of silver thread dangled weighty from the spiralled button on the crown. He had tried it on and looked at himself. It fitted well. One day he would also sit with his colours blazer buttoned to the top, the collar up, the stiff, wide-striped scarf around his neck, his hands crossed in his lap, the great iron-bolted door behind – and stare out, immortal. 'Goens' Archer, L.J.M. Full-back. And – perhaps – in the school magazine:

> 'Archer is the finest full-back in years . . .'
> In memory.
> No, in years. With the best will in the world 'in memory' was not the coach's style.
> 'He is a superb tackler . . .'
> A fearless tackler? A ferocious tackler? A courageous tackler?
> 'Archer is a courageous tackler. His boot is supremely safe. . .'
> Indivisible from this was 'Keep it up 'til Archer . . .'
> Whatever Archer wants of you. But even Archer doesn't say.

It was not only Charlie Fraser who lay on his back at night and stared at the arched beams on the ceiling. The difference was that Charlie Fraser thought of the game – the ball and posts themselves: how to beat the wind; how to beat sun in his eyes; how to set the ball for a penalty or a conversion at the perfect angle; how far to back, how many steps to take. Try both feet. Try for touch: this foot, that foot. Make them equal. Being 'got up' in his colours cap and blazer did not preoccupy his mind. A grin, in passing – yes – but that was all. He knew nothing of 'Keep it up 'til . . .' Charlie what?

And Archer was still sprawled in bed when Charlie Fraser was long gone to kick at posts. He went each morning as the sun was rising and the frost was crisp underfoot, when it was almost too dark to see. Kick and watch it fly. Trot, head down, fetch it. Trot back. Kick again.

Jarge always said to anyone who was late for anything – breakfast, prep, lessons, practice: 'Aye, you have to get up early to catch a weasel.'

Catch a weasel?

It was lost on most. But Charlie Fraser knew. Old Jarge's wily weasel wouldn't catch him out!

'I feel quite sorry for Archer,' Percy said to MacCallum the night Robbie had thrashed Archer senseless for his filthy mouth. Herbert, summoned for chess, sat very still, staring at the board. They had forgotten him.

Percy flipped a rook over and over in his hand. He qualified it: 'If one can feel sorry for Archer.'

'No one in their senses is sorry for Archer,' said Mac.

Percy took one of Herbert's pawns. Herbert took one back.

'He hasn't got certain natural advantages,' said Percy.

'Like what?'

'Some things are inbred, Mac. Little things. He can't help being a barbarian.'

'What things?'

'He'd wear his cap on the back of his head in the footer photo or have his pants too short. That sort of thing.'

'Like a soccerite?'

'Just so. He'd look quite out of place. Anyway' – satirical – 'he could hardly play soccer here! At the sight, the Head would have to be carted off feet first, Robbie following.'

'Can you imagine anyone taking a soccer ball onto Lower?' Mac grinned. And, as though the question were inevitable: 'What does his father do?'

'He's a tradesman.' Percy turned back to the board, surveyed it, lifted a brow at Herbert. Herbert was within a move of winning.

'What kind?'

'He has a shop.'

So did Herbert's father. On the farm. He shifted in his chair.

'You mean he's a shopkeeper proper, then? He's not a trader?' Mac was alarmed: his father directed a string of trading stations, an empire in the tribal territories.

'You know exactly what I mean, Mac,' said Percy. 'Your kind of trader isn't a shopkeeper.' He glanced at Herbert too – absently – as if recalling him. 'Traders to the natives are entirely different from shopkeepers. They're pioneers. They're like missionaries, bearers of civilisation. Front-runners in its spread' – Percy was enjoying himself, playing to Mac, placating Herbert – 'Adventurers. Explorers.' He paused. 'Greengrocers are not.'

Mac endeavouring to follow. 'Greengrocers?'

'Archer can play as well as he likes, but you'd rather have Fraser in the team anyway. And certainly in the photo. He bears no resemblance to a soccerite or a shopkeeper. The evidence is all in the nose.'

'What's wrong with Fraser's nose?'

'Everything's right with Fraser's nose. Not even Archer's punching it could spoil it.'

Was Percy making an elaborate joke? 'You're being ridiculous,' said Mac, irritably.

'Of course!' Percy had lost Mac long ago. Herbert remained. 'It's entirely ridiculous. But that's how it works.'

Percy turned back to the board and deftly took Herbert's queen – right from under his nose and he within an ace of winning.

'Fraser's there on merit,' said Mac.

'Undoubtedly – which is fortunate.'

' "Fortunate" ' doesn't come into it,' said Mac.

Percy shrugged. 'Anyway, nubs don't sing half as lustily when Fraser isn't playing. Altogether, he's essential.' He smiled at Herbert: it was more than nubs.

'Thanks!' said Mac: nice little barb, that.

'It's true!' said Percy. 'Anyway, this is a pointless conversation.' Percy turned to the game. 'It's just that Archer waited longer. So it crossed my mind to be sorry for him.'

'Why?'

'No one took your place, Mac.'

Who *could* take his place? Really! Mac said instead, 'It wasn't in dispute. Fraser's better.'

'Fair enough. But Archer's still disappointed.'

'Fraser got it because Fraser works,' said Mac.

'Fraser sublimates.'

'You do talk such rot, Daisy. What's "sublimates" anyway?'

Percy did not answer. He finished the game swiftly, as if closing an account. All to advantage, then suddenly trounced, Herbert stood up. Percy put the board away. 'Anything you like, Mac,' he said. 'Maybe to atone?' He picked up a book and went to the door, showing Herbert out.

Herbert walked away.

'To put off dying, Mac. Mostly that.' He said it to himself, but Herbert heard him.

Percy ambled after him, singing a mocking snatch of the school song. That was lost on Mac as well.

In the end, they all had their lonelinesses and their losses. Some very great. Some small but no less important at the time. And some carried from so long ago that the little storms had long subsided into calm and only sediment remained, dormant underfoot. Sometimes someone might be found in chapel, tucked in a corner of a pew alone, observed only by a cleaner unobtrusively polishing the candlesticks, or in one of the few bogs that still had a door, exposed by feet sticking down, inviting someone to peer over the top.

'Hey, you! Why're you drizzing?'

'Who's drizzing?' A gathering: the first scent of blood.

'Some nub is drizzing in the bogs.'

If derision didn't drive them out, the stink would.

Some were vociferous in their loss: Unwin's sobs of outrage; Archer's – tears no less present – translating into cruelty.

Loss was sometimes only known by little things. A word, a shoulder turned, a boy left without a letter when the mail was handed out, those who had given up bothering to come at all when Robbie sorted post. Even the great and glorious had been known to cry in their time: Georgie Holmes, as a small new boy, cradling his violin case and trailing something of his mother's devotion, the sensitive curve of her mouth, the bucks waiting to extinguish him; James Seymour – despite himself – when he was teased for pudginess and girlish hair. He'd obliterated them ruthlessly, almost shaved his head, worked himself to muscle, cast out knock-knees, soft cheeks, concave chest. Emerged and overcome. Sparrow, snot-nosed – half in laughter – splashing a long rambling missive from home: he could laugh himself out of anything, given time. Percy – over a book – any sign meticulously purged, all evidence expunged. Arthur, almost – only Charlie knew how close – for humiliations by the masters. Herbert when his dog died. Only then. All other tears had been ingested secretly since Charlie Fraser had saved him on the first night at school, but when the letter came from home, he'd had to let them out, knowing, somehow, that it was allowed: a fellow's dog was a legitimate cause for grief. She had died in the line of duty and devotion. Everybody understood it. He could even mourn at length. He could even be comforted. Even Davey Bennett could shed a tear on his behalf and give him a good supply of bull's-eyes from Dicks' to make him feel better. Davey's own tears at the loss of Herbert from the fort could be siphoned safely in the cause of Herbert's dog.

But if loneliness was a misfortune, a loss of validation to be grieved over, aloneness was different. It had no connection with validation or the need for regard. Percy was alone. His intellect imposed a distance others could not cross. Only the notebooks were there as evidence of need. And despite the adulation, so was Charlie.

It set them apart.

No one, not even Arthur, had ever seen Charlie Fraser cry. Herbert wondered if he ever had. It was an odd thing to wonder. Almost a heresy. He remembered Charlie, stoic in his third year, with a dislocated elbow, sitting at the side of Lower field in the first half of a House match, Arthur shielding him from jostlers, Herbert sent to tell Miss Maltby to call the doctor.

'Come with me, lad' – the coach, concerned. 'Help him,' indicating Arthur.

Rising unaided, white faced, Charlie had swayed a little. Arthur was at his side, not touching, simply allowed. They walked. Herbert met them on his way from Miss Maltby, turned and shadowed Charlie's back. Neither sent him away.

Charlie made no sound at all when they attended to him, though the doctor and Miss Maltby had to cut his footer jersey off him. Miss Maltby handed it to Arthur.

The doctor took Charlie's arm, surveying it over the rim of his spectacles, probed very gently. 'Dr James Fraser your father, lad?' he said, working briskly then.

'Yes, sir.'

Silence while the arm was manipulated. Arthur screwed his eyes up. Herbert moved towards the window, feeling the grate and click of Charlie's bones in the base of his own spine.

'Knew him long ago in Stutterheim,' said the doctor, trying distraction.

'Yes, sir,' said Charlie. Not much breath to speak.

'Good doctor.'

'Thank you, sir.'

'Very good.'

Miss Maltby unravelled bandages.

Arthur stood awkwardly by, holding the cut-off jersey as if Charlie was still inside it, as if it was heavy. He held it at arm's length.

The elbow, re-aligned, was deftly strapped.

The doctor finished. He stood up stiffly, took Charlie's pulse, consulted his watch. He cast a swift, appraising look at him, called Miss Maltby to one side and gave her a bottle of drops from his bag. 'Put him to bed. Send for me if you need me. I don't like his colour.'

'Him?' Miss Maltby was quite assured. 'Strong as an ox, doctor. No trouble. Won't hear a word.'

The doctor looked back at him. Charlie said, 'Thank you, sir.'

'Good lad, Fraser.' He seemed to examine him. Charlie sat upright, arm barely cradled. Herbert saw him glance swiftly at the doctor as he turned to go, as if he wanted to say something. His mouth moved and then set again. Drawing breath he'd lost the words. Could they be:

–My father, sir. What was he like?

–How did he speak? How did he look?

–Were you with him?

But he only said, 'Good afternoon, sir' and the doctor murmured again, half to himself, 'Good lad' and went out with Miss Maltby. Arthur sat beside him on the bench, not close, but there. Herbert picked at the peeling paint on the window-frame, not looking at either of them.

'I suppose I'll be dropped.' Charlie said. His voice was quite steady.

'Course not. A week or two, perhaps,' said Arthur.

'Sure?'

'Sure.'

'Shall we go?'

'Right.'

'Right.'

Charlie stood, legs braced a moment. He walked out. Arthur and Herbert followed.

Miss Maltby caught them at the head of the stairs. She said to Charlie, 'And where do you think you're going, my good fellow, without a shirt?'

'To watch the rest of the match.'

'Not on your life.'

She produced water and the bottle of drops and an old teaspoon and herded him into the dormitory.

Charlie shook his head. 'Don't need it,' he said. Anything longer would have been impossible.

'Do as you're told.'

'I'm all right.'

'Sit.'

'Yes, ma'am.'

He submitted. She turned her back on him while he changed, motioned Arthur and Herbert to help. Charlie managed on his own. Arthur held his rugby shorts, Herbert his boots and socks.

'Off with you now!' Miss Maltby sent them away. 'I'll keep him out of trouble, if I can.' She took the clothes and went down the dormitory.

'Right,' said Arthur, looking at Charlie.

'Right,' said Charlie.

'Right,' said Herbert, echoing them.

Miss Maltby brought him a cup of tea.

Miss Maltby had not brought any boy a cup of tea before. It was her own cup of tea as well, sugared and sent up with a little biscuit from the kitchen with the housemaid. She carried it to Charlie Fraser.

'This will give you a bit of colour,' she said.

'Ma'am.'

'Let me see you drink it now.'

She put the cup on the wooden chair beside his bed and helped him up against the pillow. He took the cup, resting it on his chest. He seemed to wince briefly at its heat. There was a trace of blood on the rim where he had sipped.

So that was how he stayed so calm. He must have bitten the insides of his cheeks quite raw to master pain like that.

Strange boy. She glanced at him. She had no sense of him, either from his locker or from what he said. He kept no mementoes among his things. Only his photo album which was always tied securely with a string and a complicated knot.

'So,' she stood at the foot of his bed, arms folded, head on one side, 'your father is a doctor?'

'My father's dead.'

It was so final an answer, she could only retreat.

'Can you manage?' she said, at a loss.

'Yes, ma'am,' he replied.

She left him with his tea and biscuit. Some time later she came back for the cup and to make it up for intruding.

He was asleep on his side, head tucked in. Locked away. She stood beside the bed, afraid to stir and wake him. His straight, fair hair was damp, a little frown between his dark brows. There was a vein in his temple where the skin was tender. It seemed so frail. A faint counter-signal to the even tread of lungs and heart. He sighed: a stumbling small sigh, quite fugitive. He caught it up, marshalled it, went on, breathing evenly.

Mysterious to be the mother of a boy like this.

Was his mother afraid to touch him too, to draw him in for comfort, turn his face against her with her palm open to the contour of his cheek, fingertips to temple?

She walked away briskly, clipping the boards with her heels.

Later, she had to admonish the fellows for making a noise around his bed. They had brought him bread from the dining-room and buttered it with lard and sprinkled sugar on it. There would be a complaint from the cook tomorrow about the empty bowls on the tables. Sparrow Bell had sugar all over his chin. Douglas Morgan was eating extra slices, one a mouthful. There would be another dislocated arm the way they were carrying on. They were contriving a human pyramid with Grant and Bell and little Herbert Cummings perched on the top. Arthur Graham was shouting instructions as if he were on parade.

'Arthur Graham, behave yourself and stop that noise at once! Mr Robinson will be up any minute with this row.'

No one paid her the least attention: Mr Robinson had gone to dinner with the Head. They knew that they were safe 'til nine, at least.

She went up later, just at lights out, to see if he was comfortable.

'Your drops, boy.' Brisk she was, spooning them out and looking just above his head at the iron bars of the bed.

'Ma'am.'

'Doctor says you should take them four-hourly. You may need them in the night.'

'I'm all right, ma'am.'

She examined his hand protruding from the bandage. The fingers were blue. 'The drops will help.'

'Ma'am.'

'Send someone if you need me.'

—Send someone if you need me. She knew Charlie Fraser would crawl to hell before he sent anyone to call her out.

He roamed around all night.

Half dozing, Herbert saw him passing his dorm door going down

111

the stairs, slowly, like a sleepwalker in the dark, good shoulder to the wall, to feel his way. He must have needed the bogs.

When Herbert woke later and went to the bogs himself, Charlie wasn't in his bed. He wasn't in the bogs either. He was sitting on the parapet outside the House, looking off the way he always did when he leaned beside the window: slipped away wherever it was he went in his head. It was as if he could disappear at will, without an explanation.

Nub: first week of the first term of the first year.

–What does your father do, Fraser? A large boy, from Stutterheim, knowing well enough that his father was dead: talk silenced when children entered a room; Mrs Fraser in the church, sitting by herself with the small boy, somewhere at the end of a pew: –Be good to little Fraser, son, he lost his father very young. Offering weapons quite unwittingly.

–I'm talking to you, nub. What does your father do?

–Nothing.

–I asked you . . . pushing power around . . . what does your father do?

–Nothing.

–What do you mean, nothing?

Others gathering, looking down at him, chests eye-level, hostile.

–Nothing. Very clear and very dogged.

–You mean he just sits around and does nothing? Laughter starting.

–Yes.

–Ah, that's a lot of rot, man. No one's dad does nothing.

He would not say that his father was dead: take his father's name and make it meaningless. There had been blood behind his eyes. He could feel the heat. And his fists were clenched at his side. Ready. He would have struck the first to say another word.

From then on, they knew he wouldn't cry.

They knew he'd fight them one by one and never cry.

–Come, my little man. His grandmother had always said,

–We'll have no tears. We'll soldier on. Walk straight. Eyes wide. Chin up. That's grand.

Something fugitive from long ago: –Could he have his father's
streak?
–He could, poor lad.
–Melancholy?
–If you wish . . .

In the morning he was up like everybody else. Arthur took his tie
and did it on himself, ducked from the loop, slung it over Charlie's
head and pulled it up like a noose, pretending to hang him with it.
They played the fool with the laces of his shoes. Arthur wouldn't
fasten the buckle of his belt.

'I want your *broeks* to fall down in assembly,' he said, 'and see what
happens.'

'Do it up, arse.'

'Not today,' Arthur said, mimicking the Head, hands behind his
back, staring Charlie in the crotch. 'Boy . . . is something amiss with
you . . . It's a sign, boy, of a shocking lack of initiative . . .'

'I'll give you a *klap*.'

Danny Grant took pity on him and did the buckle up instead.

They were down the stairs and into the dining-room. Porridge.
Bread. Old tea, rewarmed, reboiled, resteeped, pale grey with tired
dregs to read at the bottom of the cup:

'Something exciting is going to happen to you today, Douggie.'

'Probably means I'm going to get thrashed.' Doug poking about
in the leaves and undissolved sugar at the bottom of his cup and then
sucking his fingers noisily.

'Morgan! You're eating like a caddie!' Robbie casting an eye from
the top table. 'See me after breakfast.'

'What did I say!' Doug triumphant.

In the morning it was always different from the night, even if it
rained or in winter when the shadows hung about the dorms all day
and cast a deep grey gloom. Something more than darkness lifted
with the light and sent the undertow away. The legendary night adder
that lurked in the third bog after midnight was forgotten; Duncker,
who'd run away twelve years before, joined the Boer Forces and

113

returned to school with English blood on his hands, holding vigil in the chapel porch, dissolved. Perhaps, after all, Charlie, sitting on the parapet, was only something Herbert had imagined on his way up from the lavatory. A wraith-like Duncker.

What was he doing there, looking off beyond the town, so intent that if Herbert had dared to say his name, he'd have been unheard.

At night, anything was possible. In the morning, the light and the bell dispelled it. Feet on the stairs, voices, Arthur singing out of tune, Archer gargling tooth powders and water. You could hear him all over the House. There was always a line of little boys in the bogs, hair wetted flat, faces scrubbed, elbows on knees, chins cupped, contemplating the view, unconcerned by passersby or night adders, the chapel door bland and peeling in the sun, Robbie bawling instructions to those who had been sent up. Beatings before breakfast:

'I won't have a lad go hungry in fear of a thrashing. Get it over with before porridge and no harm done.'

Two or three lined up for his brisk administrations: Edwards, Mostert, Unwin.

That undertow escaped the boys who went to bed undisturbed, slept soundly and woke with the bell. They did not know it, unless they came back to the dorm in the day for something forgotten and walked down the echoing passages and stood a moment and looked at the empty beds lined up with the light coming in; or a fellow who was isolated because of sickness and had to lie hour after hour and look at the ceiling and find patterns in the struts, see mouths and monster noses, sly animals, fantastic forms. And even then, one had to hear the other echoes, have the augur's eye to see.

Loneliness was kept off with laughter. A well-timed fart to make the fellows howl, preferably just as Miss Maltby had left the room. Doug Morgan could produce them on cue, tuneful little chirrup or a trumpet call, depending. He was more reliable than Robbie's dog.

Walking down the junior dorm, nubs lined up – bed inspection. 'Parkes, did you say something?'

'No, Morgan.'

'I distinctly heard you speak.'

'No, Morgan.'

'Excuse me, Parkes, I think you made a small remark.'

Parkes convulsed. 'No, Morgan.'

'Who was it then?'

'You, Morgan.'

'Me?' Exaggeratedly looking behind himself. 'Me? That's outrageous!'

Another, quite musical. 'GB?' Pouncing. 'Report to Fraser at once. I won't have whistling in the dorm.'

'I wasn't whistling, Morgan.'

'My dear fellow, are you contradicting me?'

Another little salvo. 'There you are! What do you say now?'

GB shaking and Parkes crossing his legs.

'To attention, Parkes!'

Parkes *in extremis*.

'To attention!'

GB slung over a shoulder and delivered to Charlie's door, Parkes only making the window in time.

But if laughter kept loneliness at bay, another laughter underpinned it cruelly. Those excluded from the laughter stood exposed. Those with laughter turned against them were the loneliest of all. Laughter could betray more cruelly, maim more surely, than anger or neglect. Laughter was delivered by the pack, a coward's weapon in its carelessness: mock collectively and no one takes the buck. Only prigs fail to laugh: it is worse to be a prig than to betray your friend in laughter. Everyone knew that.

'Do you want this banana, Huddlestone?'

'No, thanks,' looking up mildly from a book.

'Why not?'

'I've just had one.'

'Have it.'

Something dawning, Huddlestone keeping the book steady, feeling other eyes. Fatty Harman shifts uncomfortably. 'No, thanks.'

'Take it, Huddlestone.'

Huddlestone takes it, sensing a tormentor, puts it to one side, continues reading.

'See!' Triumphant idiot. 'Baboons can never resist bananas!'

Huddlestone pays no attention but the tormentor cannot be diverted. Harman moves away.

'Eat it, Huddlestone.'

No response.

'Eat it, Huddlestone. Eat it.'

The chant is taken up. 'Eat it, Huddlestone!' The chant swells. Someone peels the banana. Huddlestone is held down. It is forced into his mouth. His shirt is yanked so the buttons fly off. They sit on him and examine his hairiness, fingers creeping over his chest in search of imaginary fleas: someone showing off, astride him.

'What are you boys doing?' Robbie coming in.

Everyone to attention. Huddlestone is wiping banana from his face. Robbie glances at him. 'Are you the cause of this commotion?'

'Just larking, sir,' says Huddlestone.

'Any more larking will see you in my room.'

'Sir.'

Harman breathes again. Huddlestone doesn't look at him; he takes his book and goes away.

'Was your father a pig, nub?'

'A pig?' Hopeful new boy, arranging his locker for the first time, suddenly bewildered.

'Where did you get that nose then?'

'Pardon?'

What had been belittled? His father? Himself?

Roll-call in the morning, Robbie intoning, collective unfortunates, always lumped together:

'Adcock.'

'Alcock.'

'Badcock.'

'Ball.'

Boys convulsed: Mostert's glass eye on the table at dinner, like a china hazelnut, gazing straight at the kitchen door. The waiter comes, bearing a tureen of soup.

The general wisdom after that: —Borrow Mostert's eye. It's the only way to get out of eating barley soup.

'*Tyini Thixo! Liliso lembulu!*' Holy God! The leguaan's eye! No one could mimic in Xhosa better than Mostert. He had them rolling on the floor after dinner, adding every rudery he could: Robbie wouldn't ever understand.

The waiter was off work for a week for the burns.

Which one was he?

'Uuuunnnnwin!' Bawling down the dorm.

'Uuuunnn-wwin!'

Unwin, head first in his locker, smelling damp clothes and unpainted pine boards, is determined not to hear.

MacCallum on duty: 'Are you going to shower, Unwin?'

Everyone is alert in the shower queue. No laughter yet. Wait 'til he is herded down and Mac has gone.

Edwards, Cummings, Bennett, Pringle, Mostert, Ross, a string of others.

Unwin next. Drop the towel, run in, hit the wall, bounce off, dry. The cracked bars of soap are unused on a window ledge or are dissolving to pink jelly in a puddle in a dish.

'Unwin's like a donkey!' Same old jibe: some cheerful fellow, standing unashamed himself.

'Let's see! Let's see!'

'Leave him!' Davey Bennett in defence.

'Let's see!' Someone gives Davey a shove, catapulting him into Herbert. Herbert is expert with the coiled towel, stinging bare buttocks, ducking a punch.

'You fellows!' Unwin winding up. They'd goad him on until the familiar 'I've had it! I've simply had it!' brings Mac or Robbie down.

Things said in jest – any things – are meant to pass unchallenged. Only prigs object. Jokes are jokes: laughter, laughter. Fellows have to take it.

But when Archer said, 'Unwin has endowments past your wildest dreams' and Charlie Fraser made the sharp retort 'Dream on', he'd challenged an accepted form, exposed the undertow deliberately, defending Unwin.

Such a small, inconsequential exchange, Charlie turning back to the sports page of the paper. It had passed, gone underground. But it was there. Along with the berth in the First XV. Along with the adulation of the little boys. It was there, behind the approbation of the great and glorious for the one, their dismissal of the other.

Oh, it was there.

SEVEN

Archer had had his privileges withdrawn. He was under scrutiny.
Robbie was no fool: associates of Archer's were reviewed as well. If
Archer had a mouth as foul as that, so might they. The bucks retreated.
No one would go to town for him and buy him fags and he could not
go himself. At that moment there was none less powerful than he.
Except Unwin.

Expedience came first. How to serve expedience without a loss of
face remained the puzzle. Archer circled it. In the end, it seemed so
simple. But it wasn't.

Archer sent for Unwin. Unwin came, abject, waiting at the door to
the locker room. He hovered, his face very white in the late afternoon
gloom. Archer was standing in his rugby gear, divesting himself of
his jersey. He said, 'Unwin, go to town and buy me pies.'

Unwin stood bewildered. He'd prepared himself for torture.

'Pies?' he said uncertainly.

'Pies, Unwin. You know – pies.' Being facetious. 'Pastry, meat, all
that.'

'I haven't got permission, Archer.'

'So when is permission a problem?' said Archer, walking down
and looming over him.

'If you ask Mr Robinson . . .' said Unwin. He could almost feel
Archer's boot in the small of his back.

'Mr Robinson is playing golf this afternoon,' said Archer. 'And

MacCallum?' said Unwin.

'I wouldn't want to disturb the great man,' said Archer. 'Especially not on your account. He has a particular aversion to you, Unwin. Anyway, he has just had a hard game of footer so I am sure he won't be wandering about in town.'

Again Unwin glanced behind and licked his lips. 'It's out of bounds, Archer . . .'

'So is showering late at night,' said Archer. 'I could make you shower now.'

Unwin's hands were sweating. When Archer put the coins in his palm, he'd wiped his fingers on his rugby shorts deliberately and Unwin recognised the familiar look of vague repulsion on his face. 'And Unwin?' – even Unwin divined it as the purpose for which he had been summoned – 'A packet of Flags from the coolie shop.'

'What if I'm caught?' The sweat was shoring up. Any moment now and it would burst out on his head.

'It's not worth being caught,' said Archer. He stretched and Unwin stared at the floor. He could not look too closely at so much of Archer without his jersey. 'And if you bring them back, you can have one too.'

'I . . . I.'

'Don't tell me you don't know how to smoke?' Casting the invisible skein: Unwin stumbled into it.

'Yes, I know how to smoke,' said Unwin and God-could-strike-him-dead, he'd rather lie than be thrust in the shower and scrutinised by Archer.

'And don't advertise where you've been,' said Archer. 'I'll know it pretty soon, if you do.' The peculiar lift of his voice as if he'd raised his head to scent him.

Unwin would not advertise. Unwin would not say a word.

Unwin was gone, down the stairs, out onto the back lawn with the players trailing up from the field, around the side of the House and through the gate into the street. He glanced up and down the road but no one was there. The small panes of Jarge's cottage winked back at him. The stone pines were creaking high, high up in the early wind.

Down the hill, into the dip: he could hear his steps thudding after him, announcing him. What if he met one of the other housemasters? What if he met Miss Maltby? What if the Head was taking his dog for a walk? What if Robbie was not playing golf after all?

–Just off to town, sir, to buy some fags for Archer. Cheerio, then, sir. Enjoy your stroll.

–Bother the bounds, sir. Rather have six than be stripped by Archer.

What if the prefects were just coming up from town? What would he say to them?

–Have a fag, fellows. Archer will be happy to give his pals a drag. Be my guest.

He could *see* them in his mind, a whole platoon: MacCallum, Morgan, Fraser and Graham shoulder to shoulder, sweeping up towards him.

He ducked into a side road to keep away from the main thoroughfare and hurried along it, jumping from side to side across the *sloot* that ran along its edge, up an alley and into New Street which was strictly out of bounds, even to prefects. In the late afternoon there were a few walkers and men coming home from work. Clerks and people from the bank. The sun disappeared from the narrow walkway of Cuyler Street and he ran along in the shadow of old stone walls. Reaching the High Street, he stopped, panting, looking up towards the Drostdy, down towards the great cathedral doors. There he would be on the look-out: masters, parents, Miss Maltby on an errand. But he made Dicks' without being challenged. He was sweating freely then – a cold, clinging sweat, despite the heat under his collar.

Surreptitiously he put his head inside his blazer: he could wring his shirts out with that fearful, familiar smell of fear. He pulled his jacket round him. He would have to try and wash it one day and hang it in his locker and hope it did not rot before it dried. He wondered if he could wash wool in carbolic, if carbolic would banish all that misery. He could feel, too, the clamminess of his feet in his shoes, running as he had and jumping and forgetting to go slowly.

He bought the pies and buns, glancing all the time about him, in fear that Robbie might appear, looming at him wrathfully, ready to incinerate him in the Dicks' ovens. But no one came and the shop was empty and he was out into the evening. He almost tripped across a beggar waiting in the door. He saw him in his khaki rags but he could not look at him: God did not care for beggars either. He sped down the hill, dodging alleys and the cathedral clock going 'tong' behind him. He would be late for supper. He almost forgot the Flags. He turned back, his breath squeaking. He bought them at the Indian store in New Street. No questions were asked. The Indian's daughter gave him the change with detached fingers, her little rings flitting sparks of light back at the paraffin lamp on the counter. He was running fast now, holding the packet of pies with both hands, the Flags in his pocket. He tripped in the ditch in Rose Street, tore a right-angled flap in the knee of his trousers, was up almost before he had touched the ground and the grit in the heels of his palms stung and pushed up ridges of white skin. There were damp fingerprints on the brown paper which wrapped the pies, frog-marks all over their cover. Rose Street was a cul-de-sac ending in a steep bank leading up onto the school field. A barrel-shaped mongrel barked at him from the backyard of a garden. It had yellow eyes and small pointed ears. Hackles up, it ran up and down, up and down the fence, lunging at a hole in the wire. Unwin was afraid of dogs, even when they were fenced. It was not the attack he feared, but the unexpected aggression. Even dogs hated him. Up the bank and through the fence and onto Lower field. He was in the school grounds now, no longer out of bounds. He breathed easier. He hid the bag of pies under his blazer, walking with the lump of it pressed against his clammy side with his elbow.

He was last in the dining-room. He walked in while Robbie was saying grace, standing up at the top table in his well-worn jacket with a red, wind-burned face from an afternoon on the golf course. Robbie closed his eyes when he said grace. MacCallum did not.

To walk to one's place under the dark gaze of MacCallum: Unwin could feel the sweat again, crawling along his spine. He could feel MacCallum's eyes following as he tiptoed past the lower tables to his own. He could feel how wet his socks had become. The pies were still under his jacket, the Flags made a neat rectangle in his pocket. Two tables up, Archer was staring straight ahead.

Arranging his jacket carefully, Unwin sat in his place. He examined the thick bevelling of his water glass as the soup was being ladled out, not daring to look at the seniors at either end: Arthur Graham, John Barham. From the corner of his eye, Unwin saw Graham glance up at his hands and frown as he reached to take a piece of bread. Unwin hid them in his lap. They were filthy from the gravel on the road, the blood stripes were raw, the nails black.

After soup, the empty plates were sent down. Unwin had to unfold his hands to take and pass. He almost dropped them. He left fingerprints on the rim, a smear of blood and grit on the edge.

'Eeugh!' grimaced Edwards, his neighbour, recoiling from the pile and pushing his chair onto its back legs, making it screech. 'You filthy sod, Unwin!' Under his breath he said, 'And anyway, you smell like a pig.' Every eye at the table turned to Edwards. Unwin burned.

'Edwards,' Arthur Graham said, 'what d'you think you're doing?'

'It's Unwin, Graham. He's put muck all over the plates. It's disgusting!'

John Barham looked at the plates that Edwards dumped in front of him. He made a mouth at them, dilating his large nostrils and called the waiter to take them away. He looked at Unwin with his eyebrows raised and those round, pale, prominent eyes. 'Really, Unwin,' he said in a clear voice which drifted down the hall. 'Cleanliness is next to godliness.' John Barham was fond of pompous little sayings. He used them all the time.

There was a momentary lull and Unwin, under the weight of a fearful scrutiny, felt the tide rising. But Arthur Graham banged the meat fork down on the serving dish and clattered the clean plates in front of him and said loudly, 'Pass down the bread, will you, Cummings', and the hall dissolved again into conversation. The danger had passed. Graham had diverted the dreadful moment when Robbie, sitting there at top table, might have said, 'What is the commotion down there? Will the boy causing the commotion come up to me.' He could not have gone without the pies being discovered, without leaving a trail of damp footprints behind him, without being overcome.

Unwin ate with every eye at the table on him. Did they wish him to choke in front of them, drop each mouthful in his lap and watch with fascinated revulsion? Did they want that? He could barely swallow. He looked ahead and up at the picture on the wall beyond, at the founding fathers, ranged side by side, in their clerical robes. Here a kindly face, there a profile in classic detachment. The Bishop, meditational. Like God, they were noble, they were good. Like God, they were unconcerned with him, Unwin.

The top table rose suddenly for grace, said peremptorily by MacCallum as if he were dismissing cadets from parade. The lower standards filed out, Unwin's table next. The packet of pies, now coagulated, flattened, were clenched still against his side. The Flags shouted from his pocket.

'Unwin,' Arthur Graham said, calling him back.

'Yes, Graham,' Unwin waited: Graham would send him up after all.

'I don't know why you were late – but, for your own sake, it's not a good idea to come in without washing your hands.'

'Yes, Graham.'

Arthur looked at him, his frown more puzzled than exasperated. Glancing up, he watched the boys filing out, top table, the prefects sauntering together. Unwin waited. What would Graham do? He stood, rocking slightly from toe to heel. Then he said, 'Right, Unwin,' and walked off suddenly. Except for Unwin, he was the last out of the hall: he had diverted him from Barham, saved him from the loud chafing of Edwards, given time for the others to go. Only the waiters were left, clearing the plates away. They moved with quietness, walking on soundless feet. If he could be as faceless as they were, remain unseen as they were, dissolving between hall and kitchen, only what they carried known, only what they took away remembered.

Arthur Graham might have saved him in the dining hall but he could not save him in the House. On his way to Archer, Unwin had to pass MacCallum's door. How did MacCallum know his footfall? Or was it just that, at that moment, MacCallum divined that it was time to cast his eye about his domain. The door opened and there he was. Tall, slim, in shirtsleeves with his braces off his shoulders and hanging in two loops at his sides. Distracted, he glanced at Unwin passing and then, suddenly frowning, said, 'In here.' And Unwin went into his study and stood with his arms clamped to his side and the lump welded to his under-sleeve.

There was the Red Cross nurse on the wall that everyone had talked about. He had never been in MacCallum's study before, so he had never seen her. He stared at her.

Could she see the pies?

Her face was tinted pink at the cheeks and lips. She smiled at him but in all its softness, it was a cruel little smile: she gave it to present herself. It was not for him, Unwin.

'Why were you late for supper?' said MacCallum.

'I'm sorry, MacCallum,' said Unwin, mumbling, looking past him, elbow height, at the picture.

MacCallum did not know that smile of hers and what it meant.

Unwin kept his eyes on her.

It seemed that MacCallum had touched the picture often, for it was dog-eared. Perhaps he smoothed its edges.

'I'm waiting,' said MacCallum.

'I didn't hear the bell.'

'Everyone can hear the bell, from here to the cathedral.'

Unwin looked at his feet then. There were stains on the leather, little white circles where salt gathered at the edges of the marks made by sweat. Even through the thick leather of such utilitarian shoes, those patches showed.

'I haven't got all night.' MacCallum was impatient. There was a great pile of books on his desk and the lamp drawn up to them.

Unwin said nothing. He was casting about. He couldn't think. Any moment the pies would drop out.

MacCallum stood.

Unwin stood.

Then Unwin said, 'I was in the lavatory.'

'How long do you spend in the lavatory, for goodness sake?'

'A long time, MacCallum,' said Unwin earnestly.

'I wouldn't go about saying that if I were you,' said MacCallum. 'Really, I wouldn't.'

The slow march of blood then, in his ears. What had he said? He looked at MacCallum, bewildered. MacCallum, despite the grave sameness of his face, seemed momentarily amused.

Unwin's neck burned, a slow creeping flush. MacCallum said, 'Next time you spend all afternoon in the lavatory and are late for supper, I'll send you up.'

'Yes, MacCallum. Sorry, MacCallum.'

He met Charlie Fraser in the passage as he walked away. Even in the gloom he knew his face must have been a beacon. He stepped aside into a doorway to let Fraser pass.

'Unwin,' said Fraser, glancing down at him.

'Yes, Fraser?' Truly, he could not hold the tears much longer.

But it was only a greeting and Fraser walked on and went into MacCallum's study without knocking at the door.

Unwin delivered the pies to Archer, waiting until he caught him on the way to the bogs. Archer unwrapped them and looked at them with some distaste. 'Did you sit on these?' he said.

'No, Archer. They got squashed at supper.'

Archer glanced furtively around and jerked his head and put out his hand, indicating with his fingers that he was waiting.

Unwin felt in his pockets for the Flags. He slipped them to Archer.

'Come down behind the bogs after prep.'

Unwin shifted. It was not an invitation. It was a threat. He did not know where to look.

'I . . .' he began.

'You'd better not forget,' said Archer and somewhere the image of the shower lodged in Unwin's mind.

'Yes, Archer.'

And so Unwin had his first cigarette. He had to take it voluntarily: the purpose in allowing him this intimacy was not clear, whatever bondage it entailed, undisclosed. There was no one to ask. He obeyed, sensing the deceit.

He stayed in the shelter behind the bogs with Archer. High above

126

sailed the three-storeyed lights of the House. Robbie's window was closed with the curtains drawn and MacCallum's out of view. A little hedge screened them.

Unwin was always beaten by default: his role as public nuisance. Now, if he was caught, it would have been for breaking rules. There was an odd relief, a sense of justice, in the notion. Kicking back instead of being kicked.

The idea passed: he was here because of Archer, Archer's heel firmly at his head.

Boys came and went to the bogs. Archer seemed unconcerned. He blew the smoke down, into the hedge, holding the fag between thumb and forefinger, cupped in his hand. Arthur Graham clattered into the lavatory just behind their backs. Unwin stood poised by the corrugated iron of the wall. Surely Graham could feel him standing there?

Arthur Graham sang lustily, swore lustily too, yelled, 'Who's been pissing on the seat?' It was so loud, Unwin jumped. A glare from Archer froze him.

Unwin carried a wreath of cigarette smoke back to the dormitory. He took his blazer to the basin and soaped the armpits with carbolic soap. It left a pink stain on the lining. He hung it in his locker where it smelled worse than before. He hid his damp shoes. He got into bed and lay down. He began to cough. He could not help it. Edwards threw his pillow at him and let off a string of invective.

On duty, it was Fraser who came to give them lights out. Perhaps God had taken pity after all by not sending MacCallum. Fraser walked down the dormitory, his shadow angling up against the ceiling, moving quietly above him. Unwin coughed again.

'Shut up, Unwin,' said Edwards, lashing out. Unwin put his head under the blankets, his eyes watering from the effort to control himself. Fraser stood at the foot of his bed. 'Unwin, are you sick?'

'Just a cough, Fraser.'

'Have you been to Miss Maltby?'

'No, Fraser.'

'See her in the morning.' He looked down at Unwin. 'Do you want water?'

'Yes, please, Fraser.'

'There's a jug on my desk. Take the glass.'

Unwin climbed out of bed. He went in his pyjamas, barefooted down the aisle between the rows to Fraser's study. The door was ajar, the lamp burned on the table. Fraser's camera lay in its light and his album was open. Unwin had not dared go into Fraser's study before and he had never been summoned. He went to the desk and took up the jug and poured some water into the glass. He took a sip and looked about him guardedly. The walls were bare. Where was a Red Cross nurse like MacCallum's with her cruel little smile? He turned round, looking all about him. There was a picture after all. Not of a woman or a girl. It was very small. It was of some hills with an old house in the foreground. It was faded and brown and pinned up haphazardly on the wall. Unwin bent and examined it, putting his head to one side: a hill and a little house with wooden railings and aloes and trees. Old, old trees and flowers by a fence before the veld and hills. He bent further, leaning in to look at it.

He did not hear Charles Fraser. He only felt him. He turned. Fraser stood in the doorway with his hands in his pockets. He said, quite calmly, 'Go to bed, Unwin.'

It was some days later that Robbie sent Unwin with a message to Fraser. Unwin knocked at his door. Charlie Fraser was working at his desk. He turned. 'Yes?' Unwin delivered the message and backed out. But he saw immediately that the little picture had gone. The walls were quite bare.

Expedience. Both for Archer and for Unwin. It was a strange dependence, born of need, served by fear. While it was convenient to Archer, Unwin did his bidding. Whatever he wanted, Unwin did. His trips to town became quite regular. His reward – or his sentence – the same: ten minutes behind the bogs with a fag of his own. The bucks came back, wooed with Westminsters or Flags, Cape to Cairos or Commandos – whatever Unwin could get. A word from Archer and Unwin did their bidding too, Archer just affable enough to dangle him along. It was the worst kind of menace. It sucked Unwin in. He hovered at the edges, being allowed to smile – not laugh – at Archer's jokes, being allowed to squat with a Westminster pinched between thumb and index finger like a workman at his tea-break, being adept at spitting out a shred of tobacco like Archer and Mostert and Stafford without them seeing. He began to sweat just a little less. He should have known better: lamentable Unwin.

'There's a *sloot*,' said Archer. 'It's a great long tangy that leads underground and takes you all the way across town.'

'Who said?'

'My brother used to use it. They used to get a bottle or two and take it down there. He used to use it for other things as well.'

'What brother?' said Stafford, knowing well enough he had none. Archer gave him a look.

'What things?' Stafford corrected himself.

'He had business . . .'

'What business?'

'In New Street.' No one believed him.

Put out, Archer said, with a smirk, 'I'd like business in New Street.' Unwin smirked too.

'What's so funny, Unwin?' Archer turned on him, one eye closed against the drift of smoke from the tail-end of the cigarette dangling from his lip.

'New Street . . .'

'What about New Street?'

Unwin was at a loss.

'Should we send Unwin to New Street, boys? Along the tangy and up the drain?'

They all looked at Unwin, ranged against him.

'I should think the ladies of New Street would be pretty interested to see Unwin,' said Mostert, a slow grin dawning. 'More fun than you, hey, Archer?'

Archer sent Mostert sprawling.

Unwin burned. Whatever was in New Street?

They sent him to explore the tangy. They sent him right along it by himself. They goaded him in and there was no way out except at the other end. He had to pretend he was doing it for fun. To check the route to New Street. Why New Street with its old houses and Harry Chang's greengrocer, Swan's ginger beer and the coolie shop? Surely it was better to find a route to the Great Electric Bioscope so they could bunk on Saturdays and sneak in at the back?

'You might meet mad old Kappie down there, so watch out . . .' A vagrant woman, toothless, too destitute for care, too harmless for the asylum on the outskirts of the town.

'Gangs go down there sometimes. Watch out for them.'

Unwin swallowed. Everyone knew the gangs. The shout would go up 'Caddies!' and small boys would scatter, the big and robust, like Douglas Morgan, get ready to retaliate. Caddies were scum. They threw stones. Seniors would challenge fist to fist, if they could. But caddies wouldn't fight like that – they waylaid you, lurking in a group. They crept up on you alone, in a tangy with the rats, where no one could see you and Douglas Morgan wouldn't hear. 'Come with me someone . . .' Desperate Unwin.

'Nah, Unwin . . . I wouldn't want to get my best shoes wet. Just have a look and see. It will be worth it.' Always that implicit threat. Do it, or else. Remember what happened in the locker room. Remember the showers, Unwin. Don't forget the showers.

'Unwin, have you been playing in the lavatories?' Supercilious MacCallum.

'No, MacCallum.'

'Kindly lift your shoes.'

'Yes, MacCallum.' Human or animal, dog or rat, caddies or tangy boys – he couldn't tell. Unwin felt the involuntary heave in his stomach. He kept it down. The spit in his mouth was like vinegar and iron filings.

'Just get out of the House and don't come back until you're clean. And report to Mr Robinson. I hope he gives you six. I've had enough.'

Enough of what, MacCallum? Enough of what?

'Unwin, I have been calling for you all afternoon. Where have you been?'

Silence.

'You have not been on the playing field, Unwin. Or at music, so don't give me that.'

'No, MacCallum.'

'You will explain yourself to Mr Robinson. I've had enough.'

Enough of what, MacCallum?

Four this time and Robbie barely bothering to ask why he was there.

No one looked at his stripes. No admiration. Nothing. The year before, when Sparrow Bell had got beaten – at last – all the fellows in his dorm had turned out to inspect his bum. What was so riveting? Unwin's own was a perfect hatch-work of equidistant welts. No one cared. No one came to look.

'Unwin.' Standing in MacCallum's study again. 'I did not observe you at song practice this afternoon.' MacCallum trying a satirical tone – did Percy Gilbert have some influence after all? He said, 'We have a match next week, you know. Where were you?'

Unwin kept his eye on the wall behind MacCallum, fixed on the picture of the nurse: MacCallum's darling, simpering there. Ah yes, she knew.

–Smoking in the tangy, Vincent dear.

Couldn't you just hear her? Those eyelashes, closing down and fanning out again and she, looking askance.

Unwin turned from her. There was no one to appeal to. She wasn't like the tsessebe on Robbie's wall, dark glass eyes with a strange, sad gleam in them. It, after all, had died, been cut off at the neck and sacrificed to Robbie's skill. But *she* was somewhere else, frittering her face away in a thousand pictures. She wasn't MacCallum's alone. She didn't even know him. But the tsessebe: that had been a meeting one to one – buck and man.

'Where were you?'

Where was I? Buck and Robbie; sad glass eyes; the way the horns bent up in defeat, like a broken lyre.

'Unwin! I am speaking to you! Are you a dolt? A half-wit?'

'Yes, MacCallum.'

'Yes, MacCallum? Yes?'

'No, MacCallum.'

' "Yes, MacCallum," I should think.'

'Yes.' A pause. 'MacCallum.'

–Unwin's such a repulsive little creep, I wish we could have him moved . . .

–Are you a dolt? A half-wit? Unwin, can you hear me?

–Do you know you stink?

–How long do you spend in the lavatory, Unwin?

–How long? How long?

MacCallum's litany of slights and barbs, delivered without thinking. But Unwin did not forget. And in the end, he picked over the derision as if it gave him nourishment, hating MacCallum and confirming, too, everything that he believed about himself.

'I hate MacCallum,' Unwin said behind the bogs to Archer, daring it. Archer looked at him, devised a new dependence.

'Show him, then,' said Archer.

'What?'

'Do it!'

'Do it?'

'Do it.'

'Do what?'

'Anything you like – just show him.'

'Are you mad?'

'You're as gutless as a gecko, Unwin.'

A gecko. Yes. He looked like one, heart beating in his throat, all internal organs held suspended within a strange translucent skin, as if they could be seen against the light, even with the naked eye. Here the dark-shaded liver. There the tortured gut. Here, so small, so very small, the heart with its odd, rhythmic pulse. Pulp, pulp, pulp – his inexorable little life.

–Do it! Just do it! Show him!

How could he, Unwin, show Vincent MacCallum, Head-of-House, First XV, First XI, Captain of Athletics, that he hated him. And besides, he didn't hate him. He'd have grovelled at his feet just to hear the words 'Well done, Unwin. Good lad, Unwin', and turned the hurt to veneration in a breath. Just as Archer, in hating Charlie Fraser, craved his approbation and regard, far, far more than he coveted his place at full-back.

So, Unwin took her. Unwin, sloughing off his gecko skin, wandering in some no man's land alone, searching for acceptance, anyone's acceptance – even Archer's – daring death.

Unwin took her. It was all he could think of. Mac's darling: she of the small, cruel, self-absorbed smile.

She was not an actress or a singer. MacCallum would never have chosen something as obvious. She was a nurse – all that dimpled self-sacrifice – with hand-tinted cheeks and lips and spiky lashes, artfully enhanced by the brush.

Mac used to gaze at her when he should have been at his books. She did not look like anyone in his university class or in the senior set at the girls' school. She did not look like anyone that any of the fellows had ever met, or ever would. She was an imitation woman.

Unwin took her.

Unwin took her as he walked past MacCallum's empty study on his way to choir practice. He took her on an impulse. MacCallum's door was ajar. The light was falling on her. He stopped suddenly and looked at the picture from the threshold:

–Do it!

–Do it?

–Anything you like. Just show him.

–Are you mad?

–You're as gutless as a gecko, Unwin.

Unwin took it. There – the gecko had its guts, after all.

–Show him, Unwin!

–Show who?

–Show MacCallum.

No: show Archer.

The enormity of what he'd done struck him the instant that he'd left the room. He turned to put it back.

'Unwin, what are you doing with that?' Percy Gilbert appeared

133

suddenly from the shadow of his doorway.

Unwin froze. 'MacCallum threw it away, Gilbert,' he said.

'I am sure he did not.'

'She was in the bin.' Deceit was the only refuge. He indicated the full wire wastepaper basket inside the door, awaiting removal by the housemaids.

'Put her back.'

'In the bin?'

'In MacCallum's room.'

'No.'

'My dear fellow, are you well?'

'Yes.'

'Yes? . . . Yes? Is that all?'

'Yes, Gilbert.'

'I am sure you have no use for her, so put her back.'

'Maybe he's tired of her.' Unwin held the picture against himself.

Percy Gilbert put out his hand for it, standing silent until it was relinquished. He scanned it. 'Hmm.' He raised a slight eyebrow.

'She has a very unpleasant smile,' said Unwin quite fiercely.

Percy looked him over then and Unwin dropped his eyes. Percy gave a small laugh. 'So she has.' He turned the picture, examined it upside down. 'Most perceptive, Unwin. I always wondered why I had such an aversion to her myself.'

He wandered off with the picture under his arm.

'What are you going to do with it?' It was out before Unwin could stop himself.

'Stick pins in it,' said Percy superciliously, reproving his impertinence.

Percy Gilbert closed his door. Unwin went to choir.

'What is the point of someone with whom you will never have – or ever wish to have – a conversation?' Percy had said it once, to Mac.

'I don't want to speak to her.'

'Well, what do you want?'

Mac couldn't answer. He wasn't sure himself.

Conversation didn't seem to bother the other fellows either.

Douggie Morgan used to stare at her with a foolish look on his face for minutes on end.

'What are you looking at, Morgan?' Percy with his little pipe, leaning on the door-frame. 'Morgan?'

'Morgan!'

'Huh?'

Jamie Seymour called her 'Mabel' just to irritate. 'Hello, Mabel. What's Mac been up to? Tell us, Mabel?'

Mac had the edge on all of them for having her. In owning her, he seemed to have some private right to her sophisticated candour: something they had yet to understand. No one else could boast a picture quite like Mac's.

When Unwin returned from choir and went down the passage half an hour later, there was the picture in the bin, under a small pile of sweepings and papers, this time gathered with others for collection at the head of the stairs. Glancing around, he took it out, shook off the little cloying tufts of dust and, concealing it under his jacket, he took it to his locker.

So. Percy Gilbert had believed him when he'd said he'd found it in the bin. And if he hadn't quite stuck pins in it, he hadn't returned it to MacCallum either: he'd thrown it away himself.

Unwin had done it, daring his own execution. Now Percy Gilbert was co-conspirator. Unwin was triumphant. For whatever reason, Percy Gilbert hated her as well. Unwin waited for the earthquake.

'Where's the picture?' MacCallum said, searching about, lifting books and papers. 'Where the hell is the picture?'

'I don't know, Mac,' said Percy.

'You've bloody taken it, Daisy.'

'Oh, yes, most certainly I've taken it!' Percy stretched. 'I adore her. I worship her. I lie in bed at night, sleepless, and contemplate her on my wall. I expand her, I diminish her . . . whatever. Like you, I am enslaved.'

'Bring her back.'

'I do not have your picture, Mac,' said Percy wearily, stepping a little out of reach. 'It was in the bin in the passage' – adding, acting it out, for he could see the lowering spot growing dark on MacCallum's cheek – 'I thought to myself, "At last Mac has thrown away that vapid . . ." '

MacCallum took hold of him by the lapels, shook him. 'You threw her away.'

Disengaging MacCallum's fingers one by one and then pulling his jacket straight, with a small deliberate gesture, Percy said, 'No, Mac.'

'Why d'you always do this?'

'I don't, Mac . . . You know that.'

'I'll turn the bloody House upside down. I'll horsewhip who-ever . . . I'll kill the fellow.'

'Perhaps the housemaid found it on the floor.'

'Bloody rot. It was pinned to the rail.'

'Leave it now.'

'I bloody well won't leave it.'

'It's a picture, Mac.'

Mac smashed his fist into the pile of books on his table and sent them scattering. He overturned his chair.

Percy closed the study door and stood against it. 'Stop. Temper isn't going to help.'

MacCallum opened his cupboard, stood back and slammed it with all his strength. The sound reverberated round the House, making the walls shudder.

'Vincent . . . Stop.'

There were footsteps outside. More. There must have been a congregation waiting at the door.

'Enough.' Percy Gilbert's voice was soft. He took him quietly by the upper arms, facing him. 'No, Vincent.' He half turned his head, listening.

MacCallum did not subside but Percy held him still. 'Stop before Robbie comes.' Then Percy went to the door, opened it gaily, surveyed the throng in the passage and swept his gaze around in mock surprise.

'What's going on?' asked Sparrow, hands on his hips, Danny at his shoulder; Charlie, Arthur, Herbert, juniors bunched behind them.

'Has Mac blown himself up?' said Arthur.

'No,' said Percy airily. 'I turned his bookcase over by mistake, trying to climb on it.'

'Trying to climb on it?'

'In Euripides it says the walls of Carthage were a hundred and fifteen feet high. I couldn't estimate it so I got the tape measure – and, well . . . I expect I could say it was about an inch short of Mac's ceiling multiplied by seven.'

The juniors were staring. 'Parkes?' Percy pounced on the little fellow. 'GB? Would you both like to write a paragraph or two on the walls of Carthage? Right, let me have it by tomorrow morning.' The rest of the juniors scattered. 'Sparrow? Arthur? Charlie?' he gestured with his head. As he walked away with them towards his own room he heard the key turn in Vincent MacCallum's lock. Oh, Mac, so many demons! 'Lemon syrup or ginger beer?' he said – the general panacea – and Sparrow sat on the sill, regarding him expectantly. Arthur draped himself over the corner of the desk; Charlie leaned against the bookcase, hands in his pockets.

'What's upset Mac, Daisy?' Sparrow said.

Percy measured the lemon syrup with care, diluting it with water from his jug. 'He'll get over it,' he said.

Percy knew why he'd done it. It was very clear. He had done it for Mac. The rest did not matter: self-examination was indulgent.

Besides, it was Unwin's fault.

No. To be fair, that wasn't true. He was to blame as well. He could have put the picture back in Mac's room.

If Mac ever knew. If he ever, ever knew . . .

But no one knew, not even Unwin, so it was over. The bin was gone. The housemaid had taken it. QED.

He might have returned it. But then he'd looked at it, a long dispassionate appraisal, and he'd walked to the bin and he had let Mac's darling float down from his fingers, absolving himself. She had lain bent up against the sides of the bin, only an eye confronting him from the angle at which he stood.

He had walked away and gone to class.

It was unforgivable. He knew it. But, for Mac's sake, necessary.

He had done it – or Unwin had – and he would think no more about it.

Until he had seen MacCallum's anguish. Then he'd felt remorse. 'It's only a picture, Mac.'

But he knew that she was invested with more. And not just for Mac, for both of them. It was not just an image on a card, hand-tinted pink where it mattered: mouth, skin, brows touched up with a brush. She was Mac's, and by her presence she set him apart somehow, detached from foolish boys hanging out of windows to see the croc pass by. It seemed, in Mac's room only, because of him, she was not absurd.

But in herself, she was. Oh, yes.

Percy lay with his pyjamas buttoned to his throat, his hair neatly brushed, his ankles crossed, his arms folded on his chest and observed the ceiling, conjuring her up. She was – he'd say it – in rather bad taste. That nose. It was without refinement. That lip. It was the sort that would quiver if she were crossed. There was no mystery in it, no humour and certainly no intelligence. It was unworthy of Mac to care about her. But you couldn't tell Mac that – he'd have to come to it himself. And it would be too late. For, if he married someone like this nurse, despite her chaste, starched veil, she would suck him up slowly into her domain. She would be the sort that smelled of too much talcum, the sort whose face powder drifted in little fleshy eddies among the hairpins in her dressing case, whose table was crammed with small mementoes, whose slippers were decorated with feathers that moulted gently wherever she led him. Among this strange detritus, Mac would lose the firmness to his jaw, be jowly and dark. Those shoulders would grow pale and slack. That neck. He'd wear his collars high and stiff and never pull his shirt off to glory in the sun as he did so often now. He'd have to give up his pipe. He'd join the Temperance Society at her insistence: all that bloom belied a bigot's eye. He could see it there, despite the soft blonde hair and the little tilt of her nostril and the sideways glance. Mac, under the onslaught, would go bald, have dandruff and wear a rather shabby bow-tie and patches on the elbows of his tweeds, not the sort that should be there, but the sort that were put there by a thrifty wife: Mac

138

called 'dear', Mac putting the dog out at night and making sure it did its business, Mac kept waiting – just too long – outside the primly closed door while she prepared for bed. All that, just so he could know, at last, what it was all about. To squander it – for *that*. To lose – for *that* – his swift, unblemished valour.

Percy liked that. He lay very straight, uncrossed his ankles. Unblemished Valour. It was very easily destroyed, lost its keen desire. And its passion. And *this* true-tempered passion, this Unblemished Valour, this gallant quest, all this meaning – and *that*, so much regrettable baseness in the name of love: they were two quite different things. Quite different. But Mac would never see that. There was no way of explaining to Mac the delicate difference between them because she'd muddled him. The Great Devotion, the *esprit de corps*, Belonging, Manhood at its best, uncompromised by sentiment – these were things she simply wouldn't comprehend. No woman could.

It was a tragedy.

Percy snorted. It was a small, unhappy sound.

EIGHT

The ways to gain regard are strange. Herbert had considered them. Sometimes they were futile. Sometimes self-destructive. Often cruel. So many forays to earn the notice of one's friends. It led to skirmishes for power, small betrayals. Greater ones.

If Unwin hadn't needled Archer?

If Charlie hadn't intervened?

If teams had just been chosen on another day?

If Davey hadn't gone to town?

If he, himself, hadn't asked for bull's-eyes?

Unwin, Archer. Charlie.

Davey Bennett.

There was no picture of that day. It should have been recorded. Davey, in his basher, heading off for town, his buttons done, the regulation three. Who wants bull's-eyes? Who wants pies? Who'll come with me – just today?

It wasn't recorded. And no one went with him.

'Will you fetch the photographs, please, Jones? The ones for the club and mine as well?' Charlie Fraser found him between classes and searched his pockets for the photographer's note. 'I'll see you after prep.'

'Are you going to town, Jones?' Herbert rushing into his practice gear, scattering his papers in his hurry. Blast. 'Can you get bull's-eyes, Jones?' Off without a quick goodbye.

Do this, Jones. Do that, Jones. Jones is such a very good fellow.

He never minds.

Perhaps he did and never said.

It was not recorded.

Nor was Unwin scrounging in his locker for his hidden pocket-money, the extra which he hadn't handed in for distribution on a Friday. Archer's fag money was hidden in a sock. Unwin peeped at MacCallum's nurse, as he did every time he opened his locker.

If Unwin moved his shirts, just a fraction, there was the corner of her mouth. If he moved them back it was obscured and there was only the round bland cheek without definition. If he moved his underpants, there was the edge of her eyebrow. He could make it so he saw her eyes. Or so he could see her mouth. All or some. It was good to keep her captive there under his things, suffocated. Only he and Percy Gilbert knew what the great crash had been about. And Unwin had watched MacCallum at supper, sitting at the top table in his blazer: rugby, cricket, athletics, he seemed weighed down with all that glory. His sallow face, that never had a spot or blemish – always imperturbable – looked as though he'd scraped a layer off by rubbing with a towel. Unwin observed that he did not speak to anyone. And when he rose at last to say the grace he pushed in his chair with such force that the glasses on the table danced. When Unwin went to the bogs that night, he looked up at the windows of the seniors' studies. Gilbert's, Bell's, Grant's, Graham's, Fraser's, Barham's. In the middle of them, second after Gilbert's, Vincent MacCallum's window was dark. Unwin walked half in fear, half in hot elation. He wished he'd made the great god cry.

It was he, Unwin, who'd exposed him. It was a sweet revenge. Archer had been right. And even more – even more – he'd found Percy Gilbert out as well. There was power in that. So when Archer yelled, 'Unwin!' – and quite imperious – anticipating Unwin cringing away at the thought of being sent on another mission down the tangy to buy his cigarettes, Unwin took the coins, flipped one over with his thumb and looked Archer in the eye, saying, 'Back in a jiffy, Archer,' adding, 'I did it.'

Archer did not react as he might have wished.

'Archer, I did it.' He persisted.

Dismissed already from his mind, Archer glanced at him irritably. 'Did what?'

Unwin said triumphantly, 'I took MacCallum's nurse.'

'What's MacCallum's nurse?'

'You said I should do it.'

'Listen, are you going to town or not?'

'Yes . . .'

'Well, bugger off then.'

Unwin departed hastily. He might as well have taken her and crumpled her up and thrown her back in the bin. He went off down the street, hot still in the ears. Damn Archer. Damn him. He whimpered, despite himself, when a dog rushed at the fence as he passed.

–Do it. That's what Archer had said. –Show him!

He went on, trying to march defiantly but hearing the odd sound of his shoes, like Wellington boots that are too big: all that damp and heat! He kicked at the kerb. Archer didn't know who MacCallum's nurse was. Too bad for him.

He was not the only one who went to town that day on errands for another. Ten minutes behind Unwin, Davey Bennett set out with Charlie Fraser's slip and Herbert's tickey for the bull's-eyes. He did not see Unwin glance about and disappear down the tangy. He knew nothing of Unwin's highway. He crossed it, whistling to himself, walking in the wind, doffing his hat, 'Afternoon, ma'am', to Mrs Randell, standing at her gate.

Davey collected the photographs. He went to Dicks'. He bought the bull's-eyes and a bun for himself and started back along High Street. He glanced up at the cathedral clock. It was late. On an impulse he cut down Cuyler Street and across New Street, hurrying then, knowing it was out of bounds but the envelope he carried was bulky with pictures he was longing to see. Off New Street an alley between tall houses led down to the *sloot* and African Street. Passing a yard, a small enclave where a heap of rubbish was piled by sweepers for burning, he saw Unwin. He was standing against the wall smoking a cigarette. He was puffing fast, shielding it with his other hand. Davey Bennett stopped, more in surprise than anything. He was so astonished,

142

he began to laugh. 'Un – win!' he said with exaggerated shock.

'S'pose you're going to tell.'

'Who'd I tell?'

'Don'no,' said Unwin sullenly.

'It's not very bright to smoke out in the open . . .'

'So?' Unwin's voice was high. 'New Street's out of bounds. Whatcher doin' here yourself?'

'I took a short cut.'

'If you tell on me, I'll tell on you for being out of bounds.'

'For goodness sake!' Davey Bennett said irritably. 'Put that damned fag out and come back to school.' He looked Unwin over. 'And take the packet out of your pocket. You can see exactly what it is a mile off.'

'It's not mine anyway.'

'Whose is it?'

'None of your business.'

'Come on, Unwin,' said Davey Bennett, glancing back down the alley. 'Let's get moving.'

Bennett started off, leaving him, but he heard Unwin behind him. Unwin tugged at his sleeve. 'Are you going to tell?'

'What for?'

''Cos of hating me.'

Bennett shook himself loose. 'Don't be an idiot.'

'You do. You and Cummings. You both do.'

'Rot.'

'Ever since you heard me. That time in chapel.'

'Rot.'

'You told Cummings.'

'What if I did?'

'You told him.' Accusingly.

Davey Bennett stopped and turned to him. 'What I told Cummings was that I thought you were having a hard time of it about your papers and things. Maybe worse than most. That's all.'

Unwin lumbered along beside him, saying nothing.

'Why are you buying cigarettes anyway?' said Davey Bennett more evenly. 'You'd be expelled if you were caught.'

Unwin kicked at a stone. 'I won't be caught.'

'I could have been a Bobby.'

'Well, you're not. And anyway, you're out of bounds yourself.'

'Still.'

'I promised.'

'Why?'

Unwin shook his head. 'I just promised.'

'Well, whoever you promised is a damned cad for making you do his dirty work.'

'Why?'

'He wouldn't ask you if he didn't know for sure that you were scared of him.'

'I'm not scared of him!' Unwin was indignant.

The shower. The scrutiny. –Fellows, come and look at this.

'Does he ever get his cigarettes himself?'

'No.'

'Well then, tell him to.'

'I can't.'

'Why not?'

'Because . . .' Unwin cast about. He wiped his sleeve across his nose.

'You're scared of him!'

'He's not allowed.'

'Archer.'

Unwin looked alarmed. 'I didn't say that.'

'You don't have to. We all know he's gated and no one else is *that* much of a buck to make someone else run around for him . . .' and he recalled fleetingly the bull's-eyes in his pocket for Herbert and felt ashamed of what he'd said.

Unwin wiped his lip with his index finger and rubbed it on his trousers. 'He always gives me a smoke. He lets me hang about with him then.'

'Only when you bring the fags?'

Unwin did not reply.

'He's using you.'

Still Unwin did not reply.

144

'If you buy cigarettes for him and get caught, you can hardly put the blame on him if you smoke as well. So you're a safe errand boy, aren't you? And, what's more, I'll bet he knows you wouldn't tell because you're scared of him.'

'I'm not.'

The showers. Being stripped.

Unwin wiped his arm across his forehead. 'He's nice to me, Bennett.' He had begun to whine. 'He lets me sit with him sometimes and have a puff. He's actually a decent chap.'

'Archer is not a decent chap.'

Unwin was having difficulty keeping up. 'How do you know – he wouldn't talk to you.'

'Good.'

Unwin mustered derision. 'You're too wet.'

'Fine.' Davey put Charlie Fraser's photos under his arm, feeling them consciously, and marched on, outstripping him. He wished he hadn't met him. Unwin was so wretched to be with and so disconcerting in the things he said.

Unwin hurried after him. What if Bennett told? He caught up. 'You're going to tell! You will! You'll tell Cummings and he'll tell MacCallum!' He clutched at Bennett's sleeve. 'You mustn't tell!' Davey Bennett shook him off. 'I'll kill you, Bennett, I'll kill you, if you do.' Unwin's nose had begun to run again, all his bravado gone. He dashed his wrist across it and left a mark on his coat, as if a snail had trailed across his sleeve.

'Shut up now and leave it,' said Davey Bennett. 'I wouldn't be so stupid as to say anything.'

Nor did he. But Unwin's fear of discovery outweighed his prudence. He followed a pace or two behind Davey Bennett most of the afternoon. He stood in a recess beside a cupboard when Bennett took the photographs he had collected to Charlie Fraser's study. Bennett closed the door and he couldn't hear what was said. But he stayed there anyway.

'How do they look to you?' Charlie Fraser flipped through the prints.

'Excellent, Fraser.' Davey never knew what else to say.

'This is hopeless,' Charlie flicked a finger at a picture of the croc, indistinct against the gloomy hedge on the opposite side of the street. 'Can't see what the devil it is.'

'The fellows won't mind if you explain to them. They'll still want it.'

Arthur came in and Charlie laughed, glancing up at him, 'Especially Arthur.'

'Especially Arthur what?' said Arthur and he scooped up the pictures. He picked one out and held it up. 'What the hell is this?'

'Sunset.'

Arthur turned the snap round and round. 'Could have fooled me! It's time you stopped taking romantic scenes and did something practical like asking the girls if you could go over and take some team pictures. Perhaps the cricket team or the choir or the tennis pairs. Apie would pay a fortune for a portrait of the cricket captain, what's her name, old Zeedy's daughter?' He turned to Davey. 'What's her name, Jones?'

'Josie Zeederberg,' said Davey, trying to keep a straight face: Herbert would kill him.

'Josie Zeederberg – that's the one.' He turned back to Charlie. 'I'm sure if anyone could inveigle Miss Fowler into agreeing, you could. Just gaze at her, Charlie. One look and you'll have her swooning. Anyway, I have a long list of the subjects required – at a fee – by certain other fellows,' and he cast a glance at Davey and grinned. Davey Bennett took Arthur's cue to depart.

'Thanks, Jones,' said Charlie Fraser. He put the photos in a drawer and said, 'Arthur, get your boots. Let's do gaining grounds.'

Davey Bennett came out into the passage. Unwin shrank back. Charlie Fraser put his head round his door and shouted, 'GB!' His voice echoed down the walls. 'Have you got my footer boots?'

The scamperer appeared as if conjured up, trotting from his dormitory with the pair of boots. They gleamed, rotating on their laces. 'Good fellow,' said Charlie Fraser, inspecting them. GB beamed. He would have polished the boots every hour of the day for a hundredth of the praise.

Unwin went away when the passage was empty and GB had disappeared. What had David Bennett said to Fraser? Had he told about the cigarettes? Had he told about Archer? He went back to his dormitory and sat on his bed. Bennett was with Cummings, flopped together, poring over a picture. Neither looked in his direction. He craned to see. They had a photo of cadets. They were staring at it, heads together, shoulders turned against him.

Edwards did not even cast his usual glance at him, looking for something to pick on, to put a foot out and trip him or flick a snot-ball at his head. He was reading Unwin's *Boys' Own Paper*, three issues back. He didn't even bother to ask any more. Unwin's mother's note, always tucked inside each new edition, was lying discarded where it had slipped to the floor:

'My dear son,
I hope you are well. I am glad you have settled so nicely this term. It is always a great comfort to me to know you are in congenial surroundings . . .' etc, etc, etc.

Unwin picked it up and tore it deliberately. Edwards gave a little twitch as though a fly had settled to annoy him. Unwin tore the note more slowly. Edwards glanced directly at him. Unwin turned his back. If he disappeared one day, vanished, would anybody know?
–Where's Unwin?
–Has anyone seen Unwin?
He sat, with his hands slack in his lap.
No one would notice. Not even Miss Maltby.
He got up and went in search of Archer.
Archer took the cigarettes without comment.
'I have a pack of my own,' said Unwin. 'Would you like a smoke?'
Archer, vexed. 'What?'
'I have an open pack.'
'I could get you expelled for that.'
Unwin stood. Again the bewilderment. Archer was so unpredict-able.
Archer glanced through the window. It had started to rain.

'Boxroom after prep,' he said. 'If you've got your own, you don't need mine. But someone must keep cavey, so it's you.'

'Fellows come past all the time.'

'So?'

He went back to the dorm. Again, no one looked up. He was unnoticed. But if he hung about the boxroom door, they'd notice then. Oh, yes. They'd start up a row and ask him what he was doing. That's how it was for him: intense scrutiny, then nothing. Like the waiters in the dining-hall. No one saw them 'til one dropped a plate or spilled an enamel ewer and sent it clattering against the boards. The invective then – a boil pricked and oozing – some mortal feud waiting to erupt: it was only a plate, only a jug. To be, so suddenly, the brunt of so much unexpected rage.

If he stood cavey for Archer, he'd have to hide. Get behind the door of the little toolshed and watch the boxroom through the crack. They'd find him there. They'd smell him out.

–Unwin, why are you loitering here?

Prefects – it was written in the College rules – were there 'to punish loiterers'. If hanging about outside the boxroom or lurking in the toolshed wasn't loitering, what was? MacCallum would come. Or Gilbert with his endless satirical chat. What if MacCallum marched him up to his locker and found his cigarettes? What if he found them pushed down behind his books?

What if he saw *her*, under his socks, face up, simpering at him?

–Unwin, what's this in your locker?

–Hah!

–Westminsters!

–Women!

Filthy boy!

Unwin peered across at Bennett sitting on Cummings' bed. He looked away, looked again. Bennett and Cummings were laughing at something. They glanced back at him. That sudden attention. Had Bennett told?

–I caught Unwin smoking in New Street.

–Send him up.

–He'd be expelled.

–So what?

His ploy to show his mettle with Archer had failed in every way. He had bought his own fags foolishly, to offer them, begging inclusion against Archer's rebuff. The flourish of independence, the push for notice, had gone awry.

And Bennett knew.

Bennett got up. Unwin watched him making for the door. He'd gone to tell Fraser. And Fraser, MacCallum.

It was a self-fulfilling prophecy.

'Where are you going?' said Arthur to Charlie.

'Bogs.' Charlie stretched.

'It's raining.'

'Do you want me to piss on Robbie's head?' Charlie's window was directly above Robbie's front door.

'He wouldn't notice with this rain.' Arthur was reading in a chair, ostensibly Dutch sentences, but *The Texas Ranger* was concealed inside the cover of his grammar in case Robbie made an unexpected call.

Charlie opened the door.

'I'll come too,' said Arthur, getting up.

'I believe I can manage on my own.' Charlie raised an eyebrow at him.

'You might get scared without me.' Arthur slipped his book under the chair and shoved Charlie out ahead of him, nudging at his back. 'D'you think Daisy's making tea?'

They went along to Percy's study. The Headboy, Jamie Seymour, was with Mac. John Barham sat on Percy's desk.

'A visit from The Boss,' said Arthur in surprise, hooking his arm round Seymour's neck. 'Has your house locked you out? Has Oost deposed you?'

'I'm looking for Archer.'

'Lucky Archer,' said Percy drily. 'Shall we ask him up for tea and cake?'

'Shut up, Daisy.' Seymour pulled himself up onto the desk beside John Barham. 'He's getting beyond himself at Seconds footer practice.

He's been picking on the fellows from my house and they're getting annoyed. It's bad for *esprit*. He seems to forget he's not at a house match and that they're playing in the same team. There's going to be a punch-up if someone doesn't see him right.'

'So you've come to see him right,' said Mac.

'With you,' said Jamie, deferential to another's place. 'And I've come for tea,' he grinned. 'Daisy's brand's a damn sight better than Oost's. Any excuse.'

'Such compliments!' said Percy, unfolding himself from his chair and inspecting his cups.

'Charlie?' Mac turned to Charlie standing in the doorway. 'Find Archer, will you? And tell him to look sharp. I want my tea in peace.'

'Rough him up, if you have to,' said John Barham, who took much of the brunt of Archer's spleen in the Seconds' backline.

'Oh for the muscle power,' said Percy, making an elegant fist.

'What a bicep!' said Jamie Seymour. 'Really, Daisy, you shouldn't expose yourself like that.'

'Do I excite you?' He too had a sardonic eyebrow. 'Ah well, my mother, at least, thinks I'm handsome and strong.'

Seymour laughed. 'Get on with you.' He turned to Arthur. 'Are you going too?'

'I was actually on my way to the bogs,' said Arthur. 'But I'll carry the corpse up if Charlie gets killed.'

'Right,' MacCallum said. 'Daisy, where's the tea?'

'We'll be back before it boils,' said Arthur.

Archer was nowhere to be found. Charlie and Arthur inspected the dormitory. No one knew where he was. A few of the bucks looked alarmed. 'I think Mr Robinson just sent him five minutes ago on an errand to one of the other houses,' said one. 'Shall I tell him to come up to you when he gets back?'

Charlie paid no attention to this information: Robbie was at a lecture being given by a big game hunter from East Africa. He'd been gone since before supper. If the House had burned down that night, it would have been the one occasion on which Robbie would have been quite unconcerned.

'Bunked?' murmured Arthur as they headed down the stairs.

'Could be,' said Charlie. It was raining hard. The water fell over blocked gutters, splattered up from paving into the doorway, making puddles on the floor. 'Damn Archer,' said Charlie, putting his head out and peering towards the lavatories.

'He won't be behind the bogs in this,' said Arthur.

'Maybe the boxroom then.'

'I wouldn't go into the boxroom at night.'

'You're not a desperate smoker,' said Charlie.

'Is Archer?'

'Wouldn't be surprised.'

They ducked down the path to the lavatories. They were unoccupied. Water leaked through the corrugated roof.

'God, they stink!' said Arthur.

Charlie got on with it, without comment. 'Move,' he said, starting back.

'Let a man have a piss in peace, will you?'

Charlie sheltered under the eaves of the toolshed. He was always waiting for Arthur. He seemed to have a need to mark, at length, his territory right around the school. There was a particularly luxuriant patch of nasturtiums on the bank at the south end of the rugby field which was his private preserve. Nubs used to collect the leaves along with bunches of oxalis to eat. When someone told them Graham relieved himself on them at every rugby practice, it did not seem to detract from their appeal. Charlie hunched his shoulders and thrust his hands in his pockets, half closing his eyes against the rain.

He leaned against the toolshed wall. It was damp through his jacket. He surveyed the boxroom. The door was closed but the outside bolt was drawn. He was about to move towards it when he heard the faintest sound from the toolshed at his back. He stood alert. It was less than a sound. It was as if he could hear someone breathing close at hand, as though his listening was listened to in turn.

The toolshed was also used for storage – broken chairs and desks, boys' boxes needing repair to locks and hinges. It was filled with unused sports equipment and the detritus left by boys long gone from school that was moved from place to place – too good to discard, too bothersome to allot to other owners. It was full of rats. Charlie raised a hand to silence Arthur as he came up and said in a clear, conversational voice, jerking his thumb towards the door and shaking his head slightly. 'Right, let's go up. I'm wet as hell.' He stepped over to the shelter of the House wall five yards off and stood, observing the toolshed.

He indicated that Arthur should walk away. Arthur went, clattering along the paving and round the corner of the House. Charlie knew he would move back silently.

There it was – that small furtive shifting, like a mouse, suddenly disturbed in the skirting. He heard the faint easing of hinges, saw the shadow of a toolshed door quiver. He folded his arms. Arthur breathed, 'It's the bloody ghost.'

The door gave a little squeal of protest. A small thump. Unwin came out and started towards the boxroom. Then he saw Charlie Fraser and Arthur Graham standing, dark-shaped, in the rain and he let out a shriek. The moment of reckoning had come. The two giants were bearing down on him.

They took him into the toolshed, out of the rain. Charlie Fraser said, 'Unwin, what the devil are you doing here?'

'I don't know,' said Unwin, at his wits' end.

'You don't know?' said Arthur with mock surprise. 'My dear fellow, you had better find out fast.'

Unwin's heart leapt in his throat like a demented frog. Bennett must have told. Why else would they be snooping around, looking for him?

'Well?' Charlie folded his arms.

Unwin swallowed, glanced sideways out of the door towards the boxroom, stared at his feet. 'Sorry, Fraser,' he mumbled. Charlie followed his eyes, looked quietly away.

'Were you waiting for someone?'

Unwin gave a start. 'No, Fraser.'

'Why are you here then?'

'I . . .'

'He's just relaxing,' said Arthur conversationally. 'Relaxing in the toolshed after prep. Like anyone else.'

'Yes, Graham.'

Arthur tried not to catch Charlie's eye but it was too much for him. To hide his laugh he said, 'What do you do for relaxation in the toolshed, Unwin? I can't wait to hear! Mr Robinson will be fascinated.'

'Take him to my study,' said Charlie before Unwin disintegrated and blubbed on them. He gestured with his head that Arthur should go with Unwin. 'I'll wait,' in a low voice.

Unwin glanced up at him in panic, stared again at his feet, seemed rooted. Arthur prodded him with his knee, 'Come on.'

Unwin went before, Arthur following. Charlie approached the boxroom door then, stood to the side of it, even though the rain coursed down. Arthur made enough noise going up the stairs to fool any listener into believing the entire Fifteen was ascending in their boots. Far off, Charlie heard the door of his study bang.

It was cold. Rain caught his neck, trailed down his back inside his shirt. Bloody Archer. High above, in the junior dorm, he heard John Barham call, 'Lights.' A group came down, stood a moment at the door of the House and then pelted out into the rain to the bogs, laughing and shouting, dodging puddles.

Hurry up.

Two minutes. Five.

The boxroom door opened. Charlie stood back against the wall. Sam Stafford ducked out. Archer followed. Charlie could smell the stink of Flags on their damp coats. The light from the lower windows of the House made a deep diagonal stripe across them both. They stood and listened, a yard in front of him.

'Stafford. Archer.' Charlie said, so close behind them they jumped. Archer's fists were up before he'd seen his adversary.

Charlie side-stepped the punch, put out his foot, Archer stumbled, hit his head against the wall and roared. Stafford simply stood.

Charlie leaned down and picked Archer up by the belt of his pants, turned him against the door-frame. Archer struggled to stand upright. He could outdo the height and weight but he could not equal the authority: 'Would you like to try all that again?' said Charlie in a normal voice, as if he were giving a direction: go to prep, fetch the ball, pass the salt.

'I won't be pushed around, Fraser,' Archer twisted himself up against Charlie. But Charlie Fraser raised a finger quietly and pressed it into him just above the sternum. The small power in that finger, the hand, the wrist, just restrained. Archer knew. He felt the intent behind it and forgot to breathe. 'No one will be pushing anyone around,' said Charlie, 'especially not if we intend staying in the team.'

And Charlie stood and Archer stood. The smell of cigarettes was strong. 'I'll have those fags, please,' said Charlie Fraser standing back suddenly and moving his head as if to unknot his neck. Archer reached into his pocket for the box. Sullenly, he put them in Charlie's hand. Charlie did not react. He slipped them into his shirt. 'Seymour wants to see you in MacCallum's study.' He gestured with his head that they should go.

To be dismissed like a felon with hardly a word: not derided by Percy Gilbert, nor punched by Morgan, not sent up to Robbie by MacCallum for a beating – but somehow, by the slight tilt of an eyebrow and the force of a finger, to be so shamed.

Archer went, Stafford shambled after him.

Charlie Fraser walked up the stairs behind them.

They climbed to MacCallum's study. Charlie opened the door for Archer and Stafford.

'Your tea's here, Charlie,' said Mac. 'Arthur's got The Maggot in your room, for some reason.'

Charlie took two cups from John Barham, spooned sugar liberally, nodded and went away. He left Archer to Seymour and MacCallum.

Only Arthur was in his study, engrossed in *The Texas Ranger* again.

'Where's Unwin?' Charlie said.

'Blubbing in his bed, I expect,' replied Arthur, taking a cup.

'Why didn't you make him wait?'

'To save us from being sorry for him.' He said it flippantly – but Charlie knew. Arthur couldn't bring himself to goad Unwin either.

'What'd he say?'

'Nothing,' said Arthur. 'He never has an explanation. Mac says he's always jawing him out for lurking around in the lavatories or whatever. If Dowsley or Zeedy hear we'll have another long session about how the devil carries off little boys who spend time in "self-contemplation".'

'If you tell Unwin he'll be carried off, he'll believe you,' said Charlie.

'True. I don't know what he thinks he's up to.'

'It's more what Archer's up to.'

'I hope you gave him a good *klap*!' Arthur looked up at him.

'No.'

'Why not?'

'Didn't have to.'

'I'd have done it anyway.'

'No, you wouldn't,' said Charlie.

'He's such a lout.'

'It's just that he gets it wrong.'

'I wouldn't start feeling sorry for Archer too.'

There was a knock at the door. David Bennett was standing there in his pyjamas and dressing gown.

'What's up, Jones?' said Charlie Fraser.

'Forgot to give you this,' said Bennett. He took a box of film from his pocket. 'Compliments of Mr Hepburn in the shop. He said he'd chosen one of your pictures for the window next week.'

'Which one?'

'He didn't say.'

Charlie took the film. Davey could see that he was pleased.

'It's the one of the croc, I bet!' said Arthur. 'All that breathless detail! Or the glorious sunset!'

'Watch it!'

Archer and Stafford passed on the way back from MacCallum's study. Charlie did not glance in their direction. They went on down the stairs. They sidled into Unwin's dormitory, unseen. A minute later Charlie Fraser closed his study door and Davey Bennett walked away.

'Unwin! You drivelling snot-nosed sod!' The blankets were ripped off Unwin. He snorted in surprise. A silvery bubble quivered at his nostril. He began to cry out but a pillow was pushed in his face.

Stafford kept the pillow where it was. Archer bent down. He said softly, 'You told Fraser where we were.'

Unwin shook his head. He was gasping into the pillow. Stafford lifted it. He was gagging on his own spit. 'I didn't tell.'

'You told.' Down the pillow went. 'D'you think we didn't hear you? D'you think we weren't listening?'

Unwin shook his head.

'You told!'

'No!'

Down the pillow went again. 'I didn't tell about you to Fraser or to Graham. I didn't tell about the cigarettes. I didn't tell. It was someone else. I never said anything.'

The dormitory was awake. No one moved.

'I never . . . I never.'

'Who else knew?'

Unwin screwed his eyes up. He was going to vomit. Archer put his finger under Unwin's nose, not touching him, just there. 'Who?'

Unwin could not breathe.

'Who?' very softly.

Archer slid his hand to Unwin's pyjama trousers then and swiftly pulled them down. Another tug and he had them round his ankles. He pulled them free.

'Give me my pants,' Unwin sobbed, exposed to Archer and Stafford's fascinated stare.

'Hey, fellows, come and have a look.'

'Give me . . .' the sobs were near hysteria.

'Who?'

Unwin tried to pull the blankets up around him.

'Who told?'

'I don't know.'

'Who?'

'Give me my pants.'

'Who?'

Unwin was almost choking.

'Who?'

'Bennett.'

156

'Where's Bennett?'

'I don't know.'

Archer slung Unwin's pyjama pants over his shoulder and walked away. He dropped them in the doorway. Unwin would have to cross the dormitory to fetch them.

Unwin pulled the blankets up, dragging them over his head. His bed shook unabated with the anguish. No one came to his aid.

David Bennett was sitting on Herbert's desk in the prep room in his pyjamas, trying to disengage the bull's-eyes from the sticky lump they'd formed in his blazer pocket. Davey stretched over for his pencil box which was lying on the chair. He fished out a compass. Herbert held down the ball of sweets and Davey pried them apart with the needle.

Archer and Stafford walked in. Archer came straight up to them and he said, 'You told Fraser.'

Bennett's hand was poised with the compass, his cheek bulged, a bull's-eye gently dissolving. 'Sorry?'

'Don't pretend, Bennett.'

'What are you talking about?'

'Leave him alone,' said Herbert briskly.

'Just keep out, Cummings,' said Archer, without looking at him.

'Told Fraser what?' said Bennett calmly. He transferred the bull's-eye from one cheek to the other. He put the compass down on the chair and wiped his sticky fingers on his pyjama jacket.

'You know quite well.' Archer stood above him.

'About what?' Davey said, less confidently.

'Unwin said.'

'What did Unwin say?'

'How the hell did Fraser know if someone hadn't told?'

'Told what?'

'Unwin said he told you. You're the only one he told.'

'So?' Davey Bennett coloured up, suddenly understanding. 'Why would I blab on him?'

'We saw you with Fraser and Graham, so don't lie.'

Herbert stood up and said, 'Get lost, Archer.'

Archer rounded on him.

'Stop, Goen,' Stafford dragged him away. 'You know what Seymour said.'

Archer wrenched himself free. 'Cummings is not a bloody senior.'

'Stop, Goen. Goen, stop.' Stafford interposed himself. 'Seymour will have you kicked out of the team.'

'I haven't touched him,' said Archer, putting up his hands. 'But I'm warning him. So he'd better look out because I will, some time, I promise, and bugger Seymour.' He turned away. Davey was standing bewildered in his path. Archer shouldered him roughly. Davey stumbled against the chair and fell with it to the floor. His knee caught the compass lying on the seat. The needle flipped over and went diagonally into his knee. Wordlessly, Davey rolled over, clutching it. Archer and Stafford walked out.

Davey doubled up, eyes wide. Herbert pulled the compass out. The blood ran down Davey's calf.

'I'll get him in the Drill Hall. I'll kill him,' said Herbert.

'It's all right, Apie,' said Davey, holding onto his leg. 'It's nothing.'

'What were you supposed to have told Fraser?'

'Nothing, Apie. It's not even important. And anyway, I never spoke to Fraser except about his pictures.' He squeezed his eyes closed. 'Damn,' he said. 'Damn, damn, damn.'

Much later, Vincent MacCallum walked past the dorm door, going on a final round. He stopped. Every eye of every silent boy was on him standing in the lighted passage outside the room. Only Unwin, oblivious, wept on. MacCallum bent and picked the pyjama trousers up. 'Whose are these?' he said.

No one replied. MacCallum stood, listening. 'Whose are these?' he repeated.

'Unwin's, MacCallum,' said Mostert, the boy nearest to the door, in a half whisper.

MacCallum walked down the dormitory. Unwin did not hear him. MacCallum stood at his bed a moment. Under the blankets, Unwin sobbed sporadically. Then, without speaking, MacCallum left the pants draped over the foot-rail and retreated. No one moved.

MacCallum said to Percy later, 'Unwin's got a problem.'

'What problem?'

'Why would he leave his pants lying in the dorm doorway?'

Percy laughed.

'It's a problem,' said MacCallum irritably.

'A problem?' Percy was being obtuse. He looked at MacCallum and said, 'Frankly, I don't think it's Unwin who's preoccupied.'

'You completely misinterpret me on purpose,' said Mac crossly. 'You manage to make the most disgusting things sound sane.'

Percy stretched and said. 'Oh, come on, Mac, everyone's the same.'

'And you're a bishop's son.'

'Special dispensation.'

'What should I do?'

'Nothing.'

'It sets a bad example.'

'There's that story about the beam in the eye . . .'

'Bugger off, Daisy.'

Unwin's terror of Archer, at that moment, was known, even apprehended. The fourth form dormitory was awake in silence. Even Edwards left Unwin in peace to cry himself to sleep. He had nothing to say.

But the next day – Unwin's face still mottled, lids glassy and turgid – Archer was supplanted. MacCallum took his place. The moment of Unwin's execution had arrived.

Miss Maltby found her.

Miss Maltby discovered MacCallum's nurse hidden under Unwin's clothes.

Springing locker inspection on them late that afternoon, searching for missing laundry, berating the boys for unmarked articles, she went down the row in the fourth form dormitory, opening the little cupboards. Flip, flip, flip, her hands ran along the shirts, counting.

'The next disgraceful locker will be shown to Mr Robinson.'

Flip, flip, flip, flip, pat down, open the next and start again. The boys hung about unconcerned. She was all bluster. Mostert, Pringle, White, Edwards, Bennett, Ross.

Unwin.

'What is this, young man?'

Out came MacCallum's nurse, more dog-eared than before.

Miss Maltby turned and looked at Unwin: a drubbing from Archer in a shower, full exposure to the whole school, pinned like a specimen unprotected from the light, could not have been more piercing. Every eye was on him.

'A picture, ma'am,' said Unwin.

'A picture, is it?' marvelled Miss Maltby, open mouthed. 'I never would have said so!'

'A nurse,' he mumbled.

'Indeed?'

Somewhere, someone sniggered.

'And what are you doing with this picture?' Miss Maltby was enjoying her own small moment of attention.

'Looking at it.'

'Looking at it?' said Miss Maltby as though it was a wonder. 'Looking at it?'

It was Edwards who was laughing. Unwin could feel him shaking behind him.

'Master Tom Edwards!' Miss Maltby turned her attention to him. 'Is there something amusing you?'

'No, ma'am,' Tom said, but he could not stop.

'Well, my lad, you can have your little joke in MacCallum's study, if you please.'

'No, ma'am,' said Tom Edwards, trying to control himself, catching Pringle's eye and bursting out. 'Sorry, ma'am.' Wheedling, 'Please, Miss Maltby.'

But he could not charm her, not in front of the whole dormitory. 'Indeed, Tom Edwards,' she said. 'I believe MacCallum's fond of a laugh.'

Tom Edwards went. No one else laughed then.

Unwin trembled. MacCallum would come.

Flip, flip, flip, flip, each locker door snapped closed under the practised pressure of her hand. But Unwin was listening. He heard Edwards knock at MacCallum's door way down the passage. It opened. It closed. Silence.

Flip, flip, flip flip. 'Herbert Cummings, your locker is a disgrace. Would you like to show it to Mr Robinson?' A pause. 'You wouldn't?' Another pause. 'Well, my lad, then you had better tidy it in the next ten minutes or you will find yourself busy with a very brisk interview.'

Unwin stood, frozen. He knew the conversation. He could feel the blood now, surging in his ears.

–Why did Miss Maltby send you, Edwards?

–I was laughing, MacCallum.

–Why were you laughing?

–It won't sound funny to you, MacCallum.

–Try me.

–She was inspecting the lockers, MacCallum. Unwin had a picture . . .

–What kind of picture?

–Of a nurse.

Only Unwin heard the steps for Miss Maltby was amusing herself again, berating another slovenly fellow. He did not turn to look.

'Miss Maltby?' MacCallum's voice was even, if a little high.

'Yes, MacCallum.'

'Is there a problem, ma'am?'

'No, MacCallum, but some of the more well mannered, like Tom Edwards, like to laugh when I am speaking.'

'Why was Edwards laughing?'

'Hugh Unwin has a picture which, for some reason, Edwards finds amusing.'

'Unwin?' MacCallum walked towards him.

The executioner. It was almost a relief.

Unwin did not look up.

'Where is the picture?' said MacCallum.

'On top of my locker, MacCallum.'

MacCallum turned and ran his hand along the top of the lockers. He took the picture down and glanced at it. He said to Miss Maltby, 'May Unwin be excused a moment?'

161

'Yes,' said Miss Maltby, 'if he will tidy his locker when he comes back and does it before supper.'

MacCallum dismissed Edwards from his study. Unwin stood in the doorway. MacCallum went to his table and put the picture down. He picked up a Latin grammar and placed in on top, obscuring the face.

Unwin stood: a firing squad or the hangman's noose. He didn't care which, only make it fast.

But MacCallum sat in his chair and took up his ruler and measured it between his palms, examining it. He did not look at Unwin. At last he said, 'Is this picture yours?'

'No, MacCallum.'

'Whose is it?'

'Yours, MacCallum.'

'You were aware of that?'

'Yes, MacCallum.'

'Can I ask why you have it?'

Unwin said nothing.

'I'm waiting.'

He had no idea how to say it: so you would know what it's like, MacCallum, so you would really know. So you could feel, just once, how it is. So you can hear what you say to me. Are you a gecko, MacCallum? No. You are not a gecko. You will never be one, so you couldn't understand.

'I'm waiting.'

Still he said nothing. It felt as though he had gone far away and he could only hear the wind outside and the great tide of blood beating in his ears. MacCallum was receding.

'Where did you get it?'

'I took it.'

'You came in here and took it?'

'He took it from the bin.' Percy Gilbert was behind him, standing in the door. 'Where I put it.'

MacCallum looked up. No one moved.

There would be no redemption. How could there be? She had

162

destroyed them.

Vincent MacCallum stood. He took the picture and tore it up. He put the pieces in the wire bin. Scraps of her fell out on the floor. Her temple, the angle of her jaw below the ear. He said to Unwin, 'Get out and tidy your locker.'

Unwin backed from the room. He heard MacCallum say to Percy Gilbert, 'Go.'

Percy Gilbert said, 'Vincent, can I speak to you?'

'Go.' The word was barely audible.

NINE

•■•■■■•■•

Davey Bennett woke in the middle of the night. His knee throbbed. He touched it gingerly. He turned over, trying to find a comfortable position. He looked across at Herbert asleep in the bed next to his. Herbert's breath caught in his throat, rhythmically: a catch, a sigh, a catch. Davey had often heard it. It was reassuring in its familiarity. He slept. When he awoke next morning his knee was still painful but he paid it no attention, favouring it only when he walked between House and class, a step and a hop, a step and a hop, not to put his weight on it.

He played tennis that afternoon, hopelessly beaten because he had difficulty running. He simply laughed and went to shower after games. The place where the compass had entered was hard and red. He inspected it cursorily.

It was only when he lay in bed again that night that he could feel it, a small throb-throb like a little heartbeat, counter to his own. He slept but just before morning he awoke again and had difficulty moving his leg. He touched his knee. It was hot. He lay and looked at the windows. The night outside was milky. The wind came but nothing could rock the old walls. Then the rain. He lay and listened to it, sleeting in gusts. He loved the rain when it pounded on the roof at home, drumming on the corrugated iron. He could feel it, knowing the dongas and the dry empty veld among the sweet-thorns would be drinking it in. There would be water in the river and grey herons would come down to stand at its edges, quiet fishers in slower eddies.

Here he could only hear it on the windows, for the slates, so high, high up, took the sound away.

Last holidays he had made a little house up the mountain in a top camp. The grass was soft there among the old ironstone. There were grass birds. He knew their high mountain piping. There were *ouhout* trees, the soft green of them, furry leaves against the black gnarled bark of trunks. *Rhebok* and mountain reedbuck sheltered here. Grey wraiths, they would go, always up the slope when he approached, a small whistle to alert him. There were larks and pipits of the uplands and the white high skies. That sky was different from the valleys, that air was thin and fluted among the packstones of the little house he'd made. He had built it against a huge lichen-covered boulder. A *kannabos*, white-trunked, grew up in a cleft. He had rigged a tank in it made from a paraffin tin with a pipe to let the rainwater down. The roof was thatched. One of the stockmen had come up and helped him with it. They had cut grass, lashed it with baling twine and wire. A mule had been used to bring up a small stable door and window. He had made beds from sacks filled with *rooigras*. When he had cut it, it had been sweet and soft. It had turned mouldy in the term and he had had to cut more and sew it in with a big baling needle, sitting up there in the sun, alone. There was a fireplace and an old pair of bellows, a lantern and an enamel candlestick. He had brought tools from the shed way, way below and a tin with Queen Victoria's head embossed on it which had once held a ration of chocolate his father had had in the war. On the floor was a *grysbok* skin he had cured himself, grey fawn with white soft edges.

He could sit in his doorway and smoke a little pipe he had made, filled with leavings from his father's tobacco pouch. He was at the centre and all around was a great drop of earth. Up here it was wind and space and a roaring of air. Far from school. No one was here except the old stockman, coming sometimes to inspect the sheep and the fence and the traps set for *rooikat*. He tried to recall each small detail of the little house. The smell of it and the *rooigras* and the gun oil, the paraffin and the scent of the hide on the floor. And the smell of that wind. For it had its smell: *ouhout*, *rooigras*, space, the cool of the bush in krantzes, the lifting hills. One day he would bring someone, someone who would say nothing and see it all, as it was.

He would have to wait.

Lying in the dark, he could still feel the small throb-throb in his knee. He tried to send it away. He stared straight up at the ceiling thinking of the windmill and the water pipe leading into the old cement reservoir and the pulse of water coming sporadically from the pump splashing into the tank. That throbbed too, with the beat of the pump. He tried to think of it. But the small pulse in his knee went on, ticking quietly, despite his efforts. Davey Bennett feared it.

In the morning his groin was tender. A thin red line traced up from his knee. The puncture where the compass had pierced it had become a boil. He eased his trousers over his leg. He was cold. He clenched his teeth to stop them chattering. He knew fevers well enough.

Robbie saw him going down the stairs, half sliding on the banister, to keep from having to bend his knee.

'Walk properly, Bennett.'

'Yes, sir.'

He stood and negotiated the stairs.

'What's the matter with your leg, boy?'

'I think I have a boil on my knee.'

'How did you get it?'

'I don't know, sir. It came up in the night.'

'See Miss Maltby after lessons.'

'Yes, sir.'

He stood until Robbie had gone. His eyes were hot. It was painful to blink them. Hot in a way he remembered when he was small and his mother sat by him and wiped his face with a flannel, damp with lukewarm water.

'Jones, are you sick?' Herbert asked, walking past him on the way to English.

'No. I'm fine.'

'Well, get a move on.' Herbert waited for him, half impatiently. 'Jones, what the hell is wrong with your leg?'

166

'It's a bit stiff.'

'From what?'

'The compass.'

'Let's see.'

'It's nothing, man. Go on.'

He sat in English, his book open before him. He was colder than he could remember. He could not stop the shaking. Herbert put up his hand.

'Sir?' The master turned impatiently. 'Bennett is sick, sir.'

'When will you boys understand,' said the master, 'that it is very coarse to say that someone is "sick" when you mean "ill". Write fifty times for me, Cummings Two, "Bennett is ill". Only animals become sick, not humans.' He turned back to the board.

'Sir,' said Herbert. 'Bennett is really ill.'

'What is the matter with you, Bennett?' The master put his chalk down on the table irritably and brushed his fingers on his jacket.

'I'm feeling sick, sir.'

'I'm ill, sir. Or sir, I am unwell. Indisposed, whatever. You will also write fifty times, "I am unwell" and hand it in at prep.' Bennett kept his eyes on the desk. The master put his hands in his pockets wearily and looked up at the ceiling and then back at Bennett. 'What is the matter with you, Bennett?'

'May I be excused, sir?'

'Go on then. Go back to your house.'

Davey Bennett stood. He winced. He could not put his weight on his leg.

'Take yourself off to Miss Maltby.'

Davey tried to walk to the door.

'Cummings, help the fellow. Really, Bennett, I hope you aren't creating a stir for nothing. Get on with you, Cummings, don't sit there, staring like a fool. Take him.'

Miss Maltby made him drop his trousers. It was worse than standing naked. She prodded at his knee. Davey almost cried out. 'Why didn't you show this to me before?' she said. 'You boys leave everything until it's fair rotten and then I am supposed to mend it.' She went to her cupboard, inspected the contents, fished out iodine.

167

She dabbed it at David Bennett's knee. 'I'll have to lance it,' she said. 'Why didn't you come before? You've got it infected. The doctor was here this morning. Now he's gone again. I certainly can't call him back.' A needle was extracted from the bib of her apron. 'Hold still, boy.' She touched his shoulder but it was too brief and perfunctory for comfort. 'It will hurt.'

It did. It hurt so much David Bennett thought he would faint. He swayed in the chair.

Miss Maltby eased the skin away. The boil burst. She made a strange gargling in her throat. Davey thought he would vomit. The tears would have to go away. He gripped the edge of the wooden chair, fighting.

'Go and lie down a bit,' said Miss Maltby when she had washed his knee. 'I'll tell Mr Robinson I sent you up. I'll look in later.' She glanced over at Herbert facing the window, his hands behind his back. 'Take him,' she said.

Herbert lifted Davey awkwardly under the elbow, steered him from Miss Maltby's room.

'Sorry, Jones,' he said. He did not know what else to say. Sorry, Jones. It was all he could offer.

He took Davey to the dormitory, standing disconsolately while he lay down on the bed. He pulled the blanket across him. Davey did not complain. He knew Herbert was at a loss. 'I'll be fine,' he said. 'At least we both got out of parsing.' He tried to laugh.

'I'll come up after school,' Herbert said.

'You've got footer practice. I'll still be here tonight.'

'Right.' Herbert stood, not moving and not looking at him.

'Don't bring any prep, see,' said Davey, trying to keep his voice steady. 'Tell Beef I'm sure to die, so he needn't bother. One less to mark.'

Herbert grinned. 'Lazy old bugger.'

Davey watched him walk away. The steps were loud. The dormitory was empty. Davey Bennett lay there, fingers curled around the small iron bars of the bedhead.

Do not think of home.

Do not think of anyone.

Not Mother.

Do not cry.

A day.

Two days.

Three.

Miss Maltby dosed him everything that she could think of. He had to submit to the chamber-pot with her stamping about in the passage outside. The doctor visited to dress the knee, press out the poison, bandage it up again. He had to bear it.

Four days.

Five.

Herbert brought bull's-eyes. Pringle asked to see the bandage. He got Unwin's latest *Boys' Own Paper*, fourth-hand from Edwards. Robbie came to inspect him, gruffly but kindly, morning, afternoon and evening.

The sixth day.

The morning was very quiet, the time just before tea-break when he could hear, if he lay and listened, the cathedral clock gonging softly every quarter. He waited for it now, for he had no watch, no way of telling the passing of the hours beyond the cathedral clock and the school bell marking the end of lessons. No one would come until noon and no one was about but for the laundry maids fetching the piles of sheets: '*Uyagula mfan'am*? Are you sick?' A mother's eye, looking down on him, passing on, quiet, unhurried hands twitching his covering around his shoulders, the murmur of Xhosa. There was no comfort in Miss Maltby's, 'You'll be right as rain by Saturday'. But the voices of the housemaids reminded him of a gathering of birds in autumn: absent from him but recalling home and the restfulness of the farm garden, that quiet morning-murmur. It was a sound far removed from the clatter when the fellows came up from lessons, counter to the night when, waiting in the dark, he could feel again the throb-throb in his leg, a persistent, urgent little beat. It was then he did not sleep and, if he cried, it was silent and unheard by others.

Why didn't they call his mother? Why didn't she come?

But in the morning the fear subsided and to see her did not seem so urgent any more. He could sleep again, lulled by the untroubled murmur of the housemaids, flocking somewhere close.

He dozed.

'Jones?'

He opened his eyes, startled.

'Fraser?'

He struggled up onto an elbow. Charlie Fraser stood in the empty dormitory, looking down at him, without his jacket, just in his shirt-sleeves and tie, a schoolbook under his arm. He sat on Herbert's bed and rested his elbows on his knees and linked his hands and looked across.

Davey Bennett looked back. What should he say? –Have you bunked lessons, Fraser? –Are you looking for someone, Fraser? – Can I help you, Fraser? He said nothing: no one dreamed of asking Fraser questions just to be chatty.

And yet Fraser was there, suddenly, sitting with him, not speaking. Davey Bennett was at a loss. He said, 'Do you want a bull's-eye?'

Charlie Fraser smiled.

'Cummings gave them to me.'

Charlie took one. He said, 'It must be pretty dull just lying here.'

'Yes,' said Davey.

'Do you have anything to read?'

'Don't feel like it really. Not much of a reader.'

Fraser looked to the side and down, nudged the edge of his shoe at a crack in the floorboards. Then he glanced up at Davey again and said, as if it were an afterthought, 'You like photos. So,' he cracked his knuckles, 'shall I bring my album? It might help the time go by? Perhaps, later, you could sort the new pictures. If you want.'

Would you like to have a look at my album! No one looked at Charlie Fraser's album besides Arthur Graham.

'Thank you, Fraser.' Small and hoarse.

Charlie Fraser went away and fetched it. He helped Davey Bennett up and pushed his pillow between him and the iron bedhead, patting it awkwardly, but his hands at Davey's shoulder, at his elbow, were safe, as if he'd put them there to steady him.

Davey Bennett looked away. No tears. Absolutely none.

Charlie Fraser took the pillow from Herbert's bed and propped the album against it, opening it. 'Sunny Memories' and the half-sun rising in relief from a scroll against the grey-blue cloth of the binding.

'The early photos aren't much to write home about. You'll find them boring anyway because you don't know the place.' Charlie turned a group of pages at the beginning, dismissing them. 'You'll see some of your own among the school ones. I've got more to paste in. I'll show them to you after lunch.' He glanced at the door, alert to footsteps on the stairs but they passed on down another passage. He turned back, looking from his height at Davey Bennett. 'And, Jones,' he said, using Davey's nickname. He paused – it was so brief, Davey Bennett only felt it, a beat missed to gain composure – 'I'm very sorry about your leg. Archer was angry with me, not you. It shouldn't have happened.'

'Nothing to be sorry about, Fraser,' said Davey Bennett. 'Just damned rotten luck, that's all.'

Davey could hardly turn the thick card pages of the album and his hand, out of the bedclothes, shook again with the cold and his skin was burning. But turn them he did. He went back to the beginning, to the first page which Charlie Fraser had dismissed. These were the home pictures. And in between them, intermediary, was the landscape. There were pages of them, places that he knew, perhaps landmarks along the way. From here to there. From there to here. Rivers and passes and hills and buildings and something called 'The Ruins' which Charlie Fraser had taken from every angle. There were pictures of Christmastime in the album as well: with his grandfather, a venerable, grey-bearded missionary and half a dozen old-fashioned children who must have been his cousins, for Davey Bennett knew he was an only child.

But the interesting thing about those pictures was that the school ones were all solemn while in the home ones – except where he was got up in a blazer that was miles too small with everyone standing very formally around him – he was always laughing. Sometimes it seemed that in those pictures it was not the same person, except that they were labelled: 'CWF and dog'; 'CWF and Jonah, the groom'; 'Baby, Jean, Auntie Dai, CWF' – a pair of small dark-haired girls and a stoutish woman, laughing. Charlie laughing. 'Mother and CWF': they echoed each other in the eyes, the brow, the decided chin. Charlie's mother looked out candidly. Her hand was on his shoulder: this is my son. Look at him!

Here was Charlie Fraser's home. A mission house, with a corrugated roof, a wooden railing. Beyond, the veld and a spur of hill. Here an old stone church with cattle grazing near the walls. They are small bush cattle, speckled and blotched. Hills, sky, sunsets, rivers. Aloes, grasslands. The Donsa Pass. A picture of a soldier's grave from some far off frontier war.

Then school. The teams. Cricket: house teams, the XI in their striped blazers assembled at school, at Cradock, at Bedford. Athletics: there is Rudd in all his glory from the year before. He sits dark-eyed and solemn among the abundant trophies. Rudd breaking the half-mile record, flying through the tape. That day, everyone had risen from their seats, breathless as he rounded the last bend. Even the Head in his top hat and tails had forgotten himself in the excitement and had roared him home. Everyone knew that Rudd would be the most famous of them all one day.

Then there were the footer photos: house teams, North Juniors, South Seniors, Thirds, Seconds. And then, the Firsts.

Bennett looked at each of the players in the three rows, colours blazers, collars up, striped scarves tucked in, the captain, Seymour, sitting in the centre of the middle row, his braided cap perched straight above the firm support of his ears. Bennett left the album open there, pulled his hand under the cover again, tried to still the tremor of cold.

The fever was worsening.

His eyes were heavy. He tried to keep them open. He looked at the picture with one eye, closed the other. The figures swam. He opened his eyes again, recited the names to keep himself awake: back row, left to right, say them fast, from memory, no need even to look. Then remember page 151 of the school magazine: *Characters of the First Fifteen*. He'd read it through so often, he knew it by heart. But it drifted away, left snatches with him:

Seymour: Captain. Centre three-quarter. Good kick with his right

foot but should learn to kick with his left ... *Holmes* uses his feet to advantage in the scrum ... inclined to be selfish with the ball ... a sterling game. Best record in scoring tries. *Graham* ... lightning on the wing. The tonic in the team.
MacCallum: Rather light but energetic forward ... Good jump ... uses his height to advantage.

Cold and heat were washing him away. He was lying at the edge of the sea and it was nudging and sucking. He was going out with the tide into darkness. He could hear the breakers.

Mac came back: tackles well and has a sound knowledge of the game. Fast for a forward ...
Davey slept, woke momentarily with a start, drifted off.

Bell: Centre three-quarter. Excellent kick. Courageous, plucky player. Fearless tackler.

Sparrow on the field, dashing about. He and Apie – dear old Apie – like a pair of terriers. Coach called them the 'ankle biters'. In the photo, Apie sitting at Charlie Fraser's feet, his blazer much too big. Had Apie come up to see him?
–Apie? He heard his own voice.
Nothing.
Was he standing there with a colours cap on? –Did they give you a colours cap, Apie? Let me see ...

Morgan must lose that 'bull at the gate' feeling that overcomes him at times ...

Morgan roaring. He could hear him roaring. Right across the field and all around the hills, the echoes of it. He could hear it in his chest. And chanting boys: College ... College ... College ...
Next row, sitting on the old spindle-backs from the library, set in a semicircle before the great arched door of the House. Second last on the right, middle row: *Grant*. Danny disappeared, faded out. Dan

173

gone. –Dan, come back to the line.

–Danny, come back. Davey was searching then. Night, and the wind was shaking at him, bearing him up.

Where was Charlie Fraser? He knew it word for word. He could say it still. –Say it through, Davey Jones, say it through.

Fraser: Full-back. A splendid player. Extremely cool and consistent. Excellent punt, drop and place kicker. Powerful with either foot and uses his judgement well. A courageous tackler.

Charlie Fraser went away. He was looking for him but he'd gone. He was alone in his packstone *pondok* in the mountains. He could hear the wind fluting in the walls, smell the *rooigras* in the sack, paraffin and gun oil.

–See my house, Charlie Fraser. From here you can look out across the veld and down the krantzes. Light a fire, *braai* some *ribbetjies*, boil the old *bhekile* . . . Come.

Davey Bennett woke. For a long time he lay, the album open on the page. He could see his pencil box lying on the chair beside him. To reach for it would mean putting his arm out into the cold. He looked at it. He shifted forward. How cold the sheets were! He recoiled from the little recesses of the bed where his toes found themselves. He did not know how long he lay watching his pencil box, deciding whether to reach out for it or not. At last he did, suddenly, because he had to. He drew it into the bed, under the blanket. It was difficult to slide the lid out. It had always moved so smoothly but his hand was shaking and it jammed as he pulled it back. It stuck. He eased it. It seemed like all the morning passed in opening it. He swung out the top tray where his pencils were and his nibs and his pens, his compass, feeling underneath for the thing he kept hidden. He took out the small photo of his little house. He laid it on the cover and then he slid the lid of the pencil box back into its grooves. He put it aside. He tucked the photo carefully into Charlie Fraser's album. It would be safe there. Absolutely safe.

He closed the album and pulled a corner of the blanket over it, concealing it. He could feel the rough cloth cover under his hot fingers.

Call my mother. Why didn't they call his mother? Had he asked for her? Call her now.

Miss Maltby came. Confused, he gazed about him. The dormitory was empty. Just Miss Maltby with the white enamel chamber-pot with the chips showing charcoal grey in concentric rings where someone had kicked it against a wall. He did not care any more that she held it for him. Nor could he oblige.

Robbie came. He knew the clump of his footsteps. He could hear him, see him somewhere at a distance. He was there. He was gone. He was there. He was gone. Davey did not count. Miss Maltby and Robbie. Robbie and Miss Maltby. Voices drifted in and out. He could not feel Charlie Fraser's album among the blankets any more. His hand would not move to find it.

The Doctor came. The Head. The chaplain.

There was quiet then.

Were they standing there? Why didn't anyone speak? Was it raining? Perhaps it was the wind again.

It's fluting in the packstone walls. He must fill the lamp, bring paraffin from the shed and carry it up in an old *bhekile*. He must mind not to slip at the place where water seeps from a leak in the reservoir. In the trench there is frog spawn and little purple flowers embroider the grass. Sometimes *rhebok* come to drink. The kudu are often in the lichen-grey bush where the rain doesn't reach: mist-grey, thornbark-grey, kudu-grey ... they walk so quietly, the great spirals of the old bull's horns emerge only when he moves ...

The last fence and the gate and then the short turf where sheep are sent up to high pasture in the late summer.

There is the little house against the hill. There's the *kannabos* and the great rock.

Light the lamp. Get logs, make a fire in the grate. Biltong, rusks. Boil the *bhekile*. The *rooigras* has been cut. It still smells of dust.

175

Here, inside, against the shelter of the rock, the wind can't reach.
It funnels past overhead. The walls are steady.
One day, perhaps, I'll show it to someone.
To Charlie Fraser . . .
If I can't, it will be damned rotten luck . . .
Damned rotten luck . . . that's all.

A stretcher was brought. MacCallum, Grant, Graham, Fraser: they carried David Bennett down the stairs to the doctor's car. No one spoke. Robbie and Miss Maltby climbed in the back seat. Robbie held Davey Bennett in his lap. The car turned up the hill towards the hospital.

GB and Parkes were building a soap-box on the lawn. They did not seem to look up as the car passed. But they stopped what they were doing 'til long after the dust from the wheels had settled back on the road.

Herbert went to rugby practice. He fouled so often the coach sent him for a brisk jog down the street.

On the adjoining field, Archer was warned off by the captain of the Seconds for bad language and had to sit it out in the cold in the pavilion.

Unwin went to the chapel. The Reverend Dowsley found him crouched in the choir stalls but nothing would induce him to say what was wrong beyond that God hated him. Considerably shocked, the chaplain evicted him and made a note to speak to Robbie after dinner. Unwin went and locked himself in the lavatory instead. He did not care if MacCallum found him. It was all too late.

Charlie Fraser missed rugby practice without apology and went to his study and closed the door. No one came near.

At dinner that night, when the House had assembled, it was not Robbie who stood to take grace but the Head himself. He said, 'David Bennett died this afternoon. I'd like a minute's silence.'

No one spoke throughout the meal. There was no sound but the scrape of cutlery on plates and the footsteps of the waiters until the final grace was said.

It was too far and too expensive to take David Bennett's body home.

176

He was buried in the municipal cemetery in a clearly marked plot. It was argued that it was a more dignified place than being interred under a thorntree in the veld. That's what they said, and, in time, his parents had had a marble headstone erected and a grim little iron palisade. They'd planted Christ-thorn to keep careless feet away.

But on the day that he was buried, after the service, Robbie sent all the boys but MacCallum and Gilbert out of the House so that David Bennett's parents might come up to the dormitory alone. His trunk had been packed and roped by Miss Maltby. His grandfather's tuck-box with the worn leather strap stood on top. Herbert passed it on his way outside with the others. He went off alone and sat on the bank leading down from Lower.

–Are you Basil Bennett?

–I hope not.

–Who's Basil Bennett, then?

–Gramps. It was his tuck-box when he was at school. He gave it to me, in case I felt homesick.

Ginger beer with raisins. Splashing the compartment. Talking, laughing half the night while the train rocked on to Alicedale.

MacCallum and Gilbert carried the trunk and the box out to the cab. Robbie helped David Bennett's mother in. The Head shook hands with his father. They went away. There were no more sons to send to school.

After that, nothing was said. Miss Maltby had Davey's bed taken down to the storeroom and the others moved apart an inch or two to fill the space. Having been given half Davey's territory, Herbert could see out of the window over the roof of Jarge's cottage to the trees beyond. Davey had sometimes stood there, looking out.

–Jones?

No reply.

–Jones?

A vague return.

–Where are you?

Charlie Fraser would have guessed it. On the day Davey had died, he'd gone to the dormitory after lunch to fetch his photographs. Davey Bennett had been asleep, his hand curled round the edge of the album. Charlie had lifted his fingers carefully. They were hot and dry. Davey had opened his eyes. He'd looked at Charlie but there had been no recognition. Taking the album under his arm, Charlie Fraser had hurried to Robbie's classroom. He'd knocked. 'Sir?'

'What's it, Fraser?' All the boys had looked up from their work.

'I think Bennett's very sick, sir. I think he may be delirious.'

'Tell Miss Maltby to send for the doctor.' Robbie had pushed back his chair. Charlie had known he was worried for he strode out, patting at the hunting knife. 'Perhaps you should step across to the Headmaster too, Fraser,' he'd said, swinging round and then hurrying on. 'I'll go up to the dormitory at once.'

Later, when Charlie had returned to his room, he had thrown down the album on his desk. It had slipped off the edge onto the floor. He'd bent to pick it up. Davey Bennett's photograph had fallen out. Charlie Fraser had taken the picture to the window and looked at it in the light. Obscure against the side of a boulder was a little packstone house with a thatched roof. Beyond, a hillside rose and to the side, fell off towards a gorge. A spindly *kannabos* grew up into a pale sky. A crooked stable door. A rifle rested up against the step. Along the margin, in Davey Bennett's rounded writing: D. Bennett. My Hut. Underlined.

Davey Bennett's treasure. Bequeathed, for no return.

Charlie had gone to his bookshelf, reached to the top rack and pushed the album in. He had not called GB to bring his rugby boots. He had found them himself. He had polished them, rubbing the toes with his face cloth. He had missed rugby practice. He had not even gone to kick a ball alone.

Archer inspected his pimples covertly in the small mirror in his locker. Could they grow and suppurate and eat away his face and turn it pus-green in half a day as Bennett's boil had done? He knew why they had come: he had killed David Bennett. This was evidence enough. And if they had been there before as a mark of impurity and vile habits, they were proliferating by the hour for this greater sin. He did not know how to avoid retribution. He did not know where to put the blame – but it would have to be expunged.

He did it by denial.

For the moment, brief though it was, he did not smoke.

For the moment, he did not torment nubs.

For the moment, he kept away from Unwin and the tangy.

For the moment, Goen Archer did not play the buck.

It had its rewards.

He was reinstated and he went to town himself. His skin cleared up. Robbie wrote a good report of him for the first time in four years.

So far so good. But he needed a sign to indicate that he was not to blame. He got it unexpectedly. The moment was recorded by Arthur Graham in a letter home:

'Dear Moth and Dad,
We played Crusaders on Saturday we went down to PE on Friday afternoon by train. Charlie Fraser stuck his head out of the window and got a cinder in his eye so the reserve from the seconds took his place. His name is Archer. He did well. We won. We stayed at Grey College. They laid on very good grub and there were Collegiate girls giving a recital so we all went, which was grand. No news, just slog.
Your everloving son,
Arthur Graham.'

So Archer played a match for the Firsts in Charlie Fraser's place and was even mentioned in the report in *The Journal*. It was a fleeting glory. He went about, quite affable all week. He even practised his kicking for a day or two until the rain set in.

After that, he seemed to forget. He did not notice that the rain did not distract Fraser, that every afternoon saw him on the field, punting balls.

He cadged a cigarette off Stafford. Once. Then twice.

He went to town and bought a box himself.

A nub, suddenly complacent, gave him buck, so he thrashed him with his belt.

Why not? Bennett was receding and with him the notion of retribution. Life proceeded in its regular, predictable routine. Nothing changed. He thought less about Bennett in chapel, pushed the recollection away. He hadn't meant it after all. Footer, women – women, footer: these reasserted themselves in his reveries.

He did not understand that, for most, the first – the only – keeper of the conscience, is cowardice.

He had not died. He could relinquish fear.

It was not only Archer who had killed David Bennett. Herbert, for a tickey's-worth of bull's-eyes, had betrayed his friend as well. A dozen times. A hundred times. Their fort. Their games. By leaving him to follow from the field alone. He went over and over and over it at night, trying to see the highest pitch of the roof in the dark, following the trailing light of a lantern carried somewhere down below or out in the street, listening sometimes to the sound of the mule cart going by to fetch the buckets from the lavatories. Sometimes he dreamed it, most times he lay and thought about it. Round and round and round. He heard his case and he delivered judgement. This way, that way. *He* had challenged Archer. Archer had been angry with him – Get lost, Cummings – so he'd pushed Davey Bennett out of his way. And if Herbert hadn't sent Davey for the bull's-eyes – just sending him on any whim, at any time, lackey to a hero of the First XV – and they hadn't been trying to get them unstuck at that moment . . . but then it was Davey who'd fetched the compass, Herbert hadn't told him to . . . In the chain of events, in cause and effect, where does responsibility begin and end?

Had it started in the locker room when Archer swore? Or was it what Charlie Fraser'd said to Archer when he'd found Unwin in the shower? Or was it just bad luck and unconnected, after all? An accident that no one could foresee?

Chance?

Luck?

Fate?

In the end, Herbert had asked Percy, too burdened to be silent any more. He had no other way to exorcise the thing. He came to Percy's study and he said, 'Have you time for chess, Gilbert?', sounding the petitioner he was.

Percy looked up, almost startled, but he didn't say – What's wrong? He consulted his watch. 'Just enough, if you haven't got too clever since we last played!' He yawned and leaned over to his locker and extracted the board and the little silky bag of pieces.

'Were you busy?' said Herbert, still standing at the door.

'We have History Society tonight. I was looking over notes.'

Herbert backed.

'Come in and sit, Cummings. I know what I'm going to say. It's all about whether the Turks are worthy to be included in Europe. I'd really rather play chess than think of Turks.'

If Unwin hadn't needled Archer?

If Charlie hadn't intervened?

If teams had just been chosen on another day?

If Davey hadn't gone to town?

If Herbert hadn't asked for bull's-eyes?

'About Bennett . . .' Herbert said, when he had made three foolish moves, the game destined to end before it had begun.

'Yes?' Percy surveyed the board.

'Was it Unwin's fault?' Herbert could deal with Unwin first.

'Such a regrettable fellow.' Percy sighed, taking out his little mother-of-pearl handled pocket knife to scrape his pipe bowl. 'Unwin was just the catalyst. No . . . not the catalyst, really.' He paused. 'The decoy. That's it.' He picked up a pawn thoughtfully and put it down again. 'A wooden duck, glassy-eyed, left to bob about on the water when the hunters have gone. They get waterlogged, turn turtle, belly-up . . . sink.' A gesture – pphft! – no more. The images Percy chose were as important as the subject at hand.

'Well, then, who?'

No answer.

'Me?'

Percy refilled his pipe. 'No, Cummings. You were only passing by.'

'But still.'

'You see a donkey being beaten in the street. You protest. You are outraged. You intervene. But donkeys are beaten in the street every day. You will never stop it.'

'But Bennett?' Herbert linked his knuckles, webbed his fingers.

'A casualty.'

'To what?'

'To the thing that drives us all,' said Percy.

Herbert waited.

'The need for recognition, Cummings. And the power, good or bad, that goes with it.'

Herbert chewed at his bottom lip. The sweat was behind his knees.

'It's the business of life, Cummings.' Percy took up another pawn. 'Archer's such a thoughtless sort of oaf, without wanting to be. His attempts backfire. You can't even blame him – there's nothing seriously vicious in him. He wants approval. Mostly Fraser's. He gets it wrong, that's all.'

'You make it sound, sort of . . .'

'Trivial?'

'I mean, Bennett is a person.'

'There's no parody in any of this, Cummings.' Percy made a sideways move, took Herbert's knight. 'It makes it so much worse. Think how many have been casualties to simple negligence. It happens all the time.'

Unwin – deeply bewildered, a decoy duck indeed – had been transposed, without the possibility of redemption, to limbo. He did not care. There was nothing to care about any more. David Bennett was lucky he was dead. Oblivion would have been a better choice.

He went to smoke in the tangy sometimes. He sat it out behind the bogs. He seemed suspended, as if he was waiting to dissolve: albumen in the sun, frog-spawn in a drought. He pushed off any gesture from the motley for inclusion. Only Davey Bennett seemed present. Still there, where no one else could see him. Still there, despite his bed and his chair and his desk having been stored. Still in some opaque underworld where Unwin had retreated. And sometimes he visited Davey Bennett's grave, taking the tangy, emerging quite near the station, rather aimless in his wandering, knowing – but not confessing, even to himself – where he was going. The cemetery was up beyond the lines, under the stone pines, the grass grey, growing in sparse patches. There was always wind, gusting sideways. It was a dry, spare, empty place.

He would go in through the lych-gate. It seemed reluctant to admit him. He would walk along the rows, up and down, up and down. The grave was close beside the old wall. The Christ-thorn had taken root. Ants always trailed along the loops of the iron palisade. They always met and touched and hurried on. None went by unnoticed by the rest. The older stones leaned in, the epitaphs obscured. The newer still stood upright, shouldering their words.

David Basil Bennett
3rd April 1898 – 10th April 1913
I know that my Redeemer Liveth

He sometimes spoke aloud. 'Sorry, Bennett.'

There was only stillness and a hot, dry breathlessness in the shelter of the wall.

Had he betrayed David Bennett?

He didn't know any more.

Had David Bennett betrayed him?

No. He knew he hadn't.

Not in any way?

Not in any way.

Davey Bennett had betrayed no one. Not even himself.

Unwin came empty handed. He had nothing to bring. But he came nonetheless. It was a mutual recognition.

Charlie Fraser carried it as well. He carried it most of all. It was he who had humiliated Archer. He did not try to exorcise the fact or put it aside. There could be no relief in laying the burden down by talking about it to someone else, trying to despatch it, neatly witnessed. It would be too easy to let the kindly chaplain take it up with a homily on God's Will. So he said nothing. He did not mention Davey Bennett again.

Nor did he forget him. The time of his remembrance would come. The moment to atone.

A newboy, named Jones, arrived at school and, in a while, it seemed that no one could recall that 'Jones' had once referred – emphatically, uniquely – to a slim, straight-haired boy called Bennett.

–Jones?

No reply.

–Jones?

A vague return.

–Where are you?

Oh, up on the hills in his little house, Herbert. *Kannabos* and packstone and sky; paraffin and gun oil and a fire made of thorn brush; *rooigras* bed and buckskin on the floor and the old *bhekile* steaming over coals. Not chained to plot AXXXI in the municipal cemetery. Not he.

Charlie Fraser knows it.

Damned rotten luck or not.

TEN

There was no picture of Josie Zeederberg in Charlie's album. Herbert had acquired one from the photographer's himself, using most of a week's pocket-money. Captain Josie in the cricket team, very solemn in the front row. So solemn, she might as well have been Daniel Grant with the stalwarts of the XI gathered round. Josie Zeederberg, snout to the fore. Josie Zeederberg on patrol, marching down the road so briskly her hat trailed on its strings, dipping and dancing like a kite at her back. Herbert kept the picture in his Greek grammar where it would not be seen by anyone else. He did not want Edwards pouncing on it. Josie Zeederberg was not the sort of girl one kept pictures of like Clarice White as 'The La La Maiden' or Violet Henderson as 'The Queen of the May'. She did not invite staring. She seemed to breathe decidedly, with a little white about the nostril, indication of impatience, when she saw the fellows pushing each other around on the field and playing the fool. She didn't humour them quite the way that others did. She had a disconcerting way of having the last word. Something clear – and funny – that kept them in their place like a little blast on her bugle. He sensed that Josie Zeederberg was much cleverer than all of them.

Herbert knew just where she walked when she went to school. Up the other side of the street, past the Mullinses and over the road at the crest. Always trotting, head full of errands, looking neither to right nor left, not expecting – nor wishing – to be waylaid. At the Grants' wall she stopped to inspect the fig tree when it was in fruit and then crossed the road again and went in through the gate of the Girls' School opposite: a neat circumvention of the boys' houses. If he wanted to meet her by accident he'd have to lurk about in the Grants' garden and saunter out onto the verge on cue. It was the only place in which lurking wouldn't be suspected or observed until the last moment. She couldn't change her plan then, and cross earlier.

The compulsion to do it was irresistible. The excuse? Herbert could be forgiven for scratching. The idea, he knew, was strictly bad form, now that he was counted with the great and the glorious. Being the youngest in the XV, he had the most reason to look sharp. And besides, if he behaved like a fool, what would Charlie Fraser think of him? What Dan Grant, despite Mary Clifford? Among them, only Sparrow and Arthur and Doug could stare at the croc or at Clarice, without inviting derision. They laughed at themselves – and among themselves – uproariously. It was all part of the fun.

Herbert had to do it. Do it and get it over with. Saunter up and say, 'Hello.'

Hello? . . . Hello?

Hello who?

He didn't have a clue what to call her.

More brusque, perhaps: –What did you mean that time, is Charles Fraser in my House?

No, that wouldn't do. It was too abrupt.

–Good afternoon . . . Where are you going?

–What's that to you?

What, indeed.

–Hello. The fellows want to know when you are playing cricket again so they can come and watch.

–It's hockey season.

Right.

–Hello . . . Are you Harry's sister?

–Yes.

–Harry is a good fellow. He's a friend of mine.

–*What*? Complete derision, skirting round him, but somehow walking over him: Harry is definitely *not* the right connection.

–Hello . . .

She took her clarinet to school on Wednesday afternoons. He let three Wednesdays pass before he dared.

And as for Josie Zeederberg herself, she never lurked. She marched forth, always without her hat on her head, always with it twisting at her back. Her boot laces were rarely tied. She avoided the boys' houses not because the boys embarrassed her but because they annoyed her with dangling themselves out of windows to watch, as if it were an honour of some kind to have them risking their necks to stare. Who'd want some gormless pimple-face falling out of a window for her? Really!

Besides, at close quarters, most of them were astonishingly smelly! Her mother was always expressing the wish to line them up and scrub them raw as she scrubbed Josie's younger brothers in front of the old coal stove on Sundays. But, at a distance, sitting in the cathedral, shoulder to shoulder and a view of the backs of their necks, they were tolerable. Just. She had never thought of necks at all until her elder sister Annie – such sophisticated observation – had been heard to remark to her friends, drinking cocoa in her room, 'Look at the back of the neck. It will tell you everything!' It lodged in her mind then: look at the neck, it will tell you everything, like her great-aunt's dictum:

'Never trust a man with a flat head.'

A flat head?

'Flat at the back, dear. It's very ill-bred.'

So Josie Zeederberg had taken – absently – to looking at heads and necks when she was in church – just in passing – if the sermon was boring. According to Annie, there was only one kind of neck that was acceptable. Not the kind with a groove down the nape like a little boy's, or the hairy sort or the kind that stuck up out of the collar instead of fitting it exactly. Nor were necks acceptable that appeared as if they were balanced on top of the shoulders instead of being part of the stem of the boy, connected absolutely with the tension in his legs and spine. Annie had thought this out at length, it seemed. Whatever did she mean?

'The man is in the neck,' Annie had said, looking peculiarly arch and knowing.

'Who says?' Josie had snorted.

'Off you go, Baby.' And she was shooed away.

But she looked after that. And her sister Annie was right.

Little boys had necks with heads precariously balanced, ears poised to steady them, to keep them there, to stop them tumbling off. And the light shone through those ears, illuminating them faintly, so that they glowed. Such necks were held in a way that had nothing to do with trunks and roots. Such boys had little tails to their hair at the nape, like a tadpole's.

Seniors were different: shoulder to shoulder, collar studs straining, certain jackets edged with Colours braid, pale blue on dark, only Herbert Cummings, among the younger boys, sporting such accoutrements.

'Josie, what are you looking at?' Her neighbour nudging her.

'I am looking at something for Annie, to see if she's right.'

'What?'

'Necks.'

'What?'

'Shut up.'

Looking at those senior necks was like discovering something forbidden, even slightly menacing. It was offending to his great dignity to stare Georgie Holmes in the back of the head. It was not right to stare at Seymour either. His neck was broad and strong but rather freckly and bland. Still, it belonged to Seymour. Percy Gilbert's neck was not to be scrutinised at all. It might even be sinful to look at Percy Gilbert's neck in church. Besides, he seemed so very old.

Arthur Graham had a nice neck. A shade slim, but strong and easy and brown and it certainly grew upwards rather than being attached from the top. Sparrow's still had that boy-groove and the little tail. It didn't matter. Anyone would be happy to put their nose in Sparrow's neck or blow on it like you blew on the baby's tummy at bath-time to make it laugh backwards. Daniel Grant's was close to perfect and so were his shoulders. Doug Morgan's was too thick. Vincent MacCallum's was too dark. Charlie Fraser's was sublime.

One could only peep.

Josie made her observations for her sister, noted exactly what it was that she had meant.

'Charles Fraser's is the best,' she said.

'Inevitably!' Annie, all aglow!

Having delivered judgement in favour of Charlie and seen Annie carry it around as though it were some personal triumph, Josie Zeederberg examined Herbert Cummings' neck at length. Why not? Herbert didn't frighten her at all. There – it was too long, despite the Colours braid. It was also too thin. He was not a big boy yet. But it had good sinews and it was smooth. She had the feeling that if she put out her finger and touched it, it could be teased. She almost did it. Herbert had wriggled his shoulders as if he felt her and she had sat back and behaved herself.

But when Herbert Cummings suddenly came storming round a corner and almost bumped into her, not looking at all where he was going and nearly knocking her into the fig tree outside the Grants' gate, she got more of a fright than he and her face had been very flushed.

'Watch out, will you!' she said gruffly. How did Annie do it, making fellows quake and not seem flustered herself, even if she was?

'Sorry. Terribly sorry, ma'am.' Herbert Cummings was as red as she.

Ma'am?

Josie shook herself and adjusted her clarinet case under her arm.

'Are you pinching figs?' he said. Brazen boy.

'Pinching figs!' Indignant. How dare he?

'I mean, picking figs.' Herbert's ears were warm.

'If you observe the tree,' said Josie Zeederberg, taking the advantage, 'you will see that there are no figs because it is the middle of winter.'

Herbert Cummings stared at the tree at some length. 'Yes,' he said.

'And anyway,' she continued, 'Daniel Grant said I could have them whenever I want.'

'Dan Grant said that?' That was impossible. Dan Grant couldn't utter a syllable to a girl.

'Yes,' she said. She looked at him directly. 'He only stutters badly in front of Mary Clifford.' There was a put down! Said off pat!

Herbert scratched his ear. 'What's in the case?'

'A clarinet,' she said.

'What for?'

'To play.' Patiently.

'Play what?'

'Are you being idiotic on purpose?'

Herbert was feeling a bit dry in the mouth. 'I haven't seen one before.'

Josie Zeederberg stared at him just longer than she'd intended. He had a funny little quirk at the side of his mouth and his mouth itself was wide and sort of curling and he had a dent in his chin. You could have put an index finger to it, like a piece to a puzzle. It would fit exactly. And he had a gap between his front teeth, just enough to whistle through in a way she'd always envied and couldn't emulate.

Herbert wiped his chin. Had he left his lunchtime pumpkin on it? He must have. Was there another pimple coming? He examined the fig tree again. She was standing there waiting for him to speak. Cornered, he said, 'You asked if Fraser was in my House. Why?'

'Did I?'

'Yes.'

'When?'

'The other time.'

'What other time?'

'With the cricket ball.'

'What cricket ball?'

Girls were so dumb.

'The other time.' If he didn't say something soon, she'd go away, and his chance to know her would be lost. 'Do you want to meet him or something?' he said, wading into complications – mad impetuous arse.

'Me?' back-pedalling, almost indignant: what would she do with Charlie Fraser, short of die of fright? On the other hand, if she said No and Annie found out, Annie would kill her.

190

'Well, do you?' he said.

'Don't mind.' She looked off towards the school gate.

'All right,' he said.

What the hell had he done?

–Fraser, excuse me, there's a girl who wants to meet you.

–Which girl?

–Josie Zeederberg. Fifteen years old. Plays the trumpet and the clarinet.

Instant death. No one took such liberties.

'How will I meet him?' she said.

'Ask him to tea.'

'Don't be ridiculous.'

'Well, then, ask me and I'll bring him along.'

It had got beyond him. She'd laugh at him now, incredulous, and he'd be safe.

'Come on Saturday at half past three.' She rapped it out brusquely, an instruction, not an invitation. There, Annie Zeederberg! Now you'll owe me! Favours and Benefits for at least a year.

'Don't I need a note from your mother?' Herbert was plaintive.

'My mother is too distracted for that,' she said. She walked on. Herbert stood, appalled. He watched her go: such a straight walk, such a gruff voice for a girl, such a little snout of a nose, such a decided chin. She left behind a kind of scent: winter flannels and warm soapy water and fresh bread and butter. Something like it. He wasn't sure. He went back to the House very vexed. When he saw Charlie Fraser coming up the stairs after prep, he dived off down the passage. What was he to say? He could never speak to him again! He went off miserably, unaware that events had progressed far beyond his and Josie's little subterfuges under the fig tree.

'What's to be done about that glorious girl learning music at the university?' said Arthur, stretching all of himself: he always did when he spoke about girls.

'I don't do music at the university and neither do you,' said Charlie, 'so how could I know who you mean?'

'The one we saw in the Cathedral Café last Saturday?'

'Which one? There were lots of them.'

'*That one*. You know. I showed her to you.'

'Did you.' No enquiry. Charlie knew exactly who he meant.

And as she'd looked around from the table where she was having tea with three others, her gaze – a moment before the blazers and the bashers and the schoolboy shoes made her turn away – had lingered a fraction longer than it might, on him.

So he hadn't seen her, if Arthur had. He wouldn't remember her, if Arthur must.

'I think you're blind, or dozed off half the time,' said Arthur, exasperated. 'She was the one with the sort of darkish, blondish hair. Up, you know . . . well sort of up and down at once. And the beautiful smile . . .' Arthur lay on Charlie's bed and put his hands behind his head. 'What if I wrote her a note and said I was very interested in music. Or invited her and the other students to come to the next concert? Tell them Holmes is a fine violinist and they should listen to him.'

'Then she'd be bound to run off with Holmes.'

'Yes, she'd run off with Holmes.' Gloomy. 'Why do beautiful girls always like fellows who know about music and poetry and things? I'd have thought it was all too wet.'

'George Holmes is not wet.'

'No.' Certainly, Georgie Holmes was not wet. 'Well,' casting about, 'if I took lessons down there and pretended I was in the university class with Percy.'

'Arthur, you can't sing a note in tune and you've never touched a fiddle in your life.'

Undaunted, Arthur said, 'I know her name.'

'What is it?'

'Hilda.'

'Hilda who?'

'I don't know. I was listening to their conversation. That's how I know they were music students.'

'So?'

'You must remember her, surely, Charlie. I can't believe you're that blind!' Arthur settled down, crossed his legs. 'I think she had brown eyes. I've never thought of liking brown eyes before.'

No, Arthur, not brown – green eyes, slanted elfin-eyes and a little freckle in the hollow just above her lip and a straight nose, quite firm, and her hair swept up: long neck, held just so, because she had known that he was watching, even though he'd looked out of the window and said to Arthur, 'There are footer boots at 15/6 at Stirk's or Fliers for 14/9 at Birch's. Which ones shall we try?'

'And she had this funny little laugh,' said Arthur. 'She was smashing! When we have that dance, do you think she'd come? If we need an introduction we could ask Daisy or Seymour. They must know her.'

'I'd watch out for Seymour.'

'Daisy then.'

'Since when is Daisy likely to want to dance?'

'As a favour.'

'Do you want to do gaining grounds?' Charlie got up from his chair.

'No.' Arthur made himself more comfortable. 'I want to talk about Hilda.'

Charlie sighed and sat again. Arthur had got it wrong. Whatever her name was, it wasn't Hilda. Hilda was the other one, the small dark one that Arthur hadn't noticed. He'd been staring so hard he hadn't heard a thing.

'What are you going to have, Arthur?' Charlie had said, glancing up at the waitress who was standing with her notebook, waiting.

Arthur had held the menu but he had been peering over it, transfixed. Charlie had nudged him. 'You look like a *galjoen*. Close your mouth.'

Arthur had closed his mouth, then laughed. Two of the other girls had looked over. She hadn't. But Charlie knew that her gaze was just poised at his shoe: his rather large, dusty shoe. He had not moved his foot, even though he'd wanted to.

The waitress had been impatient. 'Two teas and two iced buns,' Arthur had said, rather loudly.

'Since when do I want an iced bun?' Charlie had retorted.

'No time to look at the menu,' Arthur'd said. 'I think I'll just buy a paper.' They were beyond the tea tables on the counter. He had had to pass the girls to get it.

Arthur had straightened his shoulders, eased his neck a bit in his stiff collar, sauntered. He'd lounged at the counter, hand in a pocket, head inclined and inspected the pile. He'd searched his blazer for change, was short, coloured up and looked over at Charlie. Charlie had found a coin, put it on the table in front of him and folded his arms. He would not make himself conspicuous by taking it to Arthur. Arthur would have to fetch it.

Arthur had passed the girls again, screwed up his courage, said 'Good afternoon' in a voice that failed to materialise the way he had intended: it came out entirely wrong. Charlie had almost laughed aloud. The girls had glanced up, smiled briefly, detached as older sisters, not unkind. Arthur had taken the change without looking at Charlie and seemed to wade back to the counter, his dignity compromised. He'd inspected the headlines diligently as he'd returned. This time he'd tripped, but saved himself and, being Arthur, had burst out laughing. The girls had laughed too, spontaneously.

'Idiot,' Charlie had said, his shoulders shaking as Arthur rearranged himself at the table, getting his legs and arms under control. The waitress had come with the tea and buns.

Arthur had poured the tea, tipping the pot too sharply and the lid had fallen off. Everyone turned to look. Having thoroughly embarrassed himself, he'd played the fool for the rest of their stay and the girls had forgotten their loftiness and had begun to talk in that clear, self-conscious banter that invites response. One had just turned – pert and laughing – to speak to them when the door had opened and borne in, it seemed, on a stray gust from the gale outside, were Parkes and GB.

Never closer to death: those small shining faces were turned towards them and Parkes had said as if he'd made a thrilling discovery, 'Good afternoon, Graham,' addressing his own fag-master first; 'Good afternoon, Fraser,' GB's next. They had stood beaming.

'What dear little fellows,' one of the girls had murmured, just audibly. They'd made petting faces then. And *she* had wrinkled up her nose – the kind of small maternal gesture girls make when all the power is theirs – a condescension which, Charlie knew, had suddenly extended beyond those two triumphant nubs, to them.

And Arthur, his most diverting repartee dying at delivery, had looked as though he might have swept them up and throttled them. Hanged in the bogs or buried. Flayed alive. Parkes and GB had stared at him, wide eyed. Discretion being GB's most estimable attribute, he had nudged the bewildered Parkes to the furthest table and taken a chair facing the wall. He'd sat bolt upright 'til the waitress came.

The girls had gathered up their things. Hats, umbrellas, music, books. As they'd left, one had said gaily, with a little wave, 'Bye, bye, boys.' Arthur and Charlie might as well have sat with GB and Parkes. By her gesture, they were all the same.

But *she* had gone out last and closed the door against the wind. Charlie had seen her through the window dip her head slightly and brush away a small wisp of hair that blew across her eyes, as if using the glass as a mirror. But she had looked through it. She'd looked straight back at him.

It was the first time he'd ever felt his ears burn. He'd said to Arthur, rather roughly, 'You've got icing all over your chin.'

Arthur sat up and dangled his legs over the side of the bed and put his head in his hands and announced, 'I think I'm in love.'

'Again. What happened to Katie from Park Drive?'

'No, Charlie' – a sepulchral voice – 'this is the real thing.'

'How can you be in love when you've never spoken to her.'

'It's driving me mad.'

'That's not love.'

'How do you know?'

'Let's go and do gaining grounds.' Charlie stood again.

Arthur sat with his eyes screwed up tight as if he were in pain. 'Let's go to town and have tea.'

'It's not a holiday and we don't have any money and she won't be there and it's after five o'clock and you're getting slack.'

'Does nothing move you?'

'Fetch the ball.'

Whatever moved him might have been known to God, but not because it was divulged to Him by Charlie Fraser. He neither confided in Him nor bargained. He had never felt he had the right to ask favours or trade off good behaviour. He was the son of a doctor, the grandson of a missionary and he had been sensible, all his life, that God was overworked: having been given a few advantages in education, health and talent, he should be satisfied, stick to the rules and shut up.

And if things started to crowd in, he took the ball and went and kicked it. In doing that he thought it through himself and made his own decisions. Footer. Honour. Sex.

Love.

Death.

The first two were clear. The third perplexing and intrusive. Whatever he knew, the informal information, had been gleaned at school but his formal education in the matter had been delivered by his grandfather, one holiday back, as he'd prepared to start his senior year. It had added nothing to his understanding of the subject:

'Charlie, lad,' walking him out into the garden, pipe clamped between his teeth and looking at the far hills as if he were examining them for the first time. 'Charlie, lad.' A mournful tone. Some family skeleton about to be revealed?

'Yes, Grandfather.'

'There are things a young man ought to know.'

Indeed. Charlie looked at the hills too. There were things he knew well enough about himself. What was this then?

His grandfather cast about, as if for a sign. The vegetable patch was near, just through the wire to keep the donkeys out. 'You must always remember, lad,' he cleared his throat and glanced back at the house. Charlie smiled. Grandma had put him up to this, he could hear her:

–My dear, it's time you had a heart-to-heart with Charlie.

–Charlie and I have heart-to-hearts all the time.

So they did: cricket and footer and athletics and farming.

–He is nearly a young man. And he doesn't have a father.

–I am well aware of that, my dear.

–Well, then.

Well, then.

Grandfather had said, staring at the rows of vegetables through the netting, his voice very measured, 'Remember, lad,' considering a moment, puffing absorbedly, 'if you plant a potato, it will grow.'

'Yes, Grandfather.'

Poor old fellow. He was sucking hard at his pipe. 'Do you get my meaning?'

'Yes, Grandfather,' Charlie had said. He was trying not to laugh. Thank God Arthur wasn't there.

Giving his back a pat, his grandfather had said, 'Fine lad, good fellow.'

Was that all?

The pipe was drawing strongly.

That, indeed, was all.

Charlie had left him to Grandmother:

Well? – he could hear it – Grandma all beaky and pecking, waiting for Grandfather to tell.

–Fine lad, good fellow. Grandfather retreating into man-to-man.

–What did you *tell* him?

–That if he planted a potato it would grow.

–A potato?

–Yes.

–Oh, Charles! Really!

Poor old Grandfather would have got it in the neck.

Footer. Honour. Sex. But what of Love and Death? These he feared. For what, in the end, did Love do to Death and Death to Love? Did one change or cancel the other? Could Love transcend Death or was Death always weighted for victory? What if there wasn't time to be loved enough to be remembered? What if there was no redemption – like his father, receding out of memory: a slow, inexorable journey to nothingness. *That* was death.

–Your father's death was an unfortunate accident, Charlie, his mother had said the last time they had visited the grave.

He did not contradict her. Suicide was not an option. It was her own denial, a way of shielding him from the need to atone. But

197

atonement – somehow, sometime – was what she wanted. To atone was to assuage the fear.

　　–Could he have his father's streak?

　　–He could, poor lad.

　　–Melancholy?

　　–If you wish . . .

She had said, –We must always do our duty and not buckle, Charlie.

She had not buckled: twenty-one years old, a child-in-arms and almost destitute. She would have to be dependent on parents, siblings, until Charlie grew up.

Earnest small fellow, wearing his new long pants – embryonic man – on leaving for school for the first time:

　　–I'll build you a house, Moth. With a nice white gable and a
　　gravel driveway and a fanlight over the door.

What did Death do to Love and Love to Death?

They had stood by the grave in the wind, in that high, bleak place, with the hills a deep, distant stain of blue, lost in dust-haze.

　　Eyes to the front.

　　No sentiment.

　　No betrayal.

　　Iron love.

　　Was this how it must be?

She had not brought flowers. She had picked instead two sun-speckled roses from an old briar on the hedge, almost peremptorily. She did not look at him. He had wished she would. Perhaps they would never come here again. Perhaps the old grey cross would sink into anonymity, the letters weather out. He had taken a photograph, almost apologetically, fixing some identity. He had stooped and pulled up a small, faded helichrysum from the foot of the stone cross. He had tried secretly to coax it into growing, tending the shoot of pale, furry leaves, needing it to bud. It had withered and shrivelled into a black net of tough fibres. It had seemed like a defeat.

Charlie Fraser spent a lot of time kicking the ball. More than anyone else. The consequence – the often heard remark of the coach – 'We'll do all right on Saturday, Fraser's solid as a stone wall. His boot is absolutely safe.' It was not only his boot.

Robbie knew it. GB knew it, Arthur knew it. Herbert. Davey Bennett had known it: at the threshold, he'd saluted it. Charlie Fraser conducted himself with self-discipline and discretion. He got on with it. There would be no breach.

It was what his mother expected of him.

It was what others expected of him.

It was what he expected of himself.

But then he'd seen her.

She'd looked back at him through the window of the Cathedral Café, brushing her hair from her eyes. Green eyes, slanted elf-green, straight into his.

She'd unsettled everything. Arthur. Him. Them. Just by a glance.

So he kicked the ball more strenuously. Every afternoon before prep he took it down to the field and he kicked it. Every morning before breakfast, he kicked it.

'GB, does Fraser have a girlfriend?'

'What's it to you, Parkes?'

'Graham does.'

GB spat on Charlie Fraser's rugby boot and rubbed with his cloth. 'So?'

'He wrote to her.'

GB kept on polishing. Damn Graham: he'd been waiting for Fraser to write someone a letter and he never did, except to his mother on Sundays like everyone else and his grandparents every other week.

'Don't you want to know who to?'

'Who to?' said GB, with exaggerated indifference.

'A girl called Hilda Knight. I took the letter. I had to promise not to tell. He said he'd hang me out of the window if I did.'

'Rot.' Graham never bullied nubs.

Parkes was waiting, polishing more slowly, knowing GB would

199

have to ask: 'Is she pretty?'

'I posted it, I didn't deliver it. So I don't know.'

'Why? Isn't she at school?'

'No,' said Parkes triumphantly, with a well-rehearsed superiority. 'She's a music student at university.'

'Then how could he know her?'

'Remember in the café?'

'Then she won't write back.'

'She already has.'

'How do you know?'

'I saw her letter.'

'Did you read it?'

Parkes said nothing but he rubbed Arthur's boot with renewed vigour.

'I would never, ever read Fraser's letters,' said GB loftily. 'Not for a thousand pounds.'

'He doesn't get any.'

'If he did.'

'Graham doesn't know!' retorted Parkes. 'He left it lying on his desk.'

'That's not the point,' said GB, drawing himself up.

'Your Adam's apple's jumping like a frog,' said Parkes. 'Can't you stop it?'

GB wrenched up his collar. When he couldn't bear it any longer, he said, 'What'd it say?'

'That she'd come to the dance with him and that Gilbert had told her all about him. And that he could write back if he wanted to.'

'Which one do you think she was?' said GB.

'How should I know?' Parkes was quite offended. 'Do you think I looked?'

'The tall girl was the only pretty one,' said GB.

'Well, that's her then.'

'Bet it's not.'

'Bet it is.'

'How much?'

'Four marbles and an ironie.'

The price was high. GB rubbed away. Bet she liked Fraser more. Bet she did. He threaded the laces. 'How does Gilbert know her?'

'Gilbert knows everyone at university.'

'Do you think Gilbert has a girlfriend?'

They both laughed and spat at their boots simultaneously.

'I can hit yours. Hold it still.' GB spat again. It caught Arthur's boot on the toe.

Parkes spat back. GB deftly lifted it out of the way. He grinned. No one spat on Fraser's boots but him.

Herbert was at a loss. It was already Thursday. What was he to do? You couldn't ask a fellow like Charlie Fraser to go to tea with you out of the blue. It was unthinkable. He was in a real jam. There was no one to consult – certainly not Percy on a matter like this and Davey Bennett wasn't there. What would Davey have said?

–Ask whoever's hungriest. That's what he'd have said.

–Why?

–'Cos if you offer a tea to someone who's always hungry he won't bother too much about why you asked him.

Edwards. No. He would say something embarrassing or he'd fool around and make Josie Zeederberg laugh which might take the advantage from Herbert himself. Pringle? He'd never go to tea with a girl, even if there were fifty kinds of cake. He'd be more likely to bring his cattie along and aim it at her – bull's-eye – right between the eyes. He went through every fellow in his form. None would do. If only Davey Bennett was there. He'd have come along quite comfortably and not intruded and said all the right things and wandered off into the garden without any nudging when Herbert had wanted him to. But Davey was gone so there was no use harping on it.

Arthur saved him. It was a completely unexpected reprieve. Almost Charlie himself.

'Why are you looking so gloomy, Aap-face?' Arthur said, as they had walked up from footer practice.

'I have to go out to tea on Saturday.'

'And you're complaining!'

'There'll be lots of cake and things, but . . . ,' sending a swift glance to see if Arthur suspected him, 'it's awkward going alone.'

'I'll come with you.' Arthur was quite sanguine. He never treated Herbert as a junior. Tea with an ogre – if there was cake – was tolerable.

'Will you? Thanks, Graham.' Taking the advantage home, 'Maybe you'd like to bring one of the other fellows . . . who doesn't get out that often.'

'Sparrow?'

'He goes out all the time.' Definitely *not* Sparrow. He'd beguile Josie Zeederberg and every other female in the family just by saying good afternoon.

'Doug?' It got worse and worse. Josie Zeederberg would be furious with him. Besides it was a monstrous cheek to invite extras without consulting her.

'He'd eat up all the cake.'

'True,' said Arthur. 'Count Charlie out – he's not a tea-and-cake man and he never talks in company he doesn't know, so he's a waste of time.'

Damn.

'Ask him anyway.'

'He won't come.'

'Well, just you then,' said Herbert.

'Where are we going?'

'Zeederbergs.'

Arthur started to laugh. 'You feeling nervous, Apie?' He gave him a small shove. 'I think you should do this one alone. You don't want other fellows hanging around.'

'Please,' said Herbert, desperate. He couldn't go alone. Josie Zeederberg had only asked him because of Charlie. Why, he didn't know. It was all too complicated. He was wading about, knee deep. Perhaps he could get sick by tomorrow afternoon.

'One thing . . . is Zeedy going to be there?' Arthur was suddenly suspicious. An audience with Zeedy had to be weighed up against the standard and the quantity of cake.

'I don't know.'

Arthur looked as if he was going to back out.

'There are lots of daughters,' said Herbert, overlooking the fact that two of them, the second pair of Zeedy twins, were less than a year old and went for a ride every other afternoon along the bottom of Lower field in a large perambulator, sitting face to face with bonnets bobbing, glaring at eath other like two cross old ladies in a carriage.

'Right,' said Arthur, convinced.

'Right,' said Herbert.

Right indeed. Arthur stood in the hallway of the Zeederbergs' bulging little house and stared. And stared. Because, wafting down towards him as he waited in the hall, trailing a mist of carelessness, was the vision from the Cathedral Café: Hilda Knight, the girl he had written to; the person who had said she would come to the dance with him; the glorious girl from the music department. Percy's acquaintance. He had a letter to prove it.

Only, she wasn't Hilda Knight, after all.

'This is my sister, Annie,' said Josie Zeederberg rather peremptorily, looking vexed. Why Arthur Graham? Where was Charles Fraser? She could not look at Herbert squirming about at the door as if he'd been sentenced to the gallows. It wasn't he – appalling boy – who would be hanged! Annie was breathing death at her neck. *Where* was Fraser? Her prim little greeting, 'Good afternoon,' and her half frowning smile, could not quite hide the just-wait-'til-I-get-you-Josie-Zeederberg in her stance.

'Annie?' said Arthur. Go on Arthur, keep on croaking. You will turn into a frog in a minute. Herbert was ready to run.

'Yes,' said Josie. 'Short for Ann.'

'Short for Ann?'

'Well, long for Ann, if you like,' said Josie Zeederberg, frowning at him. Were all Cummings' friends as dumb as he was?

'Right.'

A diversion was caused by the appearance of Harry Zeederberg. He looked astonished to see them standing there. 'Graham?' he said, with due respect, 'Apie?' giving him such an exaggerated leer that Herbert could have punched him. And the nickname! In front of

Josie Zeederberg! Herbert stared a yard ahead of him. He dared not look at Annie. She was so extraordinarily lofty, he would wither away with a glance.

'Harry!' said Josie, narrowing her eyes. 'Get out of here in those boots! Mum will thrash you for bringing in mud and donkey manure.'

Harry ignored her. 'I've got fellows for tea,' he said to Annie.

'You can't!' said Josie.

'I said he could,' said Annie.

'Who?'

'Edwards and Fatty Harman, to see how much cake he can eat before he explodes.'

'My God!' said Josie Zeederberg, turning down the passage.

'Language, Josie!' A voice floated vaguely from a door to the right. Mrs Zeederberg. Poor Mrs Zeederberg. Always distracted – writing love stories with eight children and a pile of mending to attend to. She appeared, dragging yards of knitting wool. 'Go out on the back porch, Harry,' she said. 'It's very rude to bring guests to see them harm themselves. Good afternoon, boys' – absently to Arthur and Herbert – 'are you wishing to see Mr Zeederberg? He went to Port Elizabeth in the train yesterday, I'm afraid. I got a message' – bending and picking up the escaped strands – 'the dear man only packed his pipe and a newspaper. What is he to do for clothes for the rest of the week?'

Arthur laughed. It was so spontaneous, Annie laughed too. And so did Mrs Zeederberg.

'They've come for tea,' said Annie. 'Josie invited them.'

'Did she? Well done, Josie!'

Josie made her back even straighter than before. Clip, clip, clip, she marched off down the passage to the living-room in her disreputable boots.

'When you've made the tea, bring me a cup,' said Mrs Zeederberg. 'There's a loaf of gingerbread in the pantry and another in the tin on the top shelf. Take that too. And do keep an eye on Harry. I don't want any accidents or to have Mr Robinson round here complaining. He's too extraordinary. That poor child . . .' It was unclear of whom she was speaking, but one assumed Fatty Harman's fate concerned her, in passing. 'And the tea, dear, it's in the apron drawer. I hid it from Gracie. She was feeding it to her dolls. Do you want me to show you?'

Annie paid no attention to her mother. She turned to Arthur and she said, 'You can come with me and carry the tray.' Arthur trotted down the passage after her: newborn lamb, all faculties deserted. Annie turned to him, chatting over her arch little shoulder, 'What's your name?' she said. 'My sister's introductions are rather sketchy.'

'Arthur Graham.' Croak, croak, croak.

'Of course.' Oh, so gracious. She smiled then. 'You're the winger.'

'Yes. How did you know?'

'I know everything that's important.'

Josie rolled her eyes. 'Herbert is also in the Firsts,' she said loudly so her voice carried after them.

'Really?' Annie glanced back. Clearly she hadn't seen him at all. 'You're very young for the Firsts.'

'Annie . . .'

'I'll watch the next match and shout for you.' She went to the tray, already laid so beautifully, with beguiling little touches: Charles Fraser was coming to tea. She put aside the flower in the cream jug rather fractiously. She turned suddenly and said – and Arthur, if he hadn't been so mesmerised, would have known it was a ploy – 'You're the fellow from the café last Saturday! You dropped the teapot.'

Arthur grinned sheepishly.

No, her eyes weren't brown. They were green. Slanting green, almond eyes with a little scar just under one. 'It was you, wasn't it?' she was saying. 'You were with another fellow. That's it. Now I know you.' A little gesture, a finger on the sleeve of his jacket, lingering a moment, playful. She took the kettle from the stove and filled the pot. Arthur's face was ablaze: Danny at his worst, Sparrow just before combustion. He could have matched them both.

'It was you – and your friend. Sort of . . . bulky chap . . .'

Bulky? Charlie?

She used her hands, a gesture more suggestive of Douggie Morgan. 'Never seen him before.'

'Never seen him?'

205

That Arthur found difficult to believe. But then, they had never seen her before either. Where had she been while they were sprouting into their ears and feet and knees under her father's eye?

'I was at school in Port Elizabeth,' she said, divining him. 'I was too troublesome to keep at home! That's why I have never seen you or that other fellow' – dropped so carelessly – 'what's his name?'

'Charles Fraser.'

'Rather a solemn chap,' she said as though it were only a passing thought.

'He's got a lot on his mind,' said Arthur, at a loss.

'Really? Is something wrong?' Keep on wading in, boy. Annie smiled – with all her eyes – at him. 'Poor fellow! Is he all right?'

'There's nothing to worry about,' said Arthur. 'He's perfectly sound.'

'Oh?' with an encouraging little inclination of her head again. 'Sound, is he?'

'He's a very decent chap.' Arthur bent to lean on the kitchen table, almost missed it with his elbows. What if he had – and had fallen face first on the floor?

She was waiting.

'Very decent,' said Arthur. She must leave it now. One didn't get sentimental or expansive about another fellow in his absence. It wasn't Charlie who had come to tea. Thank God.

'Are you friends?'

'Since prep school.' He took the tray from her. He mustn't drop it. He breathed out instead of in when he had meant to inhale something of her, standing so close. He got it wrong. It was almost a snort. He hurried off with the tray and put it down, looking pointedly at Herbert. Herbert seemed quite at ease, not making faces at him or touching his nose or shaking his head at him to indicate that he was dangling 'dags'. But Arthur took out his handkerchief anyway and made sure.

Annie poured the tea. She did not trust Arthur with a porcelain teapot. Josie handed round the cups. No one said anything for a few minutes.

Arthur tried not to stare at Annie Zeederberg: the girl he had written to, his partner for the dance, heroine of so many hours of reckless fantasy. And she had no idea. None at all. What on earth was he to do? And *who*, in God's name, was Hilda Knight? He couldn't remember any of the others. And though Annie Zeederberg was only seventeen, younger than he, she might as well have been twenty-five with her student portmanteau and her music books and being the eldest in the family and directing things as though she were the mother. Arthur balanced his teacup with exquisite precision. He looked at her feet instead of her face.

'Harry?' Annie hearing footsteps in the passage. 'Has your friend exploded yet?'

'No, but we need more cake.'

'There are rusks in the pantry and raisin loaf on the kitchen table.'

'He won't eat that,' said Harry.

'Too bad then. He'll live to eat another day,' said Annie. Harry made faces at Josie, sent sly looks in Herbert's direction, helped himself to a slice he had not been offered. He had been followed by the family dog. The cake came perilously close to being swept away with its tongue and its tail. It was an old, squat bull terrier bitch with black patches on both ears. She looked at each of them in turn, head to the side, observing with one eye at a time. Haunched like a little warthog, stiff legged, big footed, she sat before Herbert and contemplated him – sideways and up: such a blackcurrant eye, pink rimmed and lashless. She was so astonishingly ugly, Herbert grinned. The dog grinned back.

'Petal, sit,' said Annie. Petal did not sit. Petal did a little backwards turn, a pirouette in reverse, neatly avoiding the furniture. It was clearly well rehearsed.

'Show off!' said Josie.

'How can she be called Petal?' said Herbert. 'Looking like that?'

Josie laughed. 'Petal suits her very well, I think. We always call the things we love best "Petal".'

'Why?'

'Just because . . .' Josie could not explain the family nonsense talk, the ridiculous names, the whole Vocabulary of Love. One had to be born into it to understand.

Petal was given a saucer of milk. 'She's getting on,' said Josie. 'She's already twelve.' Josie looked at her gravely. 'She's old, but feisty. She'd bite you if I told her to.'

'Nonsense, Josie,' said Annie, rising. 'Come and look at the garden, Arthur,' she said. 'I need to check on the littles. We have hordes of them and I must see if Harry's friend is plastered all over the porch.' Arthur would have walked into the wall if she'd told him to.

Annie led the way. Outside she could get onto footer without Josie listening and dissecting everything she said. She could get on to the team. She could ask about positions – half-backs and centre three-quarters. She knew quite well where Charles Winton Fraser played. She'd sneaked a look in Harry's magazine from last year. If only there had been a picture. She would get Arthur to come back again and tell him to bring his friends. Arthur was a very dear chap. Very dear indeed. Funny too. Nice crinkly eyes. Nice teeth. Nice smell.

Poor Arthur: so neatly packaged.

Fatty Harman had not exploded. Edwards stood up and greeted Annie Zeederberg most affably and did not embarrass Arthur Graham by looking at him. He was far too much in awe of the great man. Fatty Harman stood too. He always seemed so disconsolate, not the chubby-happy sort at all. Arthur leaned against a tree, put his hands in his pockets, crossed one leg over the other, most relaxed, and looked distant. Edwards and Harman must go away.

Annie went across the garden to the swing. Two small boys were fooling around on the chains on which it was suspended. Annie sent them off. She sat on it herself and asked Arthur to push her. It was a miracle that the swing – speeding back – did not knock him out: the little rush of wind she left behind was intoxicating.

Herbert and Josie Zeederberg had an argument.

'Why did you bring him instead of Fraser?'

'Fraser couldn't come.'

'Bet you didn't ask him.'

'Why shouldn't I ask him?'

''Cos you're scared of him.'

'I am not.' What rot.

Josie shrugged. 'Bet you bribed Arthur Graham with cake.'

Witch.

Getting her back, 'Are you that desperate to meet him?'

'Me? Of course not!' Rapped out roundly. In doing it – too late to retreat – Josie had given herself away. And Annie. She went red, despite herself. Now what was she to say?

'Then why did you ask me to bring him?

She fed bits of icing to Petal. 'A sort of dare.'

'With who?'

Josie hesitated.

'With who?'

'With . . . myself.'

'Why?'

–Because of you. And never mind Annie.

But she could not say it, so she said instead, 'To see if you're really such a buck as they say you are.'

'Who says?'

'People.' She meant girls.

For wearing the wide-striped jersey, for being in the XV, for knowing Charlie Fraser well enough to bring him along.

Discussed by girls.

Herbert glowered.

Josie bent down and scratched Petal's bald, scabby nose. Thank God boys were idiots: she'd had a narrow escape.

Arthur and Herbert walked back to school together: bestriding mountains up the bank from Lower to Upper, overstepping torrents at the *sloot*, swords unsheathed, armour burnished, colours streaming. Their blazer pockets were sticky with extra slices of cake.

One for Charlie. Another for Charlie.

–Charlie is not a tea-and-cake man.

Is that so?

'Charlie!' Arthur said. 'Guess what?'

Charlie turned from his desk where he was working on his album.

'I had tea with her.' Arthur tossed a piece of cake at him as evidence.

'Tea with who?' Charlie ate the slice with every appearance of enjoyment, licking his fingers and wiping them rather carelessly on his trousers.

'*Her. Her.*' Arthur took him by the lapels.

'Hilda Knight?'

'Yes. Except no, she's not Hilda Knight. I have it all wrong. She's Annie Zeederberg. Zeedy's daughter come back from PE. Why did you say she was Hilda Knight?'

'I didn't. You did.'

'I couldn't have been that unobservant.'

'You big arse, Graham. Now what are you going to do?'

'Oh, my God!'

'Quite!'

'I'll have to get out of the invitation to Hilda Knight.'

'You can't.'

'I must.'

'You know you can't.'

How the hell had Arthur managed to have tea with her?

ELEVEN

Wretched prefects wanting a dance. And wretched Miss Maltby for encouraging it, conniving with the old biddies in the other houses as if they didn't have enough to preoccupy them with laundry and housemaids. She had already spoken to Miss van Ryneveld at the university about playing the waltzes and Miss White about the flowers and Mrs Clark about the trifles and custard. She was marching about with lists that had nothing to do with mislaid socks or broken trunk hinges. It was very annoying. She had even spoken to members of something called The Quadrille Band to provide the rest of the music. The place would be overtaken by women. Bunting in the Drill Hall! It was time for the holidays and a trip by train to Kimberley and a week's shooting with a chum. Campfire, wagon, tent and a few good yarns. Sandgrouse on the pans in the morning at sunrise. Francolin at sunset. Empty veld. Empty skies. That was what he needed. Wretched boys. What business did they have with dancing? They should be packed off on Cadet Camp to practise manoeuvres in the dunes and have a few strategic skirmishes to get their mettle up. It would cure them of dancing and all the attendant mischief.

The wretched Head as well, supporting them. Just listen to it! First three holes on the course discussing the iniquities of the boys, the next three the iniquities of the staff, the last three the iniquities of the bunkers. And then:

'Well, my dear fellow,' said the Head, setting his ball and making

211

a delicate practice swing, 'I think it a good idea to let them have a bit of gentle company every now and then. Part of their education. We don't want them to grow up complete barbarians.'

Barbarians? His boys? His good fellows? It was only when females entered the scene that they started scrapping with each other or behaving regrettably. They were perfectly sound until the girls minced by. There was always a female at the core of any real trouble: foolish fellows entering the grounds of the girls' school at night to ring the bell. Perfectly sound boys dangling on the ropes like baboons! Such a great haroosh about it all. Look at the debate! Did you ever see anything like Morgan – sound, perfectly sound in the House – posturing about to make another fellow blush for him! And Grant, glowing like the rising sun and dumb as an ape because some girl offered him buns! What would he do if he had to face the firing line? And Cummings, risking his worthy neck to hang out of windows for some chit who looked like a harridan to him. And poor Arthur Graham. There was really no hope for the fellow. One could see it. He would walk gaily into some domestic morass with every appearance of enjoyment. He'd have one of those adoring wives with a way with her who would have him trotting behind her carrying her knitting or carting children about on his shoulders. He'd be bowed down by debt with a dozen little mouths to feed. And what was so wretched was he'd probably think himself the happiest man alive when he had the makings of a really first class soldier. Courageous. Strong. Steady. Undismayed. Not too filled up with imaginative nonsense not to take an order without flinching.

Even the fall-out between Gilbert and MacCallum had something to do with females. It was all very uncomfortable. At any rate, it seemed to be for Gilbert. Odd fellow. But sound. Very sound on any matter of principle. If he didn't end up a don he'd be a fine physician. A headmaster. A bishop. What on earth would Gilbert want with a dance?

MacCallum was behind it, egging on Seymour and Holmes, distracting them. MacCallum, with his levantine looks – very debonair – was the sort who might acquire, in later life, a certain

212

reputation. That was the wretchedness of women, luring perfectly sound fellows like MacCallum. One would never want, in time, to question 'character', to hear rumour – disseminated by women – to wound. Character was not what a fellow knew or did but what he *was*. And women – not all women, certainly, but the sort that laid siege to fellows like MacCallum – had a way of undermining that. They chipped away at it. They could make a man forget himself. To his everlasting embarrassment.

If they had a dance, all the senior girls would be hanging about MacCallum. He, with a carnation in his buttonhole and all that dark charm, being secretly dissected without knowing the danger he was in. And the upshot was that Percy Gilbert would be cynical for days and take himself about with a kind of careless spite that was very disturbing to everyone. And very familiar.

Women made men unreliable. That was their menace. Such dependable fellows, suddenly lost.

Only Fraser could be relied on. Perhaps it was the missionary in him.

Or the mythic.

Perhaps, after all, Fraser had been invented, clapped in armour, the fact that he was just a boy forgotten. Fraser was insurance against the commonplace and dreary: invented, without consent.

The Head was waiting for him. Robbie selected a club as though he were inspecting the armoury, found one and removed it – presenting arms – took a shot that left him in a bunker.

'It causes such a commotion,' he said.

'What does?' The Head had long since left the dance behind.

'Dances!' said Robbie, rather savagely. 'And a whole lot of misery as well.'

'Misery?' The Head laughed. 'My dear fellow, it's supposed to be an entertainment to celebrate the end of the term and the start of the holidays.'

'For the fellows who aren't able to bring themselves to ask a female to the floor – such misery.'

The Head walked down towards the bunker with him. Poor old Robbie. No doubt he was speaking of himself.

'I have already consulted Miss Fowler,' said the Head. 'It's very acceptable to her. There will be a lot of sisters and cousins which will keep it light-hearted.' The Head put down his golf bag and wiped his forehead with his handkerchief. 'They need to develop some social graces. What will become of the lads who go up to Oxford or Cambridge if they behave like colonial rough-necks? We shall be the laughing stock!'

–What if they go to war instead? There'll be no Quadrille Band and bunting then.

Robbie tramped after his senior. He said nothing.

Arthur was vexed. If he hadn't been so hasty! Damn and blast. How could he have muddled her name? It was Percy's fault!

Percy's fault? Percy would have resented that. He was far too bleak and preoccupied to bother with Hilda Knight. But he had been mean, he acknowledged it: he knew he'd handed out more essays than was fair and when Arthur Graham had come and asked him some days before if he could supply the full name of a student called 'Hilda' who was studying music, he'd been irritable and cutting. 'Hilda Knight?' he'd said, at last.

'The very lovely girl with the beautiful smile . . .'

'She seems pleasant enough,' Percy had said, taking up his pen and dipping it in the ink. He had not wished to get into any conversations about women again. What he said was always misconstrued.

'The music student?'

'The music student.'

'With the sort of' – Arthur had made a swirling kind of gesture round his head – 'hair that's up and falling down.'

'Perhaps it was a windy day when you met her.'

'Well, anyway, that one.'

'I assume so. If you say her name is Hilda.'

'Have you talked to her?'

'Yes.' Impatient and dismissive.

'Do you think it would be all right if I asked her to our dance?'

'She's not married,' Percy had answered briskly.

'I'll write, but will you sound her out, Daisy? Just test the water?'

'Miss Knight' – Percy orchestrating a conversation with the wall – 'I am sounding you out. Testing the water, as it were. There is a boy at school who is smitten and wants to dance with you.'

'No, no, Daisy.'

'He's a frightfully handsome fellow, Miss Knight, do not look alarmed.' Percy had turned and contemplated Arthur. 'He is exceedingly tall and well – heroic?' Percy had paused. 'Broad-shouldered, Miss Knight, the winger in the XV, lightning fast. Also, a splendid cricketer,' building to a crescendo, 'a prefect! . . . and, might I add, I wouldn't be surprised if he were your senior by a year or two, so don't fret that he's a baby.'

'Don't you dare say that,' Arthur had retorted hotly.

'Well, it's true, isn't it?' Percy had forgotten himself. 'Why *are* you still at school?'

Arthur had left abruptly. Percy, hating himself for taking it out on the fellow, had shoved his chair back and gone after him. 'Arthur,' he'd called him. 'I have to make a case for why a schoolboy wants to take a student to a dance. I'm sorry.'

'You fellows are at school yourselves even if you are in the university classes,' said Arthur resentfully. 'Why d'you have to bring the school bit up at all?'

'Because she's never seen you with us and she'll wonder.'

Arthur had said nothing. It always came back to the same thing. He was thick. Stupid. Ignorant. He was the last to deny it. First the maths teacher, now Percy.

Percy said, trying to repair it, 'Seymour has invited a student as well, but she's a cousin, so you've outdone the Headboy this time! I'll tell Miss Knight you ran away to seek your fortune for a year and your education was interrupted by all sorts of exploits on the diamond fields. You're destined to be the hero of the hour.'

'Stop talking rot.'

'I won't let you down.' Percy had patted him on the shoulder.

Mollified, Arthur had said, 'If she accepts.'

There was no accounting for taste, Percy had thought as he returned to his room and taken up his pen again, scratching across the paper to set his teeth on edge. Hilda Knight talked incessantly, laughed inexorably, played the piano badly and had black hair and eyes. She was a jolly sort of girl, friendly, but she would drive Arthur mad in ten minutes and she was at least a foot and a bit shorter. She'd be looking him straight in the navel!

Percy had written himself a reminder in his notebook: *Ask The Midget if she wants to go to the dance with AGG*.

A note had followed. A prettily written reply returned. Another note – a little longer. Arthur had agonised over his spelling. He had a romance before he knew it – with a girl whom he had never seen, even if she had sat two yards from him in the café. Who on earth was Hilda? It was worse than the worst mistaken identity films shown at The Great Electric Bioscope. All it lacked was a villain – Archer with a menacing cape, Unwin as a levitating corpse, Percy with a poisonous potion or a sputtering cannonball while Miss van Ryneveld trilled sinister chords on the piano, hidden behind the curtains. He was wretched. And Charlie was no help at all. He said exactly what Arthur did not want to hear: if he'd sent an invitation, he had to stick to it. Which was true. But the invitation in his head and the reality of the proposal were entirely different. Did that bind him? And what of Annie? Who would take her to the dance? Some fellow from the university classes in an evening suit, someone like Mac, sashaying around the floor with her while he heaved himself about in his old black shoes and Sunday pants that were too short for him with someone called Hilda Knight. If Percy's recent –Ah, the Midget. Sharp little thing, was anything to go by, he'd be engaged for the evening with a vituperative dwarf.

'Are you going to invite anyone, Charles?' Arthur was really very gloomy.

'What for?'

'Why not?'

'Don't know anyone to invite.'

'Who would you *like* to invite?'

–It's who *you* would like to invite, Arthur.

'No one in particular,' Charlie said at last.

But that was a lie.

And he couldn't ask her because of Arthur.

Nor did he tell him that he'd seen her when he'd walked to town on an errand for the science master. He'd been to the photographer's, and to the post office to buy some stamps. He had stopped at Birch's for a new pair of rugby socks and at Grocott's for some writing paper, drawing it out. He had walked up the street alone, in the shadow of the cathedral, glancing up at the clock which glinted gold in the late afternoon sun. Not long ago old Professor Cory had been swung out on an armchair to apply gilding to the faded figures. Charlie grinned. Imagine the old fellow, perched airily aloft in a living-room chair, leaning forward in a brisk wind with the crowd below, agape. Imagine so much eminence scattered about on the pavement!

He crossed the street. He walked alert. He always walked alert, but this was different. He was watching, scenting.

Make it happen.

And it did.

The sun was warm, the wind sharp and sudden round the corners. He passed the Cathedral Café and Radomsky's Tobacconists. Clerks were going in and out of the old Court building. Here was Mr Moorrees, one of the young masters, hurrying down the pavement. Raise your hat: 'Afternoon, sir.'

'Fraser!' Rapping it out.

He walked on past the Diocesan offices. The old tree outside was creaking in the wind. And there was the Reverend Zeederberg, coming out, wreathed in pipe smoke, a brown paper parcel under his arm, preoccupied with arranging his pockets.

'Afternoon, Father.'

'Fraser, my boy.'

Hesitate. Never hesitated for Zeedy before. Stand, barring his way, hat in hand, turning it.

Zeedy, at something of a loss, said, 'How is your grandfather, lad?'

'Well, I think, sir. I'll see him in the holidays. I heard last week.'

Absent-mindedly, 'Ah . . . good fellow.'

'He has had gout,' said Charlie. Since when had he chatted about Grandpa's gout to anyone? Grandma would be horrified. Only old men who took too much port got gout.

217

'Gout? Is he fond of wine?'

'Yes, sir.'

'Not good for gout.'

The Reverend Zeederberg did not look as though he disapproved, however. He took his tobacco pouch out of his pocket and frowned off down the street. 'I'm waiting for my children,' he said. 'They are always late.'

'Where have they been, sir?' Politely. Charlie felt the heat of the sun through his jacket.

'My daughter, Annie, took the little ones to the library. It's always too exhausting for my wife. They run about so. We are very glad to have Annie home.'

'Has she been away, sir?'

'In Port Elizabeth. There are so many children in the house. My wife's cousin offered to have her. It was so much better for her to have a little independence without child-minding all the time, so she could get on with her schooling. My wife is very busy. Ah, here they are!' Old Zeedy watched his brood crossing the street. 'Well, lad . . . there they are, then. Still don't look from right to left. Watch out! What is Annie about?'

Annie Zeederberg, with her arms full of books, was trying to guide them over before a wagon ran them down. 'Hurry up, Gracie!' She was looking cross and bothered.

Charlie watched: don't dismiss me yet. Not yet.

'Do give my greetings to your grandfather when you write,' said Zeedy, stepping off the pavement to herd the children into a group.

'I think he will be here for Synod soon.'

'Of course! So he will. I shall see him then.' Zeedy was not with him any more.

'Yes,' said Charlie.

It was the moment to go. Zeedy had forgotten him.

Still he stood, feeling the old stone wall behind him, the arch to his left, the tall white house at the corner, the sun bright on its gable. He stood, just a moment longer.

'That's Fraser, Annie,' said one of the small boys, staring over at him. 'He's the best at footer.'

'Annie knows that!' said the other scornfully. 'She asked Harry!'

'Hush,' said Annie, shifting the books in her arms and nearly dropping them.

She glanced at Charlie, dipping her head, a sort of apology. He should have stepped forward then to help her with the books but he was rooted. She looked again, fleetingly, over the heads of the children, past her father. Straight in the eyes.

Had he smiled back? He didn't think so. He didn't know. He had raised his hat. That much was ingrained. Had he stood for an hour or had he walked away?

Had the Reverend Zeederberg said, 'Fraser, this is my eldest daughter, Annie. Tom, Will and Gracie,' indicating the little ones, 'Annie – Charles Fraser, grandson of my old friend'?

'Miss Zeederberg.'

Was it an introduction or not? He'd taken his hat off and turned it in his hands again, not having anything else to say. And then he'd walked away, knowing she was watching him.

'*Who* is that boy?' said Annie Zeederberg to her father.

'Name's Fraser. Old Canon Taberer's grandson. Dear old chap.'

'Who? The grandson?' She laughed, light-hearted, making a small skip.

'Silly girl,' he said. 'The grandfather.'

'He's very handsome.' She could say what she liked to her father.

'Is he?' He patted her elbow, taking some of the books from her. 'I expect he is.'

'Do you know his grandfather well?'

'I don't see him often.'

'Where does this fellow live?'

'Young Fraser? Lives on the mission with his mother and grand-parents, I think. The father died.'

'What of?'

'Died young. Sad case.'

'Why?'

'What a lot of questions! Do you know what happens to people who ask questions all the time?'

'Bother the Devil!'

Her father laughed.

'Annie wants him to come to tea,' said Gracie.

'Don't talk nonsense,' said Annie.

'You do!'

'I don't know him from Adam,' said Annie sharply.

'Well, then why did you shout at Josie the other day for bringing those other boys to tea instead of him?'

'I did not!'

'You did! Harry said!'

Annie shook her shoulders. 'What does Harry know?'

Boy standing by the old grey-brown street wall under the trees. The late shadows of the afternoon shifting, making light prisms on his face. A boy, shoulders straining his jacket, his hat in his hands. Well-veined. Strong wrists. A little frown drawing his eyebrows in. A small pucker on his forehead.

Stop, boy. Wait. Don't walk on.

He had walked on and she had walked a hundred yards behind, seeing him going up the hill ahead. No slackening of the pace, no change in the steady, easy stride. He did not turn.

The children took the corner below the school, over the bridge and right, running ahead of Annie and their father. He was still going up the hill towards the House. It was hard to see him in the shadow of the stone pines. The sun fell across his shoulders, like a yoke he carried easily. He was gone.

But he did stop. He did turn when he knew they would be out of sight. He looked back down the hill and breathed again.

He saw her in church. Once, he saw her, way off, hurrying into Abbott's Chemist. He saw her with her family, all in a line, walking into town. He saw her pushing the Zeedy twins up the street in their carriage. She had to struggle a bit on the slope. One of the babies fell forward. He couldn't hear from that distance, but by her gesturing and her braking the carriage with her foot and her pulling off her hat and plumping it down between them and the sharp wriggle she gave the carriage by the handle, he concluded that she was having a hard time of it and had something to say! He laughed quietly, standing in the high-up window of the House. He did not move until she was out of sight behind the gable of the Head's bungalow.

He saw her all the time. He did not speak to her. Sometimes he smiled. Sometimes she smiled. Sometimes they simply looked and it seemed that she was waiting. But he could only stand clod-footed, or walk away.

Arthur sought her out when he could, however briefly, loitering after church to exchange a word, looking for the baby carriage and then sallying forth, very jaunty, as if on an errand. She talked to Arthur any time – with the babies squalling, without the babies squalling, Harry hanging about or not, Gracie entangling her legs in the perambulator wheels, small brothers scrapping – it was all the same. She was as light as a bubble, floating here and there around his head, over his head, into his head. She was there, then gone, taken by the breeze. Arthur would come back breathless, fling himself in a chair. There was nothing that he liked to talk of more, in a roundabout way, but Charlie knew. Charlie was patient. He didn't laugh.

Charlie did not tell Arthur – he could not – that Annie sometimes watched him when he kicked at posts. She did not conceal herself. She might look over the hedge, or stand at the gap, or glance up from a book she was reading on the swing. Sometimes she watched quite candidly. She might stand with one of the babies on her hip, pointing him out. It was he who was uncomfortable then: there was something in the way she did it that seemed to indicate to him that he was of no more interest than the other things which gave the babies entertainment – a hadedah dipping its beak, the ubiquitous pigeons wheeling, a donkey cart in the road. Was she really watching him or was she playing games? He couldn't tell any more.

He began to doubt himself: he developed a preference for the posts nearer the Zeederbergs' hedge rather than the others at which he had usually punted. He did not admit it to himself: he decided they were a more tricky obstacle and needed to be tackled before the Big Match. He decided too that he would frown her away if she distracted him. He did not frown. He hardly dared look in her direction.

Charlie had kicked at posts for years, done gaining grounds, run about the field quite unselfconsciously. Now, he was alert to everything. When she wasn't there, his boot was heavy and his kicking desultory. When she was, it was a little wild and inaccurate. It alarmed him. He also felt mean, as if he'd put his foot out and tripped Arthur.

So he did not mention to Arthur – what was there to mention? – that once she had taken the babies for a walk in their carriage along the upper end of the field, across the little bridge and out into the road that ran along the edge and that he had stood a long time behind the poised ball, waiting for her to pass out of range. The ball had fallen not far from her. He had run to fetch it. She had looked back then, the ball on the ground between them. The babies had bobbed balefully. He had sent her a quick sideways glance and a gruff, 'Afternoon, ma'am. Sorry about that.' He had gathered the ball, seeing her little boots a yard or two from where it lay. They seemed poised to walk towards him. He scooped up the ball, turned his back and trotted off. But he had heard her laugh. Whether she was laughing at the babies or at him, he did not know, but he felt distinctly foolish. He kicked the ball very hard the next time. It sailed straight through the posts and hit the roof of the pavilion with a satisfying thud.

Her composure had almost deserted her without the hedge between them. She had heard the kick without turning, heard the thud of his feet as he ran. She even heard the snap of the short, brown winter grass close behind her as he brought himself up to reach for the ball.

'Afternoon, ma'am. Sorry about that.'

But she had laughed to see his face, almost scowling and the babies glaring back at him. He was aware of her, after all. Oh, yes. *And* he was afraid.

She had walked on briskly.

He stood in front of the posts, facing into the sun, stepped back to kick. That thud, that dull, deep thud, the bounce on the pavilion roof, the softer fall, reached her as she watched, sideways, from under the brim of her hat.

Josie was not fooled. Coming on Annie under the fig tree in the backyard she said, 'Why're you standing out here and gawking at Fraser?'

Gawking at Fraser. It sounded so gauche.

'I am bringing in the washing,' Annie said, swiping at some clothes cast over the hedge. 'Go away, Josie,' flicking her with a pair of wrung-out drawers, dried to stiff diagonal creases. Josie had no idea of the delicacy of the dialogue she had invented: it was to do with light on his face and the way his hair, so straight, bounced spiky at his forehead when he ran. It had to do with how he stood when he waited just a moment before he kicked, head bowed. It was to do with looking sideways at the trajectory of the ball. And what he would say if he ever kicked it into her garden and had to retrieve it and what she would say if she had to fetch it for him. She wondered who he was taking to the dance. Some little girl from school – oh, condescending Annie, he's as old as you – who would admire the binding on his jacket and his XV badge and know nothing of his manly neck? Hilda was going and Helen Seymour, the Headboy's cousin. She had laughed when Hilda had told her of Arthur Graham's invitation. Arthur Graham was as bold as brass! Who did he think he was? She'd tease him when she saw him again and make him red. He was dear when he was red and crinkled up his eyes and laughed. He had strong teeth, very white, even if they were a little crooked. 'Arthur Graham is altogether adorable,' she had said to Hilda. 'If Harry wasn't such a sweet, silly boy, I'd swap them instantly.'

Annie might be gathering the washing, but she certainly wasn't looking at what she was doing. Josie elbowed her aside and stared across the hedge at Charlie Fraser. She did not care if he saw them. Annie pulled her away, drawing her back. Josie, so blunt herself, seemed unaware of the subtleties of romance. Who was 'gawking at Fraser' now?

Josie pulled her arm free. 'If he won't talk to you, why don't you just say something to him yourself?'

'Like what?' She couldn't march onto the rugby field and walk up to the lone figure and say, 'Come this way, Charles Fraser,' now could she?

'Perhaps he doesn't even know you exist,' said Josie helpfully. Annie went off then, very annoyed, very touchy. Charlie Fraser kicked the ball far off on the field. It hit the cross-bar and bounced back. Josie laughed: she bet he'd said a rude word with no one there to hear. Something very rude. Good. Very good.

Charlie Fraser was jogging up towards the try-line. She could have shaken him. What was the matter with the fellow? At least Herbert was predictable. He would simply whack the ball into the hedge at the right moment so he could talk to her. She'd ignore him as he scrabbled in the dry leaves, reaching for it. At last he'd say hello and she would turn. 'Yes?' You again!

It was always evident by the way Herbert stood, hand on hip with the ball tucked neatly under his other arm, legs apart – All right, Miss Josie Zeederberg – that he could brazen it out just as well as she.

Three days before the Big Match and the dance, Josie Zeederberg ensconced herself in the sourplum by the hedge with her recitation book. When Herbert came – so much kicking and punting and panting about as he got nearer – she slid down and made her announcement, without any preamble, 'I am playing at the dance after the rugby match.' Herbert had jogged on the spot, in case someone saw him and accused him of loitering instead of practising. 'Why are you playing at the dance?' he said.

'Miss van Ryneveld asked me.'

'It's only the prefects,' he said. He would not be there, in case she was interested.

'So?' His absence did not seem to concern her at all.

Another gaffe. He kicked his heel into the turf, screwed it round. Now what? He shifted his stance.

She wanted to laugh. 'It'll be all your starchy seniors and all of ours,' she said. 'Sounds a bore to me. Ours are making such a fuss, you'd think they were getting married.'

'Don't you like dancing?'

Josie shrugged. It depended with whom, but she didn't say. She looked away. 'Not specially.' She was non-committal.

'I can always ask Charlie Fraser to dance with you.'

She gave a little snort. 'You're such a brag, Herbert Cummings!'

'Is that so?' Herbert tossed the ball from one hand to the other, attempting the supercilious. 'Is your sister playing too?'

'Yes.'

'Good.'

'Why good?'

'Good.' There, he had her back! She mustn't think she was the only one who could ask leading questions without explaining.

She gave him a look. He laughed.

He was standing two yards off. He was sweaty. She did not mind. His hair was spiked on end. There was a little dark cow-lick at his temple. She liked it. He was rather skinny but he had nice knees. They were well-exercised and brown and sort of square. They were not the pudgy sort, like Fatty Harman's, that got yellow splodges on them when he ran around a lot, like the blubber on corned beef.

Herbert sniffed and wiped the back of his sleeve across his forehead. He bent and pulled up his sock. Say something. Quick. 'I must get on and practise.' That was not the comment to keep her standing there.

'Are you playing in the match on Saturday?' she said, quite capable of looking after herself.

Obviously. Couldn't she see the great stripe across his chest? Didn't she know what the single broad, pale band on the socks meant? 'Yes,' he said, briskly. 'Are you coming to watch?' He swallowed as he said it, silly fellow, so that it came out with a catch, as if it mattered.

'Maybe.'

'It'll be a good match.'

'You'll be beaten.'

'Rot!' Absolute scorn. 'We haven't been beaten for years.'

'Bet you will be.'

'What do you bet?' He challenged her.

'Tea at the Cathedral Café,' she said. Who was brazen now?

'Right.' He said and laughed. His lack of money was of no concern: the Methodists would never win.

Herbert bolted away then. The other fellows were coming down to practise. He could hear them tramping round the side of the pavilion with the coach. That roar! Douggie Morgan suddenly sprinting onto the field, charging about, letting it all out. Herbert was glad he was not an opposing forward. The man might as well order his coffin now.

Tea at the Cathedral Café. Hers. Not his. Herbert punted the ball ahead. It sailed across the field. He sprinted after it, a great rush of wind in his face. Someone gathered and returned it. Running backwards, arms braced to catch, he bunched and jumped. Up, up. He might as well have caught the sun.

It was not Miss van Ryneveld who had asked the Zeederberg sisters to play at the dance. But they did not know it. It was Percy Gilbert, Second-Head-of-House. He'd arranged it all, a gesture of magnanimity and a rueful penance of his own, achieved on a sudden inspiration. Percy struck the oddest bargains with his Maker.

Percy, despite his apparent boredom, had offered to oversee the music programme. Except for John Barham and a few of the others who did not play in the Firsts, most were preoccupied with the Big Match. As the week drew on, the dance was put aside, out of the heads of The Chosen. They had business to attend to. A brooding fell on all of them. Saturday and the Methodists. Nubs were more respectful than usual. There was a checking of polish supplies and a washing of laces. By Thursday, GB was very grave. Parkes saw him go into the chapel alone on Friday night.

Percy and John Barham went to town, Barham to see to the bunting and dessert and to order the ginger beer from Thomas and Son. Percy left him deliberating on how many crates were required and hurried off to the university to collect some promised notes. As he went past the music rooms and saw Miss van Ryneveld sitting at the keys, practising, the idea struck him. He did not think, he was ebullient, distraction suited him. He said on an inspiration, 'Miss van Ryneveld?'

'Yes, Mr Gilbert?' Miss van Ryneveld of the giant teeth and the lantern jaw, was very fond of Percy. He draped himself at the corner of her piano. 'I have been selected as the Music Committee for the Prefects' Dance. I wonder what constitutes a committee? Will one member do?' He smiled at her. 'Have I a *quorum*? I think I need some help. So, may I invite you, Miss van Ryneveld, to join me?'

'The Quadrille Band has been engaged and I have already been asked to play the waltzes.'

'But *what* is to be played?' He paused. 'I have been given a dozen requests already but I would like some guidance.' She was easy to coax. 'Most of the prefects are racing about practising for a rugby match on Saturday afternoon. You'd think it was preparation for war. So, while they are killing each other – brother and brother – it falls to me to organise the tunes for the survivors. I believe The Quadrille Band has an excellent repertoire.'

'Indeed,' said Miss van Ryneveld. 'I engaged them myself. They did a very creditable performance at the university dance the other night. It was a splendid occasion. I didn't see you there.'

'We're schoolboys and we're not. We're students and we're not,' said Percy. 'Neither fish nor fowl. Look at Holmes and Seymour and all the others in the Intermediate. They don't know who to play cricket or footer for – school or university. They don't know whether they should smoke their pipes or not. They wonder if they should grow moustaches and drink in a bar or stick to cocoa in the common-room. There's even a fellow I know who'd like to ask a girl to marry him, but he still has a fag, so he doesn't need a wife to polish his boots or fetch the newspaper! It's all most unsatisfactory!'

'Get on with you, you impertinent boy.'

'There you are!' said Percy lightly. 'That just proves it – one minute I am "Mr Gilbert" and the next, an "impertinent boy"!'

Blah, blah, blah, he could hear himself, leading her on. 'I expect a whole lot of casualties to be lined up against the walls, bandaged from head to foot, who will be depending on the music rather than the dancing for entertainment,' he said.

Miss van Ryneveld was lapping it up, head inclined, she with her watch chain frozen to her chest and her hennaed hair clamped into furrows like the ploughing on the new field beside the prep school.

'But I think that a clarinet and a fiddle would do very well to accompany the waltzes,' he said. 'I once heard such an accompaniment at a dance at home. It really was capital! The Archdeacon's wife was very taken with it and so was the wife of the Bishop of Bloemfontein.' The Bishop of Bloemfontein didn't have a wife, but *she* didn't know that. She just drank it up. 'And there are the Zeederberg sisters who I believe perform very well together.'

'Miss Josie Zeederberg prefers blowing that wretched bugle of her brother's!' snorted Miss van Ryneveld. 'She should have been born a boy.'

'No doubt.' Percy had not the remotest idea what Josie Zeederberg looked like even if she had passed before his face daily. Nor did he care how she played. It was Arthur he was thinking of and of rectifying his own mistake and getting him out of a pickle – partly, anyway. While dancing with The Midget, Arthur could rest his eyes on the sublime Miss Zeederberg with her fiddle. Percy would even dance with Hilda Knight to give Arthur a chance to fall at the feet of the goddess, if he wished. He owed it to the fellow. He had been cutting. Unkind. Careless. He hadn't listened when Arthur had applied to him. Of course Arthur hadn't been talking of Hilda Knight! Conjuring up the real object of desire was the least he could do now.

'I have a particular reason for asking.' Percy glanced at the door, all conspiracy and deceit. 'A young friend of mine ...'

'Now you are going to embroil me, Mr Gilbert, in something underhand.'

'Miss van Ryneveld!' Percy cajoling. 'I have got myself into a jam' – Come on, old girl, just take it. She did – 'May Miss Annie Zeederberg be your accompanist?'

'On the violin?'

'Why not?'

'I think you're up to something.'

'Not at all.'

'She's very accomplished but I don't see why we need her or her sister when we have The Quadrille Band ...'

'Miss van Ryneveld' – rather confidential – 'do help me out. It will be a very special favour.'

'I'm sure I know quite well why you might want Miss Annie

Zeederberg playing the violin!' said Miss van Ryneveld. 'You're a very naughty fellow, Percy Gilbert!'

Percy went away, hugely pleased with himself. 'You're a "very naughty fellow",' he mimicked.

He had done it for Arthur Graham.

He had also done it to punish himself. That too. Mac would home in on her like a wave to the moon, taking up the tide. Observing him would serve as penance. He could watch himself being slowly singed – paper man – from the soles of his feet. He would be discarded like Mac's nurse, torn into little pieces and left to float down into the bin. He had pre-empted it himself.

Let Mac dance. Let Arthur dance. Love was very transient. It could dissolve at a word.

The thirteenth of June.

The Match.

The Dance.

So much excitement and expectation on one day.

It came back to Herbert sometimes, drifting in – some scent, some snatch of music, seeing a grimy window pane high up in his courtroom and recalling, suddenly, the feel of his fingertips on dusty glass. And greater and more frequently, that surge of energy, as if, in watching a rugby player taking a gap, he again held the ball, tucked in his arm, firm in his hand and was darting for the line. –Go Apie! Go! –Watch Apie! Watch him go!

There was a picture of the match in Charlie's album, a vague, rather dark snap of fellows in a ruck and the church spire drifting behind the posts; another of a line-out, Mac jumping way above the rest. There was a picture of the Drill Hall too, decorated with flutes of flowers and paper bunting. Those pictures were in every album. In Herbert's own. In James Seymour's and Georgie Holmes' and Dan's and Sparrow's and Mac's. Had Percy kept an album? Perhaps a selection in his morocco writing-case, all neatly annotated in his very large, eccentric writing. Was there a picture of Percy himself, with the rose in his lapel and the frothy end of the Paisley handkerchief in his pocket?

In afteryears – laughter in recalling it – sitting in the cricket pavilion, watching School versus Old Boys, the morning sun gilding gold the Clock Tower's new-cut stone:

–Remember the Prefects' Dance in the Drill Hall? says Percy.

Laughter.

–And your rose, Daisy! Where did you get it? John Barham says, exhaling drifts of smoke.

–I took myself and a pair of scissors off to the Head's garden and cut it in broad daylight.

–Just like that?

–Just like that!

–And Mac, playing the Lothario! John Barham shakes his head.

–Couldn't help himself, poor fellow.

–You know, it was then that Mary Clifford and Dan met each other properly. Such an old slyboots under our noses!

–Thought we didn't notice, says Herbert.

–Do you remember that girl? The one who played the violin? says Edwards. –You must remember, Apie?

–Annie Zeederberg, says Herbert.

–I wonder what happened to her?

Herbert smiles, looks down towards the women seated together near the grass where children play. Their hats dip, their laughter drifts. John Barham has moved on, full of his own recollections.

–What day was it? he says.

–Sometime in June? says Edwards.

The thirteenth of June. The morning of the match. The anniversary of Charlie Fraser's father's death.

Charlie rises very early. He takes a ball and kicks at posts. On the way back to the House he goes in at the chapel door. Standing at the back in his footer gear, with an old jacket on against the cold, he stays a minute, very still.

His mother always lights a candle in the old brick church on that day. Some say she shouldn't: one must turn one's back on sin. Is there a sanction on the right to one small flame? It burns down alone, at the mercy of the draughts, the little vagaries of wind that enter through the chinks. How long it flickers on, no one waits to discover. She never speaks, only says, 'Where are the matches?' The flame lights the underside of lashes as she leans in to hold her hand about the wick, protecting it. The flare against the tender skin below her eyes shows its pale transparency. She was only twenty-one when he died.

There was no candle to light, no memory Charlie could recall, no face that he could constitute beyond the stiffness of a studio photograph, only remembrance of a little grave, in the high, barren cemetery with a view of hills. It was unadorned, but for wild helichrysums, brave and wind burned, just inside the iron palisade. He had brought one of the small plants back with him but it had died. Did it mean that his connection was not real?

He had kept the small shrivelled root, tucked away among his things.

Each has his own forms of remembrance and homage.

TWELVE

•■•■■■•■•

June thirteenth. The school awoke at dawn. The air was very still. The gods rose early. One and then another. A perfect quiet in the studies and the prefects' room. Charlie's bed had been empty for an hour. He was down on the field, looking at the posts.

Archer also woke. It would have been today, when *The Journal* might have reported, '*Archer is the finest full-back in years.*' Instead they would say it about Fraser. He turned over. The bell marked the quarter on the roof high above. He lay on his stomach with his eyes open. The Seconds were playing first. What was Seconds? What was the runner-up to full-back? Everyone would watch, but it was not the same. *The Journal* would not even mention the game in passing. The copy, and the roars, would all be kept for the XV.

And what could he say against Fraser? Nothing. No one could ever say anything against Fraser. Archer could still feel the finger in his chest. It was branded. It had been his deepest humiliation because it had been administered by Fraser. A beating from Morgan, a thrashing from Robbie, would have been nothing in comparison. And he didn't know why.

Unwin also woke. He looked across at Cummings sprawled over his bed, arm dangling, one leg crooked, frowning in his sleep. Did he play footer, even in his bed? Unwin propped his head on his hand, elbow bent, and looked at him. Cummings was quite a small fellow. Yet, you could see by the way he walked, by the way the seniors treated him, that they were grooming him for greatness. Why Cummings? Why Cummings and not someone else? Why was Cummings' life so full of expectation and busyness? Cummings was always off somewhere with someone. Cummings didn't ever hang about alone. Even Percy Gilbert, who seemed as old as Robbie himself, fed him ginger beer and played chess with him. Even Archer seemed to give him regard. Why Cummings?

There was no expectation for Unwin. Just the long dreariness. He would sit in the stand this afternoon, included perhaps, by Huddlestone and Harman, and shout for the XV, fervent that Cummings should get the ball out of the scrum, fervent that Morgan should cause the stretcher-bearers to take off one corpse after the other, open-mouthed when Fraser placed the ball end-up for a penalty or Holmes or Seymour or Graham darted for the try-line, handing off opponents as they went. Just as fervent as all the rest with the noise around him and the rhythm of feet whispering first, gathering the deeply dredged up sigh, heartbeat swelling, just as fervent as the hundreds of other voices rallying the long, panting chant: 'College . . . College . . . College'. He would shout too, feeling it in his feet, up his legs, in his groin and his solar plexus. The river rising with the word, pumped up above them into the sky while far off the town lay in the winter sunshine with the pigeons wheeling in the bowl of the valley, circling the ochre-grey of the cathedral spire. But for him, in the stand, no hand would be put out to his and someone nudge, –See that, hey, Unwin?

–Yus! Just watch!

A ball being placed for a conversion: Fraser, head down a moment, stepping back. The hush, the great breathless hush, the thud, the silence, then the roar. Oh, they would fling arms round necks, butt heads, punch arms and thighs with the fellow on either side while John Barham strode about in front of them, chanting loudly. No one to butt heads with but Huddlestone and Harman. Anyone else would spit, –Get off, Unwin, with a shove. That was his lot.

Why did he mind so much, when they seemed to accept it? Why, because they never rose to the teasing, never yelled, –I've had it, I've simply had it! Did the bucks let them eke their lives out, relatively undisturbed? They didn't even seem to mind about being at school. They had a kind of pale solace in each other and in the things they did. They didn't appear to be unhappy. Harman even had his photo in a number of albums, 'Fatty Harman', written underneath. He knew why he was there and he accepted it. Any acknowledgement would do:

   –There is a fat boy in our form. He is the fattest boy you have ever
   seen . . .

Harman's story: Fat Boy.

Huddlestone's story: Hairy Boy.

What was Unwin's story? Where was his place?

In the tangy? With the rats and the caddies?

What was wrong with him?

Unwin dressed, back to the dorm. He went to breakfast, sat in a shaft of sunlight, diverting the dusty motes. The sun was warm on his lids. Did geckos sometimes come out of their crevices and bask a little? How safe was it for them to do it? The light was in his eyes, he could see no one, only dancing dust, swarming in its own random rhythm round his head. It was warm and quiet, caught in that shaft. Warm and quiet.

'Move up, Unwin. You're hogging the sun!'

Even the sun was not his: not even a little portion of it. Not for a minute. Even the sun was subject to standing order, someone else's entitlement before his own. He must keep on the move, just out of reach, marking out the time. But even that was disallowed.

'What is that boy about?' The Head, glancing out of the window of his study.

'Which boy?' Robbie, craning to see.

'If a fellow's time-table isn't full enough, fill it. No one should be loitering about at this time of the day.'

Unwin, standing in the *bergwind* under the stone pines, just standing, waiting for six terms to go.

Keep out of sight. Go to the tangy with the Westminsters or Flags. Archer would not come any more. No one would. Even the Reverend Dowsley seemed to have forgotten him. Perhaps he had nothing to say. What does one say to a boy who curses God? One who'd killed another boy? To understand would be too tedious. He was safe. And when he was gone at last, all that would remain was his name in *The Register*. No one would ever look it up. It would simply be there, taking up a number, somewhere between 2274 and 2636. Would it read:

Unwin, Hugh Llewellyn, son of L.W.: Left Dec. 1914; b. 25.5.1897; Form I-V. Unknown after 1914?

No footer team, no cricket team, no aquatics or athletics. No drum major in the Cadet Corps, no lieutenant, not even corporal. No prefect. Nothing of his subsequent life: if there was one. Was it a record at all, asserting only that he had existed – entrance, exit, a father and a date of birth? Nothing to say: beaten twice a week, every week. No weeping. No flinching. Unwin, H.L., Tangy-boy.

–If a fellow's time-table isn't full enough, fill it.

Robbie did. He summoned Unwin before lunch.

'Unwin?'

Unwin stood, alarmed. 'Sir?' What now? Had someone reported him for sitting in the sun? For knocking his tea into his saucer at breakfast? Nothing would surprise him.

'I want you to take charge of the first-aid box at the match this afternoon and be ready to help out if it's needed. I'll let the coach know.'

The coach only knew the great and glorious. The coach did not know Unwin.

'He doesn't know me, sir.'

'He will by the end of the afternoon,' said Robbie.

'Sir.' Unwin's hands began to sweat. He pressed his palms against the sides of his legs, standing to attention.

'Go up to Miss Maltby and collect it from her and here's a list.' Robbie turned to his desk and opened a drawer. He extracted a sheet of paper. He gave it to Unwin. Unwin glanced at it. Items One to Ten, clearly marked and numbered.

'Check the box against the list. If anything is missing, tell Miss Maltby.'

'Sir.'

Unwin left Robbie's study. He closed the door behind him. The brass door-knob slid under his palm as it did when he retreated from a caning, but today it felt familiar, even unadmonishing. He rubbed the damp off it with his cuff. His face was telescoped in its curve, looking back. He took the stairs to Miss Maltby's domain in twos and knocked smartly, Robbie's list ready in his other hand.

Lunch. Fifteen silent boys among the rest. A quick irritable glance down to the lower tables where juniors were getting beyond themselves. It was not a day for levity.

Herbert knew that if he touched a mouthful, even a slice of bread without dripping, he'd throw up. He could hardly breathe. The first big match. Perhaps the last. He passed his plate to Tom Edwards.

He thought about the Methodists. Best to confront them head-on: Snyman and Osher and the famous forward with the slanting eyes, like a Chinaman, that he had seen in town last Sunday morning outside the Commemoration Church when he had gone to Holy Communion at the cathedral. Their hair was cut so short they looked like the inmates of a penal colony. They stood there, prayer books in their hands, very pious.

It was Percy who had said it: by his tone and the small sardonic smile, it was hard to know who he was mocking. 'Not fit for the gallows!' he remarked with a swift glance in their direction. 'Just look at them! What deplorable jackets! Dressed for a dog-stealing expedition! Caddies, all of them! Watch them play dirty! How can God be on their side?'

Percy had declared then – standing in the porch of the cathedral, poking at the paving with his umbrella – that God was an Anglican and that the Methodists eased in only just ahead of the Baptists, although, in fairness, the architecture of the Commemoration Church gave the Methodists a bit of leverage against them all – in this region anyway. One couldn't say what horrors were constructed on the Reef.

The juniors had nodded their heads and stared off at the boys across the square. Abominable indeed. Gilbert should know.

'What about the Catholics then?' Herbert had said, with some impertinence. He would catch him out.

'Catholics!' Percy had rolled his eyes as if the word was sacrilege in his mouth, especially standing where he was, at risk, the great steeple over his head: twelve thousand tons of stone.

Herbert had flushed.

Percy was mocking. He was laughing at him. He was laughing at them all. Idiot for mentioning it. It was good enough reason to kill Snyman and Osher when the time came. Doug Morgan would take care of the blond Chinaman. They had sized each other up from either side of the street, neither looking away. Then the Chinaman had turned his head nonchalantly and said something to the others. They had smiled among themselves. Doug had marched into church: he might as well have had spurs clanking at his heels.

'Don't fret, Cummings,' Percy had said, patting his shoulder as they collected their hymnals. 'If you fellows try not to annoy God too much this week, it'll be fine on Saturday.'

Herbert had not enquired about what manner of annoyance might offend. No doubt God had a dozen reasons for annoyance, not the least with Herbert for having punched Tom Edwards' nose on a Sunday morning before church. He'd had no choice – Tom *would* go on about Josie Zeederberg in front of the others. Maybe he'd be punished once and for all. Maybe he'd be dropped or changed to centre again and Sparrow would be scrum-half for the big match. Herbert was in a knot with church in the morning, chapel coming up in the evening and, in between, a lump of salt beef with pumpkin and grey-eyed potatoes for lunch. No wonder he had felt low.

The feeling had lasted all week – that turgid tug at his gut, mouth dry. The coach had talked to them the evening before. Had he listened properly? What had the coach said? He had been through it in his head all night.

–If you hand a fellow off, don't leave your arm outstretched. Push out, draw back, lightning-quick and strong.

He was sure that he had heard each quarter chime until the morning. He looked at the top table where Robbie and the senior prefects sat. No one spoke. Even Percy was silent and Mac was pushing food around on his plate, eyes on his water glass.

Doug Morgan ate mechanically: prepare the machine, fuel the engine, a discreet belch, fist to his mouth.

The blond Chinaman.

He must not let him slip from his mind even with his head in the scrum. Think of the face. Was he a Chinaman?

'Is he a Chinaman?' asking Mac.

'Is who a Chinaman?'

'That fellow who plays for the Methodists?'

Mac didn't bother to reply. It was quite irrelevant. Doug applied to Percy.

'Of course he's not a Chinaman, Morgan! How could a fellow of six foot with blond hair, at school with the Methodists, be a Chinaman, I ask you! He only looks like one!'

Doug was offended. 'How can he look like one with yellow hair?'

'You tell me?' As if he were five years old.

'I don't know.' And to hell with you too.

'His eyes are slanted up.' See? 'Very odd.'

'I believe all the girls at the public school are in love with him.'

'Lucky fellow,' said Percy patiently.

After a moment, Doug said, 'Well, that's a relief!'

'What's a relief?'

'That he's not a Chinaman.'

'What difference would it have made if he was a Chinaman?'

Douggie Morgan wouldn't have been able to say, but he wouldn't have been comfortable with it. He drank his tea in a gulp, cup enclosed in a fist: that was that. One more problem out of the way. The Methodist was not a real Chinaman.

Percy turned his own cup and regarded it silently. An odd thing, a teacup. How differently different boys approached the object. The treatment of it spoke volumes. Dan Grant and Sparrow Bell used a teacup with discretion, attentive to its worth. They did not leave their teaspoons standing against the rim while they sipped, they did not swill the lukewarm liquid in their mouths. Gentlemen, both of them. John Barham always trailed tea around the rim with the bowl

238

of his spoon as if exorcising germs. A school teacup was too small in Charlie Fraser's hands, yet its roundness seemed to please him. He often held one as though cradling it, cupped the curve as if its warmth were sensuous to him: a light, caressing finger. Doug Morgan, shovelling sugar and stirring as if he was excavating with a drill, broke them with tedious regularity. Percy put his teacup down carefully and moved the handle to the right. He glanced at Mac. The lines were set around his mouth, eyes averted: he was already on the field, warming up, steady and strong.

–Play well, Mac. Jump high.

Percy would shout too, feel the pull of triumph for him. He put his hands in his lap, waited for the grace.

Down the table Arthur was restless, stretching, inspecting his calf, wriggling his foot against the table leg.

'Stop it, Graham.' John Barham frowned.

'Sorry.' Arthur was unaware of why he was apologising.

Charlie Fraser sat next to Arthur. He took up the salt cellar every now and then and placed it on the table cloth precisely, as if beading it. The extremities of the pudding spoon of the fellow opposite seemed the points of reference. He remained absorbed. He ate his food. The contents of the plate were not of interest.

Danny and Sparrow leaned towards each other, quite silent and looking off across the heads of the boys through the lancets at the grounds beyond, eating in unison, alert then subsiding, synchronised as hunters stalking. They had no need for words.

GB and Parkes were at the lowest table. GB ate nothing. Parkes tried to abstain, feeling the reverence of renunciation, but unable to oblige. He was much too hungry. GB looked disapproving. He shovelled his stew onto Parkes' plate as if asking him to forage. –There now, Pig-Face.

GB was in a knot. He had got up very early and polished Fraser's boots again. And again. The laces were perfectly white, the eyes were smooth, the leather buffed and buffed until it glowed. The footer shorts and jersey and the socks were neatly laid. He had touched the jersey, running a finger along the top of the stripe. He had held the

239

boots most respectfully.

–Please, God, let him kick all the goals through the middle.

–Please, God, don't let him miss.

He talked to those boots, knelt down and placed them side by side, his hands tucked into them as if they were feet, head bent over them. Toe to toe, then heel to heel. That looked funny, so he laughed. He placed them straight again, two soldiers standing to attention, facing forward. There!

–Through the middle, God, and also into touch.

GB glanced back, suddenly feeling as though the light in the study had dimmed. Fraser was in the doorway with his arms folded but when GB turned, he undid them and said, quite easily, 'Thank you, GB. Very good job.' GB scuttled up from his knees. But Charlie Fraser still stood between him and the door. GB looked from side to side, deciding on the best and most dignified retreat. His ears were fiery. But Fraser said, 'Aren't we going to shake on it?'

GB hesitated and then he put his hand in Fraser's. Man to man. 'Good luck, Fraser,' said GB, looking Charlie in the midriff, his voice a tone deeper. Man to man.

'Thank you,' said Charlie Fraser. He almost laughed.

The Methodists walked. Some carried their boots or had them slung by the laces around their necks. Some wore shoes. Some didn't. At the front, Osher, Snyman and the Chinaman. Behind, the other stalwarts. They seemed enormous. The school followed them, coming down the hill and across the *sloot*, a strange army encamped on the far side of hallowed ground, standards waving. In the pavilion the chanting opponents were ranged. John Barham and Percy and the prefects from the other houses stalked up and down in front, little flags in fists, ready to dart out and whack a miscreant on the head who failed to sing lustily or did not know the words. The mascot, being ensconced among the second years, was warred over like regimental colours, everybody wanting a turn to hold it. John Barham confiscated it and bestowed it elsewhere. Everyone shut up: the view, from below, of John Barham's nostrils on the scent, was not encouraging.

The Head, all affability and handsome grace, his ecclesiastical collar gleaming with starch, surveyed his domain. He turned to the Visiting Head at his side. 'Ah, we're in for a good game!'

'Certainly, we're in for a good game,' said the Methodist austerely, beaming in on his troops across the field: –No, sir, not a game! It is warfare! My lads know that!

'You have some key players?' The Head all interest, even magnanimous. –Where is our danger, then?

'Certainly very promising!' His colleague gave nothing away, folded his hands on the top of his cane: –They'll take out the kingpins. They know who they are: Morgan, MacCallum, Graham, Fraser.

'We have the best side in years.' Rather lofty from the Head: we'll seize the day despite the partisan and brash encouragement from the collection of girls who have walked up from the other side of the town and who are hanging over the fence and pushing down the wire!

The Head glanced back at Robbie. Robbie sat behind with a face like a bullfrog, rheumy eye directed at the throng at the fence, mouth turned down. –What were those girls about?

The stand was full of parents, sisters, members of the Council, arranged with their wives in the shade – so much dappled colour, dipping hats, a flutter of largesse going along a row. Among them all the masters, old Jarge looking as if he was at a horse race – his favourite after golf: 'It's a certainty! Not a shadow of a doubt, lads!' Taking bets himself.

'They look very big, Mr Richards.'

Jarge appraising, 'Oh-aye, they will beat 'ee.' Sheer heresy from one of their own! Jarge in gales of laughter then. 'Beat 'ee? Course they won't, lads! You can bet old Morgan's cranking 'imself up like St George hanticipating the Dragon.'

And on the benches, on the bank, a crowd of spectators muffled against the wind: small boys rolling around on the grass with a ball, dogs sniffing stiff-tailed at each other on the ends of leashes. Behind the posts, at the far side of the field, in a little group, the workmen and the waiters and the old man who cleaned the lavatories and lit the fires underneath the laundry cauldrons outside the House. Another chant – whatever proffered glee – to see a goal soar, a try rolled over at a corner, a boy stand up triumphant and shake the glory down as if he didn't notice, or a missed chance and the voices swooping in dismay to an under-murmur.

–Bad luck.

–Damn.

–You'll get it next time.

–Next time, yes.

The Seconds played. Archer could not be faulted. He dropped a goal from the twenty-five, he converted three tries. He scored one himself, barging straight through the Methodists and scattering them like wooden men. He was a credit. A hero. Pity it was too late to be among the great and glorious for the rest of the season. But that day he was. How the School roared!

'Well played, Archer.' The coach, more than affable, making mental notes.

'Splendid fellow!' The Head at his most expansive in the centre of the frenzy. 'Really splendid!'

'Great match, Archer!' Holmes and Seymour, giving him a pat on the shoulder.

'Well done, Goens' – Stafford and Mostert, gaining glory despite the acolytes slouching round them. The bucks sat straighter, neatened up, felt reflected notice.

Even Mac grinned. Charlie Fraser came back from the bog, 'Archer?' He shook his hand.

Archer glowed.

He put on his blazer and went to sit with his team-mates in the stand. It was a transitory triumph. The man from *The Journal* was only sharpening his pencils now. The Firsts would be on in five minutes and wipe the Seconds' glory out with flying boots.

Perched in a tree by the quince hedge in the Zeederbergs' garden, prime view, two little Zeederbergs all dressed up in their uniforms, Eton collars, ties and jackets – out of deference – sprouted from the branches. And, floating about in the back garden among a huddle of friends, including some young men from the university music class, pretending indifference: Annie Zeederberg. The fellows stood at the hedge and watched. The Reverend Zeederberg brought his pipe. Harry, scrubbed and fed, had been booted through the quinces just in time for the school assembly. Josie made tea while the Seconds played. She had no interest in Leonard Archer and she didn't care who won. She had a foolish bet with Herbert Cummings. She would have to watch the Firsts to find out how much more she'd owe to Annie after all the other bets she'd made. Charlie Fraser was becoming an expensive item. He did nothing as she thought he would. But whatever he did today – even if he was carted off by the stretcher-bearers and died in a blaze on the bank – one way or another, suitably chaperoned, she and Herbert Cummings would have tea together at the Cathedral Café next Saturday afternoon. She couldn't wait! Who would pay was yet to be decided. It was likely to be her and, by then, her debt to Annie would far exceed a month's pocket-money. She would have to appeal to her mother's distraction – and her romantic soul – and get a loan.

Annie heard the roar from both sides of the field as the Seconds' game ended. The Firsts would be coming on. She looked up. Josie was marching out of the back door, banging the flyscreen behind her. Annie smiled. Watch out, Herbert Cummings! She got off the chair under the fig tree and walked across to the hedge with her friends to where her father and the young men were gathered. The little boys were hanging by their knees from a branch. Gracie had scrambled through onto the grass at the other side.

'Everyone looks funny running around upside down,' said Tom. 'Hang here, Will. Hang here next to me and see.'

GB couldn't look, waiting for the Firsts. He simply couldn't look. He picked at his hangnails and bit the skin on the side of his thumb. Parkes was sucking a sweet. It was a large bull's-eye. It must have been near the end and full of cavities: odd that a sound – of all that sugar and spit being sucked – could, in later times, recall that afternoon so sharply. More than the roar or the chant or the ululations from the other side of the field.

'Parkes!' GB gave him one in the ribs.

243

'GB?'

'Stop that noise.'

'What noise?'

'That sucking!'

'Want some?' Parkes took the sweet out of his mouth and inspected it.

'Not with gob all over it.'

Parkes was not offended. He lodged it in his cheek and went on sucking anyway.

Here they come, here they come. The tramp, tramp, tramp of boots. It turned the guts to stew. First, the Methodists. They were huge. Look at their forwards! GB stuck a finger in his nostril. Pick here, pick there. The knot in his middle was painful. Perhaps he was hungry. He turned to Parkes. Parkes was licking his sticky fingers. He had finished the bull's-eye. It was too late to ask for the last bit, after all.

Parkes said, very knowing, 'Graham better watch out for that winger.'

GB looked. The Methodist wing was a big, rangy fellow with strong knees. He was standing with his hands on his hips. He was frowning. He had great, glowering brows.

'Why?'

'He's supposed to be a tough.'

'Who said?'

'I read about him in the paper. It said he's got a wicked hand-off.'

'What's his name?'

'Osher.'

The roar went up, hats waving. Percy flourished his flag. Idiot nubs were flinging themselves about. The bawl began.

There they were, gleaming in their shades of blue, grouped about their captain, Seymour, shoulders pumping in the sunlight. Fanning out, the forwards took their places, the backs strung across the field, bouncing, running on the spot, warming legs in a small, chilly wind.

So much manly drama.

–It is really a Great Romance, Percy says, long years after, sitting on the bench behind the House, listening to the sounds of cricket drifting up from the Old Boys match being played on Lower field. He cocks his head. –Another six for Doug, he says.

–Romance? Herbert is puzzled.

–What else? The manly bonds, the manly aesthetic. Beautiful young men doing things beautifully. It is wonderful to watch.

–I am not sure I follow.

–Just making an observation, says Percy. –All that vigour and desire, so perfectly redirected. It's stirring stuff. It needs trumpets and drums, not foolish nubs howling at the sky!

Silence. The sacrificial moment just before the kick-off, the great heartbeat steadying: blood rallying, breath deep and strong. Percy watched: Arthur easing his legs on the wing, rubbing the backs of his calves; Douggie Morgan swinging his arms; MacCallum, hair perfectly brushed and gleaming, hands on his hips. He looked towards the stand briefly. He was not scanning for Percy. Percy followed his gaze: the seniors from the girls school were grouped together in their afternoon coats, another little knot stood at the hedge of the Zeederbergs' garden. The fellows were parading: the presence of women made them posture just a little, gave a reverence to how they stood.

Cummings and Sparrow Bell danced on their toes, so much smaller than the rest. Cummings was looking at the ground. Perhaps he was praying, dark head bent and, in the boy face, in this moment of solemnity, the traces of a fine, ascetic structure, waiting to emerge. If one could hear a heartbeat, Percy thought, some ardent marshalling of blood, it would be Cummings'.

Kick-off and the ball sails up. The Methodists are baying from the start. Osher and Snyman and the Golden Chinaman are everywhere. Into touch. Line-out. Penalty. Scrum: the Chinaman drapes his arms, rag-like and deceptive over the necks of his props, but his leg, thrust forward, is sprung to swing them in.

The thud. The collective grunt and Herbert darting down. He sends the ball out to the backline. Here they come. The indrawn breath, the rising shout, the great explosive joy. Go. Go. Go.

Herbert felt the rush of energy in arms and legs, winged when he dived, passing out from the scrum. He could have flown after it, airborne, when he kicked for touch.

Arthur opened the score with a try. There can never be an exultation quite the same as that. Arthur knows: the heart of the world is humming – he can feel it in his feet. In the stand, Parkes has almost wet himself.

GB cannot look. He stares at his shoes. The hush lasts for ever. He clamps his eyes shut. Don't look. Don't look. Don't breathe either. He hears the thud of Fraser's boot.

He and Parkes are locked together, bouncing heads. So they should be. Who was it who cleaned those hallowed boots? Who was it who prayed? Please, God, straight between the posts. Right through the middle.

God is certainly an Anglican!

Charlie Fraser trots to his place. He runs backwards the last few yards. Arthur Graham looks round at him. Charlie grins. A signal passes: I'll die for you, you die for me.

By the quince hedge, Annie Zeederberg smiles. Such perfect restraint. Josie, for whatever reason, is hanging upside down between the boys from the branch of the tree. She is happy to see the world upside down. Indeed, it has always been – for her – a better vantage.

The teams were even and the current dragged the ball, back and forth, back and forth between them. Holmes scored a try. Oosthuizen scored a try, Fraser converted both. Sparrow dropped a goal. Danny Grant, bleeding mightily from a cut above the eye, took the flag out in the corner with the fourth try of the day. Again, Fraser's boot was safe. As the cheers subsided, the coach led Dan Grant off. Unwin, his moment come, rushed across the open grass with the first-aid box, shoes squelching. Danny Grant sat still as the coach inspected the cut. Unwin snapped open the latch of the box and extracted iodine, gauze and a bandage. He did not flinch as the cut was dabbed. He held the gauze in place while the coach wound the bandage round Dan's head. Dan's blood was sticky on his fingers. Such glorious gore. He did not mind. He was calm and deft.

'Thanks, sir. Unwin,' said Dan, heaving himself up, touching his eye gingerly, pulling up a sock and trotting back to the field, precious minutes lost.

'Unwin, is it?' said the coach.

'Yes, sir.'

'Good lad.'

Somewhere in the stands Mary Clifford sat, half poised.

'He'll be all right,' said Clarice White.

'All that blood!' Mary breathed.

Dan's bandage glinted white, like a little talisman that she could follow with her eyes. She glanced down at Unwin with his first-aid box at the side of the field. If she could have changed places!

The Methodists fought back.

Back and forth, back and forth and the spectators erupting and subsiding, murmur to chant, chant to shout, at either side.

The try of the match had certainly been Osher's for the Methodists. Ten minutes from the end, he had almost won the game for them. Arthur could not catch him. No one could. It was a mighty race but he had gathered, ball tucked into his chest, and darted here and there, until he saw the gap. He had gone right through them all and the pennants on the far side of the field had been streaming as if a gale had taken them and whipped them to a frenzy. The girls from the public school had howled. Robbie had sat stoical and looked at the sky. Dear God, this was barbarous! It was time a wall was built along the road – good, dressed stone and six feet high. He consulted his watch. Two minutes left. The stand throbbed. A general dismay. It was twenty-seven, twenty-four to the Methodists.

The ball went out from the Methodists' half. A high kick, spiralling across the sun. Heads up, each man was bunched to spring.

Never take it straight on. If you gather on the chest it will knock you back, wind you, send you two feet into the turf.

Never think you'll miss. If you do, you will. Never hear the thunder of approaching boots, bearing down. Only watch – quite calm – as it plummets; get below and take it sideways at the shoulder, move with it, in perfect counter-balance. Steady it, then run.

Never miss.

Charlie Fraser did not miss. He felt the thud, the deep tremor through him to the ground below and, taking the momentum, ran.

He ran towards them, through them, past them, straight ahead, the posts before, eyes on the cross-bar. Head down. Go. Breathe deep and strong, blood to propel until the sudden speed of lightness takes you, the great elation rising.

He could have scored a try to equalise. Steady, Charlie, steady. Just a moment, half suspended. Poised. Then – sudden grace – he kicked. It soared, curved, arched across the cross-bar, fell. The flag was raised. Four points notched, instead of three.

The world erupted round him as the final whistle blew.

Twenty-eight: twenty-seven. Charlie Fraser, blazing glory, walked from the field, head down.

Archer stood. His shout was just as loud as all the rest. But he was pushed aside as all the boys mobbed down. Juniors ran about the field, Parkes and GB spun so fast they fell, legs entangled on the ground. Unwin checked the contents of the first-aid box, rubbed bloodied fingermarks from the metal lid, consulted the list. The teams shook hands. Here, the Golden Chinaman, Snyman, Osher, face to face, just boys.

'Well played, lads.'

'We'll see you next time.'

Good opponents. Sporting chaps. The debate about God's true denomination was forgotten, all abominations put aside, dog-stealing coats and all.

Archer walked back to the House in silence. The moment had come. It had passed. What was it like to carry all that adulation round for days as Charlie Fraser would? To never doubt, never feel disapprobation or regret. Never fail.

Charlie Fraser got a tub of clean, hot water. So did all the rest of the Firsts. The Seconds, lining up, took the lukewarm scum without complaint. It was forgotten that the highest scorer of the day had been Archer.

When *The Journal* appeared at last, the Firsts took half a page. Osher for the Methodists, Graham and Grant and Cummings for the College. Charlie Fraser had a paragraph to himself.

> 'In the dying moments the visitors worked their way towards the home side's territory. The day was saved by Fraser. This sterling young Rugbean gathered near the halfway line, and absolutely wormed his way through the whole of the opposing team, until he was practically under the goal posts. Had he wished he could possibly have notched a try, as he had a beautiful opening, but instead he coolly dropped a goal.'

And that evening, ruddy from the bath or shower, heads scrubbed, loose-shouldered and hungry as soldiers returned from a crusade, the prefects among them dressed for the dance. Archer, cold and disgruntled, passed MacCallum, Grant and Graham shaving, tapping their razors against the basin's edge and chatting: a murmuring, manly camaraderie.

Arthur Graham was peering into the water, looking for stubble, poking about with his finger. 'Got it! Come and look, fellows!'

Ha! Something to show, at last.

Even Sparrow Bell had lathered up his chin! Who did they think they were? Archer snorted. Among them, only Mac and Morgan could compete with him for what was left among the suds when the basin was drained. All that manliness overlooked and someone telling him to hurry along to prep.

THIRTEEN

•━•━■━•━•

Such a night.

'Here, *poephol*,' Charlie inspecting Arthur, standing close, protective of him. 'Put a bit of whatsit in your buttonhole. Why've you scraped your face so red?'

'I think I smell. This bloody jacket's stiff with sweat!' Arthur fanned his armpits.

'Borrow mine. I've got another.'

'Maybe it smells too.'

'Maybe it does.'

'I think I'll ask Percy for some of that hair stuff of his. It's nice, like oranges,' said Arthur.

'Stinks to high heaven.'

'D'you think that's worse than sweat?'

'Yes,' Charlie laughing, putting his arm over Arthur's neck: so much elation still. He looked at Arthur, grinned, released him and pulled his jacket straight.

–It's all right, boy. I won't go near her.

Herbert hung out of the dorm window with everyone else in the form to watch them pass. Girls in white. A cloud of scents. And voices like you'd never heard, canary sounds flitting about, very disconcerting. Robbie came in and found them. There was nothing he could do. He only said, rather wearily, 'Don't behave like a bunch of baboons, boys. Don't make pigs of yourselves . . .' He could see –

they were positively wallowing.

Josie Zeederberg went by.

Herbert watched her, all starched up herself with her hair in a ribbon. What was Josie Zeederberg, bugle-player, doing with a ribbon in her hair and her boots in order?

'What's up?' Edwards, squeezed in beside him, was looking at him, a laugh dawning. 'Who have we here, hey, Apie?' He began to shove.

'Look,' Herbert nudged him hard, diverting the danger and able to exaggerate. Anyone could exaggerate over Annie Zeederberg and be allowed to get away with it: she was far beyond their reach. Thank God she was so close behind. 'That's Harry's other sister.'

'That?' Incredulous. 'How did Harry get a sister like that? You must be lying.'

Annie was going in by the side door with her little violin case. She stopped and glanced around, scanning, turned away and closed the door behind her.

Edwards whistled through his teeth. He ran his hand across his head and folded his arms. 'Good grief.'

Here were the prefects now, coming out of the House, a floor below.

Poor Arthur. He kept walking backwards to hurry them on. Calm down, Arthur. Calm down. You'll fall on your arse in a flowerbed.

The partings in the hair, from Herbert's vantage, were iron straight, re-perfected twenty times. Even Sparrow had managed to control the little plume. They had all had a turn at dabbing it down, Sparrow finally fractious at their ministrations and pushing them off.

'Looks like a *spreeu* did a shit on your head!' said Doug, at his most gracious.

They went with the alertness of a scouting patrol: hunters in the dawn, the quarry sensed. Swift now, Mac pulling down his jacket at the back, easing his shoulders; Percy with a whole blown rose dangling from his buttonhole and a silk handkerchief in his pocket, just loping along, breezy and ironic; Douglas Morgan walking with his arms loose, big-legged; Dan Grant inspecting his cuffs. He'd be cracking his knuckles in alarm. Charlie Fraser came out last, quite at ease, it seemed.

'Back window after lights,' said Edwards in Herbert's ear.

'Robbie will be prowling.'

'Robbie?' Edwards laughed. '*Nooit*! You think he'd want to get caught looking through a window at a dance? Imagine if Miss Maltby saw him with his nose to the glass! He'd never live it down.'

'Well, the Head will be there and some of the other masters and their wives.'

'Dare!'

'Done!'

Charlie walked through the door of the Drill Hall.

–Do not look at her, Fraser.

He didn't.

He said good evening to the Head, shook hands, glanced across at all the girls. Miss van Ryneveld was at the keys, making tinkling runs, up and down. The little Zeederberg – Josie – was pulling a cloth through her clarinet. Without display, she was quite absorbed in what she was doing. Humorous little face, straight back. Pretty. He knew Apie watched her. She watched him too. To be watched like that, without deceit. It was simple. Generous. It seemed so easy.

Arthur was in an agony at the door, waiting for Hilda Knight. He had no idea what she looked like, whom to greet and claim. Thank God Percy was with him, playing the wit in his ear.

Charlie walked past the piano. He did not turn in her direction. She did not look in his. He went and stood with Dan – Dan the Beacon – up against the wall. Mary Clifford was among the seniors in a corner with Miss Fowler. Dan was not looking at her either. There they were, the two big heroes, behaving like a pair of startled girls while Sparrow, half their size, was entertaining a throng and making them laugh.

'Buck up, fellows,' Mac said, coming over – rather prefectorial – and gesturing with his head.

They followed him. It was a long walk across the floor. James Seymour was advancing with the seniors from the other houses.

Georgie Holmes. Oosthuizen. McIntosh. Lanham and Wentzel and Holdcroft. Half a dozen more. Dan fell behind, peeled off, diverted by a word from a master. Without them, he would never be able to proceed again. Charlie went back for him. 'Come on, Dan.'

'H . . . hh . . . hands're dripping.' The stutter was tuning up.

'Too bad. Just pretend you're about to score.'

Herbert had been through it all as well. The long walk. The pulse in the neck. The voice that came out half an octave up. The sweaty hands and the glass that wished to lurch from fingers to the floor, Josie Zeederberg laughing at him quietly.

But that was after.

This dance, face to the pane, with Tom Edwards breathing so hard he misted it up, was etched for ever. Arthur with Hilda Knight – she was so small she almost had to stand on his feet to look at his face, like a child being dandled by its brother; Douggie Morgan – sporting Doug – dancing with Mary Clifford and handing her over to Dan-by-the-Wall. 'Miss Clifford, do you know my friend Daniel Grant? He's a very famous fellow!'; Percy engaged in conversation with the Head over a glass of ginger beer, making it look like whisky and soda, the way he stood; Charlie Fraser, arms folded, standing alone by the table where the food was laid out in between the tall glass vases of cockscomb and lilies.

Herbert wiped the glass, stared unblinking. –Go on Charlie, ask her. Ask her when she takes a break.

He had one eye to the pane. –Ask her, damn it, or Josie Zeederberg will never speak to me again!

But Charlie didn't ask her. He waited his turn for Hilda Knight and stared pointedly at Arthur.

Arthur went to the table and poured three glasses of punch, balanced somehow all together in his hands, and took them to the performers at the piano. Miss van Ryneveld was gracious. Josie looked at him as though he'd handed her a toad. Annie took the glass with twinkling fingers and smiled at him.

'Hello, Arthur.' She inclined her head, laughed lightly. Dear Arthur.

–Ask her, Arthur.

And he did.

She went with him gaily – leading – arm linked into his.

Arthur, like a scarecrow man, feet suddenly growing out of his shoes, hands thrusting from his sleeves, all angles, breathes sometimes. She jogs him on, taps her hand lightly on his shoulder as if to emphasise a beat, rubs it out again with little gesturing fingers, almost pulls his ear-lobe. He is helpless.

Arthur, transported, a trickle edging down his temple, looks over her head at Charlie. Charlie winks. –Relax, old fellow. Hilda is chattering away. Charlie inclines his head to her but doesn't hear a word. Arthur has his back to him now, half a yard away.

Annie is facing him.

May the world stop now.

It does stop. But only briefly.

Hilda Knight tweaks his arm. She is determined to introduce him to her friend, Annie Zeederberg: she cannot dance in comfort with such a silent boy, even if he looks like a god. He is not fun and she wants Arthur back, to have him clowning and peering about and being jolly.

Hilda says, 'Annie, this is Charles Fraser. Charles, Annie Zeederberg.'

They stand a moment. Annie does not say, 'I met him in the street ... And every morning in my head, Hilda.' She says instead, 'How do you do?' and drops her eyes.

'You play the violin very well.' He sort of growls it out as though admonishing.

'Like you play rugby.' She has a flush on her neck.

Josie stares.

Annie says then, to cover her confusion, 'You had better promise to dance with me as well. I can't play all night.'

Arthur lifts a shoulder to ease a skewer in the heart for the way she speaks to Charlie.

Charlie looks away. 'Yes, ma'am.' He says it reluctantly. It sounds like an apology to Arthur.

It is.

And so he does – stiff, feeling Arthur's eyes and hearing Hilda Knight, her voice in the distance like a running stream. So much chatter but her words fading every now and then, as if she knows Arthur is not with her.

It is not a long waltz. It is not a fast one. Charlie will not dance with her again, so Help-me-God.

Here is his hand. Here, hers. Turn four fingers sideways across the palm. Here – her other hand is at his shoulder, his own is at her back. Here – a place for his foot, her foot, his knee, her knee. And speaking now, she says, quite softly so he has to bend, 'You must come to tea with Arthur.'

He makes no reply.

–No. Not with Arthur.

–Come alone.

–Not alone.

–Every day.

–In another life.

She almost looks him in the eyes, waiting. Whatever she is saying, her breath is at his ear. It is like a hidden flue drawing life to blood and stirring bedrock.

'Tea?' he says, at last: he has never heard the word before.

'Yes. On Sunday afternoon.' She moves a little in his arms, settling in, her chin is almost at his shoulder.

The music ends. They stand – so briefly – poised together. He steps back and she looks away and claps her hands, begins to laugh, to hold him there. Another dance?

'Thank you,' he says. He walks away without delivering her to her place. Mac, hovering quietly, steps in and does it for him. Mac doesn't care at all what Arthur thinks. He stays, inclined towards her near the piano. Arthur fetches Hilda Knight a drink. He tries to smile at her. Percy wanders over, takes up the thread with Hilda Knight and asks her to the floor but it's too late for Arthur. Mac has Annie by the hand and is guiding her out, looking for all the world

255

like a bloody gondolier with his jet hair slicked. She is more than vexed. Percy speaks to Hilda Knight – at least, he exclaims sporadically 'Ahha! Is that so? Well, I never!' He is saying whatever he must say to keep her with him. His jaw locks neatly every now and then, the line running at an angle down his cheek. His rose has shed its petals everywhere. Only the stalk remains, still hooked into his lapel by a thorn. He watches too. Indeed, the girl is very beautiful.

Charlie went outside and stood with his hands in his pockets by the edge of the grass. He half turned, hearing Herbert and Tom Edwards getting off the window ledge. Herbert did not stay. For only a foolish moment he glanced back. Charlie looked straight past him, not seeing him. Whatever was in his face would not be there tomorrow. It would be carefully stowed away.

As Herbert crept off on bare feet in the shadow of the shed, he saw Mr Moorrees come from the lighted door. He heard him say, 'Fraser, get in and do your duty. There are young ladies without partners. Do you want Miss Fowler to think we cultivate a lot of louts here?'

Charlie Fraser followed him inside.

Herbert went off to the bogs. The stars were low. Bright and clear, almost as clear as at home where they would hang up above the hills. Sometimes on a winter night he would hear a jackal call and feel his dog, suddenly alert, waiting for the sound again, her head under his hand.

The music started up again. The lights from the Drill Hall glowed orange-gold, making their own mist, the drift of voices laughing, more distant than the rhythmic click of crickets in the dark gardens. Here it was so still, the House in darkness, the big walls looming over him. Herbert leaned his head against the wall. There was no moon and way off he heard the sound of wheels rolling slowly up the street: the tangy-carts, starting on their rounds. Another life, barefooted men padding down the alleys behind houses, starlight glinting on the iron curves of buckets, mules' eyes catching flecks of light. He could hear the murmur of quite another kind of song, minor notes linked one to one, deep voices harmonising. In the Drill Hall, The Quadrille Band was playing a jig. It seemed a jingling, foolish sound, listening from the dark.

He felt heavy. No reason, after the glory of the day. The elation and the pulse had steadied. He felt flat. He had felt heavy too, sitting on the ledge, looking in. Tom Edwards had kept nudging him, pointing out things he could see quite well himself: Sparrow dancing with that White girl, 'What's her name?', nudge, nudge.

'Clarice.'

'Look, Grant is standing by himself. No, he's going over. Brave, hey?'

Dan had asked Mary Clifford. Herbert guessed what it had cost. But the tune had changed just as they went to the floor and the rhythm of the next was far too fast for Dan to lead. Poor Danny, so much sweat in galloping about, no time to feel his hand against her waist.

'Mac's an old smoothy-chops, isn't he?' Tom Edwards, stifling laughter, peered at MacCallum heading off towards the piano. Not the same in his evening suit as he was in his footer gear.

'Stop shoving me,' Herbert had said crossly.

'I'm not.' Tom was offended: why hadn't he brought Ross instead? Cummings was so bloody touchy. It must be Josie Zeederberg. But he didn't say it – it was a long drop to the ground below the ledge. 'That big sister of Harry's is quite the action,' he said instead.

Quite the action?

Tom Edwards had recently been to stay in Johannesburg. He had a new vocabulary. 'Mac's danced with her three times.' Another nudge. He had done it by mistake. Herbert was nearly dislodged.

'For God's sake, stop shoving.'

'I think Percy's a pansy,' Tom had said, trying to humour him.

Knock him off the ledge. Now.

'Or a daisy!' Tom Edwards had been very pleased with himself after that, very knowing.

Herbert had no idea what he was talking about. But whatever it was, it was derisive and uncomfortable. 'I'll *klap* you!' Herbert had said, almost pushing his face against the glass. The Head passed by just then, oblivious, a yard from their noses, dancing with Miss Fowler.

Tom had wriggled his legs. 'Maybe we can sneak back later and look for something to eat.'

Herbert had not replied. He had watched Josie Zeederberg.

'What are you looking at?'

'Nothing.' Intent at the pane: Josie Zeederberg, seen through dirty glass and Edwards' hot breath making prisms on the surface; Josie on her chair with her clarinet, feet straight and a wistful look, her fingers winking up and down. Had she known that he was there?

He had watched Charlie Fraser dance with Annie Zeederberg and Arthur standing off at the side with the girl who talked so much. Arthur had seemed to look across her, beyond her and hardly move in all the time the waltz was played. He was like a man helpless at a drowning, who waits on shore because he cannot swim.

The picture in the album of the Drill Hall decorated for the dance had no people in it. It had been taken in the afternoon. There was the backdrop, painted by old Lucas, hanging like a sail on a spar: the Victoria Falls in brazen blue. The practice rings were looped up, the horses stowed, the gym mats roped and stacked and the supper tables ranged along the walls, laid with white cloths and rosettes of coloured paper. On them stood the heavy fluted vases that Miss Maltby had brought up from the cellar. Each held a bunch of scarlet cockscomb, ferns and creamy lilies.

Even now, after all these years, Herbert would not have any of them in the garden.

–How about some jolly cockscomb? The cutworms don't like it a bit so we'll have some colour when everything else is going off.

–Absolutely not!

They were stained like congealed blood, contorted – half fungus, half petal – an entrail on a stake. And lilies, thick with orange pollen and great thrusting stigmas poking out. No, not pure at all, despite their drooping, bashful heads. There was deceit in them. Growing wild in disturbed and barren land, they were the flowers of the dead.

–Lilies then?

–No lilies. Hate the things.

–Don't be ridiculous, my dear love!

–No lilies.

–Really Herbert! What *can* we plant?

All memory is re-invented over years, interpretation honed by subsequent events. At the time, Herbert had been only a boy, but he'd absorbed – old augur-eye – the words, the looks that held the cipher. Under re-examination, as a man, he read them. And he remembered Charlie Fraser's face, caught in light before Moorrees came out and called him in:

–Will I betray my friend for love? And will I love my friend the more for wounding him?

Did it matter in the end?

There wasn't time to know.

But it had mattered then. Oh, it had mattered:

–I could kill you, Fraser! I could bloody well kill you! She was mine.

She was no one's.

Yes, it had mattered, light-hearted though they were. Affection and betrayal played at touch, soft-fingered and regretful.

But it was Boy-Love.

Simple. Straight. Unsoured by compromise.

It did not know the shame of self-betrayal. It did not need to slink away.

FOURTEEN

●■●━━●■●

'*We are The Strong Men!*' Only we.

The photograph would be famous for years: stared at, laughed over, found in every album which emanated from the House. Charlie had taken it the day after the dance. Sunday and the light was streaming in through the study windows.

–Who are these?

'*We are The Strong Men.*'

MacCallum, Graham, Morgan: Commander, Jester, Titan. Charlie had taken the picture of them dressed only in undershorts, indulging in a lot of horseplay. Vincent MacCallum glared into the lens, not quite as solemn as he usually was. Today, he had a touch of self-consciousness, afterglow of success. He had danced three times with Annie Zeederberg, twice with Clarice White.

Arthur Graham said, 'It's as cold as the sevens! Get a bloody move on, will you!' inspecting gooseflesh. 'Look at those muscles!' He rubbed his midriff with the heel of his hand admiringly. Last night's expectation and the attendant midnight gloom could be sent away with joking and fooling.

He would go to tea today. She had said so, never mind the way she had said it, suggesting he bring all his friends along as well. She had patted his arm playfully, looking him straight in the eyes with her head tilted. Wag your tail, Arthur, good fellow. Whatever he said – Yes or No – it was all the same to her.

He understood – Yes or No. It was all the same to him, as well, when Hilda Knight suggested he bring a friend for lunch.

–Yes, sometime. Thank you. He had been able to smile at her too, full in the face, without looking away. Such straightforward subterfuge! It made him feel low. And the fantasies had all run short: what he might have said to Annie over supper; what he might have murmured in the waltz. Bloody Mac, marching in and distracting her when it was clear she didn't want distraction.

He did not think of Charlie then. Nor did he look at him fiddling about with his camera. It was not Mac who had distracted her. But he couldn't blame Charlie either. Charlie had danced with her once and walked away. After that, she had been subdued and detached. She had gone to speak to the teachers, as if – suddenly – she was tired of boys. And Charlie? He had been Hands-in-the-Pockets-Charlie ever since then. He knew when Charlie stuck his hands in his pockets that way that no one should fool with him or ask him what was on his mind. He'd gone on retreat, like a bloody priest who'd forbidden himself to speak for a week.

They arranged themselves for the picture. Douggie Morgan was wearing a dreadful pair of old underdrawers and socks with bare heels. He hung above Arthur and Mac, Sampson-like. John Barham, neatly suited for church, sat, in contrast, in a chair in front of them, his pipe in his mouth. Percy was nowhere around. They'd gone to call him, so he could orchestrate the poses but Percy had taken himself off to visit the Dean and his wife. He did it very seldom. It was an ominous sign. Perhaps he had to breathe in ecclesiastical air sometimes, to stand by a lancet window with the light touching his head and remember where he came from. Perhaps he had to have a conversation from which the parade could be excluded, soothe away moroseness and pull himself back from wherever he had wandered or rid himself for an hour or two of the barbarians – Doug Morgan exploding from the bogs in a gale of farts, great happy horrible boy; nubs falling about laughing over something vulgar; Vincent MacCallum mooning with a picture and now, insinuating an understanding with a girl with whom he had no connection at all, marching over every opportunity that Arthur might have had. *Droit de seigneur*: as if girls – and not just Arthur – were subject to standing order too.

Percy had blundered again, inveigling Miss van Ryneveld into asking Annie Zeederberg to accompany her, thinking he'd been altruistic – never mind Mac, never mind his own odd forms of penance and self-mortification. The upshot of the whole idiot idea was that Arthur, despite his efforts, had The Midget attached like a limpet to his leg while it was perfectly plain to all that the arch Miss Zeederberg was as detached and cool as a blossom in a breeze with all of them except Charles Fraser, Full-back. Whatever quickened sap in flowers, quickened there and found response. Poor old Arthur.

Percy had tried to speak to Mac at the dance – by a gesture, or a jest, to stop the silence.

–I want to go back to the time before the picture, Mac.

–Rub it all out, Mac. Stuff it down Unwin's throat. Have a smoke at the window and discuss the cricket scores from last season, ponder whether next time we should move Doug up in the batting order and bring Holmes on earlier to bowl. Talk about the heroes from the teams in years before. Remember when Rudd bowled those googlies and took four wickets in as many balls? Remember Broster's double century?

–Pass us the ginger beer, old man, and get yourself a glass. –Would you like some help with that Greek translation?

Supper at the Head's, tea with Robbie, a walk to town together, eating Albanys at the Victoria Tearoom and buying a cheroot, for fun, at Radomsky's.

–Speak to me, Mac.

Mac would not allow him to approach. He had sauntered about the hall with Seymour and Holmes as if they were discussing the Stock Exchange, but eyes sliding out, inspecting the flocks of girls. Percy's exaggerated rose and the handkerchief – Paisley silk – which had been worn as a joke to make the fellows laugh, had earned a cold, dismissive glance from Mac. So he'd gone to tea at the Deanery. He could talk about books, his father's orchids, his plans for Cambridge. He could forget, for an hour, The Great Dismissal.

The Strong Men posed without his direction. Charlie called Herbert to act as tripod and stood on a chair for a better angle. All the other fellows pushed in at the door. Herbert tipped over with laughter and the camera was caught by Charlie just in time.

'Quiet!' Charlie bellowed, trying to focus. There was a hush. But the sound of feet, coming down the pavement, sent them all into a state of sudden alert.

'Croc!' Arthur was at the window in a flash. He leaned out and did a quick head count. 'Fourteen.'

With The Strong Men there, they cared nothing for the mistress. Only the pipe-smokers remained aloof. And Daniel Grant kept his eyes on the floor, listening.

Herbert clambered onto Arthur's back to get a better view. Josie Zeederberg was there, with her school basher dangling by its chewed ribbon and an expression of supreme detachment on her face. Then she saw him and she looked into the distance as though she were searching for someone far off. Herbert craned to see down the road but no one was there except a mongrel foraging in the gutter and some women turning into African Street with bundles balanced on their heads. But before she set off again, hastening to catch up, she glanced back once and he ducked inside, triumphant.

Ha! So she did look for him, after all! He might have spent the evening with his nose squashed against the glass, but he was not the only one who watched! *And*, whether she wanted to or not, she would have to pay for tea at the Cathedral Café next Saturday. A bet was a bet!

'Why are you so pleased with yourself, Aap-face?' said Arthur.

Herbert gave him a dig in the ribs.

'Hold the camera, Cummings,' said Charlie sternly.

'Take a picture of the croc's tail for Apie, won't you Charlie?' said Arthur. 'Just the tail will do.'

'Shut up, Arthur,' said Charlie. 'Apie, hold steady, man. Jack!' – to Sparrow, bobbing about – 'Mind your head.'

That photo was developed and everybody wanted one. *The Strong Men* were pinned to every wall. Herbert had written under the photograph himself, 'Swank!!!' Big fellows, shoulders and chests broad and deep, lungs filled, swimmers' arms folded, Arthur's perfectly honed midriff, like an oarsman's. The laugh shaking them. So much laughter, so much promise.

But the rest of Sunday drifted, as it always did in term, into the quiet winter afternoon, ebbing away with leaves falling and a donkey, escaped from pasture, trotting down the road, big head held up, hide wooled with its winter coat and braying at the *sloot*. A long, querulous complaint. There was prep to do – so much of it – and for the seniors, the Intermediate loomed. Mac and Percy were both at their books. John Barham was walking up and down under the gums with his hands behind his back as if reciting to himself. It would be Greek or Latin. John Barham was almost as good as Percy at an apt turn of phrase.

The House was very quiet. The younger boys had been taken to Howieson's Poort for a picnic by Jarge, sitting in the mule wagon, his hat at an angle, nubs clambering all over him, yelling as they trundled down the street. They would come back full of dirt and cuts and make a mess in the bogs and irritate the hell out of everyone for being in high spirits.

The Lower Fours were up at the Cradock Dam trying to round up desultory donkeys or invading the forts of the nubs in their absence, looking for scraps of tuck or something to break. Danny Grant had gone home for the afternoon with his brother. Lucky Dan, taking his preoccupations with him. He was probably lying on his bed in his room, the corner of the girls' boarding house just framed by the sash, wondering where – behind that prim facade – Mary Clifford was and if she was similarly restless.

It was almost better when it was raining, for then there could be no disappointment in a Sunday, no wish to jog off up the Cradock Road and go out beyond the golf course or raid the armoury and shoot doves and cook them on a bare spot on a hillside. This was when your dog was needed to flush a francolin, to look for buck spoor. Lolling in studies and loitering about in the road with nowhere to go was aimless. There was no likelihood of any of the girls coming in the opposite direction. The only happy fellows on a Sunday afternoon were those with sisters at the Girls' School: Morgan, Archer and a collection of smaller boys – on whom the privilege was wasted – who were allowed to visit for an hour after lunch. One could talk rot to one's sister while watching some other bloke's sister listening to the rot talked by him. Even at a distance, it could be thoroughly diverting. Morgan sailed off after lunch every Sunday as if his big, bossy sister was the dearest thing in the world. Archer steamed after him, his black hair wetted flat, positively affable, breathing toothcleaner as if his life depended. He only stayed away when his spots were at their worst. Herbert's own sister was inconvenience itself. She wouldn't come to school for at least another year. It would be almost too late.

Herbert went in search of Tom Edwards. He was with Ross and Pringle and Ainslie and White and all their dorm-mates. They were playing an informal game of footer, one eye on Robbie's window: no sport on Sundays. Herbert joined in. There was nothing else to do until the tea urn came and then there was the two-hour wait until chapel. They went on a fruit-raid down Oatlands Road. There was no fruit to raid except some scaly oranges from a garden with an empty house standing in it, so there was neither fun nor danger in the exercise. White shot stones at hadedahs with his catapult. He didn't hit them, but they made a foolish, raucous racket, enough to have some old fellow asleep on a *stoep*, *The Journal* over his head, totter up from his chair and shout at them.

When they got back, Mostert with his static eye was pushing Fatty Harman and Furry Huddlestone around half heartedly, trying to flush them out of a sunny spot by the House wall where they were reading together. Harman and Huddlestone paid no attention. They did not react when the tormentor was only fretful and looking for something to do. With no one to egg him on, Mostert lost interest and wandered off. He broke a window pane instead. He did it by mistake. Mac put his head out of his study at the sound and shouted irritably, 'You cockroach, Mostert!'

'MacCallum?'

'I've a mind to thrash you myself.'

'Yes, MacCallum.'

'Go and see Mr Robinson before breakfast tomorrow morning

and report the breakage to the carpenter.'

'Yes, MacCallum.' Thirty-two this term. Not bad. He made a rude sign at MacCallum's window when it had been banged and latched. Shower time. Where was Unwin? Let's *terg* Unwin.

Unwin had taken himself off. Sundays were the days when someone might decide a stripping in the shower was what he'd asked for and oblige him with an audience. Unwin had his own retreats.

For the rest, the fellows were confined to the House and the lawns. The sun was watery and bland behind the ridge. It was just after four. It was the time of day to write a complaint home, to feel low and seedy, to discover a boil on your bum and fear the end. That end always seemed closer, creeping just a little nearer when either Doolie Dowsley or Zeedy gave a sermon in chapel. Neither could summon the energy to be cheerful on a Sunday evening:

> *One of them went to the fields to gather herbs and found a wild vine of gourds. He cut them into the pot of stew but when the men began to eat, they cried out, 'Oh, man of God, there is death in the pot!'*

It must be Miss Maltby's favourite passage: there was always death in the pot on Sunday evenings. Whatever they ate then was thin and sour and old. Throwing up six Albanys after tea might also bring death to those who had taken the nubs' unclaimed share that day, especially breathing in the bog-bucket while one did it. The safest thing on Sundays was not to think too much and to write the obligatory letter home before dusk set in. Fading light on Sundays had a bad effect, especially on small boys, tired from a day of doing nothing. One might ponder too much on the dog or even the nameless mule that pulled the Cape cart. It was essential to make the letter cheerful – otherwise the mothers just might write to Robbie and be a nuisance. Chapel straight after letters didn't help. The words on the chapel wall, *Delivered for our Offences: Raised for our Justification*, failed to put a fellow in a light-hearted frame of mind. 'I am the vine – ye are the branches', despite the leafy motif painted round it, was reminiscent of the dreaded poisoned pot. Why had they put it right above the altar?

Everything on Sundays pointed to death. It was waiting just outside the chapel. It was inside the chapel too. All those tablets: *Horum Pietas Nobis Patriae Virtus Multum Profuit* to fellows who had fallen in the Koranna Rising or the Gaika Rebellion or the Second Matabele War. There were twenty-three casualties commemorated from the South African War, Atherstone to Williams, and sometimes more than one in a family. Only eleven years had passed and yet the names seemed old – ancient knights from another age – the brass of plaques rubbed soft by seven hundred and five weekly applications of polish. They glimmered on the walls beneath the gas lamps at evensong. What did they mean to anyone? What did they mean to little idle boys tracing the letters with sleepy eyes, an exercise to keep awake with Doolie droning on? Castell White. Horatio Hutchons. Dionysus Stone. Dionysus? What had his chums called him, then? No one with a name like Dionysus Stone could have been a boy. He probably had a large moustache in the second form and had fought in several wars before matriculation.

Write home in the afternoon, or late at night, just before lights out, if the fellows will let you. Sunday evenings are usually the time for pillow fights and horseplay. Sprained thumbs, bashed shins or smarting ears are the weekly currency: tears in the junior dorm.

'Who's blubbing?' A prefect bawling down the passage.

Some unfortunate put up for display, wretched in pyjamas.

'Have you done your letter?' MacCallum tapping his pen in his palm.

'No, sir ... MacCallum.'

'Get on with it.'

Small boy hunched over a school writing tablet, the badge in pale blue in the left-hand corner, *Nec aspera terrent*: nor do hardships terrify. So keep it brief, boy. And keep it at arm's length so as not to splash the heraldry. And no snivelling. Wipe your nose on your pyjama collar and stick your pencil in your ear and wriggle it about. It will yield enough treasure to distract you.

GB to his father, falling asleep over the page after a day in the *poort* and sunburned on the tips of his ears. The small blond hairs on them stood straight as new-born prickles.

'Dear Dad,
There was a footer match on Wensday. It wasn't important only against the publik school. We won. We played the Methodists on Saturday. We only just beat them. They have a good winger called Osher. Robbie doesnt like Methodists. What's wrong with Metodists? He said, dont worry, they only Methodists. Fraser made a drop at the end of the game. That's why we won. It was the most perfek kick, just sailing. Fraser is the best at footer, also Arthur Graham. The prefects had a dance. We were allowed to see the hall. They had trifel for pudding. Some boys had a fight in the bathroom this morning. One got a blood nose. He bombed us with blood clots so Robbie is going to thrash us all for rowing on a Sunday whcih isnt fair. We had a picnic. Parkes bashed his chin diving off a rock. It's got a stihch now. Fraser is swotting hard. He is not grumpy about it.
You loving son, Giles Braithwaite.'

What use was such news on a trading station six hundred miles away when his father had no idea who Parkes was or why Fraser should be grumpy or not?

GB cut his tongue on the edge of the envelope when he licked it. It was a bad end to Sunday. Perhaps he was wrong. Perhaps Fraser was grumpy, after all. He hadn't seemed to notice GB when he came into his study with his footer jersey folded after chapel. He hadn't asked if he'd had a good day. He didn't even mention the match. GB stood there wondering what to say. Fraser had been propped at the window with his hands in his pockets, gazing out at nothing at all.

Unwin to his mother.

'My dear Mother,
It is Sunday. It is a cold day. I am enjoying my Boy's Own. There is no news.
Your son,
Hugh Unwin.'

Be consoled, Mother. I have been down the tangy in search of something to keep me busy.

–Don't be idle, Hugh. The Devil finds work for idle hands.

There is nothing down there at all. Not even caddies. I have walked five miles round the school grounds, keeping off from anyone looking for trouble. I have no money for Westminsters, so it has been a miserable morning. I have lost the last *Boys' Own*. Someone has taken it. I think that the juniors use it for lavatory paper in their forts when they have finished reading it. I have a painful ear. Perhaps the sore will eat into my brain and kill me like Bennett, hallelujah! I may go up to Bennett's grave. At least no one will find me. If I could get a smoke I would have it under the wall and be comfortable. Bennett was a good chap. Even though he's dead, I think he may be my friend. Cummings doesn't come. I think he pretends that Bennett isn't there.

Arthur, dashing it off in his study, racing the bell for chapel:

'Dearest Old Moth,
We played the Methodists yesterday. We won 28-27. I scored a try. Charlie did a beautiful drop. It was a hard game. The Methodists are tough.
We had a dance last night. The Drill Hall had been decrated with coloured papers and things. It looked nice. We had good grub. There was cold chicken and beef and potatoes and a kind of custard and cake pud – cant remember the name – and some ices but they got melted before we got to them. The music was good. Some of the masters were there.
Your loving son,
Arthur Graham.'

Such a flat letter. What had doused the light?

'Silly old thing!' said one of the sisters to the mother, absently giving the page a kiss. 'He needn't worry, some poor unsuspecting girl will dote on him one day.' They had both laughed.

Sparrow:

'Mums,
I think I am in love. What does it feel like? It makes me sort of
sick all the time. It's a throwing-up kind of thing. We had a ripping
dance. (Don't tell Poppy what I said! Promise?) We had grand
music and very good food. Robbie is in such a bad mood because
of it all. He stomped off this morning and hasn't been seen since,
muttering and spluttering. I think he has gone to see some old
friend on a farm. I bet they're shooting even though it's Sunday.
The Head probably guesses but Robbie's a 'law-unto-himself'
(that's what Seymour heard him say). We'll see in chapel tonight
how he looks. If he's red in the face, he's been out in the veld, if
he's sort of green he's been smoking all day and discussing us!
It was the big match yesterday. Herbert Cummings was scrum-
half. I wish I had played there but he's very good so I can't begrudge
him. We only just won. Fraser kicked a beautiful drop in the last
two minutes. I also kicked a drop. Poor old Methodists. They
were very disappointed.
Can't wait to see you all. Dan Grant has asked me down to the
Kowie for part of the hols. Can I go? The fishing is first class and
there is a golf course. Dan's very good at golf. He says he'll teach
me. Some of the other fellows have been invited too. Graham
and Fraser and Morgan. I can get the train back after a week.
Please say yes. The fishing is splendid.
Your loving boy,
Jack.'

Charlie to his mother:

'Dearest Mum,
Played the Methodists in the big match yesterday. We won 28-27.
It was an exciting game. Arthur played very well. I had a few good
chances to kick, which paid off.
We had a dance last night. Good grub and decorations. There was
a band. They played very well.
Have you made enquiries yet about a posting with Uncle Sonnie

270

next year? There's no point in staying on in the university classes
if I can get a job. Anyway, I know we can't afford it. Most of the
fellows are off to England except Arthur and Morgan. Morgan is
going straight onto the farm but Arthur is looking about as well.
It would be grand if we could go up to Uncle Sonnie together.
Arthur has written to his people about it. I will go to the station
one of these days and ask about the fare. A fellow who was in the
House a few years ago wrote to Robbie the other day and said
there were places in Land Settlement. I had a word with him
(Robbie) about it. Sounds promising.
Love to Grandma and Grandfather and lots to you,
Charlie.'

What else, Charlie?
    That the day has been hollow and restless, that the tea was weak
and cold at lunch and the Albanys stale. He would have liked to get
on his bed and fold his arms across his chest and go to sleep and wait
it out. The feeling of suspension – self-awareness, whatever it was –
was tedious. The glory of the match had passed away. He wanted
Arthur to come and sit in his study with him as he usually did, but
Arthur wouldn't look him in the eye today. Somehow, he had to fill
the time up. 'Til what? 'Keep it up 'til . . .' What? ''Til he packs his
bags and gets on the train and goes home'? ''Til he packs again and
takes another train north . . .'
    –Where do you live, Fraser?
    –That's a bit difficult to answer, sir.
    –No fixed abode? Suddenly suspicious.
    –Not yet, sir. I am building a house for my mother on a plot. It is
owned by my uncle. It is only started. There is no street.
    –What shall I put here then?
    One day, a plastered house, a red-tiled roof, gables, stained glass
in the fanlights, a driveway made of gravel and a name on the
gate. One day, a car. And a borehole and a windmill and fruit trees
and a furrow.
    –Care of?
    There is no one.

He did not go to tea at the Zeederbergs. At half past three when Arthur came to find him, fair and dutiful and awkward, he said he'd been invited to Daniel Grant's and was going over to take some photos of the new Highland Terrier pups once he had done some work.

'I think she is expecting you as well,' said Arthur.

'Sorry, but I said to Dan . . .'

'What shall I say?'

'Tell her.'

'That you prefer Dan's . . .'

'Should I write a note?'

'Perhaps . . .'

Charlie took up a pen and a leaf of school paper and wrote a brief apology. He handed it to Arthur. 'Don't take Mac,' he said and laughed.

'I'm not mad.' Arthur put his hands in his pockets.

'Take Percy.'

'What for?'

'Go alone.'

'No.' He didn't say it: he knew that wouldn't please her. 'I suppose I'll have to take Sparrow or Barham or someone else.'

So Arthur and Sparrow and John Barham went to the Zeederbergs and Charlie took his camera and walked up the road to the Grants' tall stone house opposite the girls' school. He ached, his legs were heavy, his shoulder was tender where he had taken the high ball. He was weary. From the corner he could see the roof of the Zeederbergs' bungalow. What would she say? Such a brief, unfriendly little note.

'Dear Miss Zeederberg,
I promised Daniel Grant I would take photos of his pups this afternoon. I forgot to tell you last evening. Thank you for the invitation.
Yours faithfully,
Charles Fraser.'

How hopelessly it would be misconstrued. It had been done for

Arthur, written in a hurry. What would she think?

He hated subterfuge and now he was in it, up to his neck, not for having done anything, but only for having thought it. She was no longer to be watched, but to be retreated from. Defences down, there was a consciousness in the way he stood or looked or flexed his knees if her name was said. He could not go to tea.

There was a fury of small-dog barking when Charlie knocked on the Grants' door. He waited, leaning his back on the rough stone wall, looking down the cool-tiled sweep of veranda. The wisteria shadows were mauve and blue on the floor. Dan appeared. He looked half asleep and sheepish, rather solemn faced.

'What's up?' Charlie said.

Dan rubbed his hand across his head. 'Nothing.'

'That's the problem.'

Dan smiled. He had watched Charlie too. 'Come in.'

The Grants' terrier was an old matriarch. She had had her last litter. Danny led Charlie through to the scullery where the basket was kept. The old dog wagged her stump of tail and lay down again. Dan's sister was playing with the puppies on the back lawn. His brother, Frank, was rubbing down a brown gelding outside the stables. Cheery Frank, untouched by the gloom of girls. For the moment, good form in horses was of far more interest.

Dan and Charlie squatted on the grass under the fig. They didn't talk much, just sat with the puppies scrambling over them, rolled them easily between thumb and fingers, tummies up. Such unselfconscious sniffings and explorations, into pockets, over knees, under chins, busy tongues, cold, probing noses.

Dan did not mention Mary Clifford, Charlie said no word of going to Annie Zeederberg's. Both shadowed every word they said.

'What're you going to do next year?' said Dan.

'My mother's moving to Salisbury soon. My uncle is the Native Affairs Commissioner for Mashonaland. He'll try and find a post for me,' said Charlie.

'What kind?'

'Don't know. Whatever's going. Civil Service, I suppose.'

'What about your grandparents?'

'Grandfather's too old to stay on at the mission. He's retiring soon. He and Grandma will go to my other uncle in Johannesburg and live there.'

Not live – just wait it out. Grandfather would never go on living in a town. Bleakness would creep in with a low-ceilinged parish church with plain glass windows and mine dumps squatting at his door. No more mountains, no more river unwinding through pasture and bush, no homesteads scattered on the hills with aloe-kraals and drifting herds of lyre-horned cattle. He'd walk without his shadow in that new place, dying slowly with the prim responses at Communion, the unmelodic, cheerless hymns.

'What'll happen to your house?' said Dan.

'The next missionary will get it.'

It wasn't theirs to own. It was a rectory. It belonged to God.

Charlie glanced up at the walls of the Grants' house, the grey-stone masonry, the long window with the shadow of the stairwell behind it, the chimney, higher than the stone pines in the street. He edged a pup back by the leg, rolled it over. He did not say anything. That house had belonged to Dan's family for three generations. He had no doubt another three would follow. Soon, Dan and Frank would go to Cambridge like their father before them and their grandfather before that. Dan would read Law; Frank, Science. In a hundred years, this house would still be the Grants', imprinted with their history, loved by their descendants. So much continuity. So much certainty.

–Ah, yes, this is the Grant house. Been here for generations, my dear. It would be sacrilege to have it pass out of the family.

Charlie looked across at Frank, whistling to himself, running the brush across his horse's back, companionable, tossing a remark over his shoulder at them every now and then. He wished he had a brother. He looked up at the house again, the Virginia creeper lifting in the small wind round Dan's window. His house, his room, would belong to some other boy – half a dozen – who would call it theirs. No one would know he'd ever lived there. There would be no one to reminisce with – 'our room, our house, our place . . .'

'It's an exciting country,' said Dan.

Charlie – somewhere else – was leaning on his elbow, teasing a puppy with his fingers. 'What is?'

'Rhodesia.'

The puppy wormed its way into Charlie's shirt. He fished it out, scratched at the little down-tipped ears. 'I have to learn to build,' he said.

'Why?'

'My own pole and dagga hut.'

'Like a native?'

'It's all I'll be able to afford. I think my starting salary is likely to be a pound a month.'

Dan said, searching for some compensation, 'All that freedom, though.'

'Perhaps, one day, I'll have a farm.'

'Frank would like to farm too,' said Dan.

Charlie nodded. If Frank wanted to farm, there would be no shortage of funds to acquire one. 'He'll be a good farmer,' said Charlie.

'He wants a horse stud,' said Dan. 'Hey, Frankie? A hhh . . . horse stud?'

Frank turned and grinned back. 'Race horses!' he said, giving his gelding's rump a whack to send him off into the paddock. Charlie disengaged the pup from his pocket: all he had a hope of was a stretch of wild, stony, virgin bush parcelled out as a buffer against wilderness.

Tea was brought. Dan's mother, Lady Grant, sat at the table under the tree in the back garden. Chairs were drawn up. The Judge wandered out. Hatted, he sat solemnly on the garden bench. Charlie was invited to the chair next to Lady Grant. He had basked, for a moment, in the splendour of a thin sandwich on a fine plate and a slice of orange cake with glazed icing and Lady Grant asking him matter of factly, in her deep contralto voice, about his grandparents and his mother without giving the slightest indication that she had noticed the worn soles of his boots or the shortness of his cuffs.

He looked across at the Judge eating a sandwich, a crumb caught at the edge of his moustache, very grave, rather distant. No wonder Danny stuttered.

Lady Grant talked on: his grandfather's origins, his work, his mission; his grandmother, her parentage; his mother and recalling anecdotes of school over twenty years before. 'Such a one!' said Lady Grant. 'And *such* a character! My word!'

Schoolgirl exploits: he knew them all. He smiled and stayed busy with his cake, trying to balance the delicate fork and pronging his thumb at the edge of the plate by mistake.

No one would ever speak about his father. No one would recall him. No one, it seemed, had ever known him. He was a man without a character. Nothing remained but a jaunty studio shot of a young fellow with a strong chin and a rakish moustache, wearing a straw boater, set at an angle. Bow-tie, good jacket, humour in the smile. Sad eyes though, looking out and beyond. Young Doctor Fraser, MD, of Arbroath, Scotland, Medical Officer, Stutterheim, five pounds per annum as a sinecure, the real earnings got from smallpox, typhoid, diphtheria, childbirth, broken bones, delirium tremens, old age, accidents. Most paid in kind, some did not pay at all.

Who was he?

Lady Grant leaned to Charlie, patting his arm, 'My dear Charles, you look so terribly solemn!' Charlie coloured. Yes, ma'am. Sorry, ma'am. What could he say?

Seeing his confusion, Lady Grant said, 'It's very good of you to bring your camera. Let us take a picture before the puppies fall asleep. And I shall do it.' She waved him away. 'I am perfectly familiar with cameras and I notice from all the pictures Daniel has brought home that you are always behind the lens and never in the photograph itself. It will be a splendid memento for your mother. I shall have a copy made and send it to her myself.'

So they arranged themselves around the garden bench. The Judge and Dan's sister with the adult dogs in their laps, Dan and his brother Frank and Charlie, each holding a pup.

'Smile!' said Lady Grant. 'Tom, dear' – to the Judge – 'you look as though you're about to sentence someone to the gallows. Do buck up!'

They had rearranged themselves less stiffly.

'Smile!' Lady Grant had said. But only Frank had smiled and fooled with the little dog until it barked at him and made him laugh.

In Charlie's album, a large copy takes centre page. In Dan's and in Frank's, it is titled 'Sunday Tea: Cantie and Baldie and their puppies'. An afternoon in June. The garden swing stands forlorn against the old stone wall. A small dog is perched on Charlie's arm, light-pawed, head inclined, stump-tailed rump supported by a hand. Such safe fingers. Danny is next to him, sort of sheepish in his Sunday tie.

–That's my favourite! Charlie's mother had said to Herbert, pointing out the picture in the album. –Aren't they dear little dogs? She had talked on, knowing Herbert was struggling for words. –My mother always preferred sheep dogs, she had said, –But then, they were useful on the mission. But these! Dear little things! Lady Grant had generations of them – positively by the dozen. Such a gracious woman. I tried to get one in Salisbury but they were rather hard to come by and frightfully expensive. In the end it was better that I didn't. There were so many ticks on the plot. I might have had a tragedy and been heartbroken.

Prospective heartbreak – so much easier to anticipate and unravel.
–See? She had pointed, made a mother-face. –They sit so neatly.

All that redirected tenderness. It was so much safer.

In the picture, Charlie has a flower in his buttonhole. Is that redirected tenderness as well, with something else in mind? Where is he looking, just beyond the lens and over the head of the pup? It is a tenuous look, despite the decided brows.

Charlie went back to school after tea at the Grants. No one was around. The studies were abandoned, the doors ajar.

'Where is everyone?' Charlie asked a junior boy, reading on the parapet.

'I'm not sure, Fraser.' He stood, respectfully. 'I think most went out to tea with Graham.'

Charlie turned away. Even Mac was out. Surely not at the Zeederbergs? Percy? His desk was so neatly arranged, he might have left his

Last Will and Testament propped against his Athletics cup and disappeared for ever.

Charlie wandered off to his own study and cast about. It was Sunday at its worst.

–Time for church, Charlie.

–Not again! Rebelling.

–Hush, darling. Grandma will hear.

–I'm going fishing.

–No, you're not. Not on Sunday.

–Yes.

–No.

Put the rage away, Charlie. There is no place for it here.

Charlie took the ball down to the field – against rules – and faced up to the far posts. He did not look at the Zeederbergs' house or kick or dribble in that direction. He did not see the small Zeederbergs in the back garden playing on the swing, nor hear Harry Zeederberg say to the gathering in the living-room, 'Why didn't Charlie Fraser come to tea?'

Arthur and Sparrow and John Barham and Annie looked up at Harry in surprise.

'He was going out,' Annie said briskly. Despite its perfunctoriness, she had slipped Charlie Fraser's note into her pocket, in transit to the treasure-box she kept under her bed. She would examine his writing, even if there was nothing to extract from the words.

'So why's he kicking at posts on Lower?' said Harry accusingly. Someone had blundered. He suspected Josie and cast her a glance. She was gazing into space, unconcerned.

'Is he?' Annie reddened and Arthur looked somewhere else. Sparrow stared at the floor. John Barham was too involved with cake to notice.

'Shall I ask him in?' said Harry brightly.

Annie was at a loss. So was Arthur.

'Fine,' said Josie. 'Ask him in.' She fixed her eye on Harry: Annie would annihilate him when Arthur had gone. Idiot boy. And Annie – she hoped she'd blush to blood for making Arthur miserable.

Harry trotted off, very earnest, with a sense of having orchestrated something quite sensational, unaware of his impending fate. He was through the gap in the quince hedge and onto Lower, wading through the nasturtiums. He was out on the flat, heading for the far posts.

He stopped.

Charlie Fraser had gone.

Harry gazed about. The field was quite empty. He did not see Charlie way off in Rose Street, trying to poke the ball from the branches of a tree with a stick. It had been a mighty kick. Harry turned back, vexed: to tell the fellows that Charlie Fraser had come to tea would have been exceptional. Almost as good as getting Fatty Harman to explode.

Harry barged into the living-room. Annie had already fetched another cup from the pantry and pinched her cheeks while she was about it.

'He's gone,' said Harry.

'Bad luck!' said Josie triumphantly. Annie aimed a small kick at her that was observed by Arthur. The skewer that he kept underneath his ribcage – it was there still. He wished he could dislodge it. He wished it had nothing to do with Charlie Fraser.

She was at service in the cathedral that evening. She sat with her family in the third pew, two ahead. She turned and smiled at Arthur. At Sparrow. At John Barham. She smiled at Mac. She did not smile at Charlie Fraser. He did not smile at her. He burned.

Arthur had said, on coming back to the House. 'Why did you go and kick, like a *poephol*, when you'd said you were going to the Grants?'

'I did go to the Grants. I didn't stay long, that's all.'

'It was so embarrassing.'

'Why?'

'Because that arse Harry came and said you were on the field.'

'So?'

'So? What d'you think she thought after your note?'

'What should she think?'

Arthur had gone away, unreasonably angry.

–Just get it over with, Fraser. She wants you, not me. You want

279

her. Let's stop fooling each other. Only hurry.

Dearly beloved brethren, the Scripture moveth us in sundry places to acknowledge and confess our manifold sins and wickedness; and that we should not dissemble nor cloke them before the face of Almighty God our heavenly Father; but confess them with an humble, lowly, penitent, and obedient heart; to the end that we may obtain forgiveness of the same, by His infinite goodness and mercy.

Was it a sin to watch her when Arthur loved her? Decidedly. Was it a sin to imagine? Yes. And it was inadmissible. When he caught himself, it was always absurd. Ridiculous. To listen to such stuff! To say it! She was an ordinary girl who pushed the twins up the street in their carriage in the afternoons and went to lectures at the university in the mornings. She wore the same old skirt day in and day out and the edging of her hat had come adrift in two places. Her hair was often untidy and he'd heard her yelling at the small boys when she hadn't known that he was sitting in the pavilion, lacing his boots.

Beside him, Arthur was not looking in his prayer book. He was trying not to look at her. Mac made no pretence. He was tranced. What was he thinking, staring at her in that way? Charlie tensed, clicked his knuckles.

–Low tackle, Fraser. Grass him. Break his bloody nose.

There. Good. Knee in the back.

–She's Arthur's, MacCallum.

In the same pew, Percy was also watching Mac. He had no need to refer to the prayer book for the responses. He turned his head imperceptibly – I see you, Vincent – caught him from the corner of his eye.

Oh Lord, save the King.
And mercifully hear us when we call upon Thee.
Endue Thy ministers with righteousness.
And make Thy chosen people joyful.

Blink, Vincent. Hypnotics does not suit you. Your lower jaw might disengage and fall on the floor. It would be an unfortunate sight to have your tongue exposed. Percy closed his eyes. Dear God, all this commotion about a girl! Just look at Charlie Fraser – any moment there'd be blood oozing at his temples instead of sweat.

He shifted his gaze to Annie Zeederberg: wring her careless little neck, or make Morgan take it between thumb and third finger and jerk it. Snap. Quite easy. No fuss.

> Lord, now lettest Thou Thy servant depart in peace,
> according to Thy word.
> For mine eyes have seen Thy salvation,
> Which Thou hast prepared before the face of all people . . .

She was standing in the porch waiting for her father to come from the vestry. The congregation filed past. Mrs Randell stopped to speak to her mother, Annie inspected the folds of her umbrella. Josie was talking to Herbert Cummings. He pulled her plait and Josie only laughed. So many liberties! How did Josie do it with such ease? Annie put on her lofty look.

Here was Seymour.

'Evening, Miss Zeederberg.'

Here was Holmes.

'Miss Zeederberg.'

Here, Danny and Frank Grant.

'Hello, Annie.' They'd known her all her life.

Here Douglas Morgan and the wretched MacCallum staring with his teeth: shall I eat you now, Miss Zeederberg?

Here Arthur Graham and Sparrow Bell. Easy banter.

'Hello, Arthur.' Smiling. 'Sparrow Bell' – a mock frown – 'Look at you! What's happened to your collar studs?'

Charlie Fraser was behind them. He saw her and backed. Yes, he backed. Deliberately.

'Shit!' said Charlie with the tide flowing round him. He was shoved from behind. 'Move, Fraser.' He was borne on again by the throng. He said something to Edwards as they passed her, his shoulder hunched from her. It was a lame excuse. He had betrayed himself completely. He had betrayed her too. He went out into the cold of the square and stuck his hands in his pockets and walked up the street, back to the House, going ahead. The bell on the roof of the House rang the quarter. It was echoed way down in the town. The cathedral clock answered back, a deeper and more distant voice.

He went to bed without speaking to anyone. Arthur was still lounging in Sparrow's study. Annie and Clarice: Clarice and Annie. It would have embarrassed them if he'd walked in just then. And anyway, he had nothing to say. After lights out, he looked up into the dark, his hands behind his head, lying flat and open. He tried to call up the match, to reconstruct the moves, but it drifted away and was replaced.

Annie. Arthur. Arthur. Annie.

All love betrays.

–Would you betray me for love, Charlie?

–Yes, Arthur. In the end, yes.

–And you, Arthur?

–Yes. In the end perhaps.

–It may never come to that.

–At what price, Charlie?

At what price.

All love is betrayal. Even the Mother's. How can it be relied on? In the end she'll pack your trunk, send it to the station, scrub you up and march you out. There is nothing you can do to stop her. She doubts the certainty of her own heart.

–Grahamstown, ma'am?

–Yes.

–Such a little lad as that?

–Such a little man!

We'll have no tears. We'll soldier on. Walk straight.

Eyes wide. Chin up. That's grand.

She'll conspire with the girls too. Oh, yes. Together they'll deck you with bunting like the bunting at the dance – with an empty space for ribbons and a pocket for the photo and the latest letter.

–This way, lads.

—Too young! They should be in the classroom!

—Not a bit of it! Ready to a man!

—Wave the bunting. See – all the girls are crying!

—Don't betray those tears, boys: if you dare creep back they'd dry to scorn in seconds.

Ah, the mothers knew. And knowing, still betrayed them.

We'll have no tears. We'll soldier on. Walk straight.

Eyes wide. Chin up. That's grand.

All love is betrayal, even the Father's.

Charlie folded his arms across his face, pressed them down. Better. Press some more. Count. Keep counting.

The black water is rising. Not around, but inside. Not around the bones, but in them; not around the arteries and veins – but in them. Not around the heart, but in it.

Did his father leave the carnage lightly? Did the soul escape, unstained? Was the spirit cleansed? Was he afraid?

There had been a sermon in the cathedral in Charlie's first year: small boy sitting, head bowed, the points of his knees outlined against the kneeler hanging on a hook at the back of the pew in front. He had traced the line back and forward with his eyes. He could hear his own heart, the slow knell of blood beats in his ears and the words of the Dean delivered at a distance.

—It is a disgrace to take your own life. It is a mockery of God's gift of forgiveness and absolution.

—It is an end without the hope of redemption.

—It is the direst sin of all.

—It is forfeit of the soul.

—It is death without honour.

If that is so, even God's love betrays.

For where is God if there is no redemption? What is God if the journey into nothingness is so inexorable? So lonely?

—We must always do our duty and not buckle, his mother had said.

Duty to whom?

To her?

To his father?

To God?

Charlie Fraser had no notion of his duty to himself.

He was there to atone. With honour.

He turned on his stomach, heaving the blankets with him. He stuck his pillow over his head, shoved a finger in his eye, rubbing it roughly.

The First Commandment: Silence and Denial.

He knew it well.

FIFTEEN

He could not leave it. He had to make it right. He would have to speak to her or be unfair.

To whom, Charlie?

Just go and say, –Miss Zeederberg, I am sorry that I didn't come to tea.

–Miss Zeederberg, I would have liked to have come to tea . . .

–Miss Zeederberg, the difficulty with coming to tea . . .

–Miss Zeederberg, with regard to your invitation on Sunday to tea . . .

–Miss Zeederberg, I have come for tea . . . is it too late?

None would do.

But he went anyway.

Charlie walked fast, his hair washed and straight and bouncing, the starch of his collar softening inside where it was warmed. Clean, brisk, purposeful boy, going somewhere. Down the Upper field, onto the Lower field, past the pavilion, he went across the grass, sending the hadedahs up with a clatter, to the plumbago bush at the Rose Street end. He chose a sprig, pulled it rather roughly through the vent in his lapel. What would he say to Arthur?

He looked about, cursorily. No one was there. He turned back along the boundary and ducked through the quince hedge to the kitchen door of the Zeederbergs' house.

Harry Zeederberg opened it.

Charles Fraser was standing on the mat.

Harry stared at him as if calamity had struck. Harry, with his round guileless face and the little mole below his right eye and his earnestness, swallowed and said, 'Is something wrong?'

'May I speak to your sister, please.'

'Which one?'

Really – which one, indeed!

'Annie.' Charlie had never said her name before. It seemed a liberty. Only Arthur could say it freely. Annie. *Her.*

'She's not here.'

'Oh.'

'Can I give her a message?' Harry said with his eyes on the plumbago and not wanting to look.

'No.'

Harry stood. Charlie stood.

'Is it urgent?' Harry, with eyes fixed.

'Yes.' Very peremptory.

–Not Yes. No, you fool. No. 'Yes,' he said again.

'I'll tell her.'

'Right.'

–Tell her what?

'Thank you.' Charlie turned away and was through the hedge before Harry had closed the door or knew what it was he had to say and Charlie was back in the House in time to take the junior prep.

Arthur was standing in the prep room. 'Where've you been?'

'To town.' It was the only time he had ever lied to Arthur.

'So late?' Impossible. 'Why didn't you tell me? I'd have come.'

'Sorry' – not looking at him – 'I was in a rush.'

'For what?' Arthur glanced at the flower in his lapel.

–Arse, Fraser. You forgot to take it out.

The little calyxes were sticky and he had to pick the blossoms off, one by one, with great clumsy fingers. Arthur watched with a frown.

A note came. Harry Zeederberg brought it to Charlie's study after supper. GB showed him in and stood at the door, waiting. Day boys were not welcome in the House. Who did Harry Zeederberg think

286

he was, barging up after dark? And Parkes had seen him coming and heard him say, 'Where is Fraser's study?' What kind of execution did he want?

No one was with Charlie. He was working at his desk. He looked irritable when GB opened the door, flustered when Harry was ushered in.

Fraser flustered? GB stared.

'She asked me to bring it, says sorry she missed you this afternoon,' mumbled Harry.

Who was *she*? GB frowned.

Charlie took the note and unfolded it. He read it, put it down on his desk.

Harry glanced around at the walls. No pictures. Seniors usually had pictures – teams and things. Fraser's walls were bare. The books were neatly arranged, the footer ball was balanced in a corner with his boots, an old tennis racquet and a single golf club. A terrible old suitcase with chewed off straps as if the dog had been at it, was shoved under the bookcase.

Fraser said, 'Thanks, Zeederberg.'

Harry waited.

'Fine, Zeederberg.' It was a clear dismissal.

Harry hovered. If Fraser didn't reply, what would he say to Annie?

Charlie glanced at GB but GB, like a terrier keeping an intruder out, ready to rush at the ankles, refused to budge.

There was nothing to be said.

'Right,' said Charlie Fraser and picked up the note and dropped it in his bin. Harry's eyes followed him. So did GB's.

They knew the look – Get Out – and both retreated hastily. GB saw Harry down, as if, left to his own devices, he might run off with the footer photos ranged along the walls of the passage. He made sure he was gone before he turned back up the stairs.

Harry lumbered off, fuming. Damn Annie, getting him into this. Wait 'til she knew what Fraser had done with her blasted note – in the bin, where it belonged. What did she think she was doing? He'd tell her too.

Charlie knew it.

–What did he say, Harry?

–Nothing.

–Nothing?

–He chucked it in the bin.

–Chucked it in the bin?

In the bin. And not a word.

He couldn't leave it like this. He retrieved the note.

'Sorry I missed you. Please call again tomorrow afternoon.'

He couldn't go tomorrow. He had cadets. Arthur would be there. She had expected – and deserved – a reply. Damn GB, damn Harry Zeederberg for lurking about and staring. He stuffed the note into his pocket as Arthur came in.

'What's up?'

'Nothing.'

'Why're you so out of sorts?'

'Not.'

'Come on, Charlie, you're being a bore.'

The note burned his pocket.

He wrote a reply. He wrote it four times before it was right. He sealed it in an envelope. He went with it after he had turned out the lamps in the junior dorm. He went after he had walked down the rows. There was GB lying stiff as a soldier and staring at the ceiling. Charlie wanted to cuff his foot, sticking up under the cover, mollify him, let him know it was all right. He couldn't. He walked on.

He passed Cummings in the passage on the way from the bogs. 'Night, Fraser.'

'Aap.'

Herbert turned and watched him go. What was wrong with Fraser?

Charlie returned to his study, pulled on a cricket sweater over his shirt, blew out the lamp and went down the stairs. He could hear Dan and Sparrow and Arthur laughing in Sparrow's room. Gusts of laughter, a thump and scrape of furniture. A door opening and closing.

–You're being a bore, Charlie. They had not come to call him. They had kept away.

He stopped at the bogs. No one was there. He went in, not bothering with the door. Unblinking and impatient, he stared at the seat, went out past the little dusty hedge behind, out of the light, onto the lawn, down towards the rugby field, walking fast.

Archer saw him. Standing in the lee of the back walls of the lavatories, alone with his Flags, Archer saw him go. He followed, walking easily with his hands in his pockets, far enough to be unheard, close enough to see Charlie Fraser cross the field and go through the hedge at the Zeederbergs. He watched Charlie walk around the side of the house, return to the back porch. He saw him stand there a long time, hesitant. He circled again. He was out of sight at the side. He returned soon enough, stooped, slid something under the door. Then he backed and took the shadow of the hedge, the shadow of the pavilion, the edge of the rugby field. Archer saw him flit along under the overhang of the tuck-shop, pause at the corner of the chapel. He went in through the side door of the House. Archer lit another cigarette. He blew the smoke out in a milky drift at the moon. It floated like cobwebs in the still air.

Yes, indeed.

The letter Harry Zeederberg had brought was not in the wire wastepaper basket in Charlie Fraser's study. GB noticed at once when he came in in the morning. He looked specifically. What had it said? He had had to choke Parkes off the night before.

'What was Zeederberg doing here?'

'How should I know?'

'You went with him.'

'D'you think I hang about and listen?'

Parkes didn't have anything to say to that. But Harry Zeederberg had no business with Charlie Fraser. Only with Arthur Graham. So what was he doing? Hey? Hey? Push, shove, push.

'Get off, Parkes. D'you want a *klap*?'

'Dear Annie,

I am sorry that I did not send a note with your brother. Could you

meet me at the back hedge at 9.30 tomorrow evening?
Yours, Charles Fraser.'

He had slipped it under the kitchen door. He hoped it would reach her. Out of bounds, breaking rules, flouting friends – whatever – he had to speak to her and explain. Nine-thirty. How to get away would be dealt with at the time. What he would say, was beyond him.

School was very long that morning. So much droning on and Robbie's dog farting, unashamed, under Sparrow's feet. Sparrow was making faces over his maths book. He aimed a drawing pin at the dog's rump. It growled and Robbie looked up, alert.

'Get on, Bell!' Robbie barked. 'Let her alone.'

Arthur laughed aloud. Doug laughed. They all laughed. Dan Grant opened a window and stuck his head out.

They could hear Mr Lucas bawling at the juniors down the passage. 'Use your initiative, boy!' – some poor nub being goaded to his feet in front of his classmates.

Here is Unwin shambling by the door, his shirt tails hanging out. 'Unwin . . .' drifting after him. 'Where do you think you're going?'

–To the Devil, Sir. See if I don't prefer it.

Here is Percy wandering by with Seymour on his way across the street to lectures, Georgie Holmes, spruce, with a pigskin folder, following, John Barham flapping behind, duck-footed.

'You'll be voting for the Rhodes Scholar this evening, lads,' said Robbie. 'Be sure you think your choice out carefully. We want intellectual promise. We want vigour. Most of all we want character. That is the key issue. Character.' He looked about the room, patting his hunting knife. 'Unimpeachable character, that's what we want. And sporting prowess and intellectual excellence. All four candidates are worthy of the honour' – Robbie restrained himself from mentioning that two came from his own House and therefore, in his mind, had the edge: Robbie-trained, Robbie-honed for glory. Look at Rudd and his three predecessors. Just look!

'Who should we vote for, sir?' said Douglas Morgan, pouncing on a diversion from maths.

Holmes, Seymour, MacCallum or Gilbert?

'Whoever *you* think, Morgan.'

Seymour had scored more tries than Georgie Holmes but Georgie Holmes had made more runs in the cricket season. Seymour came third after Percy and John Barham in the Senior Higher but it looked as though Georgie just might beat them all in the Intermediate, he had worked so hard. And all that culture! Dramatics and the violin. Still – Jamie Seymour was Guard-Commander of Cadets and Gilbert was old enough to oust the Head. He seemed at least forty, if you thought about it. Mac was the outsider, a dark horse, but he was the surest all-rounder of the four. Not best at something, but excellent at everything. And then there were the fathers: Georgie's was the Resident Magistrate, Seymour's was a landowner, past mayor, alderman, whatever civic glory it was possible to reap, and Percy's was a bishop. Mac's was enormously wealthy, an entrepreneur with a title somewhere on his mother's side. Did this count?

'Does it count, sir, what his father does?' said Morgan.

'Certainly not!' said Robbie.

'Certainly it does,' Percy had once remarked sardonically. 'A venerable antecedent is essential. Do you think they'd choose the stationmaster's son? He might hold his knife like a pencil or sport a ring on the wrong finger or use the word "toilet" to scandalise his tutor.'

'The stationmaster's son doesn't come to school here,' John Barham had said, stating the obvious.

'If he did.'

'He wouldn't.'

'That's unfair,' said Sparrow.

Percy had laughed. 'Of course it's unfair.'

'It has nothing to do with it.'

'I'm sure it does!' said Percy.

'You're such a cynic,' Sparrow had retorted: new word – he loved to use it.

'Certainly I am.'

At nine they were voting and the Head had taken his time on the 'character' lecture.

'Character is not what you know and do – but what you *are*. Character is that which makes a boy a man in afterlife.'

Robbie had obviously caught his phrases and made them his own, for here they were again, rapped out briskly with the author's own authority.

'Unimpeachable character, boys . . . In years to come, you will be able to distinguish these scholars. Look at the record, short though it is since Mr Rhodes gave the College this glorious privilege. Intellectual prowess, boys, sporting vigour. Discipline, integrity. Modesty. Honour. In short, what we call "Character". That indefinable nobility which must distinguish the chosen. It is something that this young man will carry with him for the rest of his life. A responsibility, boys, which may not be bestowed lightly. A mantle, boys, inherited by few. Take this into consideration when you vote. Do not choose a fellow because he is in your house, or because he is your chum, or has a good tuck-box or makes you laugh! We are looking for the boy who will be an everlasting credit to this school.'

An everlasting credit. Robbie, standing at the back of the room, surveyed the boys. This was what they needed to hear at this time. Indeed, what else could the Head say? But in his more reflective moments, Robbie knew it was a myth. Such high hopes could spawn the cruellest disillusionment and glory be a burden. Too much expectation, much too soon. They were only lads.

He had seen it happen: –What became of old So-and-So?

–Never heard of him from that day to this.

The Head knew it too.

'Well, Robinson,' he had said as they'd sat that afternoon to deliberate proceedings for the voting. 'I hope the right man wins. But one can never tell. I have often seen the most promising fail. We have made mistakes before. If we look back at our own scholastic careers and follow up on all The Chosen, it might be a salutary lesson, I fear. When I was home last year, I called on a fellow a few years senior to me both at school and university whom we used to know as

Virgil. He was one of those young gods, splendid in every way. Quite splendid. I had heard he'd been ill and thought I'd look him up.'

The Head leaned back in his chair, fixed his eyes above the door. 'He had a perfectly dreadful wife, Robinson. It really was a shock.' He laughed. 'I think she would have made you congratulate yourself on being a bachelor a hundred times a day. So much gushing and palaver! They were living in a hugger-mugger state in a little room above a shop. It was midday and he was still in his carpet slippers, reading appalling romances written by women! And, at school, he could recite his namesake by the ream! And what do you think we talked about?'

'School,' Robbie said.

'Exactly.'

'We had tea and, if it hadn't been for the deplorable wife, we might as well have been in the common-room in our house at school. He seemed very much to want me to stay, but he got short of breath and his good lady shooed me out.'

He did not say, –He was about to weep. I could have wept myself to see him so.

'There he was,' said the Head, 'cooped up in that little room with the jar of camphor cream and a pile of frivolous books and an old water bottle in a pink woolly thing. It was a tragedy.'

'Our lads,' said Robbie, mustering himself, 'are good, straight fellows.'

'So, my dear Robinson, was he.'

Ten past nine. A quarter past. The bell sounded on the roof. The voting slips were handed out. Twenty past. Twenty-five past. Charlie Fraser completed his and gave it in to Robbie and went to the back of the room. He stood near the door. Arthur was in front of him, looking ahead, arms folded.

The nominees were grouped together to the side. Mac was grave and solemn, Georgie Holmes had a civic air. Seymour was red. Only Percy was unconcerned. He knew he would not be voted in. It did not bother him. And anyway, he was destined for Cambridge. To go elsewhere was unthinkable.

Archer was standing right in the doorway, blocking it. Charlie glanced at him. It *would* be Archer. The Head had started up again, a prayer this time, a blessing on their deliberations. May the Right Man win. Charlie said, 'Excuse me, Archer,' with an air of authority and walked out, down the passage through the side door, past the chapel. He ran then. He only walked when she could have heard his footfall. She must guess no urgency. When he reached her, he was almost strolling.

'Sorry I'm late,' he said. 'We were voting for the Rhodes Scholar.'

'Do you want to come in? It's cold out here.'

'Better not.'

'Out of bounds?'

'Yes.'

A little silence. He had not looked at her yet. He kept his eyes on the dark bulk of the tree by the gap in the hedge. 'I'm sorry if I was rude and didn't come to tea,' he said.

'That's all right.'

That was no help: she must ask a question to lead him into an explanation.

'I said I would photograph Daniel Grant's puppies.'

'You said so.'

'So I did.'

'Yes.'

'And then I went and kicked the ball.'

'Did you?'

This was hopeless.

'I didn't want to barge in late.'

'I understand.'

She was shivering.

'Do you want to go in?' he said. 'You look cold.'

'I am cold.'

'I'm sorry.'

Another silence. Annie Zeederberg was pulling at a tendril of hair.

'It's difficult,' he said.

'What's difficult?'

294

'To come to tea.'

'You mustn't worry if it's difficult.' A little arch. He must not think she had been the supplicant.

Not –Why's it difficult? Just –You mustn't worry. How was he to lead to it?

'I wish I could.'

'Some time, then.' Take it or leave it. That's how it sounded.

'I would like to very much. But it's difficult . . .'

'So you said.'

A pause.

'Are you gated?' she said.

He laughed then, eyebrow pulled down. 'No.' Self-mocking.

'Well, then?'

'There are other considerations.'

'Like?'

She was being obtuse. How to say it without implicating Arthur?

'Well, it's not a good idea . . .'

'And?'

'Not a good idea, under the circumstances . . .' Very firm. Nothing more.

She knew what he was saying. But she didn't let it pass.

Was she asking him to betray Arthur?

He would not betray Arthur. She had to understand that. He said, 'So I came to say thank you very much and sorry.'

She looked at him from the corner of her eye. His head was slightly bent as if the buttons on his coat were absorbing, the light from the kitchen windows planing his face into its contours and angles. He was frowning.

She laughed suddenly. 'It was only tea,' she said lightly and she touched his arm as if pushing him off with a little nudge. Don't worry.

He glanced up at her and laughed too. Only tea.

Her hand was within an inch, plucking at a leaf on the hedge. If he had reached for it, she'd have allowed it. And yet, it was incomparably absent. He might as well have caught at clouds. And her breath, visible in the cold air, drifting with his, was dissolving into nothing. This is your only chance, Charlie. What are you going to do with it? Walk off, leaving trite little words behind?

It is all too difficult.

'Is that all you came to say?' said Annie, hugging herself with her arms and rocking slightly.

Charlie did not reply.

–No, Annie Zeederberg. I came to say that you have invaded my head and I can't think of anything else.

'I didn't want to be rude,' he said.

'It doesn't matter.' Waiting.

Say it now, Charlie Fraser. Say it now. It's for you to say it. Instead Charlie glanced at the Zeederbergs' house and then back at the school and said, 'Perhaps you had better go in.'

'What if you're caught out here?' she said.

'No one saw me.'

'Still.'

Silence again.

'I had better get back.'

'Yes.'

'Well . . .'

She put her finger out. It brushed his cuff. 'Thank you anyway, Charles Fraser.'

'Right.'

He walked away, but he turned and paused. She was still standing there, looking back at him. Now, Charlie. Just go to her and say it.

Still he stood. Still she stood. Then he turned and was gone.

'Archer, have you nothing better to do than stand about and gaze at the dark?' Robbie pausing on his way past with Percy to inspect a sprained ankle: some foolish third year fallen off the banisters. –I'd thrash you as soon as strap you up, my boy!

'Sir?' said Archer.

'What are you about?' Robbie put his hand out to close the door. Percy gave Archer a look.

'Waiting for Fraser, sir.' He said it very clearly, for the benefit of both.

'Who?'

'Fraser, sir.'

Archer waiting for Fraser? Unlikely as Archer waiting for the Head for a chat. 'At this time?' Robbie said.

'Yes, sir.'

'No one has any business being out of the dormitory at this time except if they are in the WC.'

'Yes, sir.'

'Get upstairs.'

'Yes, sir.'

Archer was still there ten minutes later when Robbie returned alone. From behind, he read him. Robbie could read a boy at a glance. Archer was like a pack dog, hackles turned; about to challenge from the margins. 'Archer?' Voice rising. 'I told you to get to your dormitory.'

'I'm just waiting for Fraser, sir.'

–This is none of your business. Yet. Sir.

Robbie knew quite well what he had meant, impudent lout. Robbie said, 'Where is the fellow, then?'

'I'm not sure, sir.'

'He must be in the WC.'

'Perhaps, sir?' Robbie read Archer's are-you-willing-to-bet-on-it? glance.

'Get off with you then.'

And Robbie went, briskly, not looking back. He closed his door peremptorily. He filled his pipe. This was about footer and the House matches. This was about the berth at full-back for the House Cup Challenge. And where was Fraser at this time of night?

He simply didn't want to know. It would upset everything.

Archer was standing in the doorway when Charlie came out of the dark. He was leaning against the door-frame with his arms folded. This was deliberate. Charlie knew it as soon as he saw him there, half lounging and not straightening up when he wanted to pass.

'Excuse me, Archer.'

'Sorry?'

Charlie walked at him, brushed past him, shoulders jostling

slightly. He did not turn. He simply took the stairs and went to his study.

That look, the insolent curve of Archer's neck. I see you, Fraser. I see you.

Archer knew.

So what?

So what, indeed.

But – Charlie sensed it clearly – it was a shot across the bows.

SIXTEEN

'Gilbert,' Robbie said, on his way to class, passing Percy in the passage, 'would you come up with MacCallum and have tea after prep this evening? There's something I want to discuss. Don't mention it to the other prefects, if you don't mind.'

'Have you spoken to MacCallum, sir?'

'Yes. Seven-thirty. Does that suit you?'

'I have History Society, sir. I was to have chaired the meeting. Professor Cory is addressing us.'

'Nine then. It's important. Will you let MacCallum know the change of time?'

'Yes, sir,' said Percy. 'Is Seymour to come?'

'No, it's a House matter. We don't need to bother him or any of the other prefects.'

A House matter. Percy looked away.

Robbie went on, his jacket flapping about him – papers, pipe, knife, the grey flannels like the old skin on an elephant, wrinkled down to the ankles above the trudging feet.

Percy had not spoken to MacCallum beyond the peremptory exchange of House notices and instructions. But he knew Danny Grant had been called often to his study to discuss matters which had once been their preserve as Head-of-House and Vice. He said nothing.

Percy did not see MacCallum until noon. At lunch he walked up to his chair before taking his seat at the opposite end of the table and said, with flat formality, 'Mr Robinson invited us both for tea this evening. I have History Society so it's been postponed until nine. Is that all right?'

'Fine.' MacCallum kept his hands on the back of the chair and surveyed the dining-hall below. Percy waited but he said no more. He went to his seat and MacCallum asked Dan Grant to say the grace.

Percy was late. When he arrived at Robbie's door it was after nine. Old Cory had gone on and on. Travels round the Eastern Cape: from Clumber to Cuylerville to Trappe's Valley to Bathurst, collecting history like a butterfly collector with a net and jars. Potting it and labelling it and marching about with his great sunshade and his gaiters. Percy was impatient to be away but the fellows asked so many questions! Sparrow seemed to think the best way of making the good professor welcome was to detain him as long as possible. Douggie Morgan had fallen asleep in his chair at the back of the room. The great oaf had snorted when they'd nudged him awake. It was a poor reflection on the prefect body! If it hadn't been for Holmes knowing when to offer tea, they would have been there 'til midnight.

He went into Robbie's room. Mac was already standing by the little fireplace, his back to it. He seemed glowering and dark and, with the light behind him, Percy could not see his face.

'Ah, Gilbert, at last. Did you get caught up?' said Robbie.

'I am really sorry, sir,' said Percy. 'Professor Cory had the fellows asking questions.'

'Tea?' Robbie held up the old enamel pot which he always used. It had served at many camp fires. It had a certain battered glamour. The heads of his trophies looked down. Waterbuck, buffalo, a little springbok skull above the door. The tsessebe. Rifles in the gun-rack, a powder horn. Brass firedogs blinking in the firelight. The old Persian carpet was tattered round its edges. There were holes worn through. It also had its story.

Robbie offered Percy a cigarette. He handed the box to MacCallum. MacCallum lit a match. They bent to it, Percy last.

'Bad luck to light three,' Robbie said. 'Army rules. Didn't you know? Never let the third from the match be the last. One or two, four or five, but never three. That's the chap who collects it in the firing line.' It was an old story with Robbie, repeated often.

MacCallum inspected the end of his cigarette, took a respectful draw. Percy subsided into gloom. Tonight would be the firing line for him.

'Sit, gentlemen,' said Robbie. He drew his own chair up and settled himself. He enjoyed his cigarette a moment while Percy and MacCallum stared at the flames, then he said, 'Which senior in this house went out last night?'

Neither moved.

Robbie stirred his tea, set the small silver spoon down in the saucer. He took a sip.

MacCallum and Percy both sat quite still, cigarettes forgotten.

'I don't have proof,' said Robbie. 'Let's say it's a rumour that was deliberately sent my way.' He turned his cup in the saucer. His old dog stirred and twitched on the rug. Robbie looked at her and said, 'I won't have tale telling. Quite despicable in boys, no matter how it's done.' He looked into the fire. Then he said, 'But I can't ignore it either and I don't want my House compromised.' He leaned forward, took the poker and shifted a log. The sparks flew up. 'Nor do I wish to be obliged to bar anyone from playing in a House match . . .'

Percy smiled to himself. That would be disastrous: the trophy had to be retained at any cost. He blew a smoke ring surreptitiously, watched it drift. He did not look at Mac. He would have glared at his levity.

'You're the Heads,' said Robbie. 'Don't let this go beyond the two of you. Just deal with it. A quiet word here and there. Use your initiative.'

MacCallum said cautiously, 'Any idea of who it is, sir?'

'For various reasons, my hunch may be ill-informed.'

They waited but Robbie said no more. If he wasn't sure, he couldn't blame. He couldn't punish. He couldn't ban. Nor could they.

He went to the sideboard to refill his cup, muttered morosely, 'The very devil, every time,' returned to them with the pot and set it by the fire. 'And while we're on matters that remain within these four walls,' he glanced at them, 'do you know why Unwin might believe God hates him?' He said it awkwardly, as if paraphrasing. He pulled at his moustache. 'The chaplain came to see me about it some time ago. He caught him in the chapel on his own. And Unwin said it – straight off like that – to his face. Rev Dowsley was ready to go to the Head but I stopped him. We must deal with it ourselves. I won't have blasphemy coming from the House.'

'I doubt it's blasphemy,' said Percy, matter of factly. 'I think the child's just had enough.'

'Of what?'

'Of being Unwin.'

'That's preposterous.'

'It's very hard, sir, to be a fellow who is . . . not regular, if you like.'

'They're here to be made regular. That's why their parents send them.'

'Some can't adapt . . .'

'We make them. We rarely fail.'

'. . . or aren't clever or cunning enough to conceal it,' said Percy, speaking beyond him.

Robbie shifted, cleared his throat. 'I am not asking for a discourse on the cunning of boys, Gilbert,' he said austerely. 'And I won't have Unwin blaspheming. Could you have a word with him, MacCallum? He doesn't seem able to confide in the chaplain or in me. Perhaps he'll be more direct with you.'

'For Unwin,' said Percy, daring to go on, 'it's safer to speak to God.' He knew, as he said it, that he'd gone too far. 'He doesn't keep a cane behind His door.'

Or a picture on his wall.

There was a hush. A log fell. The ashes shifted. He had been impertinent. He said, 'I'm sorry, sir. I didn't mean to be rude.'

Robbie grunted.

Percy finished his tea in silence. Then he stood. He said, 'Thank you, sir. Good evening.' He took up his books and opened the door. He went out into the passage.

MacCallum did not rise. He did not want to follow Percy or to have to speak. But Robbie said no more and he was obliged to go.

302

Mac shook hands, said, 'Thank you, sir.'

Robbie sighed, 'It's time Gilbert went to Cambridge. He's setting a dangerous precedent with all this talk.'

'Don't mind him, sir,' said MacCallum. 'He doesn't mean it.'

'Oh yes, he does,' said Robbie, ushering him out.

Percy had waited for Mac at the foot of the stairs. Mac came up abreast, might have shouldered past, but Percy said, 'Vincent,' and turned to face him, barring the way. 'Are we going to discuss this or not?'

'Thanks, Gilbert, I'll deal with it.'

Thanks, Gilbert.

'*We'll* deal with it,' said Percy.

'I can manage.' MacCallum did not look at him.

Since the moment Percy had stood in the doorway behind Unwin and said, 'I put it there', Mac had hardly spoken to him, acknowledged him, called him by his name, except now. And now it was 'Gilbert'.

'We can manage this,' said Percy, 'and everything else.'

MacCallum stood.

'Come.'

'Where to?'

'Outside.'

'God Almighty.'

Percy turned and walked ahead of him, opened the side door, stepped out. He sat on the low wall, facing the bench in the alcove. Still MacCallum stood. 'Sit, Mac.'

MacCallum kept standing. 'Well,' he said. 'Do you know who it is?'

Percy inclined his head, 'If I did, I doubt I'd tell you in your present frame of mind.'

'I'd force you.'

'You have the power.' His voice lifted.

'It wouldn't be worth knocking you down.' Mac at his most derisive.

–That's a lie, Mac. It's exactly what you want to do.

Percy kept his eyes on Mac. He smiled, a small, wry grimace:

conciliation didn't work, only fists and rages. Mac would respect him more – and feel easy – if he took off his coat, rolled up his sleeves and slugged it out.

And let Mac blood his nose and wind him in the gut.

And stand above him while he whimpered.

There was a silence.

'It was Arthur Graham,' said MacCallum abruptly. 'I'd lay my . . .'

'You'd be quite wrong,' interrupted Percy, 'and it would be extremely foolish to suggest it to him.'

'Why?'

'Trust me.'

'Trust you?' Mac snorted.

Percy said, evenly, looking directly at him. 'I'm sorry about your picture.' A pause. 'I don't know why I did it.'

'I do.'

Percy shook his head. 'No, Vincent. I'm afraid you don't. You have absolutely no idea.'

'So can we leave it now?' MacCallum had his arms folded and was standing, legs a little astride: *We are The Strong Men*.

'It's *you* who won't leave it, Vincent.' Percy said it flatly. 'It's you who won't put it aside.'

MacCallum unfolded his arms and thrust his hands in his pockets. 'Who went out?'

'Let me put it to you' – Percy was on firmer ground. He could hazard a longer sentence. 'Would you and Robbie view it differently if the culprit didn't play footer?'

'All the prefects play.'

'I don't.'

Mac almost laughed.

'Then it wouldn't matter.'

'Well, of course it would matter! You can't bunk out!'

'Well, if it *was* me instead of, say, Graham or Grant, I could be punished and you'd still win the House match anyway. But if the fellow we are after was banned from playing – because Robbie'd have to do something to punish him – we could lose the trophy. He could thrash him instead, I suppose – but think what a catastrophic loss of face it would be for all the rank if someone that senior was beaten?'

'Stop talking rot! Footer has got nothing to do with it.'

'Everything, Vincent. Everything.'

MacCallum seemed at a loss.

'Let's look at it another way,' said Percy. 'If Unwin was the full-back or the fly-half, would he really have the need to believe God hated him?'

'What's The Maggot got to do with it?'

'Well, would he?' Percy stood then and he walked past MacCallum – carrying years – and he went to his room and closed the door and sat at his desk in the dark, looking at the night and the spine of the chapel against the sky. Then he took a candle, lit it and drew his books towards him. He found a piece of paper and wrote a note. He put it under Charles Fraser's door:

'Don't do it again. Apparently the House Cup depends on you.'

Charlie was already in his pyjamas but he was still at his books, reading by candlelight, when he heard the step outside his door, saw the note slide under it. He took it up and read it. He tore it carefully, put the scraps in his bin and went to Percy's study.

The House was already dark. Mac's door was closed. He passed by on bare feet.

'Daisy?'

'Come in.'

Percy was writing at his desk. The candle flame wavered in the draught, steadied and settled.

'Who knows?' said Charlie.

'Only me.' Percy offered him the other chair. 'But Robbie has a shrewd idea. He guessed or was told. He won't say.'

'And Mac?'

'No.' Percy touched the end of his nose. 'Mac only works with facts.'

'Who saw me?'

'Archer.' Percy crossed his legs, draped his arm over the back of his chair. 'That's what I think, anyway. He was waiting for you at the door the other night. Robbie likes to say it was a "rumour" sent his way. He doesn't really want to know, specially from Archer.'

Charlie rubbed the back of his neck.

Archer.

He glanced up at Percy and said, 'House matches?'

Percy nodded.

'Why do you think so?'

'Robbie wouldn't have been tempted to compromise on anyone else. He certainly doesn't want to give Archer your place. And Archer's worse than ratshit in his eyes for conniving at it.'

Charlie looked down at his hands. 'Sorry, Daisy. There was something that I had to do.'

'Must have been pretty urgent.'

'It was.'

'At such risk?'

Charlie nodded.

'If it has anything to do with females, Robbie won't be sympathetic.'

'I know.'

'Robbie's trying to find a way not to jeopardise the match.' Percy let out a sigh. 'You might just have put him in the worst moral dilemma of his life. Honour against Expedience. Expedience against Honour. How's he going to choose? Poor old Robbie. He won't be comfortable either way.'

'I'll tell him tomorrow.'

'Don't! He doesn't want to know. You're the last person he wants to see. He'd rather it was anyone else. Even Mac.'

'Well, it's not.'

'I can tell him I've dealt with it. I can make it disappear.'

'No, you can't.'

'And then?'

'Whatever he decides,' said Charlie.

'Mac will never forgive you. Nor will the others.'

'It's my own fault.'

Percy shook his head, fixed his gaze on him: the great fellow was sitting there in pyjamas that were too small for him, his wrists sticking out, his buttons fastened in the wrong holes and most missing and not done up at all. He looked away. 'Whatever possessed you?'

Charlie Fraser made a gesture with his hands, unlinking them. 'Thanks for letting me know.'

'*I'll* tell Mac, if you don't mind,' said Percy.

'I'll do it myself.'

'No, Charlie. It's for me.'

To score points off him or just to have a reason to speak – 'I think you should know . . .' ? Charlie did not say it. Percy was having a hard time of it. He wasn't the only one with muddled motives. Instead, he said: 'Did Archer tell?'

'No,' said Percy. 'It was a hunch.' He inspected his thumbs. 'Archer was after you,' he said. Then he laughed. 'There were other signs.'

'Like what?'

'Arthur's face.'

'Arthur's face?'

'I look at Arthur's face and interpret you accordingly. I think he knows that you went out as well. But he doesn't want to believe it any more than Robbie. Less. You'd better sort it out.'

'I was gone for twenty minutes, no more,' said Charlie. 'It was totally unimportant.' He hadn't even touched her hand. 'There's really nothing to sort out.' He did not look at Percy.

Percy inclined his head.

'Right,' said Charlie, rising.

Charlie went back to his room and closed the door.

The curtains were undrawn. The lights in the Second Master's little house across the road made neat rectangles on the pavement, side by side. Beside it, old Jarge's windows were dark. They were there each night: four lighted windows at dusk. They were so predictable and well contained. The master's lamp was extinguished at ten sharp. Jarge's long before. You could tell the time by them.

He stood and waited, ignoring the cold. The lights in the cottage went out. At last the street was dark. He went to the dormitory and climbed into bed and tried to warm his feet. He pulled the blankets up around his head.

He did not sleep. He thought of Percy Gilbert. Mac. Archer.

Need – for anyone, however it might be – exposed one. It could be a dangerous, angry thing. Was love, misdirected, worse than none at all?

Charlie Fraser showered, sluicing in the icy water, shaved, dressed, put on his shoes. GB hung about.

'GB?'

'I've come to make the bed, Fraser.'

Charlie Fraser took up his school-books. GB went to the bed. The little fellow put his hands under it and heaved. He tried again, red-faced. Charlie leaned over, one-handed, and drew it away from the wall. 'Make it quickly or you'll be late for breakfast.'

Charlie left, pulled his jacket down, set his shoulders. He went to Robbie's room.

'Fraser?'

'May I have a word, sir?'

'Can't it wait? It's five minutes until breakfast.'

'No, sir.'

Robbie, backing a step towards his desk, turned to it, said, 'Close the door.' This was it then.

'I went out at night without permission, sir.'

Robbie stood with his hands behind his back, examining the tsessebe on the wall above his high-backed chair. He cleared his throat. 'Why?'

'It's difficult to explain.'

'You must have had a purpose.'

'I needed to speak to someone.'

'In another house?'

'No, sir.'

'So you left the school grounds?'

Charlie hesitated. 'No, sir.' He hesitated again. 'In fact, I did not leave the school grounds.' He had not gone through the Zeederbergs' hedge. Both feet had been planted – however infirmly – on the damp grass at the edge of the rugby field.

Robbie grunted. It was a reprieve. Thank God. 'What was the nature of your appointment?' He paused before he used the last word.

'A message.'

'To jeopardise the House.'

Charlie had nothing to say.

'If you were in the army, you'd have been court martialled.'

'Yes, sir.'

'Or shot.'

'Yes, sir.'

'And this . . . person . . . you had to speak to so urgently, who was he?'

Charlie was silent.

'Why did he not come to the House and knock on the door?'

'That was not possible, sir.'

'Why not?'

'Sir.'

'Was there something to hide?'

'Sir.'

'Well?'

Charlie could not betray her.

Robbie looked up at the tsessebe. The tsessebe looked back. 'Who is she?' he said at last.

Charlie did not reply. Robbie turned to him. He did not drop his eyes. Had Robbie forgotten who had taught him about Honour?

Robbie pulled his hunting knife straight: he should have known better than to try and catch him out. 'The very devil!' he grunted and resumed his scrutiny of the tsessebe. 'You may recall,' he said at last, 'that there is a House match on Friday.'

'Yes, sir.'

'Does the trophy mean nothing?'

'Everything, sir.'

'Then you are a selfish, foolish, irresponsible boy to get yourself into this situation.' Robbie was working himself up, now. Anger was better than disappointment. He breathed deeply. 'What do you think the consequence of this would be if you had left the grounds?'

'Sir.'

'Well?'

'I know, sir.'

The bell rang. Charlie did not move.

Robbie picked up his books and gave a low whistle for the dog. She heaved up off the hearth rug. Robbie said, 'You will play on Friday, Fraser, not because you deserve to but because we need you. The House comes before the individual. It is not for your benefit, it is for the House. You will make a good job of it. Any honour that accrues from that, will not be yours.'

Charlie shifted.

'You will be back here at twelve thirty, after lunch. In the interests of the House I will not ban you from playing and will have to punish you in a way quite inappropriate to prefects. I am appalled at the precedent. Nothing will be said about it beyond this room.' He looked at Charlie then. 'Nothing.'

'Yes, sir.' Charlie moved towards the door.

'I don't think it is possible to be more disappointed in a fellow than I am in you.' Charlie knew he meant it.

'Sir.'

Robbie dismissed him.

GB heard it. Parkes heard it. Arthur, looking up from his locker, collecting his books for the last lesson said to Sparrow, 'Crikey, Robbie's going wild.'

'Who's getting thrashed?' said Sparrow, cocking his head.

'Probably Archer,' said Dan Grant.

'Ouch!' Arthur clutched his own backside. 'Guess who won't be sitting down to supper.'

Five. Six. Sparrow was still listening. The strokes went on. 'Holy shit!'

Seven.

Percy leaned his forehead against the wall, closed his eyes. Robbie, stop.

Eight. They all stood, hardly breathing.

Robbie stopped.

'Better wait and see who it is,' said Sparrow. 'The fellow will have to be carried.'

'Get to class, Jack,' said Percy. 'I'll deal with it. I've got a free lesson.' Sparrow looked reluctant. 'Go.'

Arthur, Dan, Sparrow. They almost tiptoed down the stairs.

Robbie's door did not open. No one came out. Percy waited. MacCallum was not in the House. Someone said that he was with the other Heads-of-House, Seymour and Holmes. They were with the Head, discussing Speech Day. The House seemed deserted.

Percy stood in his study doorway, waiting. Then he heard Robbie's step. He came from his quarters and walked heavily down the stairs. Percy heard the outer door bang. Through his window he watched him taking the path into the street. His old dog followed him. She squatted by a tree, sniffed, then scraped sand, stiff-legged. Robbie and the dog turned the corner and were gone. Trudge, trudge, trudge. Percy went swiftly down the passage to his rooms, entered without knocking.

Charlie was standing at the window, quite straight with his hands at his side.

He did not look round. He said, 'I'm all right, Daisy.'

'You couldn't be.'

'I am.'

'He was vicious.'

'No, he wasn't. It was a straight eight.'

'Two more than is fair.'

Charlie didn't answer. Percy said, 'I'll keep anyone away. No one seems to know it was you.'

'I told Mac.'

Percy went then, patrolling the stair head, glowering at small boys who did not seem brisk enough about their business.

Charlie Fraser came out some time later. He looked quite calm. He went to his study and closed the door.

At supper that evening, he sat in his usual place and ate his dinner. Arthur Graham, beside him, seemed unusually quiet and preoccupied. Mac remained impenetrable.

GB knew the truth. He watched Fraser from his lowly table, ears burning, almost unable to eat, strange spasms in the base of the spine when he thought about it. GB knew: that afternoon, when he had brought the tea, Charlie Fraser had been standing at his table doing his prep. He had remained quite still, hardly turning his head and said, 'Thank you', in a monotone as if any movement, even speaking, caused him pain.

GB had looked at him, alarmed, and said, 'I got a tuck-box today, Fraser. Would you like some cake?'

Charlie had glanced down at him, smiled an odd small grimace of a smile. 'Thanks, GB,' and when GB had returned a few minutes later with a slice gingerly wrapped in a piece of paper, he had been standing in exactly the same position, as if frozen. And when GB had left, he still hadn't moved.

But wild beast, nor boy, nor man, nor God Himself, would have dragged a word from GB. He gave no sign that anything had changed at all. He was watchful and fierce, an unobtrusive sentry outside Charlie Fraser's room. Poor Parkes got a beating for his troubles when he said, with innocent concern, 'Why's Fraser walking funny up the stairs?' GB had launched at him with fists and knees and teeth.

GB knew. And so did Archer. Archer waited for Robbie to summon him to say he was replacing Fraser for the House match. Archer waited for someone to ask, 'Why are you playing in Fraser's place?' Archer waited for Mac to call him up to his study and announce, 'You're in at back for Friday. Fraser's gated.' Archer was waiting to see Charlie Fraser sitting on the bench in the stand, marooned and disgraced.

Nothing happened. No one called him. The team notice went up and his name was not at full-back. And there was *Fraser, C.W.* where he always was. Full-back, first name on the list.

He could kill Robbie.

He did not understand it. It was grossly unfair.

Robbie had debated it with himself all morning in class. He had taught distractedly, set an unseen and meditated behind an arch of fingers poised together at the tips.

Gate him?

Thrash him?

Make an example of him?

Ignore it all?

'This boy, Fraser,' the Head had said to Robbie on the golf course the year before. 'Good fellow, is he?'

'Very sound, sir.'

'Sound, is he? Glad to hear it.'

'Fine boy. One of the best. Quiet, very quiet, but a splendid way with the other lads, especially the juniors.'

'Good, good.' The Head had inspected his ball, his club, the green, walking round the point. 'Make him a prefect by all means, Robinson. Yes.' Circling again. 'But not at Senior or at Vice.'

Robbie did not relish interference in his choices. 'Sir?'

'A matter of discretion, Robinson.'

Robbie had pursed his lips and chosen a club. The father. Of course. He took a swing, rather harder than intended.

Robbie was still debating it when the bell rang for lunch. Beat Fraser? Beat Archer?

How could he beat Archer? On what pretext? In the end, he had settled it, angry and morose at having been flushed into a corner. He had thrashed Charles Fraser, more severely than he should. His private wager with himself – his faith in Fraser – counter to the caution of the Head, was disappointed. If Fraser'd bunked out to drink or smoke or lark about in town, the punishment would have been perfunctory and over. But going out – at night – to meet a girl?

This was something Robbie didn't wish to deal with. This took fellows out of his control. Lost them.

He beat him hard.

The boy took it. There was nothing to show distress – hands calmly at his sides – but the pulse at his neck.

Robbie put the cane away and glanced at Fraser standing frozen at the window. 'Stay where you are,' he said. Not even a titan could have walked unflinching from the room. 'Go when you're ready.' And he left.

He closed the door and walked out of the House. He would rather thrash Fraser blue than give Archer the satisfaction of betraying him.

313

Honour first.

And Expedience? Fraser would play the House match under obligation and duress and if Robbie had punished him far more harshly than he'd meant, Fraser had not flinched. Remarkable fellow, Charlie Fraser. The boy had grit.

He would not fail him now.

But on Friday, when the final was played, the House lost the trophy for the first time in years. Holmes' team won. Holmes – the glorious boy – took it from them cleanly. It was twenty points to twelve. Charles Fraser missed a penalty and two conversions.

GB was in tears.

No one would talk about it. Herbert could not even think about it. They had watched, appalled, as the ball had flown all over the place. Not even Percy, in the stand, could look at Charlie's face. After the match there had been silence in the House. Only Archer had said, both triumphant and enraged, 'Fraser's not as perfect as he's made out,' which elicited a blind, lashing fist from Arthur Graham that nearly floored him.

'I don't know why you're defending him,' said Archer, angry blotches starting at his neck.

'Do you want another?' Arthur moved in.

'It's *your* girl he went to see.'

Arthur had him up against the wall. 'Liar!'

'Why d'you think Robbie thrashed him?'

Arthur stepped back from Archer. Archer shook himself and walked off. He turned at the doorway and threw back at Arthur, making his own challenge. 'Have a look at his arse next time you shower,' he said.

Arthur did not want to know about Charlie's arse. Archer left him with lava in his gut.

Did it matter? Oh yes, it mattered.

But, in the end, there wasn't time for her. No time for an unfolding as there was for Herbert and Josie. No time to find out who it mattered to. No time to say – either way – 'She's yours'. Not even time enough for some other fellow – Mac, for instance – to score off their hesitation, barge in and distract her.

No, there wasn't time for her. No quiet Saturdays in the university terms as there were, years after, for Herbert and for Josie with a matinée at the Great Electric Bioscope followed by the compulsory excursion for tea, the little bell tinkling above the door as they came in from the gusting winter rain or to escape a *bergwind* day, blistering the paving stones outside.

–Well, Miss Josie Zeederberg, the tea's on you again today, says Herbert.

–I know that, Herbert Cummings! Exaggerated look. I have had to borrow money from Annie because of all these foolish bets.

Herbert grins. Keep on betting, Josie Zeederberg!

–What'll you have, Herbert?

–Currant bun.

–You can't *always* have currant buns, Herbs! What about something different for a change?

The waitress says –Same as usual? without bothering to take out her pad. Same chairs, same table, same genteel cloth washed to transparency in the centre. Carnation in a little vase, wedge of paper under the table leg on the left to keep it steady.

Josie says every time –Let's be daring.

Herbert is severe. –Currant bun. Toasted.

–Same, says Josie, twitching her nose.

–And tea, says Herbert.

–Same, says Josie.

It's as far as their money will stretch.

–One day we'll have a whole lunch, says Herbert.

–Roast pork and crackling and three vegies and sauce and bread and butter pudding, says Josie.

–Not bread and butter pudding! says Herbert. –Miss Maltby made lethal bread and butter pudding at school. I will never eat it again as long as I live. Nor boiled pumpkin!

–One day I'll make you bread and butter pudding that will be Heaven-on-Earth. And pumpkin fritters that will have you enslaved.

315

–Impossible.
–I bet you.
–Not another bet!
Josie Zeederberg looks knowing.
Just wait, Petal dear!

'I hate Archer!' Arthur said. 'Bloody sod!' and he closed Charlie's study door and stood against it.

Charlie turned.

'Why d'you bunk?' said Arthur.

'I went to explain to Annie Zeederberg why I didn't go to tea. It wasn't a big thing.'

'Then why didn't you tell me?'

> –I have told you everything, Charlie. From the first day. Even when I crapped in my pants. Each thrashing. Katie. Annie. Even what the Head wrote home about me: 'Your son, though an ass, is a sound, straight fellow.'

'Sorry, Arthur. It didn't seem necessary.'

'What did she say?'

'Nothing much. She said it was fine.'

'What was fine?'

'That I didn't go.'

> –It's not fine, Charlie.
> –There is nothing I can do, Arthur.
> –Walk away.
> –I have.
> –If she follows . . .?
> –Would I betray my friend for love?

Yes, Charlie, you would. We all would. That's how it is.

Herbert found no picture of Annie Zeederberg in Charlie Fraser's album. Was there one in Arthur's? There might have been. Most likely, yes, something got from the photographer's in Church Square on a pretext of something else.

And he had said to Percy, sitting outside the House, on the quiet summer morning of their reunion, listening to the far off call of the

316

bowler, the murmur of the Old Boys in the stand, the shadow of the Clock Tower laid down on the grass, the cool white arums like ancient parchment among their leaves.

–It was all so serious, wasn't it, Daisy? So intense!

–What was her name? says Percy.

–Annie Zeederberg.

–I remember now, says Percy. –Zeedy's eldest daughter.

–Yes.

–Who she was didn't really matter, says Percy.

–It mattered to them.

–Not really.

–That's rather a brash assertion.

–She was far outside the real need, says Percy.

The Real Need?

–Self-acceptance, Cummings. Constituted from each other. Validation. We all want it. Only a few really get it. Percy had looked up at the walls of the House and turned his hat in his hand. –She just got in the way of it then. It wasn't the time for her. The match was more important.

–That's a simplification.

–Not at all. The simplification is all yours.

And what of Annie, loving still these mythic men? What of all the mothers, desperate for memorials to 'Valour', 'Fortitude', 'Forbearance'?

Are they for their sons?

Or are they for the grieving mothers?

What else can mothers do to assuage the loss? It is all that is left: so many knights with swords and dinted shields, with standards and with cloaks. The chapel walls are jewelled with them. The light along the pews is blue and ruby where once the morning sun came in, drifting pale as dust.

317

SEVENTEEN

The match passed into history. Georgie Holmes' team had won. It had been fitting: it was announced the same day that Georgie Holmes was chosen as the Rhodes Scholar. He glowed modestly. His fifteen men had been gladiators and Fraser's wild boot was a reprieve: Georgie's House loved him for it. The win was graciously accepted, without the usual howling rivalry.

Robbie was very disappointed: to lose the Rhodes and the match in a matter of days. If he had put Archer in at full-back, would they have clinched it? And if he had, would honour have been compromised?

It would. Oh, yes, it would.

It was outside debate now. A game. A match, won and lost, fair and square. Too bad. Too late. Good fellow, Georgie Holmes. Very good fellow. Well done, lad. Best team on the day. If there was to be reproach, he would have to take it on himself as well. He avoided Fraser as the team walked up. What could he say?

I was too hard, lad . . . ?

I gambled and lost . . . ?

The Head was right . . . ? Robbie grunted then. *That*, he would not concede.

There were mark orders to attend to and a broken window in the junior dormitory.

Call at the workshop.

Collect up the register, dog at heel.

Enough. Quite enough. Leave it now.

'He deserved it,' said Mac, brushing past Percy in the passage after the match. It was not an invitation to talk.

'What?'

'Fraser.'

'Deserved what?'

'The thrashing.'

'Why?'

'I'm bloody angry with him. It was sheer carelessness.'

Percy, standing outside his door, looked at him. Mac did not invite him in. 'He had an off day,' said Percy. 'So what? It's just a game.'

'I hate your bloody, flippant "so-what". It's always "so-what" with you. I wish Robbie'd given him ten.'

'You're not angry with him for that, Vincent,' Percy said quietly. He did not mention Annie Zeederberg. He said instead, 'You're angry with him because no one else is and you don't understand why.'

'They bloody well should be.'

'And they're not. That's what really riles you. They'd have wanted to lynch anyone else – you included – for giving the match away.'

–It was about authority, Percy says. –It's an odd thing, you know, Cummings. It's quite different from power. Mac didn't understand that.

Herbert drifts in the shade of the wisteria outside the House. The shadow in that corner is warm, a little hollow that has captured the early sun and kept it in the mauve dust of old walls and creeper. Percy says, –How we relive these juvenile triumphs to validate ourselves, Cummings! Sometimes that's all we have – the only little power we'll ever know. It's so vital to us. He laughs, takes up the end of his old school tie and examines it a minute, then pulls it straight. –That's why most of us are here today. He looks off towards the field where the match is being played: Old Boys versus School. –Authority is bestowed year after year with each induction of rank. But it's only the power to coerce that we're given. *Real* authority is something else entirely. That's what Mac didn't grasp. Herbert listens.

–Do you know why Fraser wasn't Head-of-House? Do you know why, right from the day he came to school, he wouldn't be considered?

–He would have been if he'd stayed on for the university classes like the others, says Herbert.

–No chance, says Percy. –Not even then.

–Why? Herbert is sceptical.

–His father, Percy says.

–His father?

–I asked my own about it. 'Can't take a chance on a fellow with an unstable past' is what he said. 'He might turn out the same. Dicey business.' If something had gone amiss in the House, there'd be someone who'd be first to say, 'Who was his father?'. It would have been the same if he'd been Jewish or a Catholic or a Foreigner. Just a little shadow which weighted their choices. They'd never admit to it, but it's there, nonetheless. Play it safe. Always play it safe.

Percy folds his arms and rocks slightly on his heels. Elegant, slim shoes, knife-edged turn-ups on his trouser legs. –Mac was safe. Daniel Grant was safe. I was safe. We were very 'good, straight fellows'. We also had good, straight fathers. But with Charlie Fraser, it was not the same. The House match proved it. He failed, yes. We all knew why and we took his failure on ourselves, as if we were to blame. Sort of sacred, in a way. It was all part of the aesthetic I was talking of. The great romance – an adjunct to the other manly drama. Blood sacrifice – sin, penance, resurrection – and the fatal flaw. Whatever you wish.

–Come on, says Herbert half laughing. –It was a game.

–Of course, says Percy. –Still, we wouldn't have done it for anyone else.

–Perhaps, says Herbert.

–Fraser moved us, says Percy simply. –That was the difference. Yes. Even now: Fraser moves us. Down all these years, he moves us.

The match was recorded in the school magazine that term. The

320

ignorant scribe – a master, sharpening his prejudice in favour of his own house – wrote: 'Fraser made an unpardonable blunder and simply gave the opposing team their first try.' Not even Mac, in his disappointment, would have written that. 'Silly sod,' Mac said, pushing the publication over to John Barham. Silly sod, indeed.

Charlie made no comment.

That report, brown-aged among Herbert's school detritus, was marked with a scrap of paper. Herbert had glanced at it sometimes. One slip, one lapse: 'Fraser made an unpardonable blunder . . .' Faded on a frayed page, laced at the edges by the depredations of the fishmoths in his dusty bookshelves, like the photos, there was a cipher in the words. It could be smiled at now. So great a blunder? To miss a kick? To give a try away?

Had his manliness been compromised?

The Second Commandment: not to fail at footer. Quite un-pardonable.

Was love unpardonable too? It seemed that then, it was.

Herbert kept the publication of the 'unpardonable blunder' closed away from idle browsers. It was not for outside scrutiny. Annie Zeederberg kept it too. She used to touch the place where the words were, as if, in writing them, an injury had been done him, to his flesh. She had seen it all, standing by the hedge, watching in a heat of agitation. What had gone wrong?

What indeed, Annie Zeederberg.

'Charles Fraser was thrashed for coming to see you,' said Josie, matter of factly.

Annie flew up.

Hero in the dust. Prostrated for love. Horror and triumph.

'Yes,' Harry said.

'How do you know?'

'Everyone knows,' said Josie.

'That's why he played so badly!' said Harry. Warming up, 'It was really your fault.'

'That's a lie!' retorted Annie.

'Don't look so pleased,' said Josie.

'I am *not*!' Annie was high with indignation.

Oh, yes, Annie knew: there was a kind of holiness in this sin of hers, in distracting him. It required a thoughtful, middle-distance introspection that she trailed about with her; moths wings around her heart.

It gave her grace.

–She distracted him, says Percy, lighting a Turkish cigarette, slipped from a silver and tortoiseshell case. The smoke is fragrant among the wisterias. –Robbie's spectre of the great danger to us all! Such a sin! Mac and Arthur were just as likely to be distracted but it wouldn't have mattered as much. It's always worse when a god is found to have his failings! Poor old Fraser! Never allowed to be an ordinary fellow like anyone else. Arthur'd have backed off for Charlie if he'd insisted. He knew there was no contest. You only had to look at her.

–Charlie wouldn't have let it happen, says Herbert.

–Not then, Percy says. He taps the end of his cigarette, as if sprinkling salt, watching the flakes fall off. –The mysterious imperative, Cummings. He looks beyond Herbert down towards the field. –When that became insistent, there'd be very little one could do. Just as well she stayed behind.

Percy smooths his hair with the flat of his hand. –She very nearly undid Charlie Fraser though! But not quite. The rest would have come after, as it always does. He smiles to himself: it seems to be an old joke with him. –All those splendid fellows so easily undone! What a motley collection of *has-beens* we are today, Cummings! Obedient old dogs! Look at our Once-Undaunted Douglas, reduced to pushing an infant about in a perambulator in view of the hallowed House! He didn't know *then* that all the dangerous secrets of a Lettie van Aas would lead him into this!

Herbert laughs. Indeed, there is nothing poor about Doug! Lucky fellow, despite what Percy pretends! He settles his shoulders, shrugging off other recollection, puts his hands in his pockets.

322

He is comfortable with their shape to his knuckles, comfortable with the smooth cheek of his old pipe under his palm and the little hole that had been darned by thrifty, if admonishing, fingers. The belonging of an old, old jacket. The belonging of old shoes. The belonging over years and years. Those itinerant boys, never knew the ordinariness of contentment. Or how the mystery changed, mutated gently into habit. They didn't have the time.

Yes, she had distracted him.

On the day of the House match she had watched from behind the hedge in the back garden. She had seen the unease, the strict control with which he had walked down the steps of the pavilion and bent to tie his boots. The easy lope was gone. Something pained him.

Arthur had been quite brilliant and scored three tries and caused a man to be carried off the field. The House had gone wild.

Charlie had missed every kick at posts. The dismay in the stand was palpable. It was as though his broad straight back was hitched amiss, as if his knees had been dislodged. She knew that he had seen her at the hedge. He had looked back briefly, then walked head down. She had never seen him walk that way before. And when the match was ended he went up the steps, hesitated, glanced back at the milling team in the stand, waiting. No one came. He pulled his socks up – went on then, towards the House, alone.

The season ended and the field was taken up with cricket. Charlie Fraser did not kick at posts. It seemed as if he had disappeared – overnight – and forgotten she was there. Charlie Fraser gone. He even seemed to have stopped going to the cathedral on alternate Sundays and if he was there, he did not often take Communion, for even through her fingers she did not see him walking to the rails. She looked for him whenever she walked past the House on the way to music or when she went to town. He was not in Abbott's. Not in Birch's. Not at the counter where the painted sign announced, 'College sweaters: Order now. Small Men's, Medium Men's, Fuller Men's'. He was not by the old brown wall in the shade of the oak that pushed up the paving where the white-faced house stood opposite, its shutters

323

sagging at the shoulders in the sun. The moment of recognition had come and gone. Charlie Fraser had turned his back and walked away to the House. The diffidence at the hedge remained, implacable. It was back to cake and tea on Sundays – Arthur, Sparrow, Apie, any number from her university classes, even Georgie Holmes and James D Seymour came. Even Vincent MacCallum sometimes, all sophisticated sombreness and pique at her indifference. It was letters from Arthur, despatched in a steady stream. Dear old Arthur: she could have kissed his face all over and laughed at him for the funny things he said. She teased him so he crinkled down his eyes at her. Such a boy! Such a dear old boy! He had no idea about Romance. He had no idea about the sanctity of vigil.

But then, she never knew that Arthur lay, nightly, eyes fixed on the ceiling – if not in vigil, then in transportation – far from the House, intent on some chivalrous adventure, some glorious escapade, on return from which she was always waiting:

–Arthur, Arthur! And the kiss! He had lingered with that kiss on battlements, in bush camps, burning buildings, trains hurtling to their doom – he had seen too many pictures at the Grand Electric Bioscope: *In Peril of their Lives*, *A Girl-Spy in Mexico*, *High Treason*. He could out-hero all of them. Oh, Arthur loved Romance just as much as she!

If Annie had known, she would have been impatient with all that sword-waving and ravine-leaping and fire-dousing. Her transportations were different. She, in turn, carrying melancholy like a candle – lighting her face to advantage – nursed Charlie Fraser from raging fevers in midnight tents, tended mortal wounds, prayed over his faltering pulse. She knew his eyelids intimately, his temples, the nape of his neck. She even buried him sometimes until she felt hot, fat tears slide out at the glory of it all.

When Arthur wrote, she searched his letters for Charlie Fraser's name. At tea she listened for it when the fellows talked – some illusory note – wondering if, on their return to the House, stuffed with cake and cordial, Charlie listened to them too, just to catch the sound of hers, laying secret claim. She didn't know. She couldn't tell. Charlie

Fraser had backed off, left the field.

Those letters of Arthur's were given to Harry with enough casual authority to distract observers from the glow of his ears. It was as well that she was not at school or they would have had to be delivered in secret to the wall that divided the grounds. Such letters, thrust across the barrier between the College and the girls' establishment, were strictly forbidden. If Arthur had been caught he'd have earned a six. The master whose study overlooked the packstone wall patrolled it occasionally, intent on loosened masonry which might reveal a hiding place. Arthur, a more fortunate lover, could write when he wanted and the occasional receipt of envelopes, via Harry, in return, was insurance on his claim.

Herbert had wondered, at the time – seeing fellows, skulking like felons, hauled in by the master – why girls were so unaccountably dangerous? Why Robbie had beaten Charlie Fraser in that savage way? Why letters could occasion such wrath from Cupid peering from his study window? Why Robbie always brought up the devil if a female less familiar than Miss Maltby were mentioned? Why he bristled when Mrs Woodman's daughter was serving in the tuck-shop and swooped about the dorm when the croc went by beneath the windows? Those girls – Clarice White, Mary Clifford – playing tennis or hockey or walking to church, suggested nothing sinister. There was nothing sinister about Josie Zeederberg either. She, with her disreputable boots and her chewed hat ribbon – she'd as soon give a chap a *klap* as fiddle about looking for his letters in a wall! If Annie Zeederberg herself appeared suddenly in their midst, she would doubtless cause instant alarm to little boys – but sinister?

Perhaps Lettie van Aas was sinister – Douglas Morgan had been intent for weeks to discover exactly why – but Mrs Huggins of the Salvation Army had her in her custody: she could not get at them. She left no letters in the wall, no scent to lure them out.

'I used to walk down the road with my nose in the air half a mile behind the croc,' Sparrow had once said. 'Just to catch a whiff!' He'd laughed. 'I don't know what of! And I never smelt anything except drains and pines.'

The prohibition on letters in the wall did not stop the flow. It intensified it. And the master's vigilance was a challenge to inventiveness. Mostert, bringing a bow and arrow from home – neatly manufactured from a length of *kannabos* with a twisted sinew string – shot a missive into the dorm window on the second floor of the nearest girls' residence. It did not bounce off the frame or hit a pane. It went straight through, the envelope skewered to a slim stake of wood. A moment, and then the window was crammed with girls, hanging out, plaits dangling and Mostert slung his bow over his shoulder and sauntered off, exultant.

The term was ending. There was no more time for letters or for mooning about on Sundays. The sky was white above the stone pines on the hill. The shrikes were calling. There were leaves on the oaks in gardens – and more ruggedly, the veld beyond outlying plots, playing fields and pasture, was blossoming. A fortnight before the Michaelmas holidays, the Cadet Corps, kitted out in hot, mouldy khaki, slouch hats banded in navy and pale blue, marched to the station. The Kowie. Cadet camp. Tents in wagons, boys on the trains, steaming down through Bathurst. The *mtsintsis* were all in flower against the sky and the bush shining and dark. Far off, over hills and more hills, breathing up and down, slow, quiet ebbs at river mouths – the sea. The noise in the train was unbearable. Robbie retreated to another carriage with Moorrees, his Second-in-Command.

The Martini Henrys were distributed and the rounds of blanks. The tents were struck. They grew like a haphazard field of mushrooms above the river. The ground was stony and *duiweltjie* thorns webbed the sand where big black ants plied back and forth, scurrying from boots. The wind got up and ballooned into tents not properly secured. Flies appeared from nowhere. Avoiding firewood duty, Harry Zeederberg took out his bugle and trailed about in search of harmony.

'Shut up, Zeederberg, you are putting me off my feed!' Edwards yelled over his shoulder from potato-peeling in the kitchen tent.

Robbie was looking disgruntled and morose. Unbidden, Percy boiled a kettle and made him tea. Robbie sat on an uneven limestone ledge and surveyed the terrain through his ancient binoculars.

The parade the first evening did not inspire confidence.

'More spit and polish, gentlemen. You'll assemble again at six tomorrow morning and I expect you to be decent, to a man. Find another hat for that cadet' – aiming at GB with his swagger stick – 'Besides that the fellow can't see, he'll make us the laughing stock.'

GB's slouch came right over his eyes. His ears were folded forward under the inner leather band. There was an inch between his head and the interior rim. Everyone laughed. Robbie did not.

Robbie would take no larking. Not with arms nor with discipline. 'Hold your weapon straight, boy,' adjusting a barrel peremptorily. 'It is not advisable to treat it as a club!' Stiff-kneed, he stalked up and down the lines: no more trudging, shoulders sloped under the sagging seams of his jacket. He strode, hands behind his back, stick bristling at his armpit. He halted before an inattentive recruit, absently scratching his backside. 'Wave your rifle around like that and someone will be shot. Disarm the fool,' he barked at the company officer. Relieved of his weapon, the cadet was cuffed to the back of the ranks. There was cold scorn from the farm boys, as at ease with their rifles as a platoon of seasoned troops. What could you do with a townie? Even his mates shunned him for an hour. Better to be shot than to look ridiculous.

Manoeuvres in the dunes: high, vaulting slopes of fawn-pale sand with a crown of scrub. They seamed the coast, east of the estuary, mile on mile on mile, warmed ridges facing the sun, cool damp gullies in the folds and lee. Standing in a landward dip looking up, Herbert could see the soft streaming of the sand in the wind brushing the crests high above his head. The air was still in the hollows.

Herbert, drifting, sat in the sand feeling its coolness through his trousers. Dune shadows are blue. He traced the sharp edge of shadow with his eyes, laid flat on a surface, pooled in a footprint, folded over ribbing where the wind had passed. Such a blue because of air and sea and the pale gold of sand behind to light it dimly. If he were to paint it, how would he interpret light like that within the dark?

'Move, Cummings. What'cher doing dozing here? D'you think this is a holiday camp?'

'Sorry, Morgan.'

'Move. Move. Move!' Douggie Morgan, sweating happily, thumbs

327

hooked in his belt, great thighs straining at the pockets of his trousers, roared, 'Shift your arses, you useless louts. Unwin! You'll get sand in the barrel if you fool about like that!'

Herbert slung his rifle at his shoulder and started up the slope. Two steps up, slip back one. His boots were so full of sand he was walking an inch taller and the grains were rubbing raw the skin at the arch, despite the old woollen socks. He was panting as hard as the others when he reached the crowning brush at the top and stood looking down – gull-height – at the sea below. Here the wind was brisk, skimming the margins of sand – a faint singing – and transferring it to another ridge. Ridge to ridge, ridge to ridge and back again.

'Move. Move. Move!' Douggie Morgan shouted, heaving up behind them.

Herbert gathered himself, adjusted his rifle and ran, Edwards and Unwin at his side.

Run, then spring: up and over the crest of the dune, up and over, suspended a moment in the blue air, leaping free, knowing the fall to land, calf-deep, on the other side, is soft. Run then, down the steep, concave slope: great, airborne strides, rifle high, exultation in the shout. Faster, faster, balance still precarious, down towards the flat beside the sea until the wet sand anchors boots. Stand and gulp the salt air, hair on end, arms tingling from the rush of wind, each footprint dredging up a little pool of water; mind the green-coned sea snails frilling the margins of their tracks at the water's edge, wavering here and there, being tumbled over and over by the dying tide.

Edwards turned circles until he fell and Unwin laughed, running backwards, water flying from his boots. Way up above, Herbert saw Arthur prop his gun against a bush and somersault from top to bottom of the dune. He lay spread-eagled at the foot, panting. He shook himself like a dog and went back for his rifle. Such a slope to climb again, but he didn't care. Herbert watched him, dark against the white light of afternoon, moving with a rhythm as though he might be singing. Effortless. Even Percy leapt with a yell, feet sprung to touch and fly, touch and fly.

–It was like those dreams, Percy says, –when you skim just above the ground. Once, when I went over the top, I had this strange sensation of smelling sea. If I'd looked back, I swear Morgan would have been there shouting, 'Move. Move. Move'. There wasn't much difference between the sound of guns and waves. No fear either. I think I was yelling my head off.

But Herbert knew. Run, boy. Run until the momentum lifts you just above the earth, then fly. Fly. Fly with the ball, across the line, clean-heeled from the fellows reaching for you. Hear the tumult for you from the stand, the great triumphant roar.

Fly from the dune, boy. Fly from the dune, razor-edged with wind-shear. Leap and hear the distant waves way below your feet, your ears ringing. Fall free and roll and rise and run with titan steps and let momentum take you.

Fly, boy. Fly until the boulders of the ironstone hill meeting boots cannot check their speed. Shout, boy, Shout. Curse the guns – and the silence when they cease. Here, there is no lifting southern wind with clean-crested waves below. Brace your shoulder to the weight of tropic air, pressing down. Wade it, then slow and sink among the flat-topped singing thorns, the *dongas* roped with roots.

Do dead men fly? Do they fly, swift in that moment of release, like boys leaping from the tops of dunes and turning somersaults and circles, lungs filled with exultation, ending at the margins of the waves and standing breathless where the sea snails turn in slow parabolas against the dragging of the ebbing tide?

–It was all a game, says Percy, –despite the Martini Henrys. He looks at Herbert, –We were happy.
–Even Unwin, says Herbert.
–Until he got shot, says Percy. And they both laugh.

'Surrender, Unwin!'

'What?'

'Surrender.'

'Aw, c'mon, Archer,' says Unwin, struggling up from his hiding place among the bushes, well away from officers and NCOs and trying to muster something of the old conspiracy. He flicks the butt end of the cigarette into the sand, squinting up at Archer, one eye closed against the sun.

'Surrender, Unwin.'

'Want a fag?' says Unwin, reaching for his pocket. He has two left. Caught red-handed, it's the only lure he has.

Archer does not take the bait. Who does Unwin think he is?

–Want a fag? Cheeky sod.

Archer, stepping back, swings the mouth of the barrel of his rifle towards Unwin's chest and pulls the trigger. There is a loud report. It echoes round the dunes. Unwin falls back, shrieking. Boys in camp around the headland look up from their task of laying fires. It is only a blank but the smell of cordite is strong.

'Archer says Unwin shat his pants,' says Edwards conversationally to Herbert, stirring a pot over the coals.

'Archer's going to shit his too if Robbie finds out,' says Herbert, glancing towards Robbie's tent.

Charlie was sergeant of 'C' Company. John Barham, its first lieutenant, sent him to attend to Unwin. He had found him, far down across the salt flats, at a curve of the river behind a rock, standing bare-legged in the water, washing his trousers. Charlie backed away before Unwin saw him, waiting at a distance, turned towards the camp, arms folded. Unwin took a long time.

Charlie heard the squelch of boots as Unwin laboured along the bank towards him. It was a clumsy, disconnected sound, like an animal in distress. He went towards him then. Unwin stopped, head up, ready to lumber away. Charlie reached him, standing off a little. He folded his arms again and glanced across the river at the tents.

–For God's sake, wipe your face, Unwin. It's covered with snot.

Charlie did not say it. 'Unwin?'

Unwin was shivering. His uniform was drenched. His pants clung to his thin legs. Unwin put his hand to his chest. The shivering was not cold. It was shock.

'You all right?' said Charlie.

'Wish he'd shot me.' Unwin's jaw was locked against an involuntary shaking. He seemed peeled of everything, boneless, white.

Charlie kept his distance. 'Will you come back with me?'

Unwin was silent.

'Camp.'

Unwin made a small sound in his throat, shook his head.

The wind was pushing up dark choppy patches way out midstream. The sky was pewter-grey. Somewhere a fish flopped over. The little lapping at the shore where salt-grass grew was loud between them.

'Tide's coming in,' said Charlie, letting his hands fall to his side.

Unwin's teeth were chattering.

'Just keep in step,' said Charlie. 'Right behind me.'

Unwin was wary: the retreat and vacancy of shock, like a lost dog, fear overriding need, need fighting fear. Unwin cast about.

'Come.' Charlie said it quietly. Then he turned and walked up the bank. He walked firmly. He did not look back to see if Unwin was following.

He kept a steady pace. If Unwin did not follow, it would be the end for him.

–Follow, Unwin. For God's sake, follow.

Charlie listened for Unwin's steps but he could only hear his own. He did not change his pace.

–Follow, Unwin. If you don't, you'll be finished with yourself.

Still he walked. He came to the crossing, where a tributary fed into the estuary, sandbars linked like hands, but he did not stop. He went on upstream. He looked for another ford, out of sight of the camp. He wanted no binoculars trained, no fellows fishing from the shore marking their progress. He turned a bend and searched for the shallows. He stopped and unlaced his boots. He did not look up but he could feel Unwin there. He was like a stray, clinging to the shadow of a man, will eroding, tail down: a yelp, the futile drawing of a lip

331

above the teeth.

What did you do with a dog like that? Did you shoot it? Drown it? Did you coax it back?

Charlie said, 'The water's quite deep. Better take off your boots.' He tied the laces of his own together and slung them round his neck. He waded in, up to his waist. The current was swift and cold. Could Unwin swim?

He went on, eyes on the far bank. He climbed out at the other side. He glanced back once. Was Unwin floundering? No, he had put his face in the water. He was scrubbing the snot off his cheeks.

Unwin reached shore. He was not whimpering any more. Doggedly he pushed his feet into his boots.

They walked into camp together, Charlie at Unwin's shoulder. 'Right, Unwin. Good fellow,' said Charlie Fraser and he moved off towards his tent.

He stopped, hand at the flap – Mostert's voice was clear: 'Hey, Unwin. Archer said you shat yourself.' Mostert was circling in. 'Why're your pants wet, hey, Unwin?'

Charlie Fraser stepped back, came up behind Mostert, turned him at the belt, said very quietly, 'Did I shit myself as well?'

Mostert stared at Charlie Fraser's sodden trousers. Charlie let Mostert go. Not abruptly, not with a shove. He just released him and absently flexed his hand. No one laughed. Charlie Fraser walked away. Unwin, straight-backed, went to his tent and changed his clothes.

–I wish he'd shot me.

Charlie looked across at Unwin sitting at the edge of the group by the fire made by the fourth years, eating their supper. Shoulders were turned from him, legs stretched to make a barrier from which his were excluded. Edwards sat with his hand up against his chin, arm resting on a crooked knee, closing him out. Not specifically, not pointedly – it was the way that Edwards lounged on his bed, open to Cummings on the left, closed to Unwin on the right. Is that the way exclusion started? A shoulder turned, an inattention in the eyes: –I say, you fellows, have you heard? No response. No one wants to hear.

Even Davey Bennett had had to duck when he saw him.

What, but exclusion, a small insidious undertow, could send one out: a swimmer dragged unwittingly beyond the headland by the tide? Or was it some internal darkness washing in? He felt the panic: the brief contracting of his blood. Had his father felt it?

Unwin had slipped his hand into the opening of his coat. He seemed bent across his arm, nursing his chest. Was he bruised? How did the report of the shot sound in the ears?

And what of a real bullet?

Charlie looked away.

Had he heard it? Was he sitting in his cast-iron cot, or lying under the quince hedge on the old plaid blanket brought from Arbroath by his father, nursemaid dandling leaves for him to catch at? Had he heard it, in the quiet of a Sunday morning? And had the keening of a woman's voice – his mother's – been real or had he invented it?

Did he know the sound of that lament: –No. No. No. Words falling; the swift, implacable darkness. –No, James, no.

Had he heard them?

–Oh, Charlie. Charlie.

He looked away, shifted his shoulders. Arthur glanced at him sleepily, heaved his legs straight, leaned against him, gave a mighty yawn and closed his eyes. Charlie propped him up, shoulder to spine, drifting in the old companionship. Here, under the stars, with the smoke of the fire permeating their hair, the tin of water boiling on the coals – far from the swing on the Zeederbergs' lawn, the little pile of letters tied with a string, the sudden awkwardness at her name arising or the sight of her walking the babies in their carriage – Arthur was back.

Archer, at another fire, sprawled with Stafford and the other bucks, had no cause to 'shit his pants' on account of Robbie that evening. Robbie did not know what he had done to Unwin. Company leader, John Barham, had not reported him. Fraser had dealt with it and said nothing.

He should not have been complacent. The moment came, soon enough. It was his own doing. Entirely his own doing.

The next day, calling a halt in manoeuvres for a drink at midday, Robbie allowed the Corps to rest in the shade of dune bush north of the estuary, and take out their water-bottles. He went off up the slope with his dog, Moorrees and his officers to survey the coastline with his binoculars and to choose a new route back to camp.

Unwin had dropped his water-bottle from his kit somewhere along the way. 'My water-bottle,' he began plaintively, searching about, his tone winding up: the familiar peevish pitch.

It could only be Unwin's that was gone. Wretched Unwin's Wretched Luck. The fellows near him simply looked at him, went on swilling warm liquid. No one offered him a sip. Unwin cast about, a landed fish, eyes wading.

Archer held out his bottle. Unwin, swallowing, reached for it gratefully. Archer snatched it away as Unwin grasped it. Archer laughed, coaxing him. He dangled it by its strap an inch from Unwin's outstretched hand, jerked it away again. Its buckle caught Unwin's nose at the bridge. Unwin turned his face down, dipping his head as if to duck a tide: his tears congealed to snot, edging down his lip.

Archer – insect-maiming: wings from moths, abdomen from thorax, head from feelers – stretched lazily and said, 'Find your own bottle, Maggot. I don't want you *spoeging gwells* in mine.'

Fraser, up the slope a little way, turned and looked at Archer. The half jeering, half talking of the others faltered.

'Jeez, if Fraser looked at me like that,' Edwards said afterwards to Herbert, 'I'd shit rivers!'

Rivers indeed! Archer might have wanted to, but he hadn't time to think, for as Fraser rose to challenge him, in return for Archer's belligerent, 'What?', Unwin sprang to his feet.

Hugh Unwin, tangy-boy, stepped back and swung his fist.

He caught Archer in the throat and Archer fell. Unwin, knuckles split from side to side, was on him. Snot and blood and spit: he had the rage of titans.

Charlie Fraser put his hat down, ready.

–At last! Good lad, Unwin. Good, good lad. Don't stop. Don't stop.

Unwin did not stop. Fury carried him. He fought for every humiliation, not just from Archer but from every other dismissive adversary: the yellow-eyed dog in Rose Street; the makers of the forts who did not allow him to piss in the pisspipe; Edwards' turned back, –Eeugh, Unwin, when are you going to change your pyjamas; Mostert's leering glass eye; Archer's candle held steady for a moment, lighting up his cringing naked self, the quiver of the flame as Archer began to laugh; the forays down the tangy, –Watch out for caddies, Unwin, –What are you laughing at?, –New Street, –What about New Street?, –You're as gutless as a gecko, Unwin; MacCallum's nurse, lip tilted in derision; MacCallum himself, –Unwin, isn't it time you bathed?, –Unwin's such a little creep, –I've had enough, Unwin, –Of what, MacCallum? –Of what?

Fighting all of them. Fighting Archer. Fighting MacCallum. Fighting God.

Boys are not born equal, God. You do not love them all the same. That is very clear. The Meek do not inherit the earth.

Archer may have been the obvious adversary, a great lout into whom it was good to sink teeth and know the clean, metallic taste of blood, but each blow, each wild flailing of his fists was for the others, just as much – more – as for Archer: it was better to have Archer talk about 'endowments' and *gwells* and everything else disgusting and demeaning than to have the eyes flicked across one by a good man, who, in the instant of doing it, dismissed and forgot. That was a humiliation more insidious and damning than Archer's belligerent notice or crass manipulation. And, it was a humiliation Archer knew as well as he. Oh, just as well. Unwin was not fighting an equal in strength, but he knew – beyond his own rage and hate – that he and Archer were using each other for the same end.

For validation.

For notice.

For the esteem of a good man. Any. Or one: Charlie Fraser, standing on the slope above, his arms folded, his hat cast aside. Unwin knew the ecstasy in drawing blood and tears – and in its being

335

witnessed and observed.

The boys moved in, circling them. Would there be a death?

–It was a courtship, says Percy.

–That's a very odd way of putting it, Herbert replies.

–Courtship of what?

–Of Fraser, perhaps.

Herbert is at a loss.

–They needed to be men. Simple as that. And Fraser – being Fraser – could validate them both. It had a long history, Cummings. Archer wanted Fraser's approbation just as much as Unwin did. As much as the rest of us, says Percy, looking Herbert over shrewdly and smiling. –One word from him was enough.

Robbie heard it before he reached the crest of the dune. He came up at the head of his officers, over the ridge and stood a moment, looking down at the hollow.

He stared. They all stared.

A chant had started, low among the younger boys: Harman, Huddlestone, the nameless, unremembered, Ungreat-Inglorious: 'Go, Unwin! Unwin, go! Go, Unwin, Unwin, go!'

MacCallum, their senior prefect, started down towards them, John Barham, their Company Officer, ready to supersede him. Robbie said: 'Leave them alone! It's time they had it out. Let Unwin have his say. Stop it the moment Unwin comes to his senses and Archer gets the upper hand.' He gestured with his chin to Moorrees and, turning from his officers, walked away, whistling low for the dog to come to heel.

To heel. To heel. Dog to man. Boy to boy.

'A man should not be a fool and fancy himself too much,' said Robbie to Moorrees. 'And if a fellow is ragged, like Unwin' – delivered like a litany – 'nine times out of ten, it is his own fault. But in the end – in the end – they have to find it out for themselves.'

Men fight. Boys, looking to be men, fight too. A good fight, between those equally matched, redeems. A good fight cleanses. That's what Robbie would have said, walking briskly away from the sounds of skirmish. Let them get it over with. Moorrees knew better than to contradict him.

Unwin did not win the fight. He could not have matched himself against Archer for long without injury. But his ferocity, his disregard for his gaping knuckles and his split lip, the gore with which he was daubed, were a birth, witnessed by all of them: Unwin struggling into the light. Irredeemable Unwin, redeemed. They saw him, not cringing under Archer's boot, but baying. He was almost comical. But no one laughed. It was too astonishing for laughter.

MacCallum was ready to separate them – a nod from Barham, a glance from Charlie Fraser – as Unwin, the veins in his neck strained to breaking in holding Archer off, began to buckle. He went between them, forcing them apart. Archer stepped back but Unwin ran in again, gasping. Straight at MacCallum. Straight into his solar plexus. MacCallum, more in surprise than anything, pinned his arms. Unwin shook himself free and looked MacCallum in the face.

–Do you see me? I am Hugh Unwin, Tangy-Boy. Do you see me?

MacCallum saw him. He said, 'Well fought, Unwin.'

Unwin glanced up at Fraser then. Fraser smoothed the band of his hat with his hand and put it on his head. In the shadow of the brim, the grin was swift.

–Well fought, Unwin.

Tomorrow MacCallum would forget he had said it. But everyone else had heard 'Well fought, Unwin'. And everyone saw – in passing – Charlie Fraser cuff his head, dipping it in: well done indeed, Hugh Unwin.

Archer went off to swim alone.

'Perhaps a shark will get him,' said Edwards hopefully to Herbert.

'Yesterday it was Unwin you wanted to feed to the sharks.'

'*Ja*, well . . .'

Something had changed. Edwards didn't know what it was.

'*Ja*, well . . .' he said again, at a loss. 'Maybe he's not such a bad bloke . . .' And before Herbert could say, –How come, all of a sudden?, it was best to distract him by punching his arm with the middle finger joint cocked until it was numb. They rough-housed all the way back to camp.

Better to slug it out than offer conciliation. In slugging it out, Unwin
had asserted his right to be noticed. He walked lightly between
Harman and Huddlestone. No more shambling – not today. His face
still bore the badge of battle and one eye was closed.

Percy followed behind the others. The evening light was pale
and green, the wind was in the salt grass. There were ragged gulls,
buffeted here and there. Robbie's dog trotted with her ears back against
gusts. John Barham walked with him but Percy did not encourage
him to talk. Ahead were Seymour and Holmes and MacCallum. Percy
knew Mac's footprints in the sand. He trod in them – that long, bow-
legged stride, toes turned slightly in: a silent, well-sprung step. If they
had slugged it out the night they had been called to Robbie's room,
would he have walked as lightly as Unwin now? As unguardedly as
Mac?

–It was a kind of courtship, Percy had said.
It did not only apply to Charlie Fraser. Percy does not need to say
it. Herbert knows that. He is looking at him quietly, without
scepticism, waiting. He is no longer the boy with awkward boots,
scuffing the sand, sweaty palmed and wanting to escape. He is a
thoughtful, generous man, as Percy might have guessed. *Tibi est
successio*: to you is the succession. No explanation is needed.
Percy turns his hat round and round and scans the arums in the
cool bed. They had been there – parchment spathes – the night
he had spoken to Mac:
–I don't know why I did it.
–I do.
–No, Vincent, I'm afraid you don't.
There is no validation given to those who offer conciliation.
Those who will not fight deserve only scorn. Percy had felt Mac's
derision. Mac – so upright, so austere. They should have slugged
it out instead, like Unwin and Archer. Oh, yes, they should,
however unequally matched.
Herbert says, –You once said to me you'd be unlikely to come

back.

Percy – seated on the wood and iron bench, the old stance, arm draped – glances up at him. –Old augur! he says. –Is there nothing you forget? I knew you'd bring it up. His voice is light but his eyes are on the arums again and his smile is bleak. –You know quite well why I came back, Cummings.

After supper, when the junior cadets had been down to the river and washed the pots and cans, Robbie summoned them to build up the fires and gather round.

'At ease, gentlemen.' He put his pipe aside, knocking it out on a log of wood and slipping it into his belt. He took a lozenge from the small tin box he kept in his breast pocket. He coughed in his chest, a pipe-smoker's rumble, a call to attention. Seymour ordered silence.

Robbie stood just outside the circle of firelight, his insignia glinting and multiplying hearts of flame in a multitude of facets. He stood before them, they seated cross-legged on the ground. This was in earnest. This, with the tents peaked around them and the flicker of paraffin lanterns and the turn of ropes and the shadow of a tent pole, stirred by the wind, moving like the steady hand of a metronome. This, Robbie had prepared. He cleared his throat again.

'Gentlemen . . . for many years I have accompanied the Corps to this camp ground, to practise manoeuvres, to learn the art of bearing arms, but never before have I addressed the Corps with the thought that in a time not far from now, my cadets will be soldiers indeed, called to arms, to give service to their King.'

No one moved.

'It has happened before,' he said. 'It will happen again. And if I am not mistaken, in the near future our Empire could well be matched against a foe both virile and ruthless in pursuit of its own ends.' His voice had risen, changed tone. His old dog looked up at him, alarmed. It shambled to its feet and barked loudly at the dark.

Some of the younger boys glanced about them at the bush looming in the flicker of firelight. What ruthless foe? Where? Were the natives thinking of rising up? The Boers again? Who did Robbie mean?

The old dog snorted and lay down. The boys subsided.

Robbie began to pace, looking out across the heads of his troops, but directing his words at his officers. 'I look with confidence to you boys who have been schooled here, drilled to serve, to give your manhood in your country's behalf without bluster, without flag-wagging but with cool heads, quiet tongues and hearts and nerves of steel.' Another clearing of the throat. 'We have served before with as much distinction as the men from the Old Country. We will serve again. We will see it through. We will be imperturbable in the face of crisis. And,' said Robbie, sweeping them in, 'it is known, wherever we have fought, that vigour and ruggedness are the hallmark of young men from the colonies. It is vigour and ruggedness I mean to instil in each of you in the days ahead . . .' Another lozenge and a glance at his old dog as she sighed and settled. 'So, my lads,' Robbie said, 'whatever you are called upon to do, *whatever* you are called to do, lads, it must be done with self-discipline, with self-esteem. It means, at any cost, the power of obeying. It means high ideals, high tone, manly instincts, sound judgement, patience.' He stood still then and the firelight lit his face from below, orange-etched the nostrils and the first under-ridges of his brow. 'Death in battle,' he said quietly but with a ring, as if he were drawing his sword, 'death in battle, is the most glorious and manly of ends, gentlemen. There is no more heroic sacrifice than that.' The Corps was silent, breathing as one.

Death in battle.

–We believed him, says Percy. –We really did. Perhaps we still do. We'll send our sons the same. It's all a myth, Cummings. Think of those books we read. So much bosh. And women being so sly as well! They are really the worst of all. Tell me, how can a hero die of dysentery? Only his mother – perhaps his sister – cares for that. All the rest will pass him over for the chap who had his heart shot through. Oh, and he must be an officer – that's sacred. No, Cummings, it's not all the same in war. Dying differentiates us too.

–It's not the same, Apie, Arthur had said.
Herbert had not known how to reply. No, it was not the same.

–It's like being in the Fourths at school. Or the third House team, in the reserves. No one's going to read about you in *The Register*. Especially not the girls.

Robbie ended, standing to attention before them all: Honour. Duty. Manliness. Their heads were stuffed with Glory. They were armed and ready. There was a long silence as they looked up at Robbie and Robbie looked down at them. He seemed to take them in with his eyes: this one, that one, this one, that one, marking them out.

Well could Robbie look at George Holmes or James Seymour. Well could he rest his eyes on that template of masculinity, Charlie Fraser, with his arms linked about his squarely tendoned knees. Well could he appeal to ardent Arthur, who straightened his shoulders and gazed at the flame of the fire. But what of Unwin? And what of Edwards who could shear a sheep and raise a *hansie*, fix a windmill, stalk a *rooikat*, set a trap – could he be uprooted and shipped away and turned into a soldier? One might as well try to drag a *witgat* out through ironstone. School was far enough for him! Well could Robbie appeal to Mac and Sparrow Bell and Dan, or to solemn John Barham or to Archer already planning glory at some unimaginable Front – Charlie Fraser's saviour? But what of Fatty Harman, inner thighs rubbed raw from marching up the dunes, quivering from the exertions in the heat? What of serious, introspective Furry Huddlestone, uncomplaining in the backline? What had they to do with wars and soldiering? What did Robbie's Death Wish hold for them?

Herbert had listened from the edges where he sat, eyes on Robbie. He had heard his own heart marching as Robbie went, back and forth, back and forth, beyond the firelight. The bush was dark behind the circle of the tents. Here and there, threading the river, a lamp from a house or a night fisherman floated in the dark. Then he'd heard – beyond Robbie's voice, which receded slowly from his consciousness to the same dull murmur of the distant sea – a clear low call from quiet ravines upstream, pitched beyond the polished turning of a great fish somewhere in the estuary: the cry of a barred owl, prowling bushland. So intimate a call, an augur's note, sounding

341

softer, softer, softer . . . And then it was gone and Edwards farted comfortably beside him, looking off and half pretending that it wasn't him.

James Seymour, Guard Commander, saluted Robbie and Moorrees and called up the fellows who'd been practising the songs Percy had chosen for the sing-along.

Robbie sat on a log and took out his pipe and stuffed it with care. He lit it with the end of a burning stick, picked from the nearest fire. Sparrow stood and stretched and came forward to lead them in song. Ruddy-faced in the firelight, his plume like a little golden fountain on his head, he sang the opening bars of *Glory and Love to Men of Old*. The Corps followed – hearty – but moved enough not to look at each other but to keep their eyes on the flames, each in his own reverie. Glory and Love: Arthur eased his shoulder against Charlie Fraser's back, Danny Grant and Sparrow sat, boot leaned to boot. Unwin was upright in his coat, not crouched beyond the circle. He did not dip his head from the light. Herbert, at the margin of the group, listened for the owl again.

There was no photograph of Sparrow Bell singing *The Sergeant of the Line* to the Corps, but the image, the firelight, the milky night, was imprinted in Herbert's mind, just the same: Sparrow standing, legs apart, hand to wrist behind his back, the light wedged below his chin. He stood, head tilted, and the gruff, husky voice – the soaring treble long gone – was true and perfectly pitched. Beside him Dan Grant stirred the embers with a stick.

   –Such a tableau, Percy says. He takes off his panama and turns it in his hands. His hair remains unruffled, a slight shadow at the sallow curve of his brow. The line that etches his face from the delicate inner eye, in perfect counterpoint to the angled sweep of his cheekbone, is so much deeper. –Such a tableau, he says again.
   –It could almost have been staged.
   –I remember, says Herbert.
   Percy is silent. He does not add: –Did you see Vincent MacCallum's face?

342

Of course Herbert Cummings would not have lingered there. He would have watched Sparrow singing, Dan poking at the coals, Arthur leaned to Charlie Fraser, spine to spine, propped against each other, drifting together. Only Percy himself, undetected, had kept his eyes on Vincent.

Vincent, lean and dark – the blue-black gleam of his hair and the sallow, narrow planes of his sombre face – had glowed with another light. Discipline, cleanliness and self-esteem. Robbie-honed, that's what Vincent was: cool head, cool heart, nerves of steel.

–He was quite splendid, you know, says Percy.

–Who?

–MacCallum.

Herbert hesitates. Is this a confidence? –Ah, yes. He says it tentatively. –No doubt of that.

–I wonder if he had the imagination to be otherwise, says Percy. The familiar cynicism is gentler now: on himself, on others. But he locks and unlocks his jaw, the old, wry gesture of self-reproach.

Advancing carefully, Herbert says, –Robbie kept pictures of each in his room for years, you know.

–Among the hunting trophies?

Herbert is silent. He pulls at his ear-lobe.

–Sorry, Cummings. I take it back. Percy looks across at him. – That was ungenerous of me.

–There are worse places to be, says Herbert.

–And lonelier too. Percy looks away towards the distant pavilion. And lonelier. Yes. So much lonelier.

EIGHTEEN

One of the last pictures in Charlie Fraser's album was taken on the Eighth of September. The Garden Party. The Music Recital. Prize-Giving and Speech Day. The last public glory for Seymour, Holmes, MacCallum, Gilbert. It was the day on which the foundation stone of the new memorial chapel was laid. The old would be converted into a library. *Delivered for our Offences, Raised for our Justification* would be hidden behind shelves of books. *I am the Vine* would be painted out or a map of the world, Empire glowing pink, hung across it. After this, when the oaks were in full leaf and the jacarandas had shed all their flowers, it would be examination time. Silence would sink intermittently on the senior studies and flies from the Grants' stables would drone in the torpid afternoons. GB and Parkes did well in a brand of fly-swatter they designed and made on Saturdays from wire and fly-screening. Tickey each, they sold two dozen. Fly-swatting was a desultory pastime when Dutch or Greek became too much. Doug Morgan had lined up his victims: seventy-five neatly ranked on the window sill.

Nubs did a shuttle service from the tuck-shop or from Dicks' after lessons. The matriculants were, in turn, boisterous or listless, the seniors in the Intermediate, irritable and lofty. Percy sat with his head in a damp towel and his feet in a bucket of cold water and treated himself to a few cheroots from Radomsky's. Robbie left them to their own devices. He kept order among the juniors with a swift cane. By the end of the year he seemed to have lost something of the virtuosity in his much admired swing. The bucks in Upper Four smoked almost openly. There was no one around to bother them.

But on this day of celebration and *esprit de corps* – the most festive and most solemn – before the closure of the year and the examinations, there was lightness and excitement. Robbie had trimmed his moustache and was talking rather loudly. He wore a different jacket and his Cambridge tie, his shoulders seamed straight and his pockets flat. Miss Maltby had clamped her hair into waves at the forehead and was wearing a pair of dangling little earrings. Mac spent ten minutes in the shower soaping his head with as much vigour as Jarge had polished the trophies for the prize-giving. He emerged gleaming.

Along the road, in the gardens of the Head's house, the tables were laid with white cloths and tall vases of purple irises. The air was mauve and fragrant with jacaranda and the sound of bees. The dining-hall waiters moved unobtrusively setting cups and jugs and bowls. Jarge limped about checking on this and that, a sprig of banksia rose in his lapel.

In the early afternoon the conveyances began to arrive, disgorging parents, sisters, small boys from the preparatory, the young ladies from the senior classes at the girls' school. Carriages, carts, gigs were drawn up along the road – a spider's web of spokes and wheels, the lithe tips of whips bending and crossing; well-dubbined seats, cracked canopies, brass lamps. The grooms and drivers sat or lay about in the shade. Pipe smoke drifted with the low melody of Xhosa passing back and forth from verge to verge; laughter, snatches of song. In the driveway the motorcars were parked, the doctor's dusty from an outlying journey, Mac's father's burnished black, the driver stiff-coated, his cap peak glinting. Mac stood with a proprietorial foot on the running-board, chatting to him. Small boys stared, bunched to run if the beast – or its owner – should come to life. GB and Parkes inspected it from atop a stone wall. Arthur, Charlie, Sparrow, Dan and Doug prowled around it, absorbed.

The seniors were spruced for parade. Pale blue braid on dark collars, the dull glint of silver thread, necks held so, shoes polished to gleaming by nubs. Charlie's might have been patent leather for the

345

efforts of GB with boot-black and spit. Sparrow had a patch of lint stuck to his chin, to bind the blood where the razor had nicked the tender skin. It was like a marker flag, a warning to his mother to keep inquisitive fingers from his dimples and his ear-lobe. Hands off: I have stubble. His plume had been disciplined. He had scoured out his ears: he knew she would inspect them, without seeming to. He had cleaned his teeth three times.

Arthur and Charlie walked down from the House together in the advancing throng, shoulders lined up, in step, only one button – senior privilege – fastened on their jackets. Arthur would have felt comfortable with a hand in a pocket to counter the rigid wetting of the cow-lick at his forehead, the feeling of having been starched and pressed. 'Look, Charlie,' he said. 'Just because you have no family here today, you're not to skulk off if mine's arrived, d'you hear? You're to join us. The Ugly Sisters want another look at you.'

'Miss Maltby collared me and a couple of others after breakfast and said, because our families weren't here, we'd been chosen to keep the juniors in line and supervise handing round the grub with them. I'm to terrify them into being polite. The reward might be free rein with the leftovers.'

'You hate cake.'

'That is one of the great fallacies!' Charlie laughed. It depends whose cake – but he left it. He said, 'I'll keep it for you. You can stuff yourself for the rest of the week.'

'And you're to sit with us at dinner.'

'Not allowed,' said Charlie lightly. 'Orphan boys have been put at a table by themselves. The seating's been marked already.'

Arthur had four members of his family coming. Charlie had none. It was too far. His mother could not travel alone. 'Well, anyway . . .' said Arthur, at a loss, afraid some well-meaning but officious mother would say:

–Where are the parents of that big fellow?

And some Know-All would reply, –That's the Fraser boy.

–Fraser?

–The doctor from Stutterheim. Remember? Significant looks.

–Aaah! – drawn out. Perhaps an eyeglass would be screwed into an eye to look him over, or a head turned a fraction longer than it should.

–We should ask the young man to join us: curious – wondering how to broach the subject of his parents.

–He's fine, Mother. Leave him alone. Any one of the fellows would have said it, protecting him.

Don't patronise Fraser. Don't. It's one thing he won't stand for. Nor will we.

'There they are!' said Arthur, pointing down towards the tables. Parents stood about in little knots, rather stiff, women's voices sharp, without the lilt of ease: the tea was still being poured. Groups formed and reformed, those at the edges looking about for some familiar face.

–Thank goodness! There you are at last!

–Where *is* my boy? I haven't seen him yet. Have you seen yours?

Heads turned, the mothers searched eagerly among the advancing throng.

'Go on then,' said Charlie, hand briefly at Arthur's shoulder.

'Come!' said Arthur.

'Later.' Charlie peeled off towards the kitchen. Arthur did not protest. He adjusted his button. Sparrow was suddenly at his shoulder, the little lint fluttering. They did not run. But almost.

What a report there had been in *The Journal*! Half a page – with just a note of admonition:

'The men's tweeds and boaters may have done well enough at the garden party but were not in keeping with the sacred and solemn service held in connection with the laying of the cornerstone of the new College chapel.'

The Head had deemed the remark an impertinence from a mere reporter, despite his sentiments – unexpressed – having been the same. Such sartorial slovenliness! The ladies had a better press.

'The Mayoress, Mrs Van der Riet, wore grey charmeuse and ninon

347

and a charming hat. Mrs Seymour was elegant as always, in black and white spots. She is the proud mother of the Senior Prefect, a young man destined for Trinity College, Oxford. Mrs Holmes, wife of the Resident Magistrate and mother of the incumbent Rhodes Scholar, was in mole and salmon, a becoming combination. Lady Grant, wife of the Chairman of the Council, presided with her accustomed grace at the garden party.'

Full approval was saved for the boys:

'The tea tables were decorated with tall vases of purple irises. The good things (dainty cakes) were handed round by polite and attentive boys.'

'Any horseplay with the food and I'll kick your arses,' Charlie had said good-naturedly. GB had staggered out weighed down with a tray of sandwiches, moulting threads of chopped lettuce as he went. He would not have touched a crumb without Fraser's permission. Mostert, the lout, was munching surreptitiously from his own platter. He had butter on his chin. He'd get a *klap* before the afternoon was out.

Charlie Fraser had appraised the crowd on the lawns. Parents, teachers, siblings. The dignitaries – subdued dove-grey and mauve – occupied a little space of their own apart from the chatter and abundance of the rest. He looked for Annie Zeederberg. He looked for her among the schoolgirls and the sisters and the nursemaids. Would she be there?

Maybe.

Maybe not.

Why would she have come?

Why, indeed.

He found her among the staff families, standing with her parents, Harry, Josie and one of the little girls.

Annie Zeederberg in white.

Annie Zeederberg with her hair pinned up under her tilted hat.

He worked his way towards her – and not towards her – with his trays of sandwiches and cakes. He was methodical and swift in the distribution, 'Ma'am? Sir?', not lingering for conversation. Sometimes he was waylaid. 'How do you do, sir', to Mac's father. 'Thank you, sir' – some remark on his prowess on the rugby field; a kiss on the cheek from Sparrow's adorable mama. 'Charles Fraser, you are enormously grown! I thought you were the new rugby coach, at least! How lovely to see you again.' He did not mind being twinkled at by her or having her gloved hand dabble at his sleeve.

Charlie went on with his task, offering his platter here and there, intent on reaching Annie before the cake ran out: do not let the lady in stripes bearing down, waylay the last half dozen *petit fours*: 'Young man, young man!' He side-stepped and escaped.

Annie Zeederberg in white. The sudden lift of eyes: is she watching too?

He almost turns aside, stops himself. Walk on, Fraser. Walk on.

'Father?' thrusting the plate at the Reverend Zeederberg, 'Ma'am?', Mrs Zeederberg.

Annie glances up. Her little hat is perched, the shadow of the brim curves with the small scar on her cheek. Green-eyed, elf-green, slightly slanted. There is a freckle in the cleft above her lip; Annie Zeederberg with a brooch of seed-pearl swallows swooping on a small gold bar at her throat, held by a wisp of chain and pin. 'Miss Zeederberg?' He almost tips the platter on her.

'Thank you.'

His entire purpose was to reach her: his most urgent need now is to rush away but the Reverend Zeederberg says, 'Is your family not here, Fraser?'

'No, sir. It's a long journey.'

'Of course.'

'Sir.'

The Reverend Zeederberg says to his wife, 'Young Fraser is Canon Taberer's grandson.'

'My word!' She scans his face. 'Of course! What a pity he's not here! Your grandfather is such a dear. Quite a favourite of mine. I met him when he came for Synod once.' She smiles up at him, a slight puzzlement. 'Why have you not come to tea with the other boys on Sundays?'

'Ma'am.' Damn his ears!

'Annie?' Mrs Zeederberg is vague and admonishing. 'Why hasn't . . .?' She touches his elbow, enquiringly.

'Charles Fraser,' says Charlie. It sounds as if he is giving the name of a dog.

'Why hasn't Charles had an invitation?'

Charlie does not look at Annie. He can feel the sweat at his back. Annie is brushing a crumb from her bodice. Gracie Zeederberg stares unabashed. Miss Josie Zeederberg stands behind her sister, looking shrewd:

–Hah! Annie Zeederberg! How are you going to get out of this one?

Harry snorts on catching her eye and coughs on his cake to hide his laugh.

'Annie did ask him,' puts in guileless Gracie-from-Below. 'But he wouldn't come.'

Silence.

'Get off my foot, Josie,' says Gracie crossly.

'Have I said something amiss?' Mrs Zeederberg looks from one to the other. Harry laughs, despite himself. So does Josie. Gracie says importantly, 'She did! Harry told me!'

Annie and Charlie glance at each other – sideways, down.

Charlie Fraser at a loss? Annie at a loss? Josie looks triumphant. Then Charlie Fraser laughs too.

And Annie smiles straight back into his eyes.

The Reverend Zeederberg says, 'Well, have a cup with us now, dear boy,' and goes to the table, pours one and brings it. Charlie Fraser puts his platters down at his feet and hardly dares take a sip of tea in case he gargles it by mistake for the lightness in his limbs. They all talk at once, linked about him. And Gracie, looking up, says, 'What's happening?'

What's happening?

Even if he never sees her again, he knows. Oh yes, they both know. There is nothing to be done to change it. It has always been too late.

'Why is Fraser talking to Graham's girl?' said Parkes as if it were GB's fault.

'He can talk to anyone he likes!' GB retorted.

'Graham will give it to him.'

'What's talking?'

'She's red in the face.'

'That's rouge.'

'No, it's not.'

'Yes, it is. Girls put it on all the time.'

'Rot.' Parkes gave another sidelong stare. 'So why's Fraser's red too then?'

'He's never red.'

'Is now.'

'Is not.'

'Is.'

Fraser was.

GB walked off, alarmed.

Under the trees, Arthur looks across for Charlie, to fetch him, to bring him into the circle of his sisters. –This is my friend, Fraser.

This is *my* friend . . .

Charlie Fraser is standing with the Zeederbergs clustered round him, Annie's head tilted back to look into his face. Charlie Fraser has his foot firmly planted in the middle of a platter of *petit fours*. Clearly, he has lost his senses.

He is laughing his head off.

Herbert heard him too. And saw Arthur turn with a smile, searching the crowd, buoyant and ready to call. He followed his gaze and felt with Arthur the sudden contracting in the cheeks, the tensing of the solar plexus a moment before the punch comes: Arthur dipped his head, as if he'd lost his breath. Herbert turned from him. There was nothing he could do.

Charlie and Arthur did not sit together at prize-giving. Charlie was in the front rows with the meritorious: a form prize for Latin. 'It's the ecclesiastical background,' he had laughed when he had found out. 'I recite it in a holy sort of way.' He sat among Seymour and Mac, Sparrow, Dan and John Barham. Percy and Georgie Holmes were placed on the aisle. They would be going up at least five times.

Arthur was at the back of the Drill Hall on the benches ranged behind the parents and guests, with the body of the school. He sat with Doug, the only two of their group not worthy of academic accolades. No one was going to applaud their mathematics or Greek. Sports cups were not given out that day: there was no chance of walking up in front of his family and shaking the great man's hand while the fellows cheered. Today his coveted cup for hurdles and the high jump trophy did not count, only what he kept in his head. And that, it seemed, was nothing.

–You are a lazy, dissolute boy. Not at all like your father . . .

–You are not a credit to this school . . .

–Your son, sir, though a sound, straight fellow, is an ass . . .

Arthur bit at the skin on the side of his thumb until he had made it raw. Someone was thumping his seat from behind. He turned round, 'Cut it out, Archer!' He felt like punching him hard. Archer paid not the slightest attention. He was scratching in his pockets. No doubt checking on the burned-off stubs of Westminsters or Flags in anticipation of an opportunity behind the bogs in the confusion between boys' supper and dignitaries' dinner. Stafford was flicking snot-balls at someone down the line. Arthur stared ahead. Beside him Doug was fooling about, trying to push a laugh out of him.

'Buck up!' He gave Arthur a shove with the side of his thigh. 'Do you really want to be Daisy prancing up there for all those memorial prizes and end up a memorial yourself? Look' – nudging again – 'Who's that girl?'

'Which girl?'

'That one . . .' a tilt of the chin.

'Which one?' Exasperated.

'Can't you see?'

'Where the hell are you looking?'

'The hat with cherries on it. Nice. Very nice. Tenth row from the front, four in.'

Arthur looked. 'My married sister,' he said crossly.

Doug laughed loudly enough for one of the junior masters at the back to turn and give him a glare. He pulled his shoulders straight and yawned. 'Oh God, here we go.'

Arthur settled back and gazed at the dark angled beams of the roof, the vault of white, the gold-lettered honours boards, badged and nailed to the lime-washed bricks high above their heads. The ubiquitous backdrop of the Victoria Falls hung on the wall – Arthur could even remember it being used, not just for the cricket luncheon, but for the set of a production of *Macbeth* when he was a newboy: Macbeth, the Thane of Glamis, silhouetted against the blue and tropical green of Livingstone's Africa. It had caused a laugh as the curtain had gone up. Now, it was enhanced with potted palms, in burnished brass containers and arrangements of leaves picked in wheelbarrow-loads from the Grants' garden.

'Wake me if I snore,' said Doug, folding his arms and settling himself. Arthur folded his arms as well. He would not sleep, not with his parents and big sisters, turning now and then to smile and bob at him. This was to have been a memorable afternoon if only he did not have such a pain somewhere in his side, between his ribs, leaking quietly, unnoticed by anyone: Annie Zeederberg had not looked in his direction that day. She was somewhere else.

At least his name was mentioned in the Head's speech – it was almost as good as a prize. He was singled out for special praise on manoeuvres, along with Doug. His mother turned and smiled at him. Don't do that, Mother – but he grinned back sheepishly.

There he was again in the sports results along with Charlie and Mac and Georgie and Dan. He frowned at his mother this time: it wasn't good form to be so obvious. After that he kept his eyes on the ceiling. Doug was twitching – he could sleep anywhere, at any time, even under Robbie's nose in maths. He would miss the Visions for the School, the Building Plan, the Rhodes Scholar. Georgie Holmes sat looking at his knees, his neck damp, cheers from the juniors in his house, clapping from the parents. The Head's approbation was warm. And Georgie – such a man in embryo himself – acknowledged it with a simple inclination of his head.

The Head settled into the body of his report, his predictions and hopes – it would be a good hour before all had been laid before them. There were difficult times ahead – political, financial – and school leavers must not be complacent. There were forces at work against Empire but, the Head felt assured, whatever the call, the boys had been trained to serve and serve they would. They would do their duty and defend that Empire, even with their lives.

'Cheers and applause [prolonged]' – *The Journal* reported.

'The Cadet Corps,' said the Head, 'has acquitted itself admirably while at camp.' There was no hint of what he had written to the Bishop: –The Corps is living in a state of the most appalling hugger-muggerdom down at the Kowie; or of Arthur's cheerful communication to one of his sisters, –The fellows haven't barthed for three weeks.

'There has been,' said the Head, 'thanks to Captain Robinson and his officers, a very high standard of discipline, competence and restraint.'

–Surrender, Unwin!

–Aw, c'mon, Archer.

–Archer said Unwin shat his pants.

–He'll shit his too if Robbie finds out.

Robbie had not found out – or had not chosen to. Such incidentals were not included in his report nor relayed by the Head to the audience at Speech Day. Instead, all could feel confident that their sons could bear arms and survive the privations of camp life, supported by their chums. Such close bonds, such firm friendships forged. Such co-operation and jolly *esprit de corps*!

–Find your own bottle, Maggot. I don't want you *spoeging gwells* in mine.

–If Fraser looked at me like that, I'd shit rivers!

–I hope Archer gets eaten by a shark.

The Head consulted his notes, looked up over his spectacles. 'It is in situations like that and on occasions such as this – on which we not only acknowledge the scholastic triumphs of our boys but dedicate ourselves and our school to the service of Christ in laying the foundation stone of our new chapel – that our commitment to high ideals is served. Our new chapel will stand as a memorial to those who have fallen in battle and in our daily worship we will honour those brave soldiers who gave their lives in their country's behalf. We remember, most particularly, those who fell in our most recent conflict, the Boer War, which claimed twenty- three men to whom this school is *alma mater*. It is through their noble example that our present lads come to understand the call of duty and the honour in fulfilling it. Duty to God before all else. Duty to King. Duty to Country.'

God. King. Country.

'Which country?' said Mostert to Edwards, looking sideways from his good eye.

'England, arse!' said Edwards. Then he hesitated. 'I suppose.'

Flies were circling high up in the vault of the ceiling, suspended in turgid air. Arthur watched them going round and round and round. Anticipating Doug, he nudged him just before a long, in-drawn breath ended in a snort.

The Head finished. '[Hearty applause]' proclaimed *The Journal*. Robbie was seen surreptitiously to consult his watch. Sixty-five minutes and twenty boys in the audience fast asleep, another ten being deplorable with yawnings and gawpings and nudgings enough to make him want to dart from the stage and scoop them into his study. He would be having a little chat to a few of them after supper.

'A stirring speech, designed to encourage the scholars of our distinguished College to do their duty as citizens and gentlemen,' reported *The Journal*.

It was the guest speaker's turn. A cabinet minister. An Eminence. The father of a past Rhodes Scholar. There was a stirring and a flutter among the ladies: so much distinction, such a presence. Even the palms in the pots seemed to tremble an instant as he passed on his way to the podium.

There was a hush. Then the strange pantomime of bows and greetings and thanks: the Chairman of the Council – Dan's father with his white, sweeping moustache; the Head – that most splendid example of manhood; the Bishop in his robes, quite tranquil, as if embalmed.

'By rights,' said the Eminence, 'I should be ignorant of the grown-ups. They do not count on such an occasion. Also, by rights, I ought not to see any girls in this room.' He paused, raised a brow enquiringly. 'I'm sure . . .' – a slight exaggeration in his stance – 'none of the boys wish to see them!' He waited for the laugh. 'But I have to escape these distrac . . .' – laughed himself – 'attrac . . . distractions – and concentrate myself on the boys – young and old! You will forgive me if I talk to only one section. I believe that is my mission.'

The audience settled in.

'As you may know,' said the Eminence, almost confidential, looking down at the prize-winners in the rows set aside for them, 'I have a particular fondness for dogs and I feel very strongly that a boy should be like a dog. If you have a dog, you do not like him to go down the street looking sideways with his tail down. You want him to go down the street with his bristles on end and his tail in the air and ready to tackle anything that tackles him. This is the kind of dog to be proud of . . .' – he cleared his throat and scanned the ranks – 'This is the kind of boy!'

Cheers and laughs. The small boys who had been dozing in the back rows stirred a little at the mention of dogs. Dogs or snakes or shipwrecks – any would do, just not What-the-Future-Holds or Duty-and-Sacrifice or the joys of being a God-fearing-Good-Christian-Lad. This was a man who stuck by the belief that a fellow should walk straight, talk straight, act straight, shoot straight.

Only GB slept on. Parkes nudged him before a senior turned around and swatted him. He was making little sucking movements with his mouth, twitching gently every now and then, his fist curled under his chin: too much sun, too much cake, all too much with Charlie Fraser going red and standing in the *petit fours*.

Unwin also sat at the back between Harman and Huddlestone.

A dog with bristles on end with his tail in the air?

A dog like the mongrel behind the fence at the corner of Rose Street? He had only put his own tail in the air once – and that because Charles Fraser had been there, ready to take the challenge for him. Unwin had barely been able to see his face in the shadow of his slouch hat, but he knew that look: –Now, Unwin. Now.

–Now, Unwin. Now.

A dog with bristles! Perhaps it was the master of the dog that counted, rather than the dog itself? How did one become a dog on one's own account – a good, true, bristles-on-end dog, snout-up, tail-in-the-air dog? A dog to be reckoned with? A dog to be relied on? A dog worthy of its master? Unwin lifted his nose, chin up. Fatty Harman glanced at him. Unwin looked as though he was about to bark.

'I have listened now to what the Headmaster has said about the Cadet Corps and I want to add my approbation to his,' continued the Eminence. 'I have been very strongly in favour of the Cadet Movement myself . . .' '[Cheers]' reported *The Journal*. 'I cannot conceive of anyone saying anything cynical about cadets, yet I have heard people in high positions scoff at them and say the lads play at soldiers and only wish to wear smart uniforms. This is absolutely untrue [Cheers again]. I have found lads in just ordinary blue jerseys, which are striped longitudinally and laterally – that is most practical because it does not much matter which way they grow' – the prompt in *The Journal*: '[Laughter]' followed by '[Applause]' – 'and they do just as well as a boy in a showy outfit. There is nothing one likes more than a Cadet Corps in a school. Nothing gives it quite the same tone. It indicates that the scholars are disciplined and have the power of obeying and for the boy trained as a cadet, the rifle becomes second nature . . .'

Robbie with frosty sarcasm: –It is not advisable to treat it as a club!

–Hold your weapon straight, boy. Don't wave it about like that!

–Disarm the fool!

What could you do with townies?

'With the discipline and the knowledge afforded by the Corps,' said the Eminence, 'the boy is able to lead and to command when he leaves the College. This is where our officer class comes from and the Corps is invaluable in training boys to serve in this manly and distinguished capacity.' – '[Cheers]' – 'There is no school in England in which the Cadet Corps is not regarded by master and boy as a good thing.' '[Renewed cheers]'. 'All the lads ask is for the encouragement of a fine leader, a man *au fait* with the workings of the Corps. In Mr Robinson, I know, you have such a leader.' '[A veritable roar from the lads for their CO, Capt Robinson],' enthused *The Journal*.

'Now, I do not think that at the present time there is any better military material in our Empire than there is in South Africa. It comes from the veld life, very likely from the wild and courageous exploits of your pioneering forefathers and their hunting of big game . . .'

Mostert perked up at this. He had often regaled the dorm on the elephant-hunting escapades of his great uncle who had met his end – much embellished – thrust through by a tusk. Mostert had no wish to scrutinise too carefully the truth in this bit of family mythology. It made a riveting story after lights out with his good eye open and the other popped on the chair beside his bed.

'Doing your duty, lads, as your Headmaster has indicated,' said the Eminence, patting the fob-watch in his pocket as if assuring it that he was aware that his time was drawing to a close, 'is the first obligation of a gentleman. And it is here, in this most distinguished College in the Union' – '[uproarious cheers from the lads]' announced *The Journal* (very partisan) –'that you fellows have received your education in this regard.' He swept his eyes across the audience, glaring and smiling at once. GB sat up suddenly as if he had been singled out. His ears pulsed gently, all alert. 'You boys,' said the Eminence, 'you, who have defaced the furniture of your College with your hitherto abominable initials' – should they laugh or not? – 'see to it that you make good in life your right to have carved them there!'

The fathers, in all their present distinction, laughed heartily – all boys together – knowing where initials had been left on window-frames and doors and desks a generation ago or on the board at the prep school, a living roll of honour.

  −Here's my name, see? And my father's and Grandad's! Put yours here, just next to them. And leave a space for Bibbi. He'll want to carve his too.

  −He's only six months old!

  −Well?

Robbie pursed his lips and frowned. There would be a rush to carve initials in lockers and desk tops after this, every motley fellow seeking immortality.

The Eminence delivered his finale, the laughter subsided. 'You have an object in life, my lads, and what we older people feel is that, when those on this platform have gone with me to our long rest, we are leaving to you the inheritance which we have received from our forefathers and we pray that when we are gone, we may hand it over to you and that you will maintain it to the utmost of your ability to the glory of God and to the welfare of this great Empire.'

The cheers were loud and long. It had been fifty minutes in delivery. Some of the little fellows at the back were needing the lavatory. GB was crossing and uncrossing his ankles, and scratching at his socks to distract himself.

The trophies stood in ranks on the table beside the stacks of inscribed and crested books. Percy examined their gleaming lines and traced them with his eyes, trying not to drop off, feeling the heat under his collar and smelling the damp of dissolving starch. The cups were very noble, delicately engraved − conceits and flourishes − donated by Messrs Moorcroft and Gowie. The Webb Essay would be his.

  −Perhaps your subject is a little sophisticated for the local readership, Gilbert, the Head had said drily.

Percy had laughed − a conspiracy between them. He knew the Head would miss him.

Next to the Webb Essay stood the Archdeacon Wirgman's Divinity Prize. It would also be his, and the Bishop Merriman. So much encouragement from an ecclesiastical quarter! Would they suck him in and make him theirs? His father would be delighted.

His mother would know better. Still, The Rt Rev Bishop Percival Gilbert Prize for . . . Philosophy? Perspicacity? Perseverance? Prudence? Prophecy? or Intellect? Insight? Intuition? It sounded good. He'd give it every year to Herbert Cummings if he could. And Cummings would have no idea why he had won it. That was his particular strength: his augur's eye – even if he did not recognise it in himself – and his total lack of vanity.

Percy glanced across at Mac, a row in front and to the right. How much more would Mac have applauded a trophy for boxing than the lily-chalice flute of beaten silver for Classics. And Georgie Holmes, sitting next to him, in anticipation of the Mr Abbott's Music Prize: he would be remembered by the fellows for his double century far beyond his sensitive rendition on the violin of Wierlawski's Mazurka. And Sparrow Bell, irredeemably flushed in the first row, would have preferred a handshake for a try or a drop to the Choir Prize. He'd have preferred a handshake all round to the plucking fingers of all those females who had mobbed him that afternoon at the garden party! What was it about Sparrow that ensured a nibbling sort of perseverance in mothers and sisters, like little fish delicately but irrepressibly mouthing crumbs?

–Mrs Bell, your son is adorable . . .

–A dear . . .

–A darling . . .

–A poppet . . .

Truly irksome. Poor old Sparrow, constantly having his face examined, with so much maternal delight. No wonder his ablutions were so rigorous on such occasions, his wielding of the razor so insistent. 'Poppets' don't shave, ladies!

The prize list seemed endless. Percy began to lose some of his *sangfroid* by his fourth appearance. He was hogging the limelight from worthies like John Barham and James Seymour. Georgie Holmes went up no less than seven times – for house trophies as well as on his own account. Percy watched Mac take the major Work Shield on behalf of their own House, hold it up for the cheers and applause of the members. The gesture roused the boys. He walked with such ease, his shoulders straight. He glanced at Percy as he passed his seat.

It was almost a smile.

Percy felt the heat in his neck. Our shield, Mac?

Was the smile: –Yes – just today, yours too, Daisy?

Herbert received a prize – the Senior Art Cup, despite his being only in the Fourth Form. His painting of the dunes at the Kowie was displayed in the art room with the work of other boys. Mr Lucas had chosen to mount it on an easel, with a drape of old velour trailing to the floor – a dramatic touch – too dramatic for the simplicity of an empty landscape of sand and estuary in late afternoon with the shadows in the folds and curves of the dunes, back-lighted gold through indigo. It had worked unaccountably, capturing the quality of space, the shift of air. Wind. It was an empty landscape. The quality of silence in it was profound.

For years after, it hung in the gloom of a south-facing bedroom, the hidden sunlight in the shadows on the sand undimmed. Its mount was foxed, cream card turned damp-spotted khaki, an old-fashioned frame, thin and black, a dusty chain to loop it to the brass picture-hook suspended from the rail. He seldom looked at it – but he knew that it was there.

That afternoon, after the prize-giving and the dedication of the corner-stone, Robbie had detailed Herbert to find a handful of fellows to go down to the site of the new chapel to gather up stray hymn sheets and prayer books from the benches round the podium. Herbert had chosen to go alone. A mood of odd intensity had settled in, the same as he had felt when he had sat in the bogs and heard the tangy-cart come up the street, counterpoint to the sound of The Quadrille Band playing a jig in the Drill Hall on the night of the dance. He didn't want anyone. He had sat on the rough boards of the podium and looked at the early evening sky. It was translucent. He watched it, describing it unconsciously in words and colour: layer on layer of lifting light, a dome of shell-smooth pearl and grey. The clump of stone pines on the north-eastern horizon thrust up dark in the fading light, some distant battery, sentinel at the crest of encircling hills.

Around him the earth was churned where the builders had marked out the foundations of the new chapel and dug a preparatory ditch. A barrow and spade stood lopsided in a trench. It all seemed so desolate now that the people had gone and only the foundation stone stood starkly in a trampled square of soil. That afternoon the site had been ringed about by boys in their dark jackets, boaters tucked under their arms or dangled from fingers. The mothers had stood, light and colourful in their garden-party hats, and the girls in white dresses or serge skirts had glanced across at the battalion of boys standing guard over the shadow of the apse. The choir had been ranged in a semicircle at the edge of the podium. There, Sparrow had stood in his white collar, his chin stuck out, the lint had been removed and only a small crescent of red announced his manly chin. He led the tenors. His plume had resurrected itself in the warm afternoon. John Barham, bass, also in his robes, looked as aged as the Bishop. Georgie Holmes seemed incongruous beside him: so much vigour contained in ruff and frilled cuffs. Unwin was trussed between the bulk of Fatty Harman and Furry Huddlestone, sweating rivers into the starch of his collar.

There they were, standing over the earth laid out in memoriam to the dead: Edwin Atherstone, Castell Damant White, Horatio Hutchons – all the names that Herbert had drooped over during sermons. Twenty-three of them – more than in his form, more than in his dorm. A whole cadet company gone before they were old. Were they gathered somewhere out of sight, knowing this was for them? The hymn sheets fluttered in his hand.

The Bishop had come down the walk from the Drill Hall, the clergy gathered behind him. He had borne his staff. He had tapped at the earth within the foundations of the chapel:

Enter His gates with thanksgiving and His courts with praise . . .

The boys had stood, shoulder to shoulder, all lined along the edges of the foundations, gazing down into them.

Blessed be the Lord my strength,
which teacheth my hands to war,
my fingers to battle.
My goodness and my fortress;

my high tower and my deliverer;
my shield, and He in whom I trust . . .

Horatio Hutchons, Castell Damant White – how old had they been?
Had they also sat and looked at the words on the wall of the old
chapel: *Delivered for our Offences. Raised for our Justification*, and
bargained with God, weighing this penance against that sin? This
oblation? That undertaking? If only to be spared. And they weren't.

Man is like a breath;
his days are like a fleeting shadow . . .
Part your heavens, O Lord, and come down;
touch the mountains so that they smoke . . .

There had been a donkey cart going down the road, a shabby donkey
pulling a scotch cart, wheels buckled askew and rolling with the
rhythm of a drunk taken by momentum on a slope. And on top, the
driver in a woollen cap with his whip looped against the sky and a
pair of small boys perched on the wood stack, singing. They had
stopped their singing to stare.

Herbert had stared back.

The cart had crossed the *sloot* and shambled up the hill at the
other side. The song had begun again: that song, the minor chords
and the Xhosa cadences, like a familiar bird-call, a shrike in a
territorial patch of bush beside the gate-post at home where the eye
looked out. He had heard that song clearly on the air beyond the
voices of the gathering beside the chapel stone – all the clergy and
the congregation. That song – an augur's voice – sung in neither
sorrow nor in joy.

That song: rediscovered, so long after, after grief.

Herbert took the hymn sheets and the abandoned prayer books and
walked away back to the House. There was a little wind now, got up,
tossing only the topmost branches of the trees at the edge of Lower.
He went to the old chapel and left the prayer books in the vestry. He
tapped the sheets together on the edge of a table and stacked them on

363

a shelf. He went in through the side door of the House.

There was an odd hush. The prep and common-rooms were empty. Then, far off, in the north wing, way up the stairwell, he heard the sound of fighting. He took the stairs in twos. Boys stood in the passages, heads down, hands in pockets, grouped close, some touching. Outside Charlie Fraser's closed door were GB and Parkes, standing off from each other. GB's face was ashen. Parkes stood, appalled.

'Who's fighting?' said Herbert. His voice echoed at the ceiling.

'Charles Fraser and Arthur Graham,' said Edwards reverently.

NINETEEN

'Right!' says Arthur, shouldering open the door of Charlie's study. It crashes in against the wall.

Charlie turns, not quite looking at him.

'Outside!' says Arthur.

'Here.'

Work yourself up, boy, outface bewilderment. Work yourself up, boy – it is the only way to confront all the losses, surrendered here with childhood.

–Don't cry, my little man. Men don't cry. How mothers lie, bare-faced.

'Sorry . . .' Charlie is retreating. But somewhere there is triumph, enough to make him magnanimous: how much more denigrating than a straight retort, the clean challenge of a blow.

–Don't do that, Charlie. Just fight me back.

'I could kill you, Fraser!' Arthur says, pushing the door closed with his foot so the open window bounces on its hasp. 'I could bloody well kill you.' Arthur is not looking at him: he remembers Annie Zeederberg, all laughter, putting out her hand to Charlie Fraser as they leave the chapel building site, turning in farewell as though she would reach out and touch his cheek. The gesture stalls, but her hand remains poised – just poised, in all its intimacy – inches from him. And Charlie Fraser's face, quite naked, is alight. His eyes, when he turns them on Arthur, are a man's who has out-gazed the sun: kill me if you must. It is all too late.

Arthur is first. That is fair. A square fist, squarely placed. The feel of fist on flesh is good. It intoxicates. It purges.

She was mine.

She was no one's.

She was Charlie's. It was her choice.

She had watched Charles Fraser standing with the other seniors at the north end of the foundations of the chapel. She could gaze from under the brim of her hat without him knowing, lost in the crowd of parents, masked by the clergy in their robes and the Bishop in his mitre.

He had stood with Arthur Graham. Both held their boaters in their hands. She had traced the blue of the crosses on their blazer badges, the trim of their colours braid, the squareness of Charlie, Arthur's rangy stance, legs apart, loose-shouldered. A light wind had lifted Charlie's hair. Straight. Fair. He in profile: if she could have touched his face, felt with him the moment of that distant meditation. And when the prayers were ended, she had gone to him and said goodbye. Bold Annie, knowing there would be no other time, ringed about by the noisy throng, a sudden hidden moment in the crowd, she'd said, 'Goodbye, Charles Fraser. Good luck . . .'

'Goodbye . . . Annie,' he'd said, his eyes on hers. His fingers had brushed hers then, linked, were gone.

She'd laughed – such elation – and put her hand up to touch his face. He had not moved away but she had drawn her fingers back, sensing watchers. Still, the caress was there. Oh, Charlie Fraser.

–I'll pretend you kissed me.

She had not said it. She had turned from him and walked lightly, buoyant in the wind: to have pressed her thumbs softly against his lids, to have breathed against his skin.

Mac hurries from his room, all authority, pushes GB and Parkes aside from Charlie's study door. Even GB – ready to die – cannot bar the way.

'Come now, you fellows . . .' Mac barges in.

Neither Charlie nor Arthur pauses or turns. They are fist to fist, head to head. The boys pressing in behind Mac, rapt, are live to their own blood pounding. GB crouches, arms crossed, fists balled fiercely at his armpits. His eyes are almost shut. He hardly dares look. Parkes, beside him, has forgotten to close his mouth. A trace of silver dangles like dew on a spider's thread from his chin. He gags and gobbles and stares again.

Fraser and Graham are equally matched in strength – Fraser is heavier, Graham taller. Only the intent is different. Arthur pounds Charlie. It is a great catharsis. Charlie bends into it, remains steady.

The watchers are silent, the boys at the back standing on tiptoe or crouched and looking between legs. Beyond the collective breathing there is silence.

Blow for blow. Neither flinches.

A chair is overturned. A thigh jars against the desk. Charlie's eyebrow is cut, Arthur's lip.

Charlie Fraser has his hand across Arthur's neck, holding his head in against the hollow of his collarbone. Arthur's arms, locked across Charlie's back, are straining in to break his head grip: weight to counterweight, face dipped to face, ear to ear, turned in from the scrutiny of others. They are tiring. Both are sweating. Arthur almost leans on Charlie, balanced with him. They rock, necks straining. They rock, they rock: it is like an embrace. Does Charlie Fraser say something? Arthur? Charlie? Arthur? They rock, more slowly, slower, slow: this strange, primeval dance.

No one moves.

Then – suddenly – Arthur Graham laughs.

Laughs.

It is the laugh he has when he has been thrashed for horseplay, for larking in the dorm. It is Arthur's clown laugh. Straight – and generous: even if I break my heart, who will know?

The spectators do not move but a stir is starting at the back. When Arthur Graham laughs, we all laugh.

Charlie pushes Arthur's neck down. Half cuff – all caress. The gesture is returned. They bend, each to each, palm cupped to nape.

Herbert knows that stance.

367

In time he knows, too well, its tenderness and its futility. He knows the neck – conduit of breath, channel to the heart; he knows the nape, naked as a fontanelle. Is it there the last resistance lies?

–Necks are heavy, Arthur had said. It was sudden and emphatic.
–Surely it's the head that's heavy, Arthur. Herbert had quietly replied.
–No, it's the neck, believe me.
He should know.
  –Leave it, lad.
  –No.
  –Get back now.
  –No.
  –Get back.
  –No.
  –That's an order.
  –Sir.

Arthur laughs and Charlie laughs. They butt each other with their shoulders. They tussle, back muscles straining. They punch each other. It is all play then, intimacy secure. Nothing can intrude. Ranged together, Charlie – hair awry – glances round at the fellows watching, says sternly, 'Close your mouth, Parkes!'

Parkes grins.

'What're you staring at, GB?' GB's eyes are tightly closed. He opens them and blinks. Everyone laughs again. GB turns on Parkes and punches him. They roll on the floor. Edwards whoops, gives Mostert a shove, sticks out his foot and trips Herbert. The moment explodes into horseplay. Fists and feet and yells. Above the uproar, Robbie's voice, 'What is the confounded commotion up there?' Clumping on the stairs. 'Are you boys baboons? MacCallum! Gilbert! Here!'

For once, no one pays attention.

No one hears the bell clanging for supper.

None of the seniors has changed for the parents' dinner in the Drill Hall.

Herbert looks at Percy sitting on the bench outside the House, examining the arums in their cool flutes of leaves, a late bee hovering.

–How did they do it? says Herbert.

–Magicians! says Percy. –That faultless touch.

Herbert smiles.

–Love between equals, Cummings, says Percy. –It was all in the heart.

It is still in the heart.

Once, long ago, Percy, at his most satirical, had said to Herbert over chess, –You will leave here, Cummings, with an educated brain but an undeveloped heart. It is the first duty of the school to ensure it.

It had been a lie. For Percy most of all.

And Mac, perched smoking in his cricket togs on Percy's window sill, had remarked with a small snort, –Next time you're here, as a celebrated old codger, Daisy, I bet you'll lie down on Lower with your nose in the grit and howl for love. So much for your undeveloped heart!

Percy had turned to Mac. He had rolled a pawn idly between his fingers. –Is that so?

–You also said you'd had bugger all education forced into your skull in this parochial little backwater – your words, not mine, Mac had continued. –I suppose fellows like Doug have a way of reducing Virgil to the level of the animal husbandry learned in Gowie's dairy, but still . . .

–You're beginning to sound as pompous as me! Percy had said drily, –and that's my prerogative.

Mac had laughed and blown smoke rings.

Then Percy had said, –I will not howl for love . . . Herbert had looked at the floor, for his own ears had burned for Percy. –I will never mourn 'the flannelled fool at the wicket' nor the 'muddied oaf in the goal'! Never!

The flannelled fool at the wicket? The muddied oaf in the goal? They'd have all laid down their lives for them, Percy included. An educated brain and an undeveloped heart?

Percy had always known better than that.

    –You know quite well why I came back, Cummings.

    –Yes, Gilbert. I know.

The year was drawing in. The last days had come. There was a slow retreat – boy from boy, boy from master, boy from House, boy from team. A subtle disengaging, a shoulder turned, a door closed in exasperation: –Will you fellows knock, please? Percy has bought a box of Markowitz Black and White from Radomsky's. He smokes them while tossing old setworks into a fruit-crate for the boxroom, his tie pulled askew, his sleeves rolled up. He is at a loss for essay topics for juniors. They are running riot in the dorms.

Mac is planning a new wardrobe. He has already sent his measurements to a tailor in Johannesburg. The result will add five years to his life. He will look twenty-four, at least. The young ladies at the Tennis Club will not be asking him about school. His long-lost nurse does not matter any more. He will have his smoking jackets, his father's car, the Club, a salary, Business-in-the-City, Sunday parties at the houses on the Parktown Ridge. He looks out of the window of his study at the backyard windmills and reservoirs on the plots beyond the school grounds. Vanes sail in the wind, the stone pines on the hill are dim through the dust of a *bergwind* blowing. He will not be back.

Dan has parted his hair on the other side. Not right to left but left to right – after eighteen years. The discomfort must be borne. It is a gesture of intent: he does not wish to be the cricket captain any more. It is the end to stuttering. Before he leaves he will go and tell Mary Clifford about his burning passion.

    –Mary Clifford, will you marry me?

Hang on, Dan. There is the whole of Cambridge to go still. Articles, pupillage. The Inns-of-Court. Side-bar. Bar.

There is no time. Mary Clifford cannot wait.

I cannot wait.

We are restless. It is time to go.

We have played enough rugger, enough cricket, run our races, marched in lines, done our penance in the chapel. There are letters handed out at dinner from institutions, companies: enrolment forms, bank drafts for applications. There are trips to town to buy an Old Boy's tie and blazer. The transformation from Boy to Man has begun. There is a brisk trade in travelling clothes and keen competition among outfitters in the High Street: 'We are capable of meeting all tastes however capricious and all purses however light.' Prices are compared, quality examined. We are not going home in our uniforms.

The new chapel walls are rising. They are knee-height by the last day. Only the first-years bother to play in the foundations any more. It is no longer a novelty to race in wheelbarrows. Cigarette consumption in the senior common-room has doubled. Exams begin.

Bad Greek paper.

Bad Latin paper.

Mathematics, fair.

History, deplorable.

English, tolerable.

Agriculture: don't ask Doug – he has just kicked in his locker.

Dutch, who cares?

They went at last, without fanfare. Communion, final assembly, a visit to the chaplain, a visit to the Head, a dinner with Robbie, a last cup under the tsessebe's eye.

'How did you shoot the buck, sir?' It is an idle ploy for conversation. Robbie does not elucidate. His dog's silent farts are no longer a matter for laughing – no one's farts are funny any more. They are irritating and embarrassing. We are past all that.

Tin chests and suitcases are brought up from the boxroom. Study walls are suddenly bare. Honours caps are tucked away, wrapped in a pillowcase. Charlie Fraser's album has been stored in brown paper under his rugby boots in the bottom of his trunk. Boys start to drift, hands in pockets, no one cares how many buttons are done up on their jackets. Such things are no longer fraught with meaning. The world is waiting.

Lunch: the last boiled pumpkin for some. The last junket. Doug Morgan, lingering in the dining-room, hooks his arm around

Herbert's neck, noosing it affectionately. 'So, Aap-face, when are you coming to farm near me?'

'Soon.'

'Come shooting in the hols,' giving his neck a jerk.

'Right.'

Another jerk. 'I'll organise it.'

'Right,' Herbert says, mumbling against Doug's pocket, unable to disengage himself. 'How many sheep are you running?' he says in a bid for freedom.

Doug lets him go, runs a hand through his hair so it stands up. 'Couple of thousand' – very serious – he looks off, already the proprietor of flocks. 'I'm going to get the stud going properly as well. The old man's past it now.' Herbert can see him, pipe clenched in his teeth, discussing genetics in the Rouxville Town Hall or behind an ancient desk in a shearing-shed, drinking his tea from a bottle, ruddy-faced, entering fleece-grades in a ledger. Happy Doug Morgan. A farm. A stud. A wife. He would be the first to succumb, just as Percy had said.

'There's quite a good cricket club in the district,' Doug is saying. 'Join us when you're home, Aap-face.' He glances around at everything in the dining-room, picking at the frayed splinters on the curve of one of the bentwood chairs. He goes to the wall and examines the picture of the XV, newly framed, hanging on its brass hook next to 1910, 1911, 1912, a space still for 1914 on the other side. Herbert looks away. He will not embarrass Doug. Doug pulls at his ear, turns, half grins, not meeting Herbert's eye. Then, as he walks out, he gives Herbert a shove, punches his arm numb and goes off whistling, already striding camps and pastures. Good straight fellow, Douglas Morgan. Absolutely steady.

Everyone – his House, his fellows – had turned out that afternoon to see Mac off. Each year the ritual was the same – when Sampson had gone and Rudd – middle-school solemn, fags inconsolable. It was then they had seemed old-mannish in their tweeds with their travelling bags and their stiff new hats. Rudd's address to his fellow prefects had taken the dullest into realms of the spirit where they had never strayed before. Mac's had been different: quiet, rather dour, halting. 'Well, fellows, here's to College then, here's to the House . . . all the best then, lads . . . Dan,' – a proffered hand – 'Jack.' No 'Sparrow' here. *We are The Strong Men.* 'Arthur.' A pat on the shoulder. Very good lad, Arthur. Simply the best. Mac went from senior to senior, the colonel on transfer. 'Charlie.' He shook his hand. 'I expect to cheer for you one day at Twickenham.'

Charlie Fraser laughed. 'Until then, Mac.'

Until then.

Percy was standing at the door, hands linked behind his back. Mac came to him last. 'Daisy!' It was jovial. How else could it be? 'When you're a bishop,' he said, 'I hope you'll remember me and give me some sort of dispensation.'

'For what, Mac?'

'Whatever you like. For all the wicked things I'm planning.'

Percy smiled. His jaw hitched quietly: he was in perfect control.

–For your innocence, Mac.

They shook hands and Mac was gone, down the passage, followed by his troops. Robbie stood in the porch, pulling at his moustache, rather moved. He suspected that despite his self-possession, MacCallum set forth with as much apprehension as a newboy entering the House for the first time. What was he going to, valorous Mac? Where would he find it? Robbie looked around for Percy Gilbert. He was not in the throng. Better so. Gilbert kept his guard impeccably, but even he was not invincible. Much, much better so.

Everyone lined up to shake hands at the gate. The cab waited in the road. Percy stood a moment in the empty common-room. He slipped away to his study and packed another crate of books, lifting his photos from the wall, taking down the seraglio drape, returning the room to its institutional garb. At a distance, he heard the cheers from the juniors as Mac drove away.

–You are free, Mac.

The room was very still. A small, frail spider wavered in a corner, exposed to the light where the drape had been.

In ones and twos they went. Half a dozen. Three or four, depending on the train timetable and the destination. Herbert – Great-Man-in-Waiting – had been invited to a farewell tea at the Grants. He made a speech – full of laughter and stumbling – on behalf of those staying behind. He'd rambled on about all the marvels they would see in the World-at-Large and England in particular, but how the footer there would never be the same as playing the Methodists, how thumping them was the greatest glory that they'd ever know. He'd ended with a pledge to follow that season's trouncing with another in the next. Three cheers from Dan and Sparrow and the other fellows and great slabs of cake from Lady Grant to take back to school.

Sparrow Bell was almost the last to go. Herbert walked with him to the station and helped him heave his trunk on board the train. Sparrow leaned out of the window, in his big man's hat and suit, off to the world. 'Cheerio, old chap,' he said. It sounded odd, as if he were practising for another life.

''Bye, Sparrow.'

'Kowie on the first Christmas home.'

Herbert had nodded.

'You, Dan, Charlie, Arthur, Doug and me.'

Herbert put his hands in his pockets. His teeth felt dry.

'A really grand reunion.' It seemed Sparrow needed to fill up an empty space between them.

Herbert nodded again. Why didn't the train go?

'You'd better give the Methodists a thrashing next match, d'you hear?'

'We will,' Herbert said, on steadier ground.

'Let me know.'

The carriage began to move, sliding away.

'Sparrow!' Herbert heard his voice, suddenly raised, lost in the hiss of steam.

Herbert stood in that stark sunlight on the platform. Sparrow had taken off his hat and saluted with it, waving it until the track had curved from view. Herbert watched the train retreat, listening until other sounds ebbed back. As he'd turned away he'd startled a threesome of sparrows. They had always frequented the rafters of the platform or flitted like small brown shadows among mealie sacks piled for transportation. One perched on the edge of the fire-bucket, watching him. He made a little sound in his throat. He couldn't recall if it was a laugh or a dry kind of sob.

–Jack will always be a boy, Percy had said.

–What do you mean?

–No one wants him to grow up.

But he had grown up and he had gone in a new suit from Birch's and a hat with a little feather in the grosgrain band and some hand-baggage that gave him the air of a commercial traveller. And Herbert had walked back to school alone and gone to his study and closed the door.

He felt like a small boy. He had no overcoat or briefcase or hat, like Sparrow. With these accoutrements, Sparrow had suddenly transcended comments on his eyelashes. He had looked severe and rather businesslike going to the station. No pet, this, for the amusement of girls! It was Herbert who would be the pet now. He'd been told, on good authority, that it was not his eyelashes – like Sparrow's – but his *knees* that inspired little raptures to spectators when he played footer. His knees!

Girls were very peculiar.

Now Sparrow had gone with his preposterous hat and his 'Cheerio, old chap'. Tomorrow it would be Arthur and Charlie. This evening, Percy.

And then?

Tibi est successio. To you is the succession.

He didn't know if he wanted it.

At five, Percy knocked at his study door.

'Come in.' Herbert stood awkwardly. He began to sweat as he had when he had played chess with Percy as a junior. But Percy did not have his satirical air. He was not here to entertain himself.

'May I sit a moment?' he said quietly. He took his cigarette case from his pocket and tapped the end of the oval Turkish on the lid. Herbert watched him light it with an ease so unlike the way farmers' sons struck a match as if protecting the flame from some Karoo blast, even in an airless room. Pure Percy – quite inimitable.

'Well, Cummings, here we are and what is there to say?'

'When do you sail for England?'

'Three or four months in Cape Town,' said Percy. 'Then off on the mail-ship. I am going to have an extended tour of the Continent with my parents and some time with relatives in Surrey before I go up.'

'How long will you be gone?'

'For ever, I hope.'

'And if there's a war?'

Percy looked at Herbert sceptically. 'I suppose you think it'll all be a fine adventure if there is?'

'I'll say.'

Percy turned from him and glanced out of the window. He opened it and the evening air drifted in with the smell of mown grass from the fields, a last cutting before the furlough. Beyond the playing fields was the town and the roofs of houses and the Gothic steeple of Christchurch. The dusk was mournful and limpid with the cold coming up from the ground and a little wisp of mist in a hollow by the *sloot*. 'Imagine,' said Percy – his voice sounded brittle – 'you will still be looking at this six months from now and I will be admiring the spires of Cambridge.'

'Have you ever been there?' asked Herbert.

'No.'

'Then how do you know how it will be?' It was defensive. The view was something Herbert caught in glimpses, unconsciously, but it had settled in with him, as familiar as the veld at home and the hills and the epic skies.

'I don't know how it will be,' Percy conceded. 'But I suspect. I have these intimations that it will feel right.'

'And everything here will feel wrong?'

Percy raised a brow and said, 'No need to be so prickly, Cummings – everything here will *not* feel wrong. It will just be *here*.'

Herbert did not know how to retaliate. He wished Percy would go then. Most of the fellows who had left that morning had simply said goodbye and picked up their bags and been off, via Robbie's classroom and the Head's study. Down to the station, board the train. Depart.

'I have been taking a slow tour of the place most of today,' said Percy. 'The chapel, the classrooms, the cricket pitch, the tuck-shop. I never did have a great affection for the tuck-shop, you know. All those deplorable Albanys and being expected to dally with Mrs Woodman's daughter!'

Herbert rubbed his hand across his hair.

Percy came back from the window and leaned against the bookcase. 'I wonder if we will meet again,' he said. 'On some foreign battlefield where we'll play cadets in earnest.'

'I don't know, Gilbert.'

'Or in court perhaps when I am a barrister and you are a pupil-at-law.'

'I am going to farm, Gilbert.'

'Foolish boy,' said Percy. 'Such a waste of talent.'

Herbert said nothing.

'The world is a bigger place than here, Herbert.'

'This is where I . . .' and Herbert was about to say 'love' but it sounded idiotic and he said instead, 'know.'

Percy took another draw on his cigarette and then slowly put it out. He did not look at Herbert then. He said, 'I'll miss you, Herbert Cummings . . .' – for your intuition, for discretion, for your augur's eye. 'I will remember you . . .' – longer than you will remember me. He smiled. 'I wish you well.' Oh, yes. The little hollows and narrow planes which gave his face its fine asceticism took light from the window. Herbert met his glance and smiled back. Percy put out his hand and Herbert took it. It was odd to feel those long, slim fingers in his own rough, bony ones. There were worlds between their touch but Percy's grip was firm and cool. Then he opened the door, tapped his hat against the side of his leg as if in salute and turned away.

Herbert listened to his steps receding, heard them stop. He glanced out into the corridor. Percy was standing at the threshold of Vincent MacCallum's study with a hand resting up against the frame. The room beyond was empty. His head was inclined. Herbert drew back, leant against the wall. He did not know what he had witnessed or that he had witnessed anything at all. But it was not something Percy had intended he should see.

An educated brain and an undeveloped heart?
No, Percy Gilbert. You give the lie to it.
    – You know quite well why I came back, Cummings.
    – Yes, Gilbert. I know.

Herbert was on an errand for Robbie when Arthur and Charlie went the next day. Perhaps they had gone as he was passing Mrs Randell's garden – the figs were not ripe hanging over the wall but there were still a few mulberries. On returning to school he passed the empty studies. He stood at the threshold of Charlie's, the sudden shock of adrenalin in his gut, appalled.

'Where are Fraser and Graham?' he said to Unwin.

'Gone,' said Unwin bleakly.

He fetched his footer boots and put them on hastily and tramped down to Lower field and practised kicking at the posts: over and over and over. Kick and let it fly. Trot, gather, come back and kick again. Kick and let it fly. Some juniors stood about, anxious to fetch the ball. He tried to send them scampering with a look: Get lost.

Still they stood – gormless nubs – gawping at him.

Poephols.

He missed the posts three times.

The light was failing when he returned to the House and it was drizzling. He picked a fight with Tom Edwards for nothing. Poor Tom – no reason to find fault with him when he was bumbling about, worrying at a stick of biltong with his teeth while he read *The Big Game Hunter*.

'Get out, Edwards.'

'Get out?' Bewildered.

'Get out of my light!'

'What?'

Herbert pushed him.

'Hey, Apie? What's the problem?'

'How can I see if you're lying about here, blocking out my light?'

He hadn't needed the light because the book he'd taken up was a Dutch grammar. Who would read a Dutch grammar at bedtime anyway? After a moment he said, 'Shut up with that chewing?'

'Listen, Apie, you're asking for it.' Tom lowered his book.

Herbert kept his eyes on the page in front of him. He kept on staring at it for a full twenty seconds.

Tom sniffed and read again. After a moment he said, 'Graham and Fraser were looking for you this afternoon.'

'Why?'

'They wanted to say goodbye.'

'So?'

'So – they said goodbye.'

'And?'

'And what?'

'I'll beat you up in the Drill Hall tomorrow if you don't shut up,' Herbert said and turned the page.

Tom looked at him. He did not sniff. He did not chew. It seemed that Apie meant it.

Herbert got up, flung his book down and took himself off to the bogs, even though it was raining hard. A good piss, even if he got wet and muddied the hems of his pyjama pants in the puddles, was better than sitting around, doing nothing.

The only bog with a door was occupied. The door was bolted. He marched into the adjoining cubicle. Someone else came down the path, splashing up rain from the stones. He stood still. He'd as soon *klap* someone as have them talk to him – he might even stick his head down the hole.

It was Parkes. He thumped on the closed door with his fist. 'GB?' No reply. 'Listen, *poephol*, I know you're in there.'

Still no reply.

'Braithwaite?'

'Get lost, Parkes.' No one called GB Braithwaite. Not even Robbie.

'Are you blubbing?' said Parkes.

No reply.

'Are you drizzing in there?' Parkes rattled the latch.

The door flew open. GB, all teeth and elbows, knocked Parkes down into puddles and mud.

Small boys in striped pyjamas, buttons flying loose, trouser-cords trailing, they fought – as they had learned – chest to chest, fist to fist.

Heart to heart.

Parkes sat astride GB, pushing his shoulders into the ground. GB jerked his knees and they rolled over and lay tangled together with their faces turned up to the rain, panting. If both were drizzing, no one would have known – only Herbert Cummings. He could as easily have let the water scour his eyes as it scoured theirs.

Fraser and Graham had gone. Gone. Utterly. It was the end of the Known World for them.

The rain beat down on the roof of the lavatory, beat down on upturned faces. Then GB and Parkes both laughed. That – after all – is how it is done. Laugh. There is nothing else to do. Herbert laughed too, alone in the third bog. But the sound got caught in corrugations, somewhere in his chest.

TWENTY

August the fourth, 1914: *The Journal* lay on the mat outside Robbie's door. He stooped to pick it up. He scanned the page, stood very still. So, it was here at last.

LATEST INTELLIGENCE

Before Going to Press
Reuter's Special Service

EUROPEAN WAR

Britain's Warning to Germany

A 'DAILY MAIL' REPORT

London. Aug. 3rd (5.20 am): The German attack on Luxembourg is a direct challenge to Great Britain. The Daily Mail states: 'We understand that an intimation has been conveyed to the German Government that if a single German soldier is ordered to set foot on Belgian soil the British Navy will take instant action against Germany'.

Stop Press: A page later:

Ultimatum to Belgium

> London. Aug. 3rd (2.45 pm): Belgium has rejected the ultimatum.

The shot at Sarajevo, in late June, had spawned this.

The column was slim, the print small. Robbie had to hold the paper at an angle to read it. Spanning the rest of the page, pushing the news columns to the perimeters, was an advertisement from *The Shrine of Fashion* subtitled *Great Slaughter: Bombs in all Departments* and, in letters twice the size of the print announcing the ultimatum, '44in. Embroidery Voile Flouncings; very handsome designs, 3/11; Black Brussels kid gloves, 12-button length, slightly imperfect. Usually 6/11, now 4/11'.

In afteryears Robbie remembered how, at that moment, he had watched a small furry caterpillar suspended on a thread, dangling in the space between the porch roof and the step below. The precariousness and yet the patience with which it hung – exposed to the vagaries of wind, a passing bird – the sun touching the tips of its spines, fragile as the filaments of airborne seeds. Beyond, built of venerable stone, the other houses sheltered still their sleeping cargo of boys. What would this mean to them?

It meant nothing for a while, for nothing changed. Lessons. Chapel. Prep. Sport. Small boys still lined up for a thrashing before breakfast.

The cadets went to camp again. Robbie was vigilant with armaments, fitness, drill. This was the real thing. His evening talks were to the point: weapon control, discipline, signalling, parade, –Keep your head down or you'll get a bullet between the eyes. I've seen it happen more than once.

What it was to be in the dunes with flailing fifteen year olds, their minds on grub, eyeing the river, wanting to take out the rowing boat and swim off the sandbars! Were they listening when he spoke to them? Did they understand the import of his words? Did they understand the weapons they were parading? Their attention had never been more urgent, yet here is a fellow picking his nose and there is another staring into space and another flicking his neighbour with his belt and another with his hat on back to front.

–Let's fish, fellows.

–It's our turn with the boat.

Running in the waves, leaping, diving, racing down the dunes, their yells were chimes carolling – it was all good sport, all fun, so much living. Nothing could persuade them otherwise. Yet last year's lads were already training in the Imperial Light Horse, Prince Alfred's Guard or the Cradock Commando, slogging the wastes of South West Africa, thorn-scrub skirmishes in debilitating heat. Others were trudging the railway line from Voi to Taveta, just inside the Kenyan border, mustering to take on Von Lettow-Vorbeck's bush-country brigands. And then there were those – his most glorious boys – who were continents away, in England, the Officers' Training Corps at Oxford or Cambridge, waiting to be gazetted into the sacred regiments: Argyll and Sutherland, King Edward's Horse, Royal Berkshires, Artillery. Dan and Frank Grant and Vincent MacCallum had all applied for the Royal Flying Corps. Subalterns, captains, NCOs: his boys – Robbie-trained. He knew where each would serve.

Jack Bell wrote from Keble:

'Members of the university – both graduate and undergraduate – have been hard at training in the O.T.C. Freshmen who have done service in their schools corps have an advantage, so I am grateful for the time spent at the Kowie and am putting what I learned to good use.

There will be no organised athletics in the university at present, which is a blow for good old Rudd with whom I have recently met up. He was quite brilliant in the last season and is positively famous here. For the present, however, there is no mind for the track, the river or the playing fields. Uniform is now accepted as academical dress and under-graduates are to be seen in uniform at lectures, in hall and in chapel.'

He also sent a picture of an O.T.C group in their khaki and their puttees and their shining boots, still without regimental insignia. Four boys, eighteen to twenty-two, grouped in stern camaraderie before the soaring leads of an ancient Trinity window. The print was tinted in sepia, a pallid light beyond, the ghost of a tree with weeping withies. On a carved table leaned Jack Bell and James Seymour. Cross-legged at their feet sat Rudd and Holmes. Such splendid boys. Two former Senior Prefects, a Head-of-House and Sparrow Bell – his Lads, his Corps, his School, regrouped ten thousand miles away in the Old Country. Jack wore his hat at an angle. Such a triumphant smile, eyes candid: we are quite invincible!

It was the first picture since the declaration of war that Robbie had put up on his wall.

In chapel, the Head often took the lectern now. It was like being in the presence of God, seated in the pews before him. He was so tall, so wise, so leonine to gaze at and to hear. At evensong, one Sunday, he said, placing his hands apart on the edge of the pulpit and looking down at the upturned faces, 'A German officer is believed to have remarked wryly to an English officer, "You Englishmen will *always* be fools – but then, we shall *never* be gentlemen". Perhaps he was not quite accurate. We hope we may sometimes avoid being fools, but gentlemen we are determined to remain. Indeed, it is far better to be a gentleman – if a fool – than not to be a gentleman at all. Remember this, my lads, and you will not disgrace either your own names or the name of this school in whatever endeavour you undertake.'

The boys stirred. There was much foolishness among them, they knew, but sitting upright, like gentlemen, would vindicate any lack of sense: Mostert put his glass eye in his pocket and stopped balancing it on his shoulder, pointing it at the nubs in the pew behind.

Having fixed their attention, the Head continued: 'Multitudes of our young men are giving their service to their country which is also service to God. They are fighting and dying for liberty, peace, civilisation, righteousness and Christianity. How could men die better?' He paused. Every eye was on him, even Mostert's.

'The fine schools of this country,' he continued, 'are like munitions factories and ought to be turning out a constant supply of living material. In this, I am proud to say, we are doing our share. I know that you lads will offer your services as soon as you leave school. If you fail in this, then our sacred work as a munitions factory fails too. Even if it means imperilling your lives for the honour and glory of England at the Front, you know your duty and we know that you will do it without hesitation.'

The light glowed in the sanctuary. From the pulpit, the Head looked above and beyond them, as if warriors gathered in the baptistry. Herbert turned his eyes away. He too looked beyond the regiment of fellows in the pews. The new Rood cross hung above them, painted freshly – gold and blue and rose – the *Agnus Dei* in the centre. He could hear the dry, hot wind outside, at a great distance. A great, hot wind – the nothingness beyond.

For the first time in his life he questioned the existence of God.

If He was there – why this peril? Why this fear?

Why this silence?

He brought his eyes back to the heads and shoulders in the pew in front. Familiar necks, some blossoming pustules; familiar ears – the large, the flat, the crooked. GB's were poised at right angles to his head. They did not seem so prominent any more but it was time he took a flannel to them and rubbed the backs clean.

The names of the first casualties came in: Graham Lindsay, killed by rebels at Sandfontein in South West Africa in September; Reginald Webber, died of wounds sustained in fighting the selfsame rebels; 'Fighting' Frames – so much closer, for there were those among the seniors who still remembered him.

'So young, ardent and vigorous, so full of every quality a parent hopes for in a son,' said the Head. 'He died in combat against the lackeys and flunkies of the German nation near Ventersburg.' The Head paused. His voice, when he spoke, reached the back pews and echoed in the baptistry. 'The despicable machinations of Beyers and De Wet have only served to strengthen the admiration we all feel for General Botha. It is men like him who bind English and Dutch citizens together and who link all that is best in the two races in this country.'

'There aren't only two races in this country,' said GB to his neighbour.

'Yes, there are! English and Dutch.'

'What about the Xhosa?' GB was indignant. Who did the fellow think he'd lived with all his life? What language was his mother tongue, tell me that? He said it with a loud and perfect click, so that Robbie glanced his way and frowned.

'They aren't races!' his neighbour scoffed.

'What?'

'They're natives.'

'So?'

'Shut up, GB. Robbie's watching.'

Lindsay, Webber, Frames: three to join the honoured throng who had died fourteen years before. There is space enough for all their names on the unadorned stone walls and choir of the new chapel, the plain glass windows awaiting tinted memorial saints. 'In loving memory of . . .' In whose honour will they each be filled? Through the panes, the sky and clouds can be seen, distant and clear, riding far beyond the small rectangles of lead-webbed glass.

The cricket and rugby teams for 1915 were chosen but there was no one to play against. The University was depleted, the Methodists down to a handful, Crusaders gone. There were weeds growing on City Lords. There would be no photo placed beside the glorious team with Morgan and Holmes and Seymour, Grant and Graham, Bell and Fraser.

The 1914 rugby team: fifteen lads with the trappings of dominance and fealty, collars up, scarves tucked at the throat – discreet dark silk – stockings banded in pale blue. Eyes straight. No smiles. It was the last team that played a proper match for four years. The school magazine announced:

'With the departure of Holmes and Seymour for Oxford, Herbert Cummings will be the new captain of the XV. He will retain his position at scrum-half. He is the youngest captain to have led the team in nearly twenty years. We have no doubt he will take over Seymour's captaincy with honour and lead the team to victory during the 1915 season. Tom Edwards is vice-captain.'

Where is the team of 1915: Cummings in his captain's cap – velvet and silver and silky little badge? It does not exist. They did not have a chance to play. The empty space on the wall is a memorial to something lost: a flag half-mast, a chapel plaque.

Where is a picture of 1916?

There is none.

1917?

There is none.

The coach has gone to war.

1918?

Every boy but seven has had the Spanish 'flu. Almost every master. Every servant.

But in the early days of the war, nothing daunted, Cummings and Edwards had drilled the juniors, teaching skills, organising house matches. Someone had to keep it going.

'You will never make a good touch-kicker without practice,' Herbert said to a motley group of third years: second-hand jerseys hanging out, deplorable socks, boots like clowns got from the second-hand box, no morale. 'Remember Fraser? Remember how he used to kick at posts every afternoon in the season after prep?'

'Who's Fraser?' Some new-pot.

It was not worth an answer. *Everyone* knew who Fraser was.

Back in the House, a know-all courting recognition, said, 'Fellows, come and look in Cummings' study. It used to be Fraser's. Here are Fraser's initials, see' – jabbing at the window sill with a proprietary finger. 'CWF' was neatly carved in a corner. Just beside it, 'AGG'.

'Who's AGG?'

'Arthur Grenville Graham.'

'Who's he?'

'Winger. Best ever. Parkes says he is the best in the history of the school.'

'I thought Fraser was the best!' – a bewildered nub plodding in the wilderness.

With supreme condescension: 'Fraser was the full-back, idiot!' Then, repeated like a jingle, 'The best full-back in the history of the school.'

'Who was the best altogether then?'

'Both were the best.'

'You can only have one best.'

'Are you trying to be funny, hey?'

Really! Didn't these fellows – raked in from farms – know anything about positions? Didn't they play rugby at Daggaboersnek and Cradock? Why hadn't someone drilled them better?

The fathers had all gone to war.

The brothers.

There was no one to ask.

Tom Edwards was detailed as Captain-of-Information. You couldn't have a newboy saying that he didn't know who the captains of the XV or the XI were or what Lower was. They'd better look sharp or someone'd be suggesting they get up a soccer team! It showed what wars could do!

One master left to join up and then another. Mr Lucas. Mr Abbott. Mr Moorrees. Robbie was too old. So were the Second Master and the Head. The pressure on all three was immense. 'Masterful administration of the unforeseen' was the challenge put to the Head by his weary Council at that time. Every day a new crisis arose. Even the Head looked bowed. Old Jarge, limping about, was janitor, games master, dining-hall waiter, groundsman, carpenter, handyman and adviser. His hair thinned. He did not wear his boater at quite the same angle. There was a cold wind on the fields at night.

An old master came back, bringing the greening gown and whiskers of a past century. He was deaf as a post. His classes erupted into chaos. If he wept at home, it would not have been surprising. A young master came as well, declared unfit for military service. He was a serious, thoughtful man with a curvature of the spine and spectacles thick as the lens of a microscope.

388

'Imagine not joining up?' some fellow said, appraising the newcomer sceptically.

'Can't do anything if he's declared unfit' – a more generous mate.

'I'd rather be dead,' said the first disparagingly. 'We ought to say something or do something to let him know we're not fooled.'

'Maybe . . .'

'Next they'll bring in women to teach us!'

'Don't be ridiculous!'

Even the Head would not have contemplated such sedition! He wrote to the Bishop:

'I am compelled to invite back masters long retired, many of whom, I fear, will be unequal to the task. Our sister school does not suffer as there is no shortage of excellent women teachers prepared to sacrifice some domestic tranquillity, to offer their support. Sadly, I cannot appeal to the same source for assistance. To expect a South African schoolboy to take kindly, in the name of patriotic self-sacrifice, to the thought of being taught by a woman, is to ask the impossible of his patriotism, his nascent consciousness of manhood, and his sense of humour!'

The situation might be desperate – but not *that* desperate!

The war did not occupy only the Head. It was the subject of Sunday letters home, interspersed though they were with other more pressing concerns, like teams and tuck.

A nub to his parents:

'The junier and sinier captains have been picked for the house teams. Our sinier captain is Cummings. He will be a hot shot. Our vice is Tom Edwards. We are going to thrash the other houses. We have had two debates. The first was on the scoundrelly behayvier of labour leaders in strikes on the Rand. The last one was on liker. There is a rumer that some English ships have been sunk and 10 Gergon ships. The sweets you sent were delish but the quinces were mostly mouldy. Please send more if you can.'

Pringle Mi. to his cousin, Ross Terts, at home on the farm:

'Arthur Graham wrote to Parkes. He does not give a nice description of German East. It is full of flies and mosquitoes and lions taking their trek-oxen. The cattle and the natives seem to be the greatest attraction to him. Fraser is with him. They are privates. Why privates? All the other fellows that went away are officers. Graham told Parkes he and Fraser dig bogs and polish boots and don't he and GB want to join them because they are more experienced at shit-shovelling! They have seen lots of game but can't shoot in case they give their positions away. He says Kilimanjaro is spectakler.'

Herbert, in the first flush of rank – his own study, the view of Christchurch from his lofty room – wrote gravely to his sister:

'We are collecting money for a Maxim gun for the SA contingent. The fellows have been very good about giving up their pocket-money. The prefects are intending to start a fund to educate a son of one of the Old Boys fallen in the war. So far there hasn't been any with children – but there won't be long to wait . . .'

In the Head's study was a map of France pronged with pins and string. He plotted the advance, the retreat, the redeployment of troops. Every day, as soon as news came in, there would be an adjustment. The masters gathered round. Little flags were made denoting regiments, battalions. The Head knew where every Old Boy served.

'He doesn't have a map of German East Africa,' said Herbert to Tom. 'What about the fellows there?'

'That's not the war,' said Tom.

'Of course it's the war.'

'France is the war. Everyone knows that.'

In November 1914, ten boys ran away. Archer led them out. By default, Unwin was among them.

'They went last night,' Robbie said, pacing the Head's study. 'They must have climbed down the fire-escape in South. I'm off to the station now to find out if they've boarded a train.' He drew a piece of paper from his pocket. 'The wisdom in the House early this morning is that they'd gone to join up. There was a lot of complaint, as you are well aware, when the Government withdrew its support from its early training scheme for schoolboys. My lads were fired up and they were very disappointed that it was called off.' Robbie was flustered for the first time in years. He handed the paper to the Head. 'I found this in my letter-box on my way here.'

'We, the undersigned, give notice that we have left the House and School to perform our sacred duty to God and our King and offer our services in behalf of our country.'

Among the signatories were Archer, Stafford and Mostert.

'Their first intention was to get out of writing the final examinations,' said the Head peremptorily. 'That is perfectly clear to me.' He tapped his fingers on the page.

'Some may have felt – quite sincerely – that their duty to their country was more important than the matriculation.' Robbie did not like to have others criticise his boys, even these boys. Only he was allowed to denigrate them. 'After all that has been said in recent weeks, it is not surprising!' The reproof was not lost on the Head. 'We have been positively pushing them into it, with all our talk of Empire.'

'That's the best excuse I've heard in years!' The Head was very terse. 'If your first-rate scholars had departed – yes! But a greater bunch of dunces was never gathered together in one place. Look at Archer! He's been in the senior class almost three years!'

Robbie could not disagree.

'Not one among this barbarous lot,' said the Head, 'would have passed the examinations at all or bestirred himself with any serious application! No one would have objected – we'd have expected nothing less – if they'd gone the moment term ended. It is only seven weeks away. Now I shall have to spend the day telegraphing parents and there will be no end of recrimination and fuss. Besides,' he glanced down at the names, 'Archer may be almost twenty – poor fellow – but half of these are clearly under age and a boy like Mostert will be rejected because of his eye.'

'He's a first-class shot!' said Robbie defensively.

'I doubt the Medical Board will give him a chance to show his prowess,' retorted the Head with some asperity: Robinson seemed to have his priorities muddled. If these chaps had been from another house, he'd have been all disparagement and censure and ready to call out the constabulary!

'If they are not attested, they'll be packed back to us,' said the Head. 'By which time, conveniently, the exams will be over. And then what are we to do with them? School regulations dictate that a runaway is expelled immediately – but can you imagine the uproar if we sent down a boy who has volunteered to fight for his country and was rejected on age or medical grounds and returned? He'd be seen as a misunderstood hero. A martyr. Can you think of the letters to *The Journal*? On the other hand, if we let this pass, we'll have half the school running off to war!' He went to the window and glanced out. He turned and said, hands clasped behind his back, very tall, 'The first boy discovered planning to abscond or in the process of doing so, will be summarily expelled. If we are not quite ruthless from the start, we will have to set a permanent guard at the station to round them up!'

Robbie pulled at his moustache.

The Head was not finished. 'And thinking ahead – something these foolish boys have not considered – what are they to do when they're demobilised and have no school certificate?'

'Perhaps they'll never know,' said Robbie.

There was a small silence.

Robbie went to the station.

'Ten of my lads are absent without leave,' he said to the stationmaster.

'Nine!' replied the stationmaster triumphantly. He took him into his office with the air of a demonstrator with something to exhibit: – Here is an interesting specimen. Just look at it! Abject boy!

A boy indeed, seated on an upright chair in the corner. It was Unwin.

'Found him in the goods shed,' said the stationmaster, hitching at his braces with his thumbs. 'Seems he missed the train!'

Robbie cast his eye on him.

Unwin felt the contraction in his blood, the heat inside his jacket. The sweat. It was back as it had been when he was younger, pooling in his shoes, pooling at his belt. All that fear oozing out. If Robbie beat him now, he would find him waterlogged.

'What train did they go on?' said Robbie to the stationmaster.

'This boy refuses to say a word. But my signalman saw them running for the goods train, just beyond the first bend, as it pulled out last night.' He jerked his thumb at the window. 'I couldn't have seen them from here, but he was down the line a way, checking points. It's extremely dangerous to jump in there but it's the last hope before the train picks up speed.' He cast his eye on Unwin. 'This one didn't jump in time. My signalman saw him come back and slip into the goods shed. He followed him and locked him in. I let him out this morning.' Speaking confidentially then, 'Won't say a word to me.' He addressed Unwin, raising his voice. 'Cat got your tongue, my boy?' Unwin kept his eyes on the floor.

'Come along,' said Robbie.

They walked out of the stationmaster's office. The sun was bright. The shadow of the roof struts laid their bars along the platform. They jagged across Robbie's face as he tramped down towards the entrance. Three, four, five struts: Unwin watched each shadow leap and take the cheek like a claw and then retreat again, shimmering slightly in the heat. He turned his head imperceptibly. Up there on the hill behind the station, was the boundary of the graveyard. Davey Bennett was there, Davey Bennett lying alone under iron stars at night, the iron sun in the day, enclosed in iron palings. Davey Bennett, with the black Christ-thorn above and the weight of earth pressing down on him.

Why had he done it? Why, despite his small exultation, had he been so foolish?

The evening before, the prefects and rank-holders had been announced for the next year. Unwin had sat examining his hands. He had no expectations. But his father did. His father, so far away in his civil servant's office in Bulawayo, had many expectations. His mother – blindly – nurtured them as well:

'My dear son,
We have every hope that you will do very well in the examinations and that you will be rewarded somehow for your sense of duty and for your industry. We know you will not disappoint us. Your father did not have the opportunities you have had in education and in meeting people whose society is so much to be valued. You are a gentleman, Hugh, and we know that every sacrifice that has been made on your behalf will garner rich rewards, not just for you but for your parents . . .'

Etcetera, etcetera, etcetera.
Had she seen his last report?

Mathematics: Weak. A remarkable paucity of insight. He has little grasp of basic concepts.
English: Fair but lacks confidence.
Greek: His knowledge of the subject is very slight.
Latin: His marks show lack of application.
History: Shows some promise.
Religious Instruction: [illegible: thank you, Reverend Dowsley!].
Conduct: Lacks initiative but improving.
Etcetera, etcetera, etcetera.

There was no doubt his father had read it and filed it away in a folder in his chest of drawers at the office and said nothing to his mother, too ashamed to show her. Perhaps he had even been conceived in an act of apology, or simply by default.

The respect he'd earned from the fight was not enough to overcome his own shortcomings. It had simply brought a halt to unwelcome attention from Archer: on Charlie Fraser's account more than on his own. Why couldn't he see the victory through himself?

   –Do it, Unwin. Just do it.

There was no Charlie Fraser to notice now.

He would slip into anonymity again: a dog indeed, but not the Nose-in-the-Air, Straight-Tailed, Bristles-on-End Dog that he had wished to be since Speech Day. He was an abject dog, one that bounces too much when spoken to and only succeeds in annoying; a dog with an indecisive bark, too high, too much between a yelp and a whine; a dog that smells of mange; a dog that is always underfoot when least wanted; a dog that others shun. There was nothing he could do to please. He was the sort of fellow others wanted to *klap* without direct provocation. And, having once earned Fraser's – even MacCallum's – brief approbation – 'Well fought, Unwin' – it was all he craved. He wanted to walk lightly, valorous, as he had on that distant afternoon when he had struck Archer in the throat and the fellows had gone with him, down to the river to wash the blood from his knuckles. So much elation, limbs tired but exultant.

And so, on that evening, when the prefects and other rank-holders had been announced, Unwin had prayed for anything. Anything. A badge, perhaps, for Choir, no matter how it might be derided by the others or pass beneath the notice of The Glorious.

Messenger to the editor of the magazine?

Folder of the tennis-net?

Guardian of the chess boards?

Library lackey?

Even bog-washer.

Unwin stared up at the honours boards, ranged side by side around the walls, knowing it was hopeless. Which boys, which names, besides these dimly illumined entries for 1885 or 1899 or 1901, had been ignored? Had some other fellow sat here too, knowing his would never be inscribed? If men were equal, boys were not.

God liked his best creations best, kept them for Himself: look how gloriously Charlie Fraser had walked in the sun at the Kowie, when it moulded his naked back. How it had glowed on the tendons and muscles of his strong legs, flanks, neck, head! It probably shone from the soles of his feet. God took pleasure in lions, not in slugs. He had put so much more attention into creating them. He had their names inscribed on honours boards in pale gold letters.

Name after name was announced and Unwin had applauded the Cummings' and the Edwards' and the Pringles and Ainslies and Rosses. Even Furry Huddlestone had a modicum of rank, nominated as Library Monitor. Harman was Captain of Choir. Harry Zeederberg, Band Leader.

'First Aid Badge . . .' said the Head. 'Hugh Unwin.'

Unwin did not hear him.

Harman gave him a nudge. He looked at him, startled.

'Go,' said Harman.

Go where?

He was pushed to his feet. He was walking to the stage. He could hear his shoes. Two hundred and thirty pairs of eyes were on him.

Unwin, H L. First-Aider. First First-Aider. Keeper-of-the- Box.

It might have been the last name, but it was there. In some school list, some minute – somewhere – his name had been raised: ahead of someone else's.

–Who shall we have for First-Aider?

–Can't think.

–What about Unwin? The coach says it.

–Unwin? Some of the masters have no idea who Unwin is.

–Lad in my House, says Robbie, rather abruptly.

–Handy, says the coach.

–Handy?

–When there's blood around.

The Head says, –Unwin then – (whoever Unwin is). He makes a note, moves on to other things.

First First-Aider: geckos sometimes came out to bask. Unwin looked around, feeling the warmth. Even though no one turned to him or patted him on the back, or even looked at him, for once he did not feel that slow-smouldering shame; that hopelessness; that walking away, dragging disapprobation, and no one knowing or caring.

God not caring.

The Head folded up his list, glanced down at the assembled boys and took up his prayer book. He said, 'Well done, lads' and dismissed them. Unwin walked from the Drill Hall, being jostled aside as boys went past, eager to thump Cummings on the back, eager to be noticed by Tom Edwards. No one spoke to him. No one said anything. The little glory passed unnoticed.

What was First First-Aider? Someone tell me, please? Say something.

He glanced across at Archer walking way ahead.

–What was runner-up to Full-Back?

Was this how he had felt? Elation and emptiness at once?

On an impulse he went to the tangy. He took a secret half packet of Westminsters he had been keeping in his locker for weeks. A small victory, a small defiance, before derision or some careless word swept it away, before the responsibility of being First First-Aider made it necessary to discard them. He knew his destination. Davey Bennett. Davey Bennett would have said something. Davey Bennett's silence had never been the same as other boys'.

He went, alert for caddies at the corner, alert for rival Methodists who also used the tangy to smoke. He walked a long time, his shoes in the rainbow-slimed oily puddles that gathered after rain. He went up the tangy and came out near the station, crossed rails and climbed the bank to the fence. He ducked through.

He sat on the little wall beside Davey Bennett's headstone, leaning against the iron chain. It had begun to rust. The lubricant which had kept it iron-grey for months had worn away. Davey Bennett's stone was mouldering into the greyness and the sameness of the surrounding graves, his name no longer sharp where a frill of lichen curled against the 'B'.

Davey Bennett might be anonymous in death: Unwin did not want to be anonymous in life. Not any more.

He lit a Westminster. The evening was warm. He looked about him. He was not afraid of graves. He could talk and no one would reply derisively. He could say, 'D'you know what, Bennett . . . ?' without being mocked. Easier to talk to Bennett than to God.

It was dark when he came down from the cemetery, pushing his way through the blackjacks and the ragged grass, down towards the railway line. He walked along in the cover of scrub, to cross well below the station.

He went along the track, through the bushes and came into a clearing above a culvert, just out of sight of the station building. There, seated on the bank, tog-bags between them, were Archer, Stafford, Mostert and seven others.

'I say, you fellows . . .' His voice was high.

What a fatuous beginning!

They had been looking intently down towards the station. He should have backed before they noticed him. But, even in the dusk, they knew his voice.

'It's friggin' Unwin!' exclaimed Stafford, jumping up.

'What'cher doing here?' said Archer.

'Want a smoke?' said Unwin, unsteadily.

Foolish boy! The last time he had said that to Archer, he had had a blank fired at his chest. He started to back.

'Yes,' said Archer. He was almost conciliatory. 'I'll have a smoke.' He kept his voice low. 'Come.'

He took the cigarettes from Unwin. The others gathered round, hemming him in. Archer's hand was not quite steady as he struck a match, cupping it in his palm.

The pack was offered around. No one refused. There was none left for Unwin.

'Why are you here?' said Archer. It was cautious.

Unwin said, 'I'm with you.' Half inspiration, half panic. He had no idea what they were doing.

'Who asked you?'

'I decided.'

Archer seemed to hesitate.

'He'll have to come,' said Stafford. 'That, or they'll get it out of him before we've got to Cookhouse and bring us back.'

'Shit!' said Archer. The tip of his cigarette intensified. He blew the smoke downwards, between their legs.

'Signalman coming!' hissed Mostert.

All ten were along the path and down into a *donga*. Archer dragged

Unwin with him.

'Shit!' said Archer again under his breath, straining to see the tracks.

They watched the signalman's lantern, quiet as a glow-worm, proceeding down the rail, the shadow of legs curving up the bank. They heard the soft, breathy whistle as the man stepped across the sleepers. He passed, oblivious of them.

Unwin dared not move.

'What's the time?' said Archer.

'Three minutes to,' said Mostert.

'Good,' said Archer.

Unwin shifted slightly, eased his neck. Were they going to blow up the train? Waylay it? Put pennies on the line to flatten them as they had when they were juniors . . . Unwin hardly knew what to think. It seemed that even his eyes were sweating.

'Right, fellows,' whispered Archer, alert.

They could hear the train starting up in the station, the heraldic push of steam, the sudden rush of released pressure. Now . . . Now . . . Now . . . They could feel the vibration of the wheels in the ground under their stomachs as they lay in the ditch. 'Be ready to jump!' said Archer.

Unwin said, very quietly to Mostert, 'What are we doing?'

Mostert stared at him. 'Catching the train, *poephol*.'

'Where to?' The old tobacco was like bile blossoming on his tongue.

'To the war . . .' Mostert turned on him, realisation dawning. 'Hey, Archer . . .'

Unwin was swallowing, he could feel the bile erupting slowly through his gut. But Archer was already on his feet. 'Ready?'

Unwin closed his eyes. Is this what it felt like just before the firing-squad took aim: guts turned over, inside out, bones dissolved? There was no escape.

'Are you yellow, Unwin?' said Mostert, peering into his face as he scrambled up.

'Go to hell, Mostert!' Unwin said. Was the bile oozing through his clenched teeth? He swore it was.

399

'Now!' said Archer, with the triumphant lift in his voice: –I am your leader.

–I am glorious.

–Follow me.

They ran.

The headlight was ponderous on the tracks, the goods coaches jostled unrhythmically, waiting for momentum to take them smoothly, string them out, hitch them to the heartbeat of the train.

The boys, going over the bank and down, into the narrow alley of gravel by the tracks, inches from the inexorable wheels, catch at finger-holds, jump and yell. Unwin is last. He does not jump. He does not yell.

Where to jump? Where to swing himself up? He cannot see, the wheels are thundering in his ears. The open door of a cattle-truck slides past. They are all inside. Only one of the youngest boys is still running along the track. Hands are put out for him. He almost stumbles, but is grasped. He flings himself up and rolls inside. Unwin runs too, reaches for the iron bar.

It is always sweat that betrays him.

It is the exuding of his self-doubt.

It is his fear.

His palm skids. He wrenches his wrist. His fingers snag and slip. He reaches again. His fingers grip and hold. But as the purchase lifts him – all that weight, that gathering iron, that heat – he knows.

This is not the way.

Not the way.

He is sure of that.

He lets go, turning, falling, rolling. It is different from tripping in the gutter in Rose Street. It is diving out, like Herbert Cummings at the edges of the scrum, like Charlie Fraser reaching for the ball. It is no defeat.

The wheels hiss on steel, inches from his head, speed sucking at him as the last car rattles by, steam and heat. The train is receding. There is only the wink of the signalman's light, down the line. There are only the cemetery trees, a Golgotha, gaunt against the pewter sky.

He stands, slowly. He crosses the track. The stationmaster's window is lit. The door is open. The stationmaster is standing there, back to him, smoking his pipe.

He slips into the goods shed and waits. He hears the ring of the signalman's heel against the rails, the sound of footsteps on the platform. They stop near the goods shed door. The bolt is shot home, the padlock closed.

Unwin had sat in the dark. There was no way out. He had wanted the lavatory too. He had walked round and round the shed, found a place where sacks were stacked, crept behind them and squatted. He had felt like a poisoned rodent, entrails oozing out. He had dragged a sack across the place to hide it. In the day the flies would come and betray him.

–God?

Nothing.

Hadn't God seen? Hadn't He seen him turn, roll, fall? He had done what was right.

–Brave, God.

Brave.

Right.

–God?

God had trapped him. God did not intervene for boys who defecated on municipal property. It was punishment for what he'd said in chapel. He had challenged God – and God didn't like it.

The names of those who had run away remain in *The Register*. They are not expelled *in absentia*.

–Can you imagine the uproar if we sent down a boy who has volunteered to fight for his country?

–He'd be seen as a misunderstood hero.

–A martyr.

–Can you think of the letters to *The Journal*?

–We have been positively pushing them into it, with all our talk of Empire.

–We must be like a munitions factory, turning out a constant supply of living material.

–It is your sacred duty, lads.

–The most glorious end is to die in battle.

But what to do with Unwin?

Unwin had not run away to war. On his return to school with Robbie, he had made no stirring speech about his glorious intentions. He had had none. He had said nothing. The First Commandment – Silence and Denial – was known to him quite as well as it had been to Charlie Fraser. He would not betray it now.

The Head had had no choice:

–The first boy discovered planning to abscond or in the process of doing so, will be summarily expelled. If we are not quite ruthless from the start . . .

He could not go back on his word. His word was his Honour. He had said it to Robbie. The Council would insist. It was cast in stone.

Unwin would have to go.

Until then, anyone who had ever been expelled was not found in *The Register*. Their names were removed from the hallowed lists. No publication of the fact was made. They were quietly expunged from the record as if their entrance into, and their exit from the school, had never taken place. No father, no date of birth, no house. No plaudits.

Few, indeed, had been exorcised in that long and honourable history.

And none since.

Unwin ensured it.

The Head turned it over in his mind. He stood a long time at his window looking at the stone pines on the pavement, pacing sometimes. Sensing somehow that Justice and the Expedience-of-Rules were at odds, he made a memorandum that Unwin's name – Unwin, H L, son of L W – should remain. Added to his entry, embellished with the words First-Aid Badge, was his date of exit. Who would notice that it was a month before finals? Who, in time, would inspect the document for such a little inconsistency or know

that a world of dilemma – practical, moral (you have no choice, sir)
– lay between 'November' and 'December' 1914?

Only an augur-eye. And there are few of those.

–I was browsing through *The Register*, says Percy. –It's an odd
document. It poses as an inventory of names but there is a pattern,
even an odd poetic rhythm, in its entries, like Robbie calling out
'Adcock, Alcock, Badcock, Ball' at roll-call.

–We could all recite it in our sleep, says Herbert.

–Those fellows who ran off to war are there as well, says Percy.
When I heard about it, I thought they'd be struck off – but they
weren't.

–King and Country! says Herbert drily.

Percy laughs. –So many glorious boys! He is wry – but he adds
reflectively, –How much better to be entitled to wear the Old
School Tie and be deplorable than to be an honest citizen without
the privilege or right!

–You don't believe that! says Herbert.

–Of course I don't believe it, but others do, whether they'll admit
to it or not. He is satirical then, stretching his legs out, the old
cynical Percy: –Some will take the OST to the grave like an
insurance policy or in case there's a gathering at the other side.
The object has enormous power to create insecurity in lesser
mortals!:

> 'I say,' says St Peter to the Old Boy banging at The Gates, 'are
> you here for the Methodist Reunion?'
> 'Good God, no!'
> 'Don't blaspheme!'
> 'Don't you *know* the difference, St Peter?' says our affronted
> friend, waving his tie about. 'Don't you *see* the difference
> between *us* and *them*?'

He recalls himself, says, –How many ran away?

–Ten of them, eleven, counting Unwin, says Herbert. –It was the
first House matter that I dealt with. There was a great haroosh
when it was discovered they'd gone. Chaps like Archer and
Stafford and Mostert bunked. It appears Unwin was with them.

He didn't make it onto the train. He was brought back from the station like a felon. He wouldn't say a word. Not a murmur against them. Not a murmur about why he'd gone with them at all. It didn't fit. No one ever got to the bottom of it.

–What happened to him? asks Percy.

–He was expelled on the hour. It was crucial to do it. That's what Robbie said, anyway. Precedents and all that. Half the school would have been off if he hadn't stopped it. The Head simply didn't have a choice. Dangerous times call for drastic measures.

–*Et al*, says Percy.

–It bothered Robbie enormously though. Mostly because there were ten signatures on some letter or other, signed by the absconders, saying they were off to fight. Unwin's name wasn't there. They couldn't prove he was part of the plot and he refused to say. Even to me.

–Unwin was born unfavoured by the gods, says Percy. –He couldn't get it right.

Herbert looks off towards the chapel under the trees. –He was unfavoured by *some* of the gods we honour here, but not all, he says quietly. –He found his own, Gilbert. Even the Head knew it. In the end, he got it right.

'What have you to say, Unwin?' said the Head.

Unwin was dumb. He was beyond the Head's reach, beyond Robbie's.

'Whose plan was it?' The Head was patient.

'I don't know,' said Unwin. It was not a lie – he didn't.

'I won't have deceit, my boy.'

'Sir.'

'This will be a terrible disappointment to your father.'

Never a truer word was said.

'Sir.'

'Your mother will be grieved,' continued the Head.

'Yes, sir.'

  –My mother grieves all the time, sir. Take no notice of her grieving. She has her own truth. Like me. It is her business.

'Why did you do it?'

'What, sir?'

'Try to run off to war.'

'I didn't.'

'Then what were you doing at the station?'

  –Talking to Davey Bennett. Rejoicing with him. No one else
  does.

Silence.

'What do you have to say for yourself?'

'Just rotten luck,' said Unwin.

  –As Davey Bennett knows, sir. As you know. As we all know.
  Rotten luck for you too, sir: you have a precedent to see to.

'I beg your pardon?' The Head looked more closely at him. The
child was not altogether sensible.

  'When am I to go?' said Unwin. He was almost brisk.

  –When you have given a reasonable account of your
  extraordinary conduct.

The Head changed his mind. He said evenly, 'Mr Robinson will
take you to the station when I have wired your parents and had their
acquiescence for sending you alone by train.'

  'Sir.'

Hugh Unwin's case was clear-cut. All quite simple. It was something
of a relief: he had been running away from school on his own account.
His intention had been self-serving. No possible glory could be
attached to his actions. He had written no Declaration-of-Intent.
The King had not been mentioned. He went later that afternoon.
He would change trains at Johannesburg and proceed to Bulawayo.
His father would meet him there.

Unwin packed his bags. Harman and Huddlestone hovered, bringing
his vests from his locker. Cummings came in and out, looking
troubled – somewhere between his new senior rank and his old quiet,
steady gaze. If anyone sensed the truth, Cummings did. Unwin was
thankful to him, despite his silence. There was no necessity for words.
As he left the House, his dorm-mates – half admiring, half bewildered

– stood in the passage to see him pass. Here, a proffered hand, there a word: 'Goodbye, Unwin', offered in salute. Some did not know where to look, but Unwin understood. He trod firmly down the stairs.

Cummings went with him as far as the gate in front of the House, then Robbie sent him back.

'Keep an eye on things, Cummings,' he said. 'Take prep if I'm delayed.'

'Sir.' Herbert looked at Unwin then, quite directly. 'Unwin,' he said. He put out his hand. Unwin took it. Cummings did not wipe his palm when he withdrew his fingers. He stood with his hands at his sides and watched them go.

Unwin followed Robbie, dragging his old suitcase. He did not turn or look back. He walked in the middle of the road, quite straight, head up. Behind, the House watched.

Perhaps it was because of the war that Herbert had kissed Josie Zeederberg. Perhaps, because of seeing Unwin's solitary figure walking off down the road into nowhere that he'd had the need to do it then. Right then. Before she too disappeared.

Fraser, Graham, Grant, Gilbert, Bell. Unwin. Once they were there, as certain as the smell of the bogs or the sound of Robbie's step. Then they were gone. Quite gone. Into nothing. Even Davey Bennett seemed more reachable than they.

Josie Zeederberg is standing under the Grants' fig tree. She is standing in the late light of that quiet afternoon as if she is waiting, knowing he will come.

He has no hesitation.

Josie Zeederberg, her hat falling down her back, humorous little mouth, oatmeal soft, slightly salty, laughs when he is done.

Warmth is pushing in through all his veins, a deep, narcotic infusion. Her breath is at his eyes, his face. He is floating.

–I love you, Josie Zeederberg.

Instead he says, 'Do you want me to climb up and pick you a fig?'

He will pick figs for her all her life, if she will allow him to.

He will pick her figs as long as there are figs to pick.

TWENTY-ONE

●■●━━●■●

1923. The dedication of the Memorial Clock Tower, built by subscription for The Fallen. In each school report the donations are noted:

Fifty pounds from a former Council Chairman.

A hundred pounds from a mining house.

Two-and-six from the pocket-money of a nub.

Five guineas from a veteran wounded in France.

Ten guineas from the Rhodes Scholar in Oxford.

Two guineas from a mother with a letter to shake the heart.

The invitations have gone out for the event. Old Boys versus School at cricket; cadet parade; formal dinner with eminences invited from the Cabinet, the Church, all professions, civic dignitaries; a concert. The church service and the dedication. The Roll of Honour. One of the houses – *The* House – has been made available to Old Boys for the night: they may relive their youthful escapades without inhibition. Miss Maltby will be there to welcome them. The new Housemaster and his wife will be their hosts.

Appeals and invitations for the Memorial Fund and Clock Tower have been sent as far as London. They are received in pigeon-holes in Cambridge and in Oxford. They are delivered – less gloriously – to country post offices in Bedford and Adelaide, Cradock and Graaff-Reinet; to suburban houses in Cape Town, Johannesburg and Kimberley.

The Old Boys gather, some with wives, others leaving them behind, to relive, unencumbered:

–What's happened to the bloody bogs?

–My God, but the poor old place needs a face-lift after all these years.

–It's not the same without Robbie and his dog.

–What dog? Some wife pricking up her ears and trying to be part of it.

–It used to let off the most terrible smells!

–Don't be childish!

Childish?

There will be a great turnout. It is the time for re-forging bonds, for discovering who is gone and who is left. The need to belong – at this time – is compelling. They come, mustering, almost as they'd mustered once for war.

Percy Gilbert, standing by the gate of the House with Herbert Cummings and surveying the cool, creepered facade, said, 'It is the sameness here that makes the rest so disjunctive, so appalling.'

A wagtail walked about on the lawn, a little signaller, its tail tapping out its morse on cautious feet. Every now and then, it hawked something. That ritual feeding would have gone on quietly here in the shadow of these walls in all the ten years since they'd been gone.

The plumbago at the corner was in flower. It was Charlie who had loved to put a sprig of it in his lapel. In almost every picture in the album in which he wore a jacket, there it was – a jaunty talisman. In anyone else it might have seemed an affectation. No one questioned it in him. If it were mentioned he would laugh quite unselfconsciously. He liked flowers, that was all. There was one picture of his father in his album, tucked in loose between the leaves. Dashing Dr Fraser. He wore a buttonhole as well. Had his mother put it there?

Later?

After?

Herbert and Percy stood in easy silence. The shade at this south wall was soft. There was a *bergwind* breathing in the trees: the warm scent of stone pines. Way off, they could hear the pock of the cricket bat and the stirring of the spectators – too distant to intrude, but a counter note, in another key. It reminded Herbert of the night he had sat in the bogs after the Prefects' Dance, hearing the tangy-boys coming up the hill, the turning of the wheels of the mule cart, and, at a distance, Annie Zeederberg's fiddle and The Quadrille Band in the Drill Hall; the sharp lights falling from the windows and the doors on the paving, and, in counterpoint, the moonshadows of the trees across the lawn, muted and ghostly.

The wagtail walked before them as they strolled past the new chapel, flew up, alighted on the steps of the great stone Clock Tower. The School Standard fluttered on its flagpole against a pale sky.

They went on down towards the pavilion, walking in silence, companionship between them, turning each other's words in their minds. It seemed that this conversation had been prepared for over years in the knowledge that, one day, it would unfold, quietly finding resolution; that all the things they had spoken of on the bench behind the House when they were boys were a precursor – a preparation – for what they'd said today. They had talked all morning, the undertow of their understanding untouched by the comings and goings of others or the inconsequence of intrusion: 'Gilbert, Cummings, my dear fellows, how are you?' Intrusion did not matter. They took up each other's thoughts in harmony. It was as if they sat with the chessboard of twelve years ago in Percy's quaint seraglio and moved the pieces, mind to mind, equally matched. That is how it was through the later years when Herbert, assiduously coached by Percy, sometimes beat him at his own game.

All through that day, their own internal conversation was taken up, put gently down, unselfconsciously resumed. They had allowed reflection to emerge bit by bit, testing the current: here – yes; there – silence is wiser for the present. In between an innings each – Percy notching up a creditable sixty-four, Herbert twenty-nine – they had brought out the years, knowing that neither would damage or profane them by a careless word. They did not participate in the 'I say, what happened to old . . .' or 'Tragic business about James Seymour and only two weeks before he was to enlist with the Flying Corps. Holmes

409

knows about it but he doesn't want to say . . .'

Percy Gilbert's way of speaking had not changed, although the mocking, acerbic note that he had cultivated as a student had gone. But even then, despite it, all those years ago, he had spoken to Herbert in the same, oddly intimate way. If it had alarmed Herbert as a schoolboy – sweat behind the knees – he had always known that Percy's conversations were self-exploratory and that there was no need to respond except by being there, to act as witness. Despite his earnest wish then for a quick escape, not wanting to embrace dissidence or be singled out by someone as singular as Percy, Herbert had recognised Percy's self-deprecating wisdom. In the boy, it had often disturbed him. Now, he felt a deep and intuitive kinship with the man. He walked beside him, moved.

They found a place in the stand among the Old Boys. John Barham made a space for them, said, 'There you are at last! I was about to send out a scouting party!' He glanced down at the field. 'Doug Morgan's still batting.'

Herbert greeted fellows behind and in front, shook hands over the shoulders of others, raised his cap to a clutch of young wives talking on the benches below. He turned his eyes to a group of players standing on the bank. There was Parkes, there GB, side by side, deep in conversation, arms folded. Parkes seemed no different with his sandy hair and his neat round head but GB had topped six-foot-two. Who would have believed such a scamperer could grow? His ears looked quite acceptable now.

About them were farmers from Bedford: Rosses Major and Minor, Ainslie Terts and a collection of Pringles from the Baviaans, ranging in age from eighteen to eighty – the complications of their relationships as confusing as the boundaries of their farms or the entanglements of intermarriage and inheritance.

There were other farmers from Somerset East and Salem, from Trappe's Valley and Pearston. There were lawyers from the town, students from the university, businessmen from Port Elizabeth and East London. There was Tom Edwards and Harry Zeederberg and Douggie Morgan and John Barham. There was Mostert, being led by a lad, quite blind. He walked with his head up as if trying to scent things. He fumbled for a handshake. There was Goens Archer, half his jaw shot away. Some of the schoolboys sat around him in evident awe. His reputation went before him. His heroisms had been the subject of discussions in the classroom or sermons in the chapel, quietly put, with no exaggeration or Robbie's hated 'flag-wagging': something inspiring for the boys, something to think on while they ate their boiled pumpkin; something to keep their minds off their stomachs and their disbanded rugby team and their dead brothers.

–Our men have been magnificent. You will not remember Leonard Archer, but he was a big lad, here some years ago. Not a lad of any great abilities although he was handy with the rugby ball. But when the hour came to give his all, he responded to the call in a way that can only earn him our deepest gratitude and admiration . . .

'He won an MC and bar,' John Barham said in a low voice. 'It seems a VC would have been more apt. Apparently he was a man possessed at Delville Wood. It only goes to show . . .'

Percy refrained from retorting, show what?

Barham, he knew, had no idea of what it showed: should never know, if he valued his sanity. Beside him, Herbert Cummings was very still. What a long and lonely and misguided struggle it had been for Archer to achieve – at last – that validation he had craved and failed to find at school.

'We lost a number at Delville Wood,' said John Barham, the Fount-of-Information. 'The two young Pattisons. And Fatty Harman.'

–I've brought fellows for tea, Annie, Harry Zeederberg had said.

–Mostert and me are going to see how much cake Fatty Harman can eat before he explodes.

–It's very rude to bring guests to see them harm themselves, Mrs Zeederberg had said.

Now Fatty Harman had exploded, without the benefit of cake: Fatty Harman, struggling up the dunes at the Kowie in slouch hat and sweaty khaki. What business did he have in Delville Wood? What business, in the end, did any of them have? And the Pattison brothers from the little rectory at Southwell, the old house under the *mtsintsis*: it would have been more fitting to be buried in the cemetery

411

alongside their father's church, ringed about by an aloe and plumbago hedge, than to lie in some great anonymous grave-factory in France.

Georgie Holmes was sitting with the Head, with the polished air of a man who had long shrugged off the parochial travelling suit he had bought in the High Street on his departure from school. At graduation, did Oxford bestow such patrician presence with its ermine-edged hood? No doubt Jamie Seymour would have looked the same.

To the left, ranged along the steps, was the school XI, kept back for the first few days of the holidays to play the Old Boys. They were full of high spirits, certain of victory against a motley team, distinguished, with a few exceptions, by its portliness and lack of wind. Watching them, Percy said, 'Splendid little fellows, aren't they, Cummings? Did we look as ingenuous as that? I suppose we did.'

'Even more,' said Herbert. 'We lived in a different world from these.'

'No doubt these are the great *meneers* of the school, just as we thought we were!' Percy laughed. 'I'm sure there are legions of eager little nubs ready to lay down their lives for them!' Percy was searching in his pocket for his cigarette case. 'We all seem so extraordinarily old in comparison!'

So very old and only ten years between them: it was decades; it was lifetimes.

Herbert watched Douggie Morgan at the crease. A great, heroic fellow still, as full of laughter as he'd always been, almost with the swagger of his school days: *we are The Strong Men, only we*. But Herbert knew him so much better now. Behind the laughter and the *bonhomie*, Doug was often sombre. He would simply say, 'It's the old bugs gnawing at me, Apie,' referring to the after-effects of malaria and dysentery which had nearly killed him in German East Africa and had had him invalided home for weeks of recuperation in the Albany Hospital. 'I'll have to go and visit the quack and ask for more of his magic juice. Works like a charm!' But it wasn't that. It was something else. Herbert knew that it was something that the doctor couldn't cure.

Herbert allowed the voices of old companions to wash over him.

He heard the sudden sharp report of the ball being hit to the boundary, the murmur of wives and mothers sitting in the stand, the glee of children, a far, triumphant shout from the captain. Beside him, Percy called, 'Well batted, Morgan!'

The sameness of sitting in the pavilion, with the sound of the bat chocking at the ball and the murmur of the crowd and the groundsmen under the trees at the far side of the field, applauding their favourites in the school team and the drift of their Xhosa coming across, a laugh and a shout of encouragement and then – as if the exuberance had burst out too loudly – subsiding into a deferential silence.

–It is the sameness that makes it so disjunctive, so appalling, Percy had said.

Now, indeed.

But then – in those first years of a distant war? It was the sameness in the daily round at school that allowed incomprehension.

The sameness – and their innocence.

What could they know of trenches? What could anyone know, at any time, unless they were there? How could a schoolboy – ardent for battle – sitting on the familiar old bench with the sound of nubs yelling in the bogs or sneaking off across the lawn in leguaan formation in the dusk to raid another house, understand, when everything about him was so much the same?

If nothing changed – what was death?

And then the casualty lists began. The names came in. One, then two; four, then five. The men of 1899, the lads of 1910, the boys of 1913.

If someone had taken the pictures of the 1913 cricket team or the First XV, pinned them up and, every week, at random, marked a fellow off, they'd have had the measure of that swift destruction. Today we'll take the eighth man; tomorrow, how about a wing? On Friday – centre. Or, perhaps, a half-back. It was inexorable.

When Davey Bennett had died, he'd done it so quietly, so without fuss, that it had come and gone without disrupting for an instant the routine of their days. One morning he was asleep in his bed – lucky sweep, not having to go to class – and the next, Miss Maltby was folding up his sheets as if she were on an ordinary laundry inspection, except that she didn't have *that look* and the groundsmen came in and carried the bed away to the storeroom. By the evening it seemed as if Davey Bennett had simply packed his bags and taken the train home.

Sparrow had also taken a train.

–Cheerio, old chap: Sparrow practising for another life in his hat and travelling suit.

That other life had been short.

Herbert, shunning other boys, sitting in the dusk on the bench outside the House, had been unable to grasp its mystery. If Sparrow was dead – why was everything else the same? *How* could it be the same? Only his blood seemed to have sensed change: its rhythm slowed, it pushed thickly through his limbs, numbing them.

–Kowie on the first Christmas home. You, Dan, Charlie, Arthur, Doug and me.

There would be no Christmas home.

And yet, the Kowie would keep on flowing down towards the sea between its euphorbia-covered banks and the *boerboons* and the aloes would bloom in their season and the wind would shear the sand from razorbacks in an endless regeneration.

If this went on – the great unending cycle – how could Sparrow Bell, so much more vital, so alive, be dead?

The news of Sparrow's death had come in the morning. It was the week of the 1915 finals. The day of the Dutch paper. Chapel on a Monday morning. Herbert had wanted to bunk, to push a last few verbs into his head. He couldn't. He was Head-of-House. The usual dreadful Monday breakfast – old bread and old tea; complaints; Robbie's dog was more flatulent than usual. He had followed the juniors as they had filed into chapel, a scrap of last minute crammings stuffed into his prayer book to check during matins.

Robbie was not in his usual seat. Through the open door, Herbert could see him walking about under the trees. Robbie bunking chapel?

Herbert was about to go out to him – but Robbie held himself in a way that invited no intrusion. Even his dog squatted at a distance, watching him.

The Head had taken the lectern and read the verse himself. Then he had removed his reading spectacles and folded them and put them down on the Bible in front of him, balancing them carefully, as though he were executing something delicate. He cleared his throat. He did that carefully too. He said, 'I know that the seniors are writing an important paper today. The examination will start at nine o'clock, as planned.' He paused a moment. 'What I have to tell . . . now,' another pause, 'will come as a great shock to the senior boys – but they will understand the need to honour 'business as usual'. That is their duty. I know they will not fail me. Nor will they fail Jack Bell.'

It was as if they drew breath together. The silence held.

'This morning I received a letter from Jack's father.'

The Head seemed to steady himself. He moved his fingers along the rim of the lectern. He said, 'Jack has died of wounds in France. He was serving with the Royal Berkshires as a subaltern. His father encloses a copy of the letter sent by Jack's commanding officer. I will read the relevant passage:

'Allow us to share with you and Mrs Bell, your great grief. Your boy, always known to us as "Sparrow", was cheerful, courteous and most gallant. He was an officer that any battalion might envy and in the months to come I know that 15 Platoon, D Company, will do great credit to the young officer who trained them and that they will amply avenge their fallen leader.

I was the last to see him as he was carried out of the trenches. It was a chilly day and we made him as comfortable as possible, moving him into the sun, where he waited with great fortitude and patience for the field ambulance to come. He chaffed us and made light of things and was as cheery as could be. His pluck was enormous and a great example to his men who were, of course, considerably older than him. He was such a splendid boy: all of us loved him, and what is perhaps a great deal more, his men loved him too and would have done anything for him.'

415

Another pause. The Head did not look beyond the boys in the pews. He could not meet their upturned faces. His eyes were on the Bible on the lectern. He mastered himself but his voice faltered on the last sentence.

'If ever I have a son, I shall be proud to know he was like your boy – lovable, courteous, brave and altogether delightful.'

He turned away, stood with his back to them, facing the altar. He adjusted his shoulders, straightened. No one moved until he faced them again and walked alone down the aisle.

The school filed out without singing the last hymn. The choir followed in silence. Once, the soaring treble: Sparrow with his little plume, steadfast on his head.

He is buried in Corbie Cemetery near Amiens. On his stone, his parents had inscribed *Nec Aspera Terrent*: the motto of his school.

–Jack will always be a boy. No one wants him to grow up, Percy had once said.

Even in death, it had not been allowed.

Nec Aspera Terrent: nor do hardships terrify, nor adversity dismay.

–Wouldn't you just *know* it! Sparrow might have said, half pride, half exasperation, jutting his manly chin.

One after the other.

And another. And another.

First Sparrow. Then Jamie Seymour. McIntosh. Tunbridge.

–A half-back here?

–What about a wing?

–Take the centre next.

–There is a long way still to go. Who else is chosen?

Dan Grant is chosen.

Involuntarily, Herbert glanced down at the row of wives and young women gathered together, heads and hats bent to each other, oblivious of the cricket. Mary Clifford was among them, hands folded in her lap. Her hair was bobbed short but she carried her head in the same graceful way she always had when she wore a ribbon at her

416

nape and a high collar, almost to her chin. She sat as she had at the debate so long ago, quiet and composed, when she'd gazed at Dan-the-Beacon until the words had stuck in his throat.

Doug Morgan was still in. He had settled at the crease and even the school's wiliest spinner could not prevail.

'Only a Dan Grant would have been able to shift him!' said John Barham.

–Dan Grant is the best cricketer in the history of the school! says the ubiquitous Know-All.

–Not another one! The nubs are wearied by it all.

Best. Best. Best. Why is everyone who is dead always the best?

Sparrow is the best.

Dan is the best.

Today the first bat. Tomorrow the spinner.

'I bet he'd have got an international cap if he'd had the chance,' said Tom Edwards.

'Indeed,' said Percy. He kept his voice a little lower than Barham or Edwards: Judge and Lady Grant and Frank were sitting with the Head two rows behind them, quite within earshot. In his lean suit, both hands resting on the top of his cane, the Judge watched the match, rarely taking his eyes from the batsman. Around them – at distance enough for deference – were gathered the other members of the Council and their wives. No one encroached and only the Head leaned in every now and then to remark, or Frank, whom Lady Grant kept close beside her, hand on his sleeve. At her feet sat a young Springer spaniel. It looked up at her every now and then, imploring release, but the order did not come until tea when it dashed about the field, nose to the ground, making a wild zigzag across the grass, belly down in search of some subterranean wanderer. It went to dig on the bank leading down to Rose Street but, after a moment, as if to a silent command, was back again. No one but the Head or Georgie Holmes spoke to the Grants when the gathering rose to go to the tea tables – a small space remained around them – but everyone fondled the dog. Even the Head. It went to Mary Clifford. It sat at her feet. She did not look at it, but her hand was constantly at its neck, caressing and smoothing.

Herbert could not bear to watch.

Dan's dog: mother of the pup at Mary Clifford's feet. She had been a little bitch with liver spots and silky ears. He had got her when he was serving with the Royal Flying Corps in England. It had been given to him by a family friend, a vicar at Elstree, whose spaniel had had a litter. Dan had chosen one, neither the largest nor the smallest, but the pluckiest. 'She'll be going home with me,' he had said. 'She'll be living quite a different life out there. We'll be fishing together at the Kowie.'

He had called her Flossie.

'Why Flossie?' his brother Frank had said. '*Flossie*!' He had laughed at Dan.

Dan had left her with her mother and the vicar until she should be old enough to come back to barracks with him. He would visit in the meantime, if Frank would sometimes lend him his old motorbike and side-car.

Dan and his dogs. Cantie and Baldie and their puppies. A litter every year. Dan in the photograph in Charlie's album, sitting with a Highland Terrier pup in his lap on a Sunday afternoon, looking rather melancholy – Mary Clifford on his mind – Frank teasing and laughing, Charlie's shoulder touching his, little dogs alert in their big-boy hands.

–It's my favourite picture! Charlie's mother had said. –Such dear little dogs!

Nineteen squadron, RFC, was flying into France, scouting. It was the most dangerous branch of operations. Knowing it, both Grants volunteered. Invincible boys. Dan is growing a moustache. It is another change, like his hair, parted on the other side. He wants Mary Clifford to see a picture of him with this dashing new addition: proof he needn't stutter any more. He and Frank go to a shop in town and have a picture taken. Dan is solemn, Frank irrepressible. Dan puts the receipt in the pocket of his flying jacket, Frank too scatterbrained to be trusted with it.

'Collect it Thursday,' says the photographer cheerily.

418

Thursday.

September 16th, 1917.

An autumn day over England. An autumn day over France. The destination is the Ypres-Menin Road. Frank goes. Dan goes. They sail the skies – they do everything together – chasing under wisps of cloud. Below is the sea and the tracery of coast creeping under them; above, a vault, blue as lobelias. It is a shining day.

September 17th, 1917.

The mist came down, unaccountably, that day. There was no sun. It was wet at the airfield. Frank Grant did not have permission to take off: no one would have stopped him, not even his CO. He had made a wreath of ivy and flax and small flowers that he had found about the perimeters of the runway. The aircraft went off alone, lost quickly in the fog.

He crossed the channel. He flew the route that they had flown the day before. He flew through cloud, buffeted by gusts of rain. It cleared across the foreign coast. He flew low – too low, much too low for safety, much too low for prudence – almost skimming, with the ribbon-road beneath.

He did not care.

Dan's plane, flying straight into the guns, had gone down over a wood. It had bounced and somersaulted into trees. Circling in, Frank could see the silent wreckage. The fields around, gun emplacements hidden, had blazed against him. Frank Grant circled, heedless. He circled that place in the broken trees, almost stalling, pulling out in time. He tossed the wreath of English meadow flowers. It turned. It spiralled down, trailing streamers of ivy.

This is for Dan.

Dan, the cricketer.

Dan, the centre.

Dan, the debater.

Dan-the-Beacon, who stutters for love.

Bashful Dan.

Great-hearted Dan.

419

Dan, my brother.

Frank, impervious to the fury turned against him – wild, reckless Frank – flew in again, dipped his wing, pulled the nose up and turned for England, his fuselage tattered with shot.

The airfield was deserted when he landed. He sat a moment on the runway, peering through the rain. It seemed no one had expected his return.

He fetched the photograph from the photographer's shop. He did not have the slip. The assistant found the print. Frank barely glanced at it but took a pencil from his pocket and wrote on the back: 'Big Swank – Dan's moustache!' He dated it for the day it was taken: 15/9/17 and he put it in an envelope and posted it to Mary Clifford thousands of miles away. He walked briskly away from the postbox on the corner, collected his motorbike and drove out in the early evening to fetch the little dog. Neither he nor the vicar spoke. He loaded the pup in a basket and took her back with him to barracks. The next day he caught the train to London, to his mother.

'Her name is Flossie,' he said to her, putting the puppy on the floor at her feet.

She took the little dog up to her shoulder, smoothing it. Only Dan would have had a Flossie!

A week later Lady Grant embarked from Southampton for home. Flossie travelled with her in the ship: a strange horizon, a stranger hunting-ground. The puppy did not leave her side.

In afteryears, when Flossie died, Lady Grant had a grave specially dug. She chose a place in the deep shade of milkwoods in the coastal bush near the Kowie where Dan had fished and swam and putted on the grass banks with his clubs. A little headstone was carved for her.

If it is redirected tenderness, no one says. It is her prerogative:

Flossie
Born Elstree (England)
Died Port Alfred

———————

Good Hunting

It is simpler than the memorial in the new school chapel erected for Daniel Grant: a marble profile of a flying officer: rank, age, place of death, parentage, dates and text. Beneath is carved a verse. It concludes:

> *Sunshine and Laughter and Youth,*
> *All he gave in Sacrifice.*

Where is he, Herbert wondered.

Is he in Flanders, in Tyne Cot Cemetery, plot XXXV. A. 24, under a cold northern sky, or is he here?

It is said that Mary Clifford has visited his grave but Herbert doubts it. It is more likely Flossie's that she knows. She never ventures far – there is no need. When Flossie was alive she used to walk her sometimes for Lady Grant. Now, she walks the young dog in her place. She is a familiar figure at the edges of the playing field where the cricket pitch goes brown in winter. She is still sometimes seen in the chapel, bringing flowers on the sixteenth of September every year. No one follows her in there. If Dan is anywhere – he is here with her.

The cricketers left the field for tea. Groups wandered up towards the tables set under the trees. Harry Zeederberg had Mostert by the arm. The boy who usually led him had been reprieved and was eating cake by the pawful. Archer was with them. He walked with a limp, his hands linked behind his back. All the belligerence was gone. He stood a while and looked at the Clock Tower. He went inside and read the names.

Could it really be Archer?

Voices were raised in affable welcome when he rejoined a group at the tables. He helped Mostert to another cup of tea: good old fellows all come back together.

Percy and Herbert stood with John Barham and Tom Edwards in the shade.

'Remember when Daisy handed out the essay on the walls of Carthage?' said John Barham.

'You were the terror of nubs!' said Tom Edwards.

'Talking of which, have you seen Parkes? He was here a moment ago with that amusing fellow – what's his name?' said John.

'GB,' said Tom. 'Giles Braithwaite.'

'Didn't recognise him at first. He's such a tall bloke and he used to be the smallest nub in the school.'

'Charlie's fag, wasn't he?' said Barham.

'And so devoted!' said Tom.

Herbert turned away and poured the tea. Percy took a cup from him and stood in the circle, his saucer balanced in his slim brown hand, his cricket jersey slung about his shoulders. In that mauve shade, the olive planes of his face were finely taut across the high-winged ridges of his cheeks.

'Here comes Doug,' said Tom, looking down the path. Douglas Morgan was strolling up towards them. His wife walked beside him, holding the hand of a very small boy. He was pushing an old perambulator. Doug came on, without the slightest show of embarrassment.

'I never thought I'd see the day,' said John Barham, 'when Douglas Morgan would be found in the grounds of this school pushing a baby carriage! What would Robbie say!'

'Robbie would say, "I told you so!" ' Percy was triumphant. '*And* – believe me, with a good deal of envy too! He'd have been as pleased as punch – whatever he pretended.'

'Have you fellows seen his lady?' said Tom Edwards, in a lower voice. 'Old Morgan looks bemused by his luck. If I'm allowed to say this about another bloke's wife – she's an absolute stunner! And that little chap, as well as the baby in the pram, are both enrolled already. I bet Douggie gave his first-born a rugger ball at his christening.'

So he did, Tom. So he did.

Doug and his wife stopped a way off to talk to Lady Grant and Frank. A little throng gathered round the carriage. Herbert could hear the laughter and the lilt of voices.

John Barham turned to Percy. 'That was a mighty six you hit this morning, Gilbert. Almost too hard to catch!'

Percy laughed. 'Just as well I lobbed it,' he said. 'I'd had my innings, done my business. It was time to go.' He paused and glanced down towards the cricket pitch, locked his jaw, rocked slightly on his heels.

–Next time you're here, as a celebrated old codger, Daisy, I bet you'll lie down on Lower with your nose in the grit and howl for love.

Percy's teacup rattled in its saucer. He steadied it, then put it down on the table's edge, adjusting the spoon with care.

'Talking of business,' continued John Barham, unconscious of another dialogue in progress, 'I wondered what line of business you're in, Gilbert? I didn't catch what you said when you were speaking to Tom here.'

Percy was brief. He was in import-export in Cape Town. What kind of trade it was, he did not say. It did not seem to interest him. Business: despite all the honours he had garnered at Cambridge, the promise of a contemplative, academic life. He intimated with a light laugh that a clergyman's son – even if that clergyman was a bishop – had to make his way, in spite of other inclinations.

John Barham talked on bluffly about the wool trade in which he was engaged and about import and export, trying to draw Percy on the subject. Percy listened, head slightly cocked, giving his attention, commenting when it was expected, but Herbert knew he was impatient to be elsewhere and his eye wandered to the House across the lawn with its ornamental pond and the pergola where the wisteria grew. The old door into the wing of South was ajar. Early that morning they had sat together in the shade: wisteria and moss and dusty sunlight all together in that small corner where the wind didn't reach. They had sat on the old bench. They had talked and talked until Georgie Holmes had come in search of them and called Percy down to bat.

Herbert's tea was cold, his plate untouched. John Barham's voice intruded suddenly. 'Of course, the price of wool is not what it should be at the moment. Also, the volume we are handling is below average. You fellows must be rather worried,' turning to Herbert, 'although I fancy at Molteno things are better than further west . . .'

'I'm not a farmer any more,' said Herbert, recollecting himself. 'I have recently taken up the law.' He glanced at Percy. Percy suppressed a small, wry smile.

'Well, what about you, Tom? I trust you're still in wool' –John Barham turning to Edwards who was cramming his face with cake.

'Same recipe, I'll swear,' said Tom. 'If you were a good, polite boy on Speech Day you could hand these round and slip a bit into the old pocket every now and then. Tastes almost as good as it did, even without the fluff and threads. Sorry, John, what did you say?'

Herbert walked slowly away, giving no offence. He too could have gorged on cake like Tom and discussed the price of wool with John Barham and been affable to the ladies coming up past the chapel with small, empty peals of laughter. The careless indulged their husbands' fierce little loyalties with amusement, the more thoughtful, with tact: this place did not belong to them.

He looked beyond the pavilion roof at the hills, at the copse of stone pines on the crest, leaning to the prevailing wind and the road winding past that Charlie Fraser used to stare at, far from all of them.

Herbert turned. Nearer, across the road, was Holmes' House on the rise with its corner stones laddering the angles of the tall walls; Jamie Seymour's, not as lofty, left and just beyond. Boxroom, bogs and bell. All were there. And where the Head's old bungalow had been the new chapel stood – not Unwin's chapel, not the site of *'Delivered for our Offences, Raised for our Justification'* but a noble, solid Romanesque building, blocking out the road. It might have been there for ever: warm ochre stone, rough-hewn, and a red-tiled roof and fine teak doors.

And to the side, the only unfamiliar thing: the Memorial Clock Tower.

Would anyone remain unmoved to see it?

One hundred and twenty-five names were carved inside it: Apperly to Wronsky.

One hundred and twenty-five to add to the twenty-nine for whom the chapel had been built. How many more would be added over decades, how many other wars were required to claim commemoration from each window, each choir stall, each pew? Why were beautiful things only built for the dead?

They are built for their redemption.

They are built to bring them home.

Percy was at his shoulder. 'Old augur eye,' he said. 'I've been watching you. You're gathering them in, aren't you?'

'Perhaps.'

'Come.'

They went in through the side door of the House.

'It's impossible to believe that Robbie isn't here,' said Percy.

'I think he is,' said Herbert.

'Like the rest of them?'

Herbert laughed then. 'If they are – who else could be Captain of the Corps, but him?'

'Are the buck heads still up in his rooms?'

'No,' said Herbert. 'There are English cottage scenes at regular intervals on the walls and a tea trolley by the door, with wheels that squeak.'

'That's a travesty! Next they'll be putting curtains at the dorm windows.'

They climbed the stairs to North. The odd silence, the echo of the pipes, the hollow plopping of a drain, a window rattling in the wind. Do you smell lozenge? Do you smell the mangy dog? Percy twitched his shoulders, patted his belt – Robbie, feeling for his hunting-knife? They passed the locker room, the wash-room. They went into the dormitory. It was just the same. Except Arthur's bed. Its present owner was much neater. There were no runnels under the old woven bedspread. The towel on the foot was folded. The room looked no different from the picture Charlie Fraser had taken the day he had left school. Only the colour of the space was not the same – the quiet grey of afternoon. The sun was not lying down on Charlie Fraser's bed today.

'You know the stories,' said Percy, walking slowly down beside the rows of lockers. He stopped at Vincent MacCallum's bed.

'Not all of them,' said Herbert. 'There is one I haven't heard. I wanted you to tell me.'

Percy's face is steady. 'MacCallum's?'

'Yours.'

It is the same thing.

425

'I suppose you saw the school magazines at the beginning of the war?' Percy said.

'Not after I left,' said Herbert. 'I was in East Africa in the bush. I didn't see a letter or a book for weeks on end. Certainly not the old mag.'

'My mother sent mine on to me,' said Percy. 'First at Cambridge. Then in the army. It was light relief after all the gloomy news.' Percy leaned on the window sill and looked out towards the other houses. 'In one of them there was a letter from John Barham in France and another from Seymour in Palestine. There was even a mention of the fellows in East Africa slogging it out with malaria and being pestered by lions. It was like a reunion, sitting there in my hut in snowy Bécordel with my valet trotting about, just as useless as my fag at school, with a mug of tea and the old magazine! It was almost like being back in the House. And then there was this report by MacCallum. By its tone, I knew he'd written it for Robbie. I've never known him so loquacious or so racy! It was about bringing down a Zepp.' He gave a small laugh. It steadied him. 'It was a better yarn than all the "raw-nature-tooth-and-claw" we used to sometimes dredge up in the library. Unwin's *Boys' Own* glorified!'

His voice had taken on the old satirical tone. With what care he must have cultivated it then. Now, Herbert was not as easily deceived.

Mac had written:

'There have been great doings, these last few days and of course you will have heard about the Zepp being brought down. I suppose you wondered if I was up as well. These are things I'll never forget as long as I live. I climbed to 11,000 feet and saw a Zepp in the beam of a searchlight. Of course, I swung round and made for it. The anti-aircraft guns were going for all they were worth. I couldn't hear the shots – the noise of the engine makes this impossible – but I saw the flashes from the ground and then the bursts in the air. I was getting my gun ready to strafe the Zepp, saying to myself – Now, here's a chance you might not get again in a thousand years and you'll need every bit of pluck you have, not to mess the show . . .'

'Imagine MacCallum having a conversation with himself at 11 000 feet?' said Percy lightly, when he had recounted the details – almost word perfect. 'The longest dialogue in history and no one there to hear!'

The account had continued:

'There was a streak of flame and suddenly the Zepp was licked by fire and fell rapidly. I thought she was going to fall on me. I stuffed the nose of my machine down and did a sharp turn out of the way. My word! I was excited and cheered and yelled for joy and stood and waved my arms about like mad. The sky was lit up for miles around and I could see London, just as if it had been day . . .'

Mac yelling and cheering? Once boys had yelled and cheered for Mac on the cricket pitch. Now he was doing it for himself – at 11 000 feet with no one to share the exultation.

'Good for Mac!' Percy said. 'I like that! After all, if anyone had been with him, he'd have given a sardonic grin and said nothing at all and not had half so much fun! We all ducked when he was angry, but I wonder if we knew when he was happy . . .'

Herbert did not interrupt him.

Percy came down the rows of beds and faced MacCallum's. 'He should have gone down with the Zepp,' he said. 'In a great eruption of iron and flame.'

He sat a moment, looking before him. Herbert waited.

'He was courting it,' said Percy, 'daring it, despite the "thousand years". The end' – that pure unblemished reckless valour – 'was not as he'd have wanted or deserved.'

'He didn't die in his bed,' said Herbert.

'No, indeed.' Percy examined the backs of his hands. 'But a collision in the air, an accident, is like a bad call at cricket. Mac never made bad calls for runs. He was much too shrewd.' He paused and Herbert averted his gaze. 'To be smacked while you're buckling on your armour for battle would have appalled him.' Percy mastered himself. 'Mac's timing was always impeccable – except, it seems, when it mattered most.'

Again, Herbert said nothing, let the words turn on themselves: Percy was safe with him.

'He was so magnificent,' said Percy.

Now, he would always be magnificent.

Percy stood. His voice was clipped. 'When it happened I was almost glad. I thought – well that's that.' Percy looked at Herbert then and smiled. It was neither sardonic, nor bleak. 'You want to ask why I was glad, Cummings, but you are too diffident in case you hear something you do not wish to hear. There is nothing to hear, nothing to conceal. I made him immaculate, that's all. How could that ever be sustained? He died. He is himself now, beyond my invention. And for me, he was an invention.' He turned from the row of beds and went towards the door. He said, 'He was really quite a simple, unimaginative chap.'

Herbert stood to follow him.

'I thought it saved him from domestic death,' said Percy, almost flippantly. He was taking control, retreating. He gave a small laugh, turned his hat in his hand.

Herbert did not know what to say. Would that have been so terrible a fate for Vincent MacCallum? His own 'domestic death' was blissful: his chair, his pipe, his reading lamp.

His wife. His small twin sons.

–What are you doing, Herbs?

–Working.

–So much law to cram into your old head in one night!

–Do you have any suggestions about how I can improve my concentration?

She laughs, stands behind him. She has.

Oh yes, she has. She always has.

–Come, Petal, she says.

'I was wrong about domestic death, you know,' Percy said suddenly. He put an arm lightly about Herbert's shoulder. 'I am married, Cummings.'

Herbert knew the words would come out wrong. Percy knew it too. He said, almost gaily, 'There is no need to congratulate me,

Cummings. I am quite happy to congratulate myself!' Despite his words, his smile was not satirical. 'I met my wife at Cambridge. You would call her a blue-stocking. And she is. But, indeed, that's not all.'

They walked along the passage towards the stairs.

'We have a daughter,' said Percy, with a touch of triumph.

'A daughter?' It is almost a croak.

'She is still an infant,' said Percy. 'That's why my wife has stayed at home.'

He stopped and looked at the floor. He tapped his hat against the side of his leg, as he had on the day he said goodbye to Herbert, standing in the doorway of his study. He said, 'I am a contented man.' He cocked his head, seemed even whimsical. 'Old augur eye that you are, Cummings, you didn't see that in your shaman's dream!'

Confessions take strange and obtuse forms. They are almost always brave.

They walked in silence together. They passed the open door of Vincent MacCallum's room. They did not stop.

–That keen unblemished valour.

It was MacCallum's after all.

There is a graveyard at Lijssenthoek in Flanders. There are cedars. They are very old, spreading widely. In the summer the Flanders poppies grow abundantly in the grass. On a holiday from Cambridge, Percy had taken a bicycle and ridden across the French border from Dainville. He had found the cemetery. He had walked the rows, searching in the green-blue shade. He had found the stone.

He had put neither poppies there nor any other flower as tribute. He had taken no photograph. The stone had simply stood in that hot sweet summer blue. He had picked up a pebble from the raked gravel at the edge of the memorial. He had put it in his pocket.

–I will take this home, Vincent, he had said.

–Not to your home, Vincent. Not to your house in Parktown with the iron gates and the pointer dogs and the gleaming cars. To our home.

So brief.

–For me, so absolute.

–Why did you come back, Herbert Cummings had said.

–You know quite well.

Ah, yes, he did. But no one knew – not even Herbert – that when Percy Gilbert's score had stood at sixty-four that morning and he had waited at the crease on Lower field for the next delivery, he had taken a small stone from the pocket of his cricket ducks and dropped it, nudging it into the ground with the toe of his boot: a small stone from the cemetery at Lijssenthoek, ten thousand miles away. And on the next ball he had stepped back and sent a six soaring out. The ball had traced an arc – the grey-ochre steeple of the cathedral, the tall slim spire of Christchurch, the distant town – and the crowd had held its breath.

It fell. And someone, with a whoop of exultation, caught it. It was just as Percy had intended.

He stood a moment before he walked. Vincent MacCallum had stood here many times before, facing affable Jamie Seymour in a house match, facing the perilous speed of Georgie Holmes. Vincent, open shouldered, mighty limbed, sending a ball – with perfect grace – into the sun.

–Next time you're here, as a celebrated old codger, Daisy, I bet you'll lie down on Lower with your nose in the grit and howl for love, Vincent MacCallum had once laughed.

Indeed.

Percy walked, swinging the bat.

TWENTY-TWO

By the principal door of the chapel are two windows. One depicts
Valour – a warrior in a red cloak, sword sheathed. When the sun
shines through, the deep blue of the background hovers on the
woodwork of the pews. Young fellows, not concerned with the sermon,
might trace the shifting lozenges of light with exploratory fingers.
Next to Valour is Fortitude. The warrior is helmeted with broken
sword and dinted shield. Beneath each, set into the sill, a soft brass
tablet commemorates a soldier. Valour: Sparrow Bell, lost in France.
Fortitude: Jamie Seymour, killed in Palestine. The choir stalls on
which are carved the names of each of the fallen are given in memory
of Vincent MacCallum – who never sang in tune and shunned the
choir – but with the Roll of Honour under his curatorship, scrolled
on the backing of the choir stalls, he is Head-of-House again. Dan,
'Sunshine and Laughter', guards the nave.

There are smaller plaques from the families of other soldiers, a
pair of embroidered kneelers, a brass salver, the silver communion
vessels, a tall candlestick.

'I see that Archer has put in twenty guineas in memory of "A
Sportsman and a Gentleman",' Percy said to Herbert. 'I suppose it's
not good form to ask for whom, if he has chosen not to say. But I can
guess. Death makes it possible to overlook what might have been
construed presumptuous in life. But it's rather fitting' – he said it half
to himself – 'and generous. Yes, even that.'

The Memorial Service for the dedication of the Clock Tower begins with the Dead March, the Lord's Prayer and Psalm 23. The officiants are the Head, the Reverend Dowsley and the Reverend Zeederberg. The Bishop leads the procession.

Percy occupies the place he had always occupied at school, Herbert to his right. Between them, however, neither eating lozenges nor sniggering at the Reverend Dowsley's homily, is Herbert's wife. Her hat is somehow disreputable. It looks as if it might slip right over her very particular nose. A pew in front, her sister turns and smiles at her. There is something tentative about her this morning: it is in the way she moves her mouth – a little flicker, like a gazelle; the way she dips her head; the curve of her neck. Her husband, Douglas Morgan, sits square shouldered beside her, inspecting the hymnal for what is most familiar – the school hymn:

> *Jesus calls us: o'er the tumult*
> *Of our life's wild restless sea.*
> *Day by day his sweet voice soundeth,*
> *Saying, Christian follow me.*

How the boys had bawled it out on break-up day! The little fellow on his lap is resolutely trying to turn the page. No doubt, in time, he will bawl it out as well, if something doesn't cut him down. Doug Morgan holds his son between his knees and takes his wife's hand. It is slim – the competence of a nurse's fingers, comforting and sure.

She pats his hand with her other, gentle, not intense, coaxing him, taking charge. She had done that week after week as he had lain in the Albany Hospital. Of all the volunteers brought in to help where qualified nurses had gone to the military hospitals, she had been the most trusted. Eyes followed wherever she walked. Her presence made morale soar. But Douglas Morgan had had her tenderest care.

Over time, there was an odd interdependence. As much as he had needed her – 'Come, Nursey' – pretending helplessness, just to feel her hands tucking in the sheets and have her dipping over him, so sublimely beautiful, she, by his proximity, could hold her own myths close: he was one of them – from the beginning.

He knew he was a substitute.

He was loved – oh, he knew he was dearly loved.

But he was not beloved.

If she had married Arthur Graham, which she might have done, she would have loved him too, just the same, most dearly, with the same soft-fingered tenderness.

If she had married Charles Fraser, she'd have sacrificed her soul completely.

He knew, despite her green-elf eyes, her slim, caressing hand, he and Arthur would have toiled far behind, plodding on the earth.

But Charlie Fraser was dead. Arthur Graham was dead. And Annie Zeederberg was his. This little fellow on his lap was theirs. No dead soldier could undo the reality of that.

All that redirected tenderness is his.

And her fierce, her immutable love is for her sons.

His sons.

Herbert looked up at the Rood Cross with the *Agnus Dei* above. The Head's voice, reading the Lesson, had receded, as Robbie's had on the evening at the Kowie when, in his way he'd prepared them for this day. The Roll of Honour was being read. Herbert stood with the congregation: the Head recited each name, each rank, each regiment. He called them back, man by man. And among the hundred and twenty-five:

Lieutenant John Matthew Bell, Royal Berkshires

Flight Lieutenant Daniel Lovell Grant, Royal Flying Corps

Sergeant Henry William Falchurch Harman, South African Infantry

Captain Vincent Joseph MacCallum, Royal Flying Corps

Captain James William Seymour, Argyll and Sutherland

Sergeant Samuel Egbert Stafford, South African Infantry

Private Arthur Grenville Graham, Second Rhodesia Regiment

Private Charles Winton Fraser, Second Rhodesia Regiment

This time, Herbert did not barricade the breach against his grief. An arm was slipped through his, a head rested at his shoulder.

433

The congregation stood.

If it was bad form to speak about them, it was not bad form to sing, eyes to the front, feet firmly planted.

O, valiant hearts, who to your glory came,
Through dust and conflict and through battle flame,
Tranquil you lie, your knightly virtue proved,
Your mem'ry hallowed in the land you loved.

Splendid you passed, the great surrender made,
Into the light that never more shall fade,
Deep your contentment in that blest abode,
To wait the last clear trumpet call of God.

The Last Post: Harry Zeederberg, veteran, limped down the aisle with his trumpet case to stand in the baptistry. He played manfully: the last clear trumpet call of God.

Percy and Herbert sit on the steps of the Clock Tower after dinner. Both know that here the conversation will end and they will go their ways. Percy has taken out his cigarette case. The smoke drifts. Their voices hum softly in the vault of the tower – a strange acoustic whisper.

'Tell me,' Percy says.

'Even though he was the last,' Herbert says, 'I'll start with Arthur Graham.' Herbert glances at Percy, adjusts the cigarette between his fingers. He is not telling it to Percy, he is telling it to himself, as Percy used to long ago. Meanings do not always emerge in sequence. They echo and reflect, layer to layer, dormant until some catalyst coaxes out the core.

The order of the telling is Herbert's choice. He must end where the present is.

And where the present is, there is Charlie Fraser.

'Do you remember Unwin?' Herbert says. 'It's one of those odd ironies, that Unwin, so despised by all of us, should have been there. He was a medical orderly with the Rhodesians. Apparently, after they sent him away from school, his father packed him off to some outpost where he'd be out of sight and out of mind. He joined up as soon as he was the right age. He was attested on his eighteenth birthday. Anyway, there was a doctor called Dolbey who was running the hospital and Unwin was a sort of factotum for him.' Herbert traces his cigarette along the edge of the step where he sits, delicately shaving off the outer layer of ash. 'Unwin was very handy with the morphia syringe – and, my God, he needed to be, with the injuries they dealt with.' He looks over at Percy and grins. 'Imagine poor old Arthur, riddled with malaria, arriving at this God-forsaken, hot little field hospital in the middle of nowhere to find Unwin – like a bad smell just come in from the bogs, and almost as urging as he always was?'

'But not a fool,' says Percy. 'I always suspected that.'

'There were things he understood about us that others didn't, when it mattered,' says Herbert. 'It made it much easier not having to explain . . . all that. He might have driven Arthur to drink with some of his fussing and officiousness – but, in the black times, he knew exactly what to do. He was like a sort of dog that senses thunder long before there's a cloud in the sky, amazingly annoying, but absolutely deft.' Herbert turns his cigarette around in his fingers, examining it. 'We were privates with some pretty uncouth dolts over us. Unwin was a sergeant. Despite that, he had another sense of rank. Not from the army. From here.'

        –Do it, Unwin. Just do it.

'It was a hellhole in the heat,' says Herbert. 'Men raving for morphia, having to be kept from it, Unwin up and down the ward trying to make them comfortable and dealing with other things – like half the roof blown off in a storm and drenching everyone – then festering in heat and wishing, more than anything, for rain. The bogs were something else! There were long trenches with forked sticks at intervals to squat over. The stink and flies were past description.'

'Men got so weak from dysentery they sometimes fell in, trying to balance themselves.' Herbert glances at Percy. He knows he does not have to explain to him about human excrement – he had spent months in the trenches. 'You cannot understand what happens to a

man in that heat when he lies in shit and is too weak to crawl out,'
Herbert says. 'You might as well just shoot him and put him out of his
misery. A couple did it for themselves. It wasn't common – but it
happened.'

Percy knows. He had always been chosen to write the letters to
uncomprehending relatives.

'Dear Madam, your son . . .' The long pauses, the long silences,
pen poised at camp tables, turning words, turning them over and
over . . .

'The battle there was against insects,' says Herbert. 'Mosquitoes
decided the outcome of that war – not men. It was how many were
down with malaria, how many with blackwater, that exercised the
minds of the COs. It was flies, maggots, jigger fleas. Bugger the lions
or the bullets!'

Percy is listening. It was a very different war from his.

'You should see the Pangani River!' says Herbert. 'It's Eden on
the first morning.' He adds ruefully, 'but the serpent isn't intent on
the Fall-of-Man from the Grace-of-God. Serpents are a minor matter
– and there is certainly no Eve for hundreds of square miles to distract
Man from combat! It was insects, parasites and heat that sent us
mad!'

A moon is rising. It is caught among the stone pines on the
northern hill, an ember lodged behind the trunk-black bars.

'Before Smuts and Van Deventer came, the English generals sat
in Nairobi in HQ, drinking gin,' says Herbert. 'And in the lines, men,
oxen and horses were dying by the hundreds – not to mention the
African porters. But of course they didn't count! They were tallied
with the mules. The Indian troops and the Cape Corps were tallied
with the oxen – one notch up. And we were tallied with the armoured
vehicles – beautifully put together and quite useless in the bush!'

Herbert links his hands about his knees. Percy is leaning against
the parapet of the Clock Tower's shallow steps.

'And then there was the food,' says Herbert. 'Sometimes we went
for eighteen hours without it – and with a full day's marching thrown

in. The only thing there was too much of was plum and apple jam! Absolutely deadly! Once we came across some sacks of dried beans in a shed on a deserted German plantation. We cooked them. My God, we were ill! Von Lettow's askaris had poisoned them. We dragged two men out of the bog-trench the next day, dead.'

The wind that had scudded on the cricket pitch that afternoon has dropped. The air is blood warm. The moon is lifting clear. It floats in an empty sky. The road past the stone pines glints iron-blue.

'There were few medals in our war,' Herbert says. 'Who is going to win an MC against an enemy comprised mostly of black askaris? They were good soldiers, they knew the bush. They were a pretty daunting foe. But as Edwards once said to me, "That's not the war. Only France is the war." Everyone still believes that.'

Percy hears the note in his voice. 'Dying is dying, no matter where it's done,' he says.

'Not quite true. Being buried at Pozieres or Warlencourt has a lot more cachet than Taveta.'

Percy says, 'You mean the King isn't going to come and lay a wreath!' The old sardonic note in his voice makes Herbert smile.

'At best, a couple of bush fowls will scratch on your mound, so you don't feel too neglected!' says Herbert, taking up Percy's tone. 'You might even get a mealie-field planted over the place you died or a cattle byre full of emaciated cows! No Flanders poppies there. No poetry. No for ever England!'

'Or *Land of Hope and Glory*!'

'They're such empty, unknown little battlefields,' says Herbert. 'You can't even see that they're there. And who's ever heard of Latema Nek or Salaita Hill when you've got Passchendaele and Vimy Ridge with all their grandeur? Who's ever heard of Taveta when you've got Tyne Cot and Poelcapelle?' Herbert gives a dry laugh. 'Dying's not the same, Gilbert. There are places to do it and places that don't count.'

'And ways of dying.' Percy is reflective. 'David Bennett's was an accident. Charlie's father . . .' he pauses, searching for words, 'perhaps it was a sort of surrender to sorrow.'

'Arthur Graham made me understand the differences in war,' says Herbert.

437

'Arthur?'

'When Arthur knew that he was going to die, he minded very much that it was not in battle, but in hospital.'

–It's not the same, Apie. It's like being in the Fourths at school or the third House team in the reserves . . .

'Arthur got malaria,' says Herbert. 'He called it his "inconvenient little illness". Like all of us, he'd been grappling with it right through the campaign. He wouldn't stop though. He fought at Salaita and at Latema, so sick he could hardly stand. He collapsed in the end. Our South African Infantry was at Taveta, just inside the Kenyan border, when a wagon-load of Second Rhodesian hospital cases came in one afternoon. They'd been travelling in the most appalling heat. I saw him being unloaded by the medical orderlies.'

' "Hello Aap-face",' says Arthur, as though he'd seen me the day before.' Herbert smiles. 'I thought he was going to tell me to get my footer boots and come and do gaining grounds with him.' Herbert's voice is unsteady then. 'He was so ravaged by sickness, he could hardly get to the latrine. That's when Unwin popped up . . .'

'Like a genie from a lamp?' says Percy.

Herbert laughs. 'It was sort of comic, really.'

'Unwin could always be trusted to deal with bogs,' says Percy.

'When Arthur saw me,' Herbert continues, 'he says, "Here I am, six thousand miles away from school and there's a bloody welcoming party from the House! Only difference is that I don't have to report you for smoking, Unwin, and can bum a fag off you myself." ' Herbert looks off towards the rugby field. He says, 'Arthur couldn't smoke. He was too ill to lift his head.'

The hospital is in an old mission school. The flamboyants are dropping flame-red petals over the red earth. This is a place of ant-heaps, grotesquely shaped, occupied by bushes, snakes and meerkats. The doctor is exhausted. The men mostly nurse themselves. The operating theatre has a mosquito net over the door. It is the only insurance against pollution.

'In those situations, it's little things that take on a particular meaning,' says Herbert. 'They seem so sentimental now – like Dan's dog.

All that . . .'

'We make it so,' says Percy. 'To obviate the horror. There's no other way.'

'At one time, when we were inside GEA, some abandoned farmsteads were raided for supplies. It wasn't policy to plunder civilian property but Unwin told me the field hospitals were critically short of bedding. A whole lot of Hunnish linen was brought in.'

'I bet the chaps would've rather burned it than slept in it,' says Percy.

'It was an obsession at first,' says Herbert. 'But they had to get used to the idea. Unwin told me there was nothing like linen sheets to make a man recover. "Almost as good as his mum!" That's what he said. He told me about a sergeant with dysentery who got hold of a child's cot pillow and slept with it under his chin. Unwin said he used to fondle it. He didn't know that he was doing it – he was too busy dying – but he wouldn't let it out of his sight. Unwin said he popped the cushion in the sack with the corpse! He said he couldn't have let anyone else touch it.'

Percy does not speak.

'And then there was Arthur's mouse. It was a funny little grey job. It made a nest in his boot. No one was allowed to disturb it.'

Arthur's boots had been laid on their side. Herbert had leaned down to right them.

–Don't touch, Arthur had said. –Watch. The flicker of a grin.

–What? Herbert had glanced round. No one else was listening. The rows of beds were full. Herbert had not breathed too deeply for the stench, nor looked too far.

Arthur had moved his hand, signing patience and watched the skirting intently.

A mouse had come. Grey and unobtrusive, it had edged round the heel of Arthur's boot and along the instep with the small sudden clockwork-movements of the wary. The tail had disappeared behind it into the mouth of the boot.

–She has babies in there. Arthur had been triumphant.

–They'll eat the boot.

–So what.
So what indeed.

'He used to watch that mouse, Gilbert, as if it was the dearest thing in the world to him. In the short while that we were billeted nearby, I used to visit him every day and get a progress report on all the mouse babies. Once that was done we'd talk about other things but Arthur used to keep a watch on that boot. He'd have killed the man who touched it.'

    –Can you see the babies, Apie? Arthur had said. –What do you think their chances of survival are?'
    –Pretty good if the boot stays where it is and you look sharp.
    If the boot stays where it is and you look sharp. The words had been suspended. Somewhere outside a pack-mule had lamented in the quiet afternoon.

Herbert is watching the moon. He is tracing the curve of the road leading up the hill, north-east.
    'What did you talk about?' says Percy.
    'We usually talked about school. Robbie. Footer. Cadets. Unwin used to come along sometimes and spew out the most unadulterated rot about forts and smoking in the tangy and New Street and the caddies. We used to laugh until someone complained about the uproar. But then Arthur got worse. Unwin knew exactly how to deal with him. He also made sure the mouse wasn't disturbed. By then, Arthur was drifting – sometimes with us, sometimes not. Unwin was very fierce about that mouse. He didn't seem to care if people thought him daft. He was generous like that. I never heard him whine the way he did at school.'
    'Did Arthur ever mention Fraser?' Percy asks.
    'Only once, when I was alone with him,' says Herbert. 'There was an odd incident. Arthur told me about it, when he was still lucid. One night, when Charlie and he were on guard duty together, two fellows came and asked for a cigarette and Arthur got out his box. He struck a match and Charlie reached in and snatched Arthur's fag away before he smoked it. He dragged on it himself.'

'But Charlie never smoked,' says Percy. 'He hated it.'

'It was the third cigarette,' says Herbert.

Percy let his eyes trace the dark outlines of the House, Robbie's old unlit window.

–It's the third that gets it every time.

'Arthur was distraught,' says Herbert. 'He knew what it meant – like all of us.'

'Atonement for betrayal,' Percy says simply. 'Charlie's way of seeing Arthur right.' He pauses, links his hands. 'And a death-wish. A symbolic sort of suicide.'

'Charlie did not commit suicide,' says Herbert emphatically. 'How can you think that?' The notion is untenable.

'No,' says Percy. 'He only had to obey orders. He knew what the consequence would be.'

'We all obeyed orders. We had to.'

'Certainly – and tried like hell to make it through. But then we weren't looking for atonement, were we? He was. He began from a different premise altogether. I bet he marched straight into the guns. He set himself up for it from the start. His own blood sacrifice. To pay.' Percy flicks the stub of his cigarette onto the grass, shifts his back against the parapet. 'I watched him. He was merciless with himself,' he says. 'Charlie always knew what he was doing.'

Herbert is silent for a long while. Then he says, 'When he was getting worse, Arthur said, "I should have lit that fag and gone out in a blaze of glory instead of dying in this bloody bed!" Unwin and I tried to make him laugh it off – superstition and all that – but he couldn't. We knew it haunted him. He thought he was responsible. What did he say? "Charlie wouldn't have died of malaria! Mosquitoes didn't bite him! They were too damned respectful! He should have left the fag to me." '

The quarter sounded from the cathedral clock. The tone echoed in the dome of the Clock Tower above them.

'Did Arthur talk about himself?' says Percy.

'Just once,' says Herbert. 'It was the first time his cheerfulness seemed to slip. "I wonder . . ." he said. I said, "Wonder what?" and he said, "What it's really like". "What's what really like?" ' Herbert

441

laughs then, does not look at Percy. ' "It," says Arthur. "That." '

'So what did you say?' says Percy.

'I couldn't answer. I was eighteen – I didn't know myself then. I wish I could have told him.'

'So he never found out,' says Percy.

'No, he never found out.'

'Did it really matter?'

'Oh yes, it really mattered.' Herbert is silent.

There is noise and laughter coming from the Drill Hall. Someone is playing the accordion. It may be Mostert. It is something he has taken up to keep him active.

Herbert says, 'The day we spoke about it' – pausing – 'Arthur also mentioned Annie Zeederberg. It was the only time he spoke about her. He had written her a letter. He kept it in an old sock under his things. It seemed as if he had been carrying it around for a long time, adding to it, because it was quite grubby. He gave it to me and said I must post it. "Don't post it now, Aap-face," he said. "Just when you're ready." '

'He had meant – when it was right, when I could add the necessary postscript.' Herbert swallows. Percy waits. 'It was a fat letter, rather blotty,' Herbert says. 'I brought an envelope for him. I left it unsealed.' Something catches in his throat. 'I think he'd written to her about Charlie. He never mentioned him to me again,' he says. 'He couldn't. I couldn't.'

–Just let sorrow leak without a sound. Lie still, quite still. And in the end, it will leak inward, undetected.

'It was very bad the last few days,' says Herbert. 'He was battling to breathe. He was half delirious, taking tiny breaths as though he was just sipping at the air. He lay and watched his boot for the mouse. He never complained, never asked for anything. The last time I visited, he was racked. Our battalion was about to move. I knew I wouldn't see him again.' Herbert stops. Percy flicks the butt-end of his cigarette away. It glows in the dark below the ornamental wall.

'That day, Unwin said to me, "The mouse has gone." He was beside himself. He didn't show it in the ward, but he was. He was

442

sweating so much, he was squelching in his boots. It was like a portent. He knew it. I knew it. So did Arthur.' Herbert speaks slowly. 'When I went in to him, Arthur had his face to the wall. "Cheerio, old chap," I said.' Again, Herbert's words catch. 'God, what an idiot thing to say!' He wipes his wrist across his forehead. ' "Aap-face," Arthur said. I could hardly hear him and he couldn't look at me.' Herbert laughs suddenly. 'Imagine – "Aap-face" – as the last thing your pal says to you while Unwin, of all people, is standing there, his feet in puddles, like on the first day at school . . .' Herbert's voice breaks.

Percy waits with him. Herbert draws a breath. He says, 'Arthur died that night. Unwin was with him to the end.' Percy does not speak. Herbert says, 'Unwin said he asked for his mother. It was the last thing he said. Simple as that.'

Herbert had sent the letter as instructed.

–Don't post it now, Aap-face. Just when you're ready.

He had written the postscript. The writing had not been especially legible but the message was very clear.

'He's buried in a little cemetery near where the hospital was,' says Herbert. 'Unwin wrote and told me. He said it was a jaunty kind of cemetery, not like Taveta which is bleak and stony. He said there was a picket fence and masses of bougainvillaea and the locals go by to the market. He said there was always someone singing or shouting or gossiping with someone else and that Arthur would find things to laugh at!'

Unwin, well acquainted, knew it. He did not find it a gloomy place, not like Davey Bennett's little palisaded plot above the station; not like the stark and lonely stones at Taveta ranked below the iron hills and the far, dispassionate eye of the great mountain floating in its tropic dreaming, crowned with snow.

–The battlefields and cemeteries don't have all the grandeur or the names.

But they are just as haunted and much more lonely.

The letter took three weeks to reach Annie Zeederberg. It was late in

April, on an autumn day, when it arrived, slipped unobtrusively through the brass letter vent on the front door of her parents' house.

Annie Zeederberg is coming home from the hospital, walking in an April evening, with the dust on plumbagos and the boys on Lower field kicking a ball into the slanting light. There are running feet, the dive for the line, the panting, tumbling bodies, the hollow thud of boot on ball – the silence, then the cheer as it clears the posts. She stands to watch. She smiles, walks on. It is a perfect evening. First star in a green dusk. The stone pines on the far hill where the road winds up are always leaning to a wind. They stand at the end of the world. It is a cut-out landscape, black silhouette of hills and church and windmill, paper backdrop for shadow puppets casting up their dark reflections.

She remembers, as if it is the very last coherent sound of her life – the flyscreen on the back door clattering behind her as she goes in through the kitchen.

There is a letter on the table in her room, waiting.

Josie is waiting too, sitting on her bed.

She has also heard from Herbert.

There is a stillness in a person numbed by shock. A sort of primal scenting, frozen from flight. It is not beautiful to see. It is the wringing of the soul. It is drowning without the benefit of water to anaesthetise and cushion. It is the nakedness of *No*, before it overwhelms.

That same evening, in the chapel, there is no hope of flight for GB.

No drowning. Not here. Not now.

Unlike Annie Zeederberg, he may not cry.

Charlie will not have him cry.

Perhaps when he is old he will seek the benediction of tears: old men often cry. There is nothing shameful in it.

GB is quite still, Parkes beside him. The Head is saying – there have been so many, they have almost forgotten to listen: –I have a letter here from Herbert Cummings, our rugby captain of 1915.

444

He writes from German East Africa. He says:

'Hugh Unwin, who is a medical orderly with the Second Rhodesians, has sent me a picture of Charlie Fraser's grave at Taveta. It is quite neat, with a wooden cross, and piled with stones at present. He was killed on March 11th. Unwin has also seen Arthur Graham's grave. He died of pneumonia on 7th April. Graham was Fraser's closest friend.'

So bald. So flat.
It was the way they would have wanted it.
It honoured the First Commandment.
It *was* the First Commandment.
GB sits. Parkes sits beside him. They sit as others have before them. Frozen.
GB keeps sitting through the sermon and the hymns and the final blessing. Somewhere, out on the field, a groundsman has disturbed the hadedahs. They are circling: so much raucous noise.
Someone says, glancing over, 'Jeez, GB's gone yellow!'
Robbie passes. He does not speak.
Two more boys, Robbie-trained.
His grief is dry. It is rooted in his bones. He calls his dog to heel. He does not bend to her. He'll allow no redirected tenderness. The tenderness – the great, great tenderness – is all inside. Invisible, except to God.

–Braithwaite's fagmaster was killed. Nubs gather round.
–Who was he?
–Fraser, arse, weren't you listening in chapel?
–What's so great about him?
Heretics should burn!
–The best full-back in the history of the school.
–Not another one!
–And what about the other bloke? Graham?
–The best right-winger in the history of the school.
–Ah, bullshit, man.
–Listen, fart, do you want a *klap*?

GB makes it to the lavatory with the door. He is disintegrating, breaking up. He stands with his hands against the back wall and vomits into the pit. He sits, foot jammed against the planks, while his life seems to drain. All of him has turned to ooze.

Parkes, knowing, is patrolling.

Parkes will not weep. He has forgotten how. Only his heart feels unfamiliar – much too large – bumping at his sternum, as if it would desert him. He wonders vaguely (and aloud) what Annie Zeederberg will do now. It worries him. She will have to be a spinster, she with her beauty and her violin: perhaps, in time, he, as Arthur Graham's successor, will be allowed to rescue her. Or perhaps she will die for the love of two fallen heroes?

It is something of a disappointment to Parkes when, in his final year, she marries Douglas Morgan in the school chapel. Morgan is certainly heroic enough – but it would have been more appropriate if she'd succumbed to a broken heart.

Parkes, in his time, will learn that hearts don't break. They are simply maimed and go on beating.

The music has stopped. The accordion has been put away. There are shouts of laughter from the door of the Drill Hall. Someone is ringing the school bell.

Percy says, glancing over his shoulder and cocking his head, 'Silly fellows, trying to be nubs again! Edwards has had far too much wine!'

Archer's and Mostert's voices ride the quiet. They clatter off towards the House together where a Reunion Dormitory has been arranged by Miss Maltby for the returning heroes. Aged, but still in harness, she is waiting to greet them at the door.

'There won't be any locker inspection tonight,' says Percy wryly. 'Only laughs and larking. No "Strip that bed yourself, my lad"! No examination of pustules!'

Far off the House door bangs, but even from where they sit they can hear the familiar sound of feet herding on the stairs.

'And now, Cummings,' Percy says. Herbert turns to him. 'It's time to tell what you've been waiting to say for seven years.'

'I don't know how it was for him,' says Herbert. He looks off across the rugby field. 'How can anyone know how it really was for Charlie Fraser?'

'You have a sense of it.'

Yes, he has a sense of it.

He holds it sacred: to reveal it, to risk its being profaned, to destroy its fragile integrity, its meaning, would be irredeemably careless. Herbert wavers.

'The First Commandment is understood,' says Percy. He will not let him down.

'And the second,' says Herbert, taking a long breath, 'doesn't matter any more.'

TWENTY-THREE

Saturday, March 11th, 1916: Four o'clock and the light coming up. A pale green morning, a sheen of white at the horizon, the clean, bleached promise of the day. There is still a star. The old myths linger: I am the morning star, the early hunting lynx, the red of sunrise in my hide, the green of morning in my eyes, darkness in my points, night and morning in my tread. The singing thorns are silhouetted now, a tracery against the sky. Latema and Reata wait, cool in shadow. They are without menace. Two bush-clad hills. Not majestic, not ravined, not mysterious. Here, within two hundred yards, the ruins of a little wattle and daub house. The mealie fields have been overcome by weeds. A fowl-run, abandoned, but, shifting across the yard in wind, husks of millet, winnowed once. No different from a hundred little homesteads, scattered across these plains. Way off to the west is the presence of the great mountain. Kilimanjaro hangs suspended above the morning cloud, her cone turned towards the sun. The first warmth belongs to her snows, cloud-white in cloud.

The tents are unobtrusive in the bush. Pitched in steady rows, tattered from months on campaign. The early fires are lit for the sentries' tea. Someone nudges at the embers with a boot. They flare and fall again, the billy boils.

There are stirrings. Men wander to the perimeter. They have marked their territory like any predator over and over, alert to the bush: the ritual is the same, except they brace their legs instead of lifting them.

Only the sentries, weary from a long watch, have seen the lights on Latema Hill. Hidden, like the eyes of small nocturnal animals – far away, inconsequential – they do not alarm. But the scouts have been out all night, working up the gully at the far side, and returned. Big guns are in place, well hidden at the crest and in the trenches all along the base where the bush thins.

Tea. And sleep before the heat sets in and the flies come to settle, and moisture brings the maggots out of fly-blow, hatching on the hair of legs, of arms and heads, unspeakable. Arthur had once felt a stinging pain in his thigh, hastily pulled down his pants, seen the skin split open and the red-brown head of *putsi*-fly larva edge out. It had humped away, trailing his own watery plasma behind it. He had gazed with revulsion at the wound left behind, sunk in on itself like a sea polyp, with a residue of brine in its mouth. The hole had gone septic, turned into a boil. He'd lanced it with a thorn. 'I'm rotting from the inside, Charlie. All of me is maggots. Do I stink? I can't smell anything any more.'

'Like a hyena.'

'So do you.'

'I thought you couldn't smell.'

It rained one night, a great, unexpected storm. They had lain side by side behind their tent, quite naked, and let it drum into them. To lie under such lancing rain and feel it run and run, dissolving them slowly into the mud, as if their backs were bonded to the ground. Rain in hair, in ears, thumping at the hollow of the throat, the lids, the groin. Lie and let it run and run. And run. Mouths open, washing, washing, licked clean. It was a great caress, some echo of support in the cupped, steady palm of some omniscient mother, half anointing, half cleansing, all-caressing. Safe.

Who will wash them if they die? They cannot go unwashed. It is the first task after birth – to wash away the signs of struggle and of blood: to smooth, to lay down tenderly to sleep, to turn the head in comfort to the breast.

There are no mothers here.

And if there are no mothers – who will wash the blood away, look once more at lids and wrists, the temple where the heartbeat echoes? Who will turn the head and touch the nape, trace the lines with fingers, as a mother maps her infant?

They turned on their stomachs and let it pound on their backs, their necks. 'Stick your arses in the air, boys,' the sergeant major had yelled. 'They'll come up bright, sweet as a baby's.' They hung their dirty clothes on the bushes to wash. Then someone got a ball. They played rugby, turned red – strange, daubed, ancient Woad-men, baying at the sky. They stood again and let the mud wash off, laughing. The tins were ranged out in the open and when they boiled tea it was hot and rich and sweet. They inspected one another then, for lice, for maggots, for boils and jigger fleas – strange primates these, in the light of lamps in every tent, fingers creeping unrepelled through hair washed clean, tending feet, scrubbed like bleached bone, cool again and pure. Their skin could breathe. They could sleep.

But this day, there is no rain. The cicadas pulse in the bush, a damp line of heat is breathing on the horizon. Reata, further to the east, shifts in a low mirage.

No 1457 has come in from sentry duty to his stretcher. The tent is still. It has been a long watch, the sky cloudless, the stars heavy. The moon had risen late: misshapen moon, gravid orange moon. He unbuckles the belt, eases boots and puttees. There is freedom in legs allowed to cool. The stinking clothes are cast aside.

Too tired to care.

Hair stiff with dust.

Too tired. He lies as he had at school, unprotective of himself, across the stretcher, arm crooked under his cheek. This is the way that children lie who are unafraid. Sleep. Arthur is across the sandy divide, tangled in his own clothes, mosquitoes feasting.

Does Charlie dream? And if he does, what dream is it?

Home?

Charlie does not have a home.

His had been a rectory. It belonged to God.

In time, his house, his room, would be taken by another boy – half a dozen – who would call it his.

450

–Perhaps, one day, I'll have a farm, he'd said.

School?

The old stones, the deep recess of windows, the view out towards the hill where the pines lean from the wind. The road north-east. The blue distance, the heliograph leaves flashing back the eye of the sun.

School: the timepiece, marking the hours and echoing back – the great cathedral clock; old Jarge limping to the bell to portion out the lessons. Had they spent all their lives counting hours?

Lower field? Here is the wind, taking the ball and curving it towards the posts. Here is the little *sloot* and the plumbago bush – blue, pale blue like late skies. Here, the Zeederbergs' quince hedge. Annie Zeederberg?

–I'll pretend you kissed me.

He had kissed her many times. He had eons to linger at her eyes. Abandoned to sleep, head bent in to his chest, he knew her.

Boy-neck: still perfection. Crooked knee, a hollow at the flank, nothing slack. His limbs are deftly honed.

He wakes, suddenly alert. Sound or dream? He does not know. Morning is streaming in, somewhere in the stillness a raptor mews: such a small, guileless sound, tapping at the edge of sleep. Warmth drifts through the canvas of the tent, leaving soft pools of light on the ground. He looks across at Arthur stirring. Arthur always has a good scratch before he opens his eyes. It is as if he is ensuring all his old friends – fleas, jiggers, *putsis* – are still with him in the morning. Absent scratching but rigorous, from head to toe. Same bits first, same bits last.

Arthur opens his eyes and looks back at Charlie. No nonsense talk about a beautiful girl who has visited him from the ether.

–Shut up, Arthur. You're distracting me.

Today Arthur is looking directly at him – and not looking at him, but beyond him. He is very still. A little frown hovers between his brows, like when he had been puzzled in class.

'What's up?' Charlie says quietly.

'We're going in today.'

'Who said?'

'Heard while you were on watch.'

Charlie looks down at the sand. 'Right,' he says.

Arthur looks at him directly. 'Right.'

They do not move.

'Did you write home?' Arthur says.

'No.'

'Want some paper?'

'If you like.'

'Time for tea.'

They rise together, face to face, bare-chested. An inch apart – hands, shoulders. Today. So Arthur gives Charlie a small shove and Charlie shoves him back. Shoulder matching shoulder; flesh – flesh; heads down; a little spar, a little tussle.

Yes, today.

There are no clean clothes. They have to bear the stiff restriction of the puttees, the boots past rotten, the shirts made fragile by the sun.

–Stick your head in your helmet. Keeps the maggots in, the flies out, is the advice to new troops.

Charlie makes the tea, nudging the ashes of the fire into life. He squats, arms balanced on his thighs and the mug between his hands.

The sun, a blazing disc, slips up across the horizon. Kilimanjaro shimmers, white and distant, fading in the glare. Dawn is over. Morning comes. Charlie leaves his tea mug by the fire, forgetting it. Arthur puts his down as well. They lean against each other, baking dry.

Charlie writes the letter. It is brief. The sergeant is blustering about. Gunners are called. He dashes it off, folded unequally and written in pencil. What to say?

'Dearest Moth,
It is terribly hot and we only have a gallon of water a day – so we're not very nice to be near. Saw a lot of game yesterday. Not allowed to shoot for obvious reasons.

452

How is the plot coming on? The house? Have the thatchers come from Uncle Sonnie's to do the roof? I will sink a borehole as soon as I get back. And we must get a dog. I want a good hunting dog. Can't say where we are or what we're up to but all's well and Arthur sends love. He nearly injured himself seriously playing rugby in the rain! Next time he must wear pants!'

What to say? A house and a borehole and a dog.

'Chin up, Moth. I'm well and fit.'

He folds it and puts it aside for the censor and his blue pencil – he can't say anything at all.

–I dreamed of rain again, like the storm. I dissolved in it. I could taste it, seeping down through mud, choking me. Then I was writing maths in Robbie's class. I couldn't understand the theorem. He was shouting. Davey Bennett came. I have never dreamed of Davey Bennett but I did last night. We were looking for our photographs. We were looking for the picture of the hut he'd built. It is up in the mountains against an old grey rock. Davey said, 'I will show you my hut now, Fraser. Come.'

I dreamed of you. You were washing me as you used to when I was a very little chap. I could feel your hands.

–Ah, I see you, my son. Long ago I watched you take those first steps, knew the small, downy shoulders, the curve of your arm in the palm of my hand. Those hollows at your flanks. That longer spine. I know them. And the little sac like two leaves ribbed together with a spider's thread pulled tight to bind them: another mystery, like the nakedness at the hip where the small blue of a vein feeds inward, concave hollow between trunk and thigh. Once, you were barrel-bellied with a small boy's abdomen. I could press a finger gently in the spot below the sternum, feel the place where the breath is anchored.

Primal-mother-grooming, picking over the little tender secrets; I would cradle you to wash.

Who will hold your head, my son? Who will cradle you?

–It is March 11th. I am going to die today.

The other night, two sentries came for a light. Arthur was with me. He was the third to use the match, but I took the cigarette from him. The third to use the match – he is the man who dies. I lit the cigarette for him. They laughed because – dispensation – I don't smoke. They said it wouldn't count. But it will.

I don't want Arthur to blame himself. I did it. It's too late to change it now.

Arthur won't die today. But one day soon.

Annie Zeederberg will have to marry someone else.

I wished to love.

I never knew.

What did I lose?

The colonel comes. The staff car from Taveta is drawn up out of range. The medical orderlies are arranging their tent just behind the lines. Unwin is there, quite calm.

'Fall in, men.'

'It's time.'

One o'clock and the sun is beyond its zenith. Arthur and Charlie go down to the transport. Charlie stands quietly by a pair of mules. The little yellow eggs of flies are deposited precisely on the end of each neck hair: so much design and balance for one small maggot life. The mule looks out. It is very patient.

There is the sound of rifles way off. The Baluchis are drawing the enemy fire.

–I see everything. Everything is very clear.

'We'll go in, boys, and take the firing line forward. The KAR, the Baluchis will be flanking us,' says the lieutenant, busy with his notes.

The colonel has just arrived. He has a word of encouragement to say. Splendid fellows, these. Tough colonial lads. Always the best.

Why doesn't the order come? Why doesn't it come? The bigwigs behind the lines are dragging it out. Malleson has retired – he is indisposed. Capell is here at last. It's all right. He's here.

–I will die today. And there is no retreat.

They start.

'Fall in, men.'

Arthur is walking, down wind, like he walked at school – that easy lope – like cadets. Only the sea isn't just over the dunes, there are no aloes blazing in among the coastal bush, canary creeper, the old blue buttonhole-plumbago.

Latema is ahead. And the vlei. The sun is blinding. Latema is in shadow. Such a little hill, long and dipped on the eastern side and then a promontory.

Where is the enemy?

Were the scouts wrong?

The sun is behind, blazing up against the black ridge. We are here, in the open plain, ant-men moving into the sun.

Into the sun.

Interminably into the sun.

The sky is yellow, a slow-leaking bile.

The fire is sporadic. As they advance, it intensifies. Intensifies to shake the earth. They go forward. Already the medical orderlies have their work cut out. The stretcher-bearers move back and forth, back and forth.

Arthur and Charlie are bringing up the boxes of ammunition. Arthur this side, Charlie that. They are priming the guns in the advance line.

Prime the guns.

Prime them.

The noise does not matter any more. The noise batters them. They are past exhaustion or fear. Their skin is thick with dirt and sweat. The enemy guns roar from the black shadow of the hill.

Three o'clock.

'Fraser!' shouts the subaltern – frantic gestures, angry now – 'Get back, man. Load and *get back*.' The earth is flying round them.

Four o'clock. The barrels are so hot, there are burns – raw to under-flesh – along the inside of his arms.

Five o'clock. The sun is lowering, but the ground is molten.

Five thirty.

Drawing in, the earth shakes, but below the din of rapid fire –

through the feet, through the worn soles of boots, out of the heart of the earth, slow-coming – the deep, deep boom of the Königsberg naval gun.

The deep long boom.

The silence: just a moment – like an indrawn breath.

Still the silence – just a moment more.

The explosion.

Even the mountain, in its far aloofness, seems to tremble.

The stretcher-bearers took Charlie back behind the guns. They'd called Arthur.

'Get Graham. Get him now.'

Arthur came. His lungs were full of embers. He could hardly see.

It took ten minutes.

Only ten minutes to end it all.

Blood was pumping into the stretcher, Charlie's right leg hanging by a thread.

Kick the ball and let it fly. Kick and let it fly. This angle, that. Away from the sun. Into the sun.

Into the sun. Straight to the sun.

So deft.

'Talk to me, Charlie.'

Arthur held his hands under Charlie's head, nape cupped as if to raise it above the blood that drowned him. Arthur could feel the great strong thudding of his own heart through his fingers.

'Say it, Charlie. Say it.'

But Charlie Fraser only says – a small sardonic little grimace – a smile, a joke? 'Damned rotten luck.'

Damned rotten luck.

That is all.

'Go now, lad.' The bearer said to Arthur. 'We'll carry on.'

Go?

'He'll go with me.' Arthur handed him off.

The bearer was an old man. He said, 'It's over, lad.'

Arthur looked at Charlie. His neck was still in his hand. Heavy,

heavy – but warm, pushing warmth into his fingers. That look: half frown, half smile. That stance. Shall I fight you now?

Essential Charlie. Never over.

'Leave it, lad.'

'No.'

'Get back now.'

'No.'

'Get back.'

'No.'

'That's an order.'

'Sir.'

Arthur went then. His gun would have razed hell. That night they stormed the hill, blazing away until a late moon rose and the enemy guns were still. They carried him home next day, slung over the sergeant's shoulder, insensible.

'Is he injured?' Enquiry from the lieutenant.

'No. Not a scratch. But something else is bust.'

Something else is bust.

The sergeant laid him on the stretcher. His back was turned on Charlie's bed.

Wake and he'll be there. Wake and he'll be lying on his stomach with his arms crooked under his head or flung out over the edge. He'll lift his head with his hair in his eyes and his eyebrows drawn in and then he'll growl or laugh – or both – and stretch.

–Charlie, what do you think about?

In retreat, or a slow smile. –Things.

–But you never say.

Laugh. –Things.

So?

So.

Herbert stands. He places his legs astride, as if he is at ease, but alert, on sentry duty. He says to Percy. 'The next day we helped the Second Rhodesians bring in their dead. It was the least we could do. They were shot to hell. We brought the mule carts and took them back to Taveta.'

He had walked beside the mule cart. The driver was a Xhosa, serving with the Infantry. Very far from home, they had exchanged quiet words. He was an old man who drove his mules without comment, waiting for his load. He wore a slouch hat moulded to his head by sweat and rain and heat. Walking at the side of the cart as it jostled ruts, Herbert had seen the great volcanic snow-crest of the mountain noosed by the thong of the driver's whip:

−Touch the mountains so that they smoke.

All the earth had smoked: the great heat, the great dust and tumult. And beyond – beyond – the mountain floating and indifferent, the high snows like cloud banks way across an empty sea. Silent. Then the old man had begun to sing to himself in Xhosa, some small repeated refrain to urge the mules along: a song recalled from a distant afternoon when boys, riding on a passing cart, had fallen silent as they'd turned their heads to stare at all the gathering about a podium and a memorial stone, bunting fluttering.

Herbert had put his hand on the shoulder of the front mule and listened to the song, sounds displaced in this strange fierce landscape. The driver had kept on singing, over and over, with the turning of the wheels – almost a lullaby – and Herbert had walked, eyes on the distant mountain beyond the ranks of singing thorns. That song, this song – boys and man – echoing each other. That time, this time, and the wheels jarring ruts in the track. That cart, this cart, laden with their cargoes, burdened to the slope. One had carried dry wood home – the other, men.

'I went to find Arthur,' Herbert says to Percy, as if returning. 'He was in his tent, asleep. More dead than asleep. It seemed wrong, or impossible, to wake him.'

−Arthur? You awake now? Herbert on his haunches at the entrance of the tent.

−Aap? Arthur half-opens his eyes. −What day is it?

−Sunday, the 12th.

Arthur moves slowly: fingers only. Head. −Sunday? Dredging up the dream.

−Look sharp, Arthur. Herbert says it gently. −It's time.

–Right.

–Right.

Herbert sets the can to boil. The water is sandy. He brings a log to the fire. Arthur comes from the tent.

–The mugs are here, says Arthur. They stand, leaning into each other as they had been left the morning before, baked dry by the sun. Rim to rim, balancing each other, weight to weight. Arthur picks them up. He smooths his boot over the small indents in the sand where they had stood, concentric rings, just touching.

'We fetched spades,' says Herbert. 'The sarge was giving orders. The padre was waiting with the other grave-diggers. Unwin was overseeing the bodies.'

Unwin moves among them. He has placed them side by side. There is no shade at mid-morning to lie them in. He squats beside a corpse, hand – in benediction – on the canvas that covers it.

'Arthur and I dug Charlie's grave together. We didn't allow anyone to help,' says Herbert. His voice has a touch of fierceness. Percy waits.

Unwin keeps his charge among the covered bodies. Arthur goes to him, squats beside him, lifts the cover on the face. His hand is very still.

Herbert looks away.

> *Man is like a breath;*
> *his days are like a fleeting shadow . . .*
> *Part your heavens, O Lord, and come down;*
> *touch the mountains so that they smoke . . .*

The words repeat over and over in Herbert's head.

–Touch the mountains so that they smoke.

'Arthur carried the body to the grave. Unwin and I helped him lower it . . .'

Herbert and Unwin and Arthur return the soil and rocks and roots and earth to their place. They work in silence. When it is done, Herbert and Unwin take up the three shovels, shoulder them, walk away. They do not turn.

Behind them, Arthur stands.

'That night I was on guard duty at the graves,' Herbert says to Percy. 'The hyenas had been a nuisance all the night before. I can remember walking up and down the perimeter. Charlie's grave was away to my left as I went up, to my right as I came down. I kept thinking of the night at the Kowie, when Robbie spoke to us. That night was the forerunner. It was very clear. That night . . . even then . . . I knew.'

Patrolling the perimeters of the graveyard in the heat of a tropic night, Herbert watches the sky, the battalions of stars, the ranks of storm clouds pressing down that cobalt dark. Along the far horizon, he sees two brooding hills – Latema and Reata – low in the blackness of the plains unlit by fires, scorched of human habitation. Fifty yards ahead, the small pile of stones, heaped on Charlie Fraser's grave. He walks the boundaries with an even, steady tread. Up and down. Up and down. A sentinel defending: just as Charlie Fraser had, so long ago. He listens for some familiar sound – anything, an echo, augur's voice or not – to take him back. He stands in that bleak cemetery, rifle at his side, eyes closed against the weight of dark, recalling the swell and suck of a running tide in a distant estuary, the turning of a great fish under southern skies: it is only his own blood surging in his ears, overwhelming him.

If he could only barricade the breach against his grief and hear instead the barred owl call.

Just once.

But nothing stirs.

Herbert had felt the tremor then, the inexorable shift of bedrock. And sorrow leaking inward.

'I went to see Fraser's mother some years later,' Herbert says.

Percy lights another cigarette, hands it to Herbert. Herbert takes it and cups it in his palm. 'Someone had to go. The letters from the COs are so often clumsy. She had to know.'

Percy does not comment. He lights his own cigarette.

460

–You went for yourself, Herbert. To say it all to someone who cared even more than you.

'She lives alone in a little room in a boarding establishment in Salisbury,' Herbert says. 'Charlie had been building her a house. But there was no point any more. And no money since he wasn't coming home.'

'What is she like?'

'Like Charlie,' Herbert says. 'There was something particular about her. She made me know why Charlie could wear a flower in his buttonhole and not look foolish. Nothing sentimental about it. There were simply meanings others wouldn't understand.' Herbert seemed at a loss.

'Perhaps I'm not explaining very well . . .'

'Yes, you are,' says Percy.

'I said I wondered about his being a private when he should have been an officer,' Herbert says. 'She sort of clucked – a Charlie smile and frown all at once – and said he hadn't felt it would be appropriate. And when I asked why, she said, "That's just Charlie" as if I ought to know better.'

–Charlie will never be Head-of-House.

–Can't take a chance on a fellow with an unstable past.

–Just a shadow which weighted their choices.

Percy inclines his head. 'He did it to atone.'

'For his father?'

'For his father.'

Way off, frogs are chiming in the *sloot*. Beyond the quince hedge on the east side, the lights of the Zeederbergs' lamps are soft behind drawn curtains.

'Did you tell his mother what happened in the end?' says Percy.

'Yes. I told her,' says Herbert. 'And in the middle of it all, she suddenly got up to make tea and she talked about the little dogs in the photo with Dan. She could see I was having a hard time of it. If we talked about the dogs, I'd manage.'

'Charlie's faultless touch . . .' says Percy.

Herbert nods.

'All in the heart,' says Percy.

461

'All in the heart.'

–Iron love to guard the fragile flame within; iron love to keep intrusion out.

'She gave me his photo album,' Herbert says.

'Why do you think she did it?'

'So he'd survive her.' Herbert does not hesitate. There is no need to explain the contradiction.

'A way to put off dying?' Percy's words echo back from long ago. 'She knew the old augur when she saw him.' He is almost triumphant.

She knew, indeed.

She had given it to him because he understood the cipher.

She had given it to him because he would honour it.

She had given it to him to restore the boy to his belonging.

    –Who is this?

    –Name's Charlie Fraser.

    –Charlie Fraser?

    –Yes.

    –Who is he?

    Not –the best full-back in the history of the school.

    –Just a boy.

Herbert says then, looking up at the lines of the Clock Tower. 'She sent two guineas for the Memorial Fund. It was all she could afford. She laughed when she told me. She said, "Poor old Charles! He is only my two-guinea son!" '

The moon is white and high. The lights of the town are settled in the hollow about the tall cathedral spire. The sky around the edges of the hills is dark, but darker yet the stone pines silhouetted at the crest, sentinel beside the old road leading out across the ridge.

Herbert brings his eyes back to Percy, says, 'There is something his mother didn't tell me. I went to Salisbury Cathedral to look for Charlie's plaque when I'd left her. I found it after a long search. It's rather high up on a side wall. I wrote the inscription down:

To the Greater Glory of God
and in Loving Memory of
No 1457

462

CHARLES WINTON FRASER
Killed at the battle of Latema Hill
German East Africa
11th March, 1916
Aged 19

Splendid he Passed

Herbert's voice is low: his story ending. 'The old native verger helped me find it. When he saw which plaque it was, he told me that, every week, a woman came with polish and a cloth. He said that he would bring a chair for her so she could stand on it and rub.'

' "She is the soldier's mother," he said. "The soldier was very young."

"Did she tell you that?" I said.

"No," he said. "She doesn't talk when she is here. But only the mother of a boy who is dead has eyes like that." '

Herbert and Percy stand. They walk slowly towards Lower field. On one side the moon is sending the shadow of the rugby posts along the ground, at the other the Clock Tower lays its darkness on the grass. They know the way, even without light. There is nothing more familiar or sure.

–Why did she give it to you, Cummings?

–So he'd survive her.

And he has. Oh, he has.

That vigour, that sheer presence, is not expunged from memory. He ensured transcendence: it seems that Charlie Fraser always knew that there was someone who'd believe.

CONTRIBUTORS

•■•▬▬•■•

My warmest thanks are due to the following who supported me in so many different ways.

St Andrew's College, Grahamstown: the Headmaster, Antony Clark and Brigitte Clark; Peter Betts, Percy Callaghan, Rose and Jerry Catto, John and Jean Creese, Brendan Doolan, Kenny Kilkenny, Lettie Rivett, Dodie Springer, Chris Terry and all the staff of the Teaching, Library, House and Administrative departments. Thanks are due to Headboys and Vice-Headboys, Ian Booth and Mark Wienand (1997), Greg Mullins and Mel Elliott (1998), their respective prefect bodies and their fellow students for the delight of being invited, as their guest, to share in their experience of school. The same is due to the Headmistress, Mrs Sue Hummel, and staff of the Diocesan School for Girls and Headgirls and Vice-Headgirls, Natalie Morgan and Alison Paterson (1997) and Catherine Wynne-Jones and Sally Munro (1998) and their fellow students.

Old Andrean Community: Messrs Robert Ball, Roger Clark, John B Clarke, Dennis Claude, Robert Cowen, John and Robin Cullingworth, Anthony Gilfillan, Chris Glendining, Norman Hutton, Jon Inggs, John Kettlewell, Gordon Laurie, James Macgregor, John More, Lorraine Mullins, Rob Mullins, Nick Neil-Boss, Michael Neser, John Nicolson, John C Oosthuizen, John V Oosthuizen, Peter Pauling, Edward Parkes and family, Don Porter, Will, Oggie and

Denham Pringle, Victor Pringle, Duff Rennie, Ken Ross and family, David Sampson, Richard Sherry, Arthur Short, Terry Stevens, Tony Taberer, Vere Tanner, Peter Terry, Duncan Thomas, James Thompson, David Walton, Charles White, Mike Wienand, Neil Wright. Drs Julian Anderson, Robert Caldwell, John Perrott and Angus Pringle. Professor Francis Wilson, Sir Michael Edwardes and Sir Stanley Rees. The Honourable Justices Tom Cloete and Donald Kannemeyer.

Friends, family and helpers: Patrick Bell, Air Commodore Crichton Boxer, Phil Brereton and the extended Brereton family, Lovell Carter, Susan Clarence, Elizabeth Compton, the Venerable Archdeacon Christopher Cook, Jane Cullingworth, Elizabeth Currie, Nan Dobrowski, Susie Dwyer, John Emery, Lorna Hall, Nicki Hamilton, Jenny Herschell, Caroline Kennard, Mary Laurie, Jacques Lemmer, Bart Logie, Denise Louw, Joan Lowe, Rubecca Luckan, Adrian Luckhurst, Marion Mangold, Tuan Marais, Lesley Mason, Jock McLean, Sue Mullins, Dee Nash, Maureen Needham, Jillian Nicholson, Vicki Oliver, Rose Oosthuizen, Michael and Fennis Parkinson, Torquil, Lynette, Alison, Hillary and Robin Paterson, Gill and Caitlin Pringle, Norman Purdon, Joy Rennie, Brenda and Robert Richardson, Matthew Roper, Bambi Rose, Frances Rouse, John and Pippa Rudd, Dorothy Shaw, Penny Silva, Nerine Stevens, Mark Stewart, Hilary Stipcich, Charles Taberer, Chris Thomas, Leigh Voigt, Alan and Janet Webster and Terry Winstanley. Drs Jean Branford, Peter Middlemost and Robert Morrell. Professors Guy Butler, Anthony Davey and Dave Woods. The Honourable Justices Frank Kirk-Cohen and Christopher Nicholson.

I remember with love and thanks, the late John Axe, Mervynne Danckwerts, Brian Godbold, Bee Rennie, David Roper and Susan Imrie Ross.